girls

in

trouble

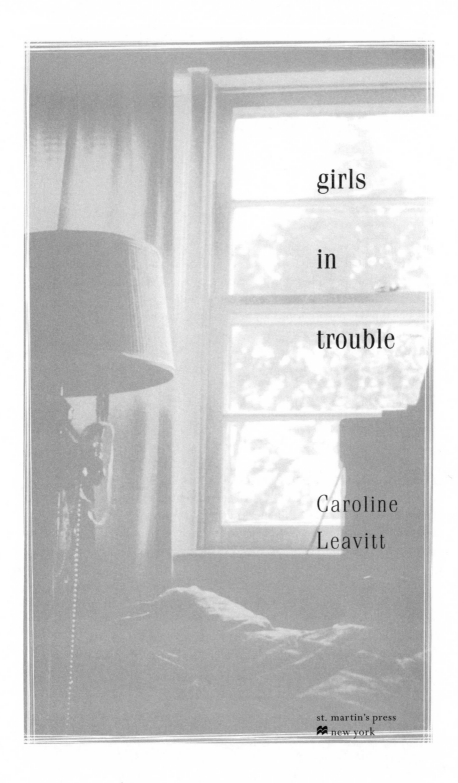

girls

in

trouble

Caroline
Leavitt

st. martin's press
new york

www.stmartins.com

Library of Congress Cataloging-in-Publication Data

Leavitt, Caroline.
    Girls in trouble / Caroline Leavitt.
        p. cm.
Summary: Abandoned by her boyfriend and at odds with her parents for choosing open adoption, Sara, a sixteen-year-old honor student, is sustained by her relationship with her daughter's adoptive parents until they become threatened by her increasing obsession with the baby and make a decision that has devastating consequences for everyone.
    ISBN 0-312-27122-0
    [1. Teenage mothers—Fiction. 2. Mothers and daughters—Fiction. 3. Adoption—Fiction. 4. Pregnancy—Fiction.] I. Title.
    PZ7.L4643Gi 2003
    [Fic]—dc21

                                                    2003009127

First Edition: January 2004

10 9 8 7 6 5 4 3 2 1

For Jeff

and Max

with all my love

acknowledgments

I must have been unbelievably good in a past life to have the sublimely wonderful, warm, smart, and funny Gail Hochman as my agent and friend in this one. Never was any writer luckier, more blessed—or more thrilled. Thank you, thank you, thank you, Gail. Huge thanks, too, to the absolutely wonderful Joanne Brownstein.

A multitude of deepest thanks goes to my terrific editor, Jennifer Weis, and her assistant, Robin Carter, at St. Martin's, and to all the stellar souls at St. Martin's.

For reading, editorial advice, and support way beyond the call, huge thanks to Jeff Tamarkin, Jo Fisher, Jo-ann Mapson, Liza Nelson, Linda Corcoran, Jennifer Robinson, Mickey Pearlman, and Jane Praeger. Very, very special thanks to Katharine Weber, Rochelle Jewell Shapiro, and M. J. Rose.

For help in getting my facts straight, huge thanks to Elaine Abdow, the adoption social worker at Catholic Social Services of Fall River, Massachusetts; and to Bill Bentzen, Peter J. Salzano, Lindy Judge, Jim Lambros, and Dr. Joseph Towbin.

And for many, many kindnesses, thank you to Clea Simon, Jane Bernstein, Janet Falon, Victoria Zackheim, Gayle Brandeis, Mary Morris, Karen Templer and the wonderful denizens of Readerville.com; my mother, Helen Leavitt; my sister, Ruth Rogers; and Jonathan and Hillary.

And, of course, this book—as does everything in my life—owes endless thanks to my funny, loving partner-in-crime, my writer-across-the-hall, my most beloved Jeff. And to our miracle of miracles, Max.

girls

in

trouble

chapter

one

Sara's pains are coming ten minutes apart now. Every time one comes, she jolts herself against the side of the car, trying to disappear. Everything outside is whizzing past her from the car window because Jack, her father, is speeding, something she's never seen him do before. Sara grips the armrest, her knuckles white. She presses her back against the seat and digs her feet into the floor, as if any moment she will fly from the car. *Stop,* she wants to say. *Slow down. Stop.* But she can't form the words, can't make her mouth work properly. Can't do anything except wait in terror for the next pain. Jack hunches over the wheel, beeping his horn though there isn't much traffic. His face is reflected in the rearview mirror, but he doesn't look at her. Instead, he can't seem to keep himself from looking at Abby, Sara's mother, who is sitting in the back with Sara. His face is unreadable. He keeps pushing back his hair, thick and brown, dimmed with grey. He punches the radio dial from station to station, smearing the sound.

"Jack, for God's sake," says Abby. "Just pick a station." Abby hands Sara a hard lemon candy to suck on. She rubs Sara's shoulders, helps her wedge the pink rubber ball into the small of her back to press against the pain. The dress Sara's been living in for months, a blue denim that's two sizes bigger than the one she used to wear, soft from many washings, is soaked with sweat, pasted to her. Her hair snarls to her shoulders, the same rust red as her mother's short, styled cut, only hers is damp, frizzy with curls. No matter how frosty the car gets, Sara can't stop sweating.

"Nineteen eighty-seven and it's the worst heat wave in Boston in fifty years!" the radio announcer says. He keeps saying his name, which is Wild Bill, and every time he says it, he laughs, and the laughter gets under Sara's skin, crawling like some sort of insect. "We've never seen a July like this one!" He's got a crackling, gleeful voice that pops and snaps as if it were carbonated. "Keep inside, keep cool, keep tuned in. There's a health hazard warning for elderly and pregnant women." Sara feels a small shock of recognition, as if the announcer were talking directly to her, but Abby keeps rubbing her bare shoulders as if she hasn't heard anything, and Jack purposefully zips into another lane. Abby's face is coated with sweat. Perspiration beads on Jack's neck. "Two people have died already," Wild Bill says and Sara thinks, amazed, *I'm dying, too.* He talks about drought and blackouts and crime waves because people are going crazy from the heat. No one can be counted on to behave reasonably. An elderly woman was found by a neighbor, panting on her floor by her open refrigerator. A white teacup poodle has nearly suffocated in a car left in a parking lot, but was revived when his desperate owner gave him mouth to mouth. "Even Wild Bill isn't wild enough to do *that!*" Wild Bill says.

Sara swears his voice is growing louder and bigger, crowding out all the room in the car, all the air, and she can't stand listening to it another moment and she's about to say so when another pain grabs at her and instead she cries out.

"Oh, honey," Abby says, turning to her, trying to push back Sara's hair, which is so wet now it's strings. "It's almost over. Almost over now."

Pain crunches down on Sara. "No," she gasps. "No, it's not."

"Soon," her mother promises. "Soon." Her mother's hands float over her.

Jack punches in another station. A long, itchy slide of jazz comes on, making Sara flinch. "Here's the turn," Jack says. His voice is low and determined.

Jack has taken a day off. He's an accountant and his cell phone sits beside him on the seat, and the only reason he's brought it is in case they need to call the doctor, or the car breaks down, or any number of disasters that surely couldn't be any worse for everybody than this one. Abby's a dental hygienist in Belmont and she's taking off a week, something unheard of for her. Usually she's so concerned with everyone else's teeth, she neglects her own when she comes home, but now it's different. "Everyone can take care of their own pearly whites for a change," she says. Every time Abby looks at Sara, Abby changes into something Sara's stopped recognizing. Abby's beauty leaves her. Her eyes, usually blue and soft as felt, become distant. Her mouth takes on a funny slope. And sometimes, when Sara least expects it, Abby's face saddens with regret.

Sara has a lawyer Abby had found, a woman at a Newton adoption agency named Margaret Robins. Every time Margaret talks to Sara, she asks pointedly, "Do you understand?" Abby asks that same question, too, but Jack won't discuss anything with Sara anymore, not even a thing as simple as how he feels. Instead, he's gone mute.

The car bumps, like a reproach from her father, and Sara winces at the flash of pain. Abby rubs her back. "It'll be over soon. Think of your future. Think of school."

Sara is an honor student. Sixteen years old and her guidance counselor already is pushing early admission to Columbia. To Harvard. She loves to say Sara can write her own ticket, which is something Abby repeats like a mantra. "You're smart," she says, but what Sara hears is that Sara may be smart, but she isn't smart enough not to be pregnant.

Sara used to have her life planned. She used to want to be a doctor—a psychiatrist—a decision she made the first time she picked up an issue of *Psychology Today* and couldn't stop reading it. When she was twelve, Abby gave her her own subscription, which Sara devoured, saving all her issues on a special shelf, highlighting the articles that caught and held her interest. Abby loved to leaf through the issues herself. "Nothing wrong with improving my mind, too," she told Sara. "It's terrific you know what you want now. A girl has to know what she wants early and stick to it, or she can get robbed of her life."

"Robbed?" Sara had looked up from the article she was reading, "Body Talk!" She glanced at herself in the mirror to try and decipher her own string-bean build.

"Oh, I'm just being melodramatic," Abby said, waving her hand, but

Sara studied her mother. Abby was folding towels, her prim white lab coat over a shocking-pink dress with a ruffled hem. Her back was hunched, her mouth tense. Abby used to want to be a dentist; she had finished a whole year of dental school when she met Jack. She had shown Sara the photograph of her in school, standing in front of a big brick building, her arms loaded with books, her red hair flying, her face flushed with joy. "Why'd you give that up?" Sara had asked her, and Abby had continued folding. "Easier," she said. "I met your father and got married, then you came along, and who else was going to stay home and raise you? Your father didn't trust anyone else but me."

"You could go back," Sara said, and Abby shrugged. "Now? How could I do that?" Sara looked at Abby with interest. "Why are you looking at me like that?" Abby asked.

Sara held up the magazine. "I was just trying to read your body language."

"I'll translate for you," Abby said, rubbing at her temple. "I'm fluent in headache."

Sara no longer knows what her future holds. *Psychology Today* comes in the mail, the cover so glossy it reflects light back at her, and she doesn't even open it to see what's in the table of contents, because, really, what does it have to do with her now?

Shortly before her stomach started to swell, she went to a fortune-teller, one of those five-dollar places with a turbaned woman on a ratty couch. All Sara wanted was to be told good news. She walked inside and sat on the edge of the couch and the woman gave her a cup of tea that tasted like dishwater and then dumped the cup upside down on a plate. "Ah," she said, poking a finger into the leaves. "Seventy dollars and misfortune is gone."

"I don't have seventy dollars," Sara said and the woman shrugged.

"Then you have misfortune," she said, but Sara didn't need a fortuneteller to tell her that.

"Grab on to me," Abby says now, offering her arm. Sara wrenches away. If she touches her mother's arm, she's afraid she'll beg for help, she'll scream, she'll do whatever it is Abby wants if Abby will just take this pain from her. She looks at the locks on the car, the windows sealed shut, the way she's so trapped. There's no air. She can't breathe. Surely, she's dying. She concentrates on the slow *whomp, whomp, whomp,* inside of her, like some strange animal coming closer, biding its time to strike. It's the most astonishing feeling she's ever had. She suddenly thinks of this movie she once saw called *It's Alive!* Babies born with teeth, vicious killers who devoured their parents.

Whomp. Another pain and Sara starts feeling more afraid. She starts thinking, *What was that? What have I done? What's going to happen?* She's been so stupid about her own body. She kept telling herself, *If I don't think about it, it won't exist.*

A contraction buckles Sara over, banding her stomach with fire. Panicked, Sara grips the seat. "Mom," she says uneasily. "Mommy—"

If she hadn't bitten her fingernails, she would have dug them into the vinyl. "Pant," Abby orders, sucking in her own breath, but Sara can't. All she can do is ride the pain, hold on fast, and pray it will end. Sara had never actually believed she would give birth, and now there's no escape. "First births can take eighteen hours," one doctor has told her, and Sara had thought he was just trying to scare her, to punish her, even. Another pain, deeper this time. *Whomp.* She winces and Abby grips her hand. Sara presses her hands along her back and the pain stops a little. Or maybe it just tightens, like a steel garrote.

Jack skids, flinging Sara against the side of the car. "Everyone all right?" he asks.

"Jack, for God's sake!" Abby says. And then something happens, a wave of pain shoots down Sara's back. It has a life of its own, an unstoppable force. She gasps and she's suddenly drenched from her waist on down. Something is pouring out of her, uncontrollably, like pee, like bathwater. The floor of the car is suddenly soaked. Sara locks eyes with Abby. "It's okay," Abby says, taking her hand, speaking calmly, but Sara can feel how her mother's hand trembles. She feels the sound of the road deep within her skin. She hears the whisper of the other drivers, flowing through her like river water. Her grip tightens. She makes a sound, harsh, scraped from her throat, and Abby stiffens. "Jack, can you please just go *fast,*" Abby says. Jack's hands tighten on the wheel.

The pain zigzags down Sara's spine, stronger, more intense, making her suck in a breath like Jell-O through a straw. She tries to roll herself into a ball, to get away from the pain, but she's too big, and anyway, she knows there's no escape from this. "Hurry," Abby tells Jack. She touches his shoulder with one hand, and there's something new in her voice, something urgent that makes Jack look at Sara for the first time. There's sweat beaded on his lip even though the car is so cold it's practically freezing. His lips are chapped and his shirt is unpressed. "Okay, baby girl," he says. Baby girl. She hears it in wonder and for a moment the pain fades. Baby girl. He used to call her that all the time, making her groan, making her friends giggle. He wouldn't let her pick up anything heavy or go anywhere by herself because he'd worry what might happen. Once, he even reached out to hold her hand when they were crossing a street, just as if she were six. *Baby girl.* At sixteen, she's no baby, but still, hearing him call her one now is comfort. Now she wishes he would call her that again, but instead, he's hunkered over the wheel, weaving in and out among the other cars, like an accident getting ready to happen.

A new bolt of pain shoots along her spine and Sara feels like laughing because her doctor is clearly wrong. Her baby isn't going to take eighteen hours to be born. Her baby is coming now and there's nothing anyone can do about it.

There ahead of them is the hospital. There's St. Elizabeth's. Big and squat and brown and full of traffic, people, and doctors. Jack pulls up by the ER. "I'll let you get out, park, and find you," he says. His voice sounds like someone she no longer knows. Sara squints out at the front door, panic rising in her throat. She can't breathe. She can't move. She can't survive. Frantic, she tries to speak. "I don't see them," she suddenly rasps. "Where's Eva and George?" Abby tightens; Jack snaps the wheel around. It's the first time she's spoken those names in the car because of the way Jack and Abby react, but she can't help it now. It feels like there's too much at stake for her. Another bolt of pain curls her over. Sara tries to sit up, and finds, to her surprise, that the pain won't let her. "Easy, honey," Abby soothes, jumping out of the car, opening Sara's door.

It's a shock to feel all that heat. Things waver in the shiny air and for a moment Sara is listing. For a moment she thinks her whole life is a mirage about to pass. She tries to arc her legs out of the car and the pain forces her down, insistent and angry, a line of pure fire making her still. *I can't survive this,* she thinks in wonder. "Sara?" Abby bends toward Sara. "Honey, here's a hand," Abby says, and Sara grasps at her mother's fingers. She holds on tight and pulls herself up and she's suddenly dizzy, and another cramp grabs her, *whomp.* And *whomp* again and *whomp,* and she tries to breathe, to stand, and she can't do either. She buckles over. "Sara?" says Jack, his voice cracking. Huh-huh, hee-hee, ho-ho, Sara pants and the pain, insistent as a fist, suddenly collapses her into Abby's arms.

chapter

two

A nurse sped Sara down the corridors, skimming along a bright green line. "It's okay," Abby said, racing alongside. The wheelchair bumped and Sara screamed, soaked with sweat, terrified. *I won't die until they get here,* she told herself. Faces blurred past her, but she didn't recognize a single one of them. Her panic spiked like fever.

"What can I do?" Abby pleaded. She tried to grab on to Sara's hands, but Sara was digging them into her thighs, against the pain.

"Where's Eva?" Sara cried, bunching over. "Where's George? They said they'd be here! They promised!" *I can't do this without them,* she thought. *I'll die.*

Abby's face hardened and got that distant look. "Here's Dad," she said, and Sara heard his steps, then she felt his hand on her shoulder, a touch, before he took it away.

"Here we are," said the nurse, pushing through a set of grey doors marked DELIVERY, into a small white room. *Where's Eva?* Sara thought, as the nurse helped her out of her dress and into a flowery johnny. "Up we go," said the nurse, gently guiding Sara onto a long green table. *Where's Eva?* Sara thought, keeping her eyes on the door, right up until the pain hurtled deeper and she shut her eyes. *Where's Eva and George?*

"Smile, you're going to get a baby out of this, Mrs. Rothman," the nurse said, and for a moment, out of habit, Sara looked at her mother, the only Mrs. Rothman she knew.

Next door, someone was screaming, wild shrieks splashing into the room, making Abby blanch and Jack look down at his sneakers. A new nurse wrapped a monitor belt about her belly, a fat band of white, a clumsy plastic buckle. A machine whirred and beeped next to her, a green line forked up and down on the screen at each contraction.

"Do your breathing," the nurse admonished. The scream tore into the room again and Sara was so frightened, her breath stopped. "Breathe, I told you," the nurse repeated.

The woman next door shrieked again. "Is she dying?" Sara asked.

The nurse tightened the monitor belt. "That woman's Orthodox Jewish and she won't take any medication."

"What medication? Give me some medication!" Sara screamed, a wire of pain cutting across her belly. The Orthodox woman screamed in harmony.

The nurse took a blood pressure cuff and wrapped it calmly around Sara's arm. "The doctor will be here any second. Now you *breathe*."

Sara panicked. Her mind was so fogged with fear and pain, she had forgotten everything she knew. The breathing Eva had helped her with. The lucky charm George had given her to keep in her pocket, a small silvery angel she loved. Where was the charm? Where were they? She needed them. She looked desperately at the door.

"Concentrate, Sara," Abby said. "Every time you get a contraction, focus on me."

The nurse glanced at Sara and then, resigned, she gripped Sara's hand. "Purse your lips," she ordered. "Pant. Hoo-hoo hee-hee." Sara tried it, but the nurse's face was smooth and calm, and Sara's felt as if it were crumpled like a ball of paper. "Hoo-hoo," panted Abby encouragingly. Jack leaned against the wall, closing his eyes, defeated, and then there was a new fist of pain, and Sara bolted up. "Hoo-hoo, hee-hee," the nurse urged.

"Get her an epidural!" Abby said, her voice growing insistent. The nurse ignored Abby. "Get her something! What's the matter with you!" Abby said, and the nurse looked at the monitor again and her face turned soft, sympathetic. "It's too late," the nurse said.

Abby moved closer to Sara, brushing back Sara's wet hair. "I'm right here," Abby said to Sara. She made low, soothing noises, clucks of her tongue. "I'm right here."

The nurse glanced at Sara's chart, frowning. Then she looked evenly at Jack and Abby. "So. You're going in the delivery room? You're the adoptive parents?"

"We're the *real* parents," Abby said. "Sara's real parents." She held Sara's hand.

A doctor Sara didn't know whisked in, six younger people behind him, all of them in green scrubs. "Where's my doctor?" Sara said. Her doctor was a woman, young and sympathetic. This doctor was male and older and had a blue Band-Aid on his nose, a bad omen if she ever saw one.

"In delivery. I'm Dr. Chasen. Don't you worry, I've delivered hundreds of babies."

"No, no," Sara cried. She didn't trust this doctor, didn't like the way he was beckoning the other people forward. "Check the centimeters," he said to them, and Sara locked her legs as another pain shot through her. "What's going on?" Abby said. "Who are all these people?"

"This is a teaching hospital," Dr. Chasen said quietly. He put his hands on Sara's legs. "Don't worry. You won't even notice them. You're going to be so busy, a flying saucer could land in here with us and you wouldn't notice that either." The students laughed, a sparkling of sound, and then Dr. Chasen parted Sara's legs and quickly, before she could protest, thrust his hand up inside of her and drew it out. Humiliated, she jerked away. "You're going to have your baby now," he said, then he turned to the nurse. "Get my girl into delivery," he said, and Sara shivered because she didn't feel like anyone's girl, not his, not her parents', not Danny's anymore, either. He whisked out of the room, the students trailing.

"It's going to be okay, honey," Abby said.

"Where's Eva and George?" Sara screamed and Jack drew back.

Abby was purposefully putting on a long green gown, tying on a mask. Someone was pushing Sara's hair into a cap. Hands and bodies were about her. "It's showtime, folks," said the nurse, undoing Sara's monitor. The gurney was wheeled back in. The nurse lifted Sara onto it. A wire of pain tightened across Sara's belly. It owned her now.

"I can't do this!" Sara shouted, and then she was settled on the gurney and as soon as it moved, she felt something pound within her, deep and insistent, and stunned, she searched for help. She'd apologize for anything, she'd do anything, be anything, if only this pain would stop. *Please,* she thought, squeezing her eyes shut. *Oh God, please,* and then, zooming into the room was Eva, in a blue summer dress, her long, pale hair flying about her in a silken sheet. There was George, tall and bald and all in black, with a silver bolo tie. He was holding Eva's hand and Sara felt so relieved she started to cry.

"Oh, sweetie, I'm sorry, I'm sorry—traffic was so horrible!" Eva cried.

"We're here now," George said, "we're here!" He dropped Eva's hand and took Sara's. His hands were big and warm, covering hers, and Sara burst into fresh tears.

"Don't cry, don't cry. It's all going to be wonderful." Eva leaned down. She glowed like a pearl. "How do you feel? What's happening?" Eva asked, bending toward Sara.

"She's going into delivery, that's what's happening," Abby said sharply, and Eva looked at Abby and Jack for the first time.

"Abby. Jack," Eva said, nodding. Jack nodded back.

"Let's go, let's go—" the nurse said. "Get into scrubs if you're coming," she said to Eva and George. "Looks like it's going to be a full house."

"I'll be in the waiting room, honey." Jack touched Sara's shoulder awkwardly.

"Daddy—" she said, panicking.

"You'll be fine," he said, but his voice sounded unsure to her. It made her more panicky. "Daddy—" she repeated, but when she looked up, he was gone.

The nurse handed Eva and George scrubs. She began wheeling the gurney, out of the room, down the hall. Abby was keeping pace, stroking Sara's hair, her shoulders, murmuring something that Sara couldn't hear. Sara heard the nurse's voice, but she couldn't make out what she was saying, either. She heard the Orthodox woman screaming again. How could anyone scream like that and not be torn in two? And then Sara noticed another sound, like a thousand angry bees humming about her head. She felt the air thickening, heating up around her. She looked up and saw two new doors. Abby was beside her again, scooping up one of Sara's hands, holding it tight. "I won't leave you," Abby said. "We'll get through this together," and the bees grew louder, angrier, until they seemed to be screaming, too, and Sara, terrified, jerked her hand from her mother's and screamed, "I just want Eva!"

"I'm here, I'm here!" Eva, in green scrubs, was running, catching up with Sara. She waved her hand at George, stopping him in his tracks.

Abby froze. "Honey——" she said. "This is crazy——"

Abby looked like a statue to her, like Lot's wife, who had turned into salt the moment she had looked for something she shouldn't have, so sad and hurt, it made Sara ache. "Mommy?" she said, and then her gurney pushed through the double doors, and the thought disappeared in a bolt of pain, and she flung a hand out and grabbed Eva's, holding on as if her life depended upon it.

Everything in the delivery room seemed to be bathed in blue light. Sara was lifted up onto a table, her feet put in stirrups. Masked faces lowered toward her, peering. Frantic, she searched for Eva. "Right here," Eva said. Sara locked eyes and gripped Eva's hand. "It's okay," Eva breathed to her. "Do like we practiced. Remember?" Sara tried to remember. Tried to put herself back in Eva's sun-splashed house, in Eva's yellow living room where they had sat and talked and planned, in Eva's big backyard where they had lounged on chaises and sipped peppermint tea and measured Sara's belly as it grew.

"Push!" the doctor ordered. She wouldn't look at him, wouldn't look at the students peering down at her. "Good girl," the doctor said, "now push again. A better one this time." Where was her doctor? Why was she the one to get stuck with this stranger?

"Get mad at the baby!" he shouted at her. "Push that baby out! Get mad! Get even!"

Eva leaned down so close to Sara she could whisper in her ear. "You can do it."

"Sara, you're not getting mad enough," the doctor said, "I need you to *push*."

She pushed, dissolving.

"Push, goddammit!" the doctor said. Something was being torn from her body, and then Sara was suddenly flying away, leaving her body, floating up. She was moving deeper and deeper into a white-hot core. *So this is how you do this,* she thought, *this is how you die.* And then she felt something boring out of her, she felt herself spinning back down into her body, and what was pushing out of her was as big as the scream she couldn't contain, and then she pushed and wept and screamed and the baby was born.

Dr. Chasen held the baby up, white and cheesy, dotted with blood. He whisked it away and brought it back, placing it on her belly. "Just for a minute," he said. It didn't look or feel or seem like any of the babies she had ever carried. She was about to stroke the baby's face, to touch its nose, and then Eva bent over her and took the baby from her, bursting into happy tears. "My little one," she breathed.

"Baby's name?" someone said.

"Roseann," Sara said, the name popping into her mind. Little Roseann. Sara remembered sitting on Eva's couch, making up lists with her and George. Each of them would take a turn. Alice. Clarisse. Names so beautiful they hurt you just to hear them. "Here we are," Eva whispered, "Anne Cheryl Rivers," and for a moment Sara thought, *Whose name is that?* Where had those names come from and when had that been decided? Wait, she tried to say, but her lips were too heavy to move even into a sigh.

"Thank you," Eva breathed. "Thank you, Sara." And then Sara closed her eyes.

Sara woke: *Something is wrong.* For a moment, she thought she was with her boyfriend Danny, in his basement, lying on the red plaid pullout couch, tense and awkward and naked, dizzy with need and desire, waiting for Danny to come downstairs to her. He liked finding her naked. "Surprise me," he used to say. She used to kiss the tip of his nose because she didn't know what else to kiss, because she was so shy.

"Danny," she said. Her voice sounded strange and hoarse in the room. She blinked and the room turned white. Danny was gone. She heard coughing and laughter and she twisted her head and there was another woman in a fussy white nightgown in the bed next to her, surrounded by flowers and wrapped gifts and two other women, whose faces were bright with excitement. "We saw your Tom. He's so thrilled!"

"He wants five more," Sara's roommate said, and everyone laughed.

"Everyone at work misses you like crazy," one of the women said.

Sara felt herself growing smaller and smaller. She used to have friends, too. And then the bigger she had become, the more she had withdrawn and the less often her friends had called her, the less they had to say to her, too. And now, they didn't call at all. "Come on, Mom. Let's take a walk so you can show us off to your daughter," one of the women said.

"Mom!" the other woman said, tickled. The women all stood up. One of them looked over at Sara, and then quickly looked away. She knew that look. She had seen it on the faces of the nurses. They glanced and then looked briskly away. Only a candy striper had dared to ask, "What are you doing here?" as if it were a mistake. "How old are you?"

"Sixteen," Sara said and the girl looked shocked.

"Quit your kidding," she said. "Get out of here."

Sara lay in bed, her hands on her belly. It was big and pouchy, as if she were still full of baby, but she felt this strange, terrible loss. "Soon it'll be over," Abby had said. And some of it had been. "How can I be anyone's father?" Danny had asked her when she had dared to tell him she was pregnant.

A nurse carrying two yellow plastic pitchers came into the room. She came closer to Sara. "There weren't any private rooms. I'm sorry," she said. She patted Sara's arm and Sara looked up at her, confused.

"You're doing a brave thing," the nurse told her, reassuringly. "I have two adopted kids of my own."

"Where's my baby?" Sara said and the nurse gave her a long, careful look.

"Are you sure that's what you want, honey? Most birth mothers find—"

"I can see my baby," Sara interrupted, her voice rising. "It's an open adoption."

The nurse put the pitchers down. She started to say something and then her mouth closed, and she left the room. Sara slunk down in bed, turning her face to the window, but moments later, there was the sound of wheels skittering along the floor. "Here she is," said the nurse, and Sara got out of bed. "I'll be back for her in a while," the nurse said.

She stared hard at the baby, her toes curling on the cold of the floor. The baby was as small as a minute, swaddled in a striped rainbow blanket just like a surprise package, her head half covered with a tiny knit cap with "I got my first hug at St. Elizabeth's" embroidered across the brim, making Sara think wistfully: *Who else has hugged Anne?* Sara bent lower toward the baby, who smelled of powder and soap and something Sara couldn't recognize. Anne's eyes were open and slate grey and they held a strange, mischievous expression, as if she knew something no one else did. Sara had read that new mothers studied their babies to make sure they had all ten fingers and toes, that every limb was in place, but Sara studied Anne looking not for perfection but for Danny's green eyes, for his strong nose and full mouth, but this baby didn't look anything like him, or anything like Sara, either, for that matter, and a wave of sadness coursed through her. Gently, she took off the baby's cap, and a soft fuzz of red hair sprang up, just like her own. "Oh!" Sara said, delighted, and the baby's eyes fastened on Sara's, and then Sara couldn't help herself. Bending, she picked up the baby, a warm, soft presence, like a little cat. "Anne," she said out loud, as if she were test-driving the name. She brought her carefully over to the bed and lay down with her. She felt as if she were all glass inside, breaking apart deep within her. Gently, she started to open the swaddling, to catch glimpses of her daughter's toes, her knees, her belly, and then she heard footsteps outside, a burst of laughter. Quickly, she swaddled Anne, she held her and waited, expectant.

Flowers came into the room first, two big bundles of golds and pinks, and then she saw George's face behind them. She saw Eva following, carrying a huge silver package. As soon as they saw the baby, they stopped. "Oh! Isn't she beautiful!" Eva cried. She put the packages on the bed, she reached for the baby, taking her easily from Sara's hands, and as soon as she did, Sara felt empty. She tucked her hands under the sheet.

"There's our girl!" Eva said and Sara half-smiled before she realized Eva wasn't talking about her. Eva rocked Anne in her arms, and then

George bent low over the baby, his face bright and expectant. "Look at that red hair!" he said. "Isn't that funny!" He looked from the baby to Sara. "Not your mouth, though."

"I swear she has my mouth," Eva said. She turned to Sara, and for a minute Sara thought Eva was going to ask her if she wanted to hold the baby again, which she ached to, but instead, Eva's smile grew. "You look terrific," Eva said. "You were astonishing."

"I was?" Sara said.

Eva nodded at the package on the bed. "Open your present," she said, gleefully.

Sara unpeeled the tissue. Pale pink, a soft satiny nightgown flowing like cool lake water through her hands. "Why shouldn't you look beautiful?" Eva said. Sara flushed. No one had called her beautiful in a very long while. "Hold it up against you," Eva urged, but when Sara lifted her arms, her breasts hurt. All this morning she had listened in on the lesson a nurse gave her roommate on breast-feeding. She had heard the woman wince. "You have jaws like a barracuda!" the woman told her baby, and then she had told her friends how she planned to bring a pump to work and let anyone dare to stop her.

Sara drew her johnny tighter against her chest. They were giving Sara a drug to dry up her milk because Eva wanted to use formula right from the start.

Sara studied her flowers, the only ones she had. She opened the card. There was Eva's delicate schoolteacher script. *"Perfect baby! Perfect you! Love, Eva and George."* Sara traced the words with one finger. Perfect, she was perfect. "Thank you," she said.

George took out a camera and clicked Eva holding the baby. He turned and took a picture of Sara. She blinked at the flash. Then he turned to the baby. "My turn," he said and lifted Anne up. He studied her mouth. "She's going to have great teeth," he decided.

George was a dentist, something Sara had hoped might bond him to Abby, but instead it made Abby angrier. "He should know better," she said wearily, but Sara didn't know what that meant except that there was probably a lecture in it for her if she dared to ask.

George swayed the baby in a kind of dance. He hummed something, so low and sweet-sounding, it just about broke Sara's heart. She watched him, and yawned. "You poor thing," Eva said. "I bet you're exhausted. Don't mind us, you can sleep."

Sara struggled to stay awake. Her lids floated down, her breath evened. She was half-dreaming, and then she heard the door push open. Her roommate, Sara thought. Her roommate's friends. Her roommate's baby. She opened her eyes, just a hair, just enough to see Eva. "You little beauty!" Eva said, kissing the baby gently, just as Jack and Abby came into the room. As soon as they saw Eva and George and the baby, all the air in the room froze.

Eva spoke first. "How nice to see you again," Eva said politely. George put his hand out and Jack shook it stiffly. "Sara's fast asleep," George said quietly.

"Isn't she beautiful?" Eva said. Abby lifted an arm toward the baby, then lowered it.

"Doesn't Sara look wonderful?" Eva prompted.

"She's a lovely young girl who's been through a lot," Abby said quietly.

"This never should have happened," Jack said.

"But it did," Eva said quietly. "And now we're making something good from it."

Sara felt as if she were outside her body, suspended above all of them. She felt exhausted, her lids began to droop. All she wanted to do was sleep again. Her eyes shut.

"She's still sleeping," Jack said, astonished, as if he couldn't fathom how Sara could sleep at a time like this. Sara, though, knew better. Put all of them in a room, and the smartest thing to do was remove herself from the scene, to keep her eyes shut and slow her breathing. She breathed. In and out. Deep as a trance. And then she couldn't have moved even if she had wanted, which she didn't.

"Well, delivery isn't easy," Eva said.

"Nothing's easy when you're sixteen," Abby said. The baby started to cry. *As if she knows something is up,* Sara thought, and then the baby abruptly stopped.

"Well," Eva said. There was silence. "Here. Would you like to hold her, Abby?"

Sara tried to open her eyes and failed. Her heart hammered. Was Abby holding Anne?

"We know we don't have to tell you that you and Jack are, of course, welcome to visit the baby, too. Anytime you like," Eva said. The silence thickened.

"Yes, we all share—" George started to say.

"Share what? This tragedy?" Abby interrupted. "Why do you have to get so close? How can that be good for any of you, especially for a child?"

"This way's more beneficial for everyone involved. No secrets. Everything out in the open just the way it should be," George said. "It's better for the baby."

"Which baby? Sara or Anne?" Jack said.

"Sara's a sixteen-year-old girl who should be allowed to forget," Abby said. Sara heard rustling. Abby must be pacing, the way she always did when she was annoyed. And if she was pacing, then she wasn't holding the baby, and if she wasn't, who was?

"Oh, Abby," Eva said. "How could she forget? And why would you want her to?"

There was a strange, edgy quiet. And then Jack said, "Maybe we should just let Sara sleep, instead of talking in here."

"Here, I'll take her, Jack," Eva said. "I'll bring Anne back to the nursery."

Her father had held the baby, Sara thought, amazed. He never even talked about it, not the whole time Sara was pregnant. Sara heard footsteps, the dull whine of the bassinet wheels on the floor. It all grew fainter. The room grew completely silent. Everyone had left, she thought. And then she started to open her eyes, and she saw her parents holding each other in the center of the room, pressed together like a seam. Neither one of them saw her wake. And then she heard Abby snuffling, and when her parents broke apart, she saw they both were crying.

"Come on," Jack said, putting his arm about Abby. He dug out a handkerchief and daubed Abby's eyes with it, and then his own.

"I shouldn't have held her," Abby whispered. "I shouldn't have."

"Come on. I'll get you some tea, you'll feel better."

And then the two of them were gone.

Sara half-dreamed on her bed. Imagine. Her parents had held Anne. They had held the baby and they were determined not to do it again. Fresh start, Abby had said. That was Abby's favorite set of words, Sara thought. Like a cooking recipe. Life as a cake mix you hoped might be delicious and to ensure it you just had to be extra careful about the ingredients you chose. As soon as Abby had known Sara was pregnant, that it was too late to abort, Abby had told Sara that it was, of course, impossible for her to keep the baby. Impossible for them to adopt and raise it as their own because how could Sara get a clean start then? Instead, she found Sara the adoption agency in Newton, the adoption lawyer who insisted Sara call her Margaret. "Thank God we live in modern times," Abby had told her. She sat down beside Sara. "When I was growing up, there was a home for wayward girls right in my town," Abby said. "The Girls in Trouble House we called it, even though its name was just St. Luke's. It was terrible. Just terrible. The stories we heard! There was such a stigma! You went to a place like that and your life was over and everyone knew it. The girls couldn't even keep their real names when they were there, just first names, because they didn't want to encourage friendships. They couldn't go outside the grounds. It was a relief when they closed the place down, put a Star Market there instead."

"Did you ever see the girls?" Sara asked.

Abby sighed. "I saw them standing at the gates sometimes, like they were prisoners. Asking for cigarettes. Asking us to call their boyfriends for them."

"Did you?"

Abby straightened up. "Of course I didn't." She rubbed at her temples and then studied Sara. "You're lucky you don't show. I didn't either until nearly my eighth month. And if, God forbid, you do start to pop, the school can't make you leave. Not the way they used to."

"Leave—I can't leave—" Sara tightened. What if Danny came back? How would he find her if she was at another school?

"Look," Abby said. "This is a private matter. No one's business but ours. With baggy clothes, you can finish the school year. You can stay inside this summer until the baby's due. Then, fall comes, you'll be back in school with no one the wiser."

Abby and Jack didn't even want Sara to know who was taking the baby, but how could she do that? As terrifying as it was to contemplate having a baby, giving it away was like giving away a part of Danny. She had to have some contact, some connection, or she'd be undone. "Closed adoption," Abby suggested, and then, to Abby's annoyance, Margaret had presented open adoption. "As much contact as both you and the adoptive parents want," Margaret said. Sara felt the air-conditioning cooling her skin, and she sat up straighter. "Yes. That," she said.

Margaret warned them open adoption was enforceable only in Oregon. "You'll want an agreement with everything spelled out," she said, but Sara kept thinking of that corny Joni Mitchell song her mother sometimes sang about not needing any piece of paper.

"We'll all talk about it," Jack said, but once they got outside the office, all he said was that he thought it was a bad idea. "It's what I want," Sara said, stubborn. Her father shook his head. "You don't know what you want. You're too young to know," he said.

Late at night, while she lay in bed, Sara heard them talking, their voices rising and falling like crashing waves. "They said it's not really that open," Abby said. "Contact almost always diminishes. People get on with their lives. They make new lives."

"Are we doing the right thing?" Jack asked, and then there was silence again.

Abby had gone to the agency with Sara and looked through the photo albums of couples wanting her baby, read the ridiculous letters that all seemed the same. *"Dear birth mother, we know how brave a sacrifice you are making."* The handwriting spiked and curlicued, the paper always soft blue or yellow. *"We want you to know we will love your baby the same way you would."* The words were insinuating. As though they knew something about her. The photographs were worse. Bland-faced couples staring out at her. *"Here we are at the beach, but we love the city, too!"* One couple posed with two big dogs on their bed. *"Every child needs a dog or two! This is Scruffy! He loves kids!"*

All those 800 numbers so you couldn't know where they were calling from, or how they might lie to you, like a childhood taunt: *Nyah nyah, I can see you but you can't see me.*

She wouldn't let her parents be around her when she called the 800 numbers, though they offered. "We can help you," Abby said. "I know just the questions you should ask." But Sara shook her head. If she were going to give something up, if she were going to ruin her life, then she wanted to ruin it all on her own. She sat upstairs, her heart racing, the door firmly closed. She spoke to the women, who cracked bad jokes, who were eager to please, who said her name in every sentence, over and over like an incantation.

And then one day, Sara was having a conversation with a woman in Maine, when the woman blurted, "Do you know who the father is, Sara? Do you realize why it's important to know?" And then Sara heard her sigh. "I'm sorry. I don't really want to denigrate you—" The woman cleared her throat. "I mean I don't intend that remark in a bad way."

"In a pejorative way, do you mean?" Sara asked.

"Oh," the woman said. "Whoops."

"I know what *denigrate* means. I'm an honor student."

"Of course you are!" The woman laughed politely.

"And I know who the father is."

"All I wanted to know!" The woman sighed, relieved, but Sara never called her back.

The adoptive couples skirted around her, acting like she was white trash or stupid, their voices fake and bright as tinsel. Chatting, they told her they were having fried chicken or McDonald's, that it was Shake 'n Bake night again, even as she heard a male voice in the background whisper, "Where's the crème fraîche?" They lied outright, trying to turn themselves into what they thought she wanted. "Are you religious?" Sara asked. Not that she cared, but she just wanted to know. "We're . . . spiritual," said one woman.

"They're lying to me," Sara said to the agency, amazed, but Margaret waved her away. "Well, you have to realize, some of these people are yearning so hard for a baby, they let their common sense fly out the window. You can't hold it against them. You let us find out the truth," Margaret told her. "You concentrate on connecting to someone."

"Please call back anytime," the callers all said, and Sara never did.

"No one yet?" the agency asked Sara.

"When are you going to make a decision?" Abby prodded. She wanted Sara to choose a family who lived in Texas, who had a big dog and who said they'd be happy to send pictures, but just for a few years. "What's wrong with these people?" Jack said, pointing to an album from a family who were moving to Spain.

And then, like an afterthought, the agency had sent over George and Eva's scrapbook. "I don't know if this is right for you—" Margaret said. "But it's worth a shot, right?" Abby hadn't liked George and Eva the moment she saw their scrapbook. "They look like aging hippies," she said, pointing to Eva's filmy long dress, George's cowboy boots. She shook her head at the picture of Eva with her preschool class, all of them, especially Eva, covered in poster paints. Abby said they were too old—in their forties, for God's sake. Forty-three! Abby was forty-three and you didn't see her talking about having a baby! Plus, they were too close, just twenty minutes away. "This isn't a good idea," Jack said.

But Sara liked the way they looked. Real. Natural. Like they wouldn't snow her. She liked the letter, which was the only one that didn't start out "Dear birth mother," but instead just said, "Hello," as if it were going to be the start of a conversation instead of an advertising pitch. She dialed Eva and George's number, and as soon as she said her name, Eva said, "Oh, sweetie," in a voice so rich with feeling, that Sara couldn't have hung up even if she wanted to. Sara spoke to Eva for twenty minutes and the whole time Eva didn't ask her about the doctor, about the father, or about anything other than what movies and books Sara liked, and then Eva had gotten quiet. "This is so hard for both of us, isn't it?" Eva said. "How can either one of us know what the right thing to do is?"

"You can ask me anything," Sara said. "But only if I can do the same."

"Deal," said Eva.

Oh, how she had loved talking to Eva. She called her the next day to see if she still felt as relaxed talking to her, and she had. She called her the day after.

And she wrote her, too. Spilling out how she felt about being pregnant, how she felt about her parents, how she worried about the future. *I hope this is okay I'm telling you all this,* she said. *I'm just a little scared. It helps to write, like getting it in print gives it less power.* Almost immediately after she sent her letters off, she got a response, always from both Eva and George, always soothing and happy, and always with a photograph of the two of them, or the yard, or the special room in the house that might be the baby's.

Sara was walking home from school one day when she saw a young mother trying to hoist up a bag of groceries in one arm and her baby in the other. The woman looked at Sara helplessly. "Please, can you help me?" she said. As soon as Sara lifted up the baby, something sharp nudged against her ribs, from inside, and she tightened her grip.

"Thank you, thank you," the woman said profusely. By the time Sara got home, she was in tears. She walked into the house, her face streaming, and there was Abby. "Honey, what happened!" Abby cried, alarmed. She sat Sara down, she put one arm about her.

"A baby," Sara choked. "I held a baby."

Abby stiffened. "That's just your hormones talking," she said, rubbing Sara's back. "When you're pregnant, things upset you more. You should have seen me when I was carrying you. Detergent commercials made me weep. Another month, you'll feel better."

"What if I don't?" Sara whispered, but Abby shook her head.

"Come on now. Go wash your face and I promise things will look brighter. Maybe after dinner we can all go out to a movie. A comedy. How about that?"

But Sara hadn't gone to the bathroom. She heard the noisy drone of the vacuum. She went to her room, bringing the phone in with her, shutting the door, and she called Eva, bursting into tears as soon as she heard Eva's voice. It horrified her. She hadn't even met Eva in person and here she was crying! "I held a baby today," she said.

"Oh, how hard for you!" Eva said. "I'm so sorry!" Eva's voice was a soft blanket.

"Am I doing the right thing?"

As soon as she said that, she thought, oh God, how could she ask such a thing of Eva? Of course Eva would tell her she was, because as her parents kept telling her, what they wanted most was Sara's baby, that that was the only reason they were being nice to her.

"What do you think?" Eva said gently. "What feels right for you and for your baby?"

Your baby. Her parents never called it "your baby." Never called it anything at all.

"I don't know," Sara cried.

Eva sat listening to Sara, and then Sara heard George's voice, low and grave and full of concern. "Tell her I'm here for her, too," he said, and Sara felt a new flush of warmth.

Eva didn't sugarcoat, she didn't make her situation out to be perfect. "The baby won't have a lot of relatives, and George's father is pretty old and set in his ways and not in the best of health," she admitted. "But we have good friends, and they love children."

"Well, I can tell you'll be doting," Sara said, and as soon as she said it, she felt calmer, as if all her tears had been wrung out of her. "I feel better now," she said.

"I think it's time we all met," Eva said.

"You really want to meet them?" Abby had asked Sara. "You think that's wise?"

"I have to meet them."

"Well, you can't go over there alone," Jack had insisted. "We'll all go."

They had all trooped over, Abby in her best black dress, Jack in a suit and tie, Sara in her blue pregnancy dress. As soon as Sara had seen the house, warm and friendly, and as soon as she'd seen George and Eva, holding hands, Eva in bare feet, George in a worn denim shirt and jeans, something slowly had begun to uncurl inside of her. "Oh Lord," Abby said under her breath.

Abby was stiff and silent, and Jack kept looking down at his shoes, but Eva was so excited, her face shone. She kept laughing, kept grabbing for George's hand. "I'll make herbal tea," George offered, jumping up.

"Coffee?" Jack said. "With plenty of caffeine and sugar? We don't really drink tea."

But what had really turned her parents against George and Eva was when they talked about making the adoption completely open. "There's no reason Sara can't be over here as much as she likes," Eva said. "Even every day if she wants."

After that, things didn't go too well. The more Eva and George talked about how Sara should truly be a part of their family, the more interest Sara showed, the more Abby frowned, the more Jack cleared his throat. "Sara already has a family," Jack said.

"Yes, of course she does, but there are all kinds of different families—" George said.

"We want her to go on with her life," Abby said. "To have what's best for her."

"So do we," Eva said quietly. "We've been doing so much reading, talking to other adoptive parents. It's really a whole brave new world."

"Our daughter's not an experiment."

"I like the idea," Sara interrupted, and everyone turned to her, as if they had just noticed she was in the room. "Well, I do," she said.

"Well," Abby said. She stood up. She held out a hand to shake Eva's, and then George's. "We should get going. Thank you for the coffee."

As soon as they were outside, Abby's shoulders unsquared. "Choose anyone else," Jack told Sara when they got to the car, but it was too late, because in her mind, Sara already had chosen, and the more her parents objected, the more certain she became.

Eva and George began calling the house, just to talk. They called because they were on their way to a new Van Gogh exhibit at the museum and thought, hey, would Sara like to come? They were going miniature-golfing or to the park. "Come over, I'm making bread from scratch," Eva said one day, and Sara had, taking a cab Eva paid for. Eva's kitchen was bright and sunny, and the two of them wore big red aprons, their hair pinned up with Eva's barrettes, and they kneaded dough. "Like putty!" Sara giggled. She held up her sticky hands and then pushed her elbows into the floury dough to knead it more.

"Now that's an unusual method," Eva said.

"Whatever works, right?" Sara said, and the two of them laughed.

Afterward, while the bread baked, they sat on blue chaises in the leafy backyard. George came out to join them, carrying a camera. "You just glow," Eva told Sara. "I could look at you forever." She turned to George. "Isn't she beautiful?" she demanded and George pointed the camera at Sara. "Say Gruyère," he ordered. "Say smoked Gouda!" When the next-door neighbor opened her back door to let her collie out, Eva waved happily. "This is *the* Sara!" Eva called. "Isn't she fabulous?"

"You told her about me?" Sara asked, surprised.

"Of course I did," Eva said. "Why wouldn't I?"

They fit her into their future. When Eva started talking about going to Maine to a lake, she turned to Sara and asked, "You like lakes, right?" When Eva and George talked about fixing up the spare room, George mused, "We could fit an extra bed in there," and Sara knew they meant it for her. The one Saturday she couldn't make it, Eva and George surprised her the next day with a green paper cone of jonquils, with a ring with a tiny yellow stone. "What can I say? We missed you," Eva said. "And we wanted to show it."

"They're trying to buy you," Abby said, when she saw the gifts, but Sara knew different. "There's nothing to buy," she said.

Eva and George wanted her there as much as Jack and Abby didn't, and as soon as school was out, Sara was there all the time. Sara knew her parents wouldn't stop her from going there, knew they were more afraid that at this late date she'd change her mind about Eva and George, and they'd have to start finding an adoptive couple all over again, or worse, that she'd suddenly refuse to consider adoption at all.

One day, Sara woke up to find Abby in her room. Already she could feel the shiny heat pouring in from the window. The mowers from next door were going, a loud, angry buzz, and when she sat up, for the first time, her stomach seemed to be in her way. Astonished, she put her hands on her belly. Abby was bustling about the room, drawing Sara's curtains open, plucking up Sara's laundry. "It's such a gorgeous day, why don't you and I do something fun together?" Abby said.

Sara had planned on spending the whole day in Eva and George's backyard. "Mom—" she said, and then Abby sat on the edge of the bed and Sara saw the look on her mother's face, the way her mouth had gone all soft, like she was waiting to be disappointed, and Sara suddenly knew that if she left, she'd see that look all day and she didn't think she could bear it.

27

"Could we go to the Van Gogh exhibit at the museum?" Sara asked.

The two of them went. The museum was empty and cool, and Sara was transfixed by the paintings. They took their time, Abby because she had to study every nuance of the paintings, Sara because it was harder to walk now that she was bigger. They were rounding the corner of one room, wandering into another, when Abby suddenly took Sara's arm. "Let's go this way," Abby said firmly, guiding her in the other direction.

"But we haven't seen that way," Sara protested, and Abby's grip tightened.

"Abby? Is that you?"

Abby turned, smiling, and there was a woman Sara didn't know. "It *is* you!" the woman said, and then her gaze flew down to Sara's dress, to the swell of her belly. "Is this your daughter?" Her eyes glittered.

"Sara, this is Margie Meuller, one of my patients."

Sara held out her hand and Margie shook it vigorously. "I've heard so much about you!" she said. "I was just on my way to the café. Would you like to join me?"

"We'd love to but we're running so late—" Abby said.

"Ah—another time then."

They stood in place, watching Margie leave. "Don't worry," Abby said quietly to Sara. "I'll think of something to tell her."

The day felt spoiled and they went home, and as soon as Sara walked into the house, Abby looked at the dress Sara had tossed on a chair that morning, picked it up, and smoothed it. "It takes so little to hang up your clothes," Abby said. Everything in this house reminded Sara of all the wrongs she had ever done. She wanted to go to George and Eva's, where everything reminded her of all the rights, where Eva made a point to introduce Sara, where there was happiness in every corner and she was the cause of it.

"I think I may go out for a bit—" she started to say.

Abby blinked at her. "Just like that? You don't even call them first anymore?"

"They said I didn't have to."

"You act like their house is yours. I can't imagine they really like that."

"Yes, they do," she insisted.

"You act like you're in love with them."

"Maybe they're in love with me, too," Sara said.

Abby straightened. "We're having an early dinner tonight," she said lightly. "I could use some help making it, if you want."

She didn't want, but she felt as if she should. So she stood side by side at the counter, thinking about how she and Eva had giggled making the bread, and here she was, working in silence with her mother, rolling out dough for pizza, cutting up green peppers and onions and shredding cheese. At dinner later, she sat at the table, dreaming she was at George and Eva's, where everyone talked at once, and here, the major sound was the clinking of forks, which made her so crazy she couldn't think of anything to say, either. "Mom?" she blurted, but Abby jumped up to get more soda from the kitchen. "Daddy—" she said, and Jack gave her that long, sad look that made her deflate.

Her father was the one she always used to count on to fix things. When she was little, she came to him for everything: a doll with a missing shoe, an insect that had gotten loose in the house, a question about why the sky wasn't green. If someone looked at her the wrong way or scolded her, he was the one she ran to. Delighted, he bought her a T-shirt that said, "That's it! I'm calling my daddy!" and she wore it everywhere. When she was eight, and had broken a tooth playing submarine in the bathtub, Abby had immediately, purposefully, scooped the tooth from the bathwater and dunked it in milk. She had called the dentist she worked for and made him agree to come to the office and put the tooth back in. "Right away," she urged. "We can't waste a second." Abby was all business but Jack was the one who had held Sara and comforted her.

"So what, it's a broken tooth," Jack had said. "At least it's not a broken heart, right?" Well, she knew all about broken hearts, because she seemed to have broken his. When she had told Jack about the baby, he hadn't said a word, and when she was finished, he quietly stood up. He looked at her as if he didn't quite know her anymore, and he stumbled out the back door, letting it slap behind him, and when she dared to look outside, she saw her father crouched in the garden, pulling up the jonquils he loved.

* * *

29

By nine, the hospital began to quiet. Visitors were gone, doctors left. Sara shifted in bed, plucking at the sheets, trying to get comfortable, and then she drifted into sleep.

She was dreaming. She was standing in Boston Garden watching the swan boats floating across the river. And then, she smelled her mother's perfume. Lily of the valley. She couldn't seem to open her eyes, and she waited, wondering what would happen next. She heard the soft pad of her mother's shoes tiptoeing into the room. She felt Abby standing over her, and then Abby touched Sara's face, quietly left, and as soon as she did, Sara's eyes opened. She yearned to have her mother back in the room. She wanted the hand back against her skin, like the brush of a curtain against a breeze.

And then, with a jolt, Sara woke completely and sat up in bed. Her roommate was sleeping, but her friends and her baby were gone. Sara's baby was gone, too.

Sara drew the sheets around her. If you asked Sara, she couldn't tell you how she felt about this baby now. She was all confused, maybe even more than she had ever been. It had been different when she was pregnant. Then, she had focused on the externals, on the way her body kept betraying her. She had been so used to being flat-chested, slim as a swizzle straw. Pregnant, Sara's breasts were full and lush, her stomach so swollen her belly button jutted out. The only big thing about her was her belly, and from the back, no one could even tell she was pregnant, which was how she was able to hide it so well in school for so long. But she knew, under her baggy clothes, she was all baby. She first felt the baby kick when she was in precalculus class and it had terrified her so much, she had clapped one hand over her mouth. And in honors history, she had a sudden bout of morning sickness. She had to get up and leave, gagging, barely making it to the girls' room where she threw up into the toilet, and when she got back, slinking into her seat, everyone bored holes through her with their staring. The girl behind her had tapped her on the shoulder and handed her a small white pill. "For stress," the girl said conspiratorially. "I got it out of my father's medicine chest. I couldn't do this class without them." She winked at Sara. "Everybody's on them. You want more, I'll give you the standard deal."

The larger Sara got, the more confused she became. Sometimes she actually agreed with Abby. She thought the baby was the worst thing that had ever happened to her, that she had been so stupid not to have had better birth control, not to have taken care of it the first week she had found out she was pregnant, not to have been so dumb she thought things might work themselves out. "Be thankful you don't have to go to a home," Abby said, and then she told Sara another Girls in Trouble story with an unsettling ending. A girl who wasn't given any pain medication because the nuns felt she should suffer for her sins. A girl who came back to her parents' home to find the locks changed. "How do you know this?" Sara whispered. "How do you know this is true?"

"I know," said Abby. "I just know."

Sometimes, though, Sara had loved the baby inside of her, had watched it in wonder when it rippled across her belly, when parts of it bumped and stretched up against her skin. "Elbow," she thought, touching a curve. "Knee." If the baby was on the left side of her, and she tapped her right side, the baby would surf its way toward her hands. As if it knew her. As if it wanted her comfort. Or maybe it wanted to comfort her.

She lifted up the sheet and looked at her stomach. How could she feel so empty?

She stared at her roommate. Her roommate's friends would probably be back. Her husband. Probably handsome and doting, the kind of man Abby would refer to as "darling," a man who would sleep on a mat by her bed if the hospital would only let him. Sara stared at the phone. Even if she dared to call them, she knew her friends wouldn't be home. Her friends were in labs or libraries or at their computers, studying even though it was summer. Especially because it was summer. They were with tutors, pushing to get their As into A pluses. Sara had been like that, too, right up until she met Danny.

She knew her friends' phone numbers by heart. Judy Potter, her study partner, a slim, funny girl with a fizz of sandy hair. They had spent hours quizzing each other, thinking up the most challenging questions. Judy believed in creating your own reality. "If we can dream it, we can be it," she said, and what Judy dreamed was for the two of them to go to Harvard. All Sara's friends had been smart girls. Smart girls who protected themselves. They were on the pill or had diaphragms or they had themselves fitted with IUDs. They wouldn't dream of sex without protection because too much was at stake—scholarships and college and all the future they wanted for themselves. And if they were foolish and unlucky enough to miss a period, they didn't wait around the way Sara had, hoping things might change, refusing to believe the truth, because really, how could such a thing happen to Sara, the one everyone said was a shoo-in to be the valedictorian? No, they took care of the problem, the same way they would an experiment gone wrong. They had safe, clean abortions done by good doctors and some of them went out dancing that same night, as if nothing had happened. They didn't look back. They got smarter and stronger and zoomed right ahead even as Sara got bigger, clumsier, and her mind and her future seemed to turn to mush.

Sara's roommate snored and then stopped. Abruptly, Sara reached for the phone and dialed. Three fours, a six, a nine. Robin Opaline. Robin used to be her best friend and lived less than three blocks away. They used to see each other all the time, used to tell each other everything, but Sara couldn't tell Robin she was pregnant, not until she was too big to hide it. She had run into Robin a month ago, just walking down the street, and Robin had looked at her as if Sara were a complete stranger. "Why didn't you trust me?" Robin asked, but all Sara could think about was whether she could trust Robin now, whether Robin would tell. And whether that would matter to her anymore.

The line rang three times and then caught. "Hello?" Robin said, but Sara couldn't make her mouth move.

"Paul? Is that you?" Robin said, and her voice took on a strange new quality Sara couldn't help but recognize. Love. "Bunny rabbit," Robin whispered. "Honey."

Sara hung up the phone. She pleated the sheet in her hands and told herself she wouldn't cry, then she turned away and looked out the window. From this floor, all you could see was another building across the way, a twinkling of lights.

In one more day, she could go home. Eva and George would take Anne home. Jack and Abby would take her. She would leave this room forever. And then, as soon as Sara was settled back home, she could get up and take the train from Brookline to Waltham, where George and Eva lived, just a half hour away. She could spend every day with them, and two weeks later, when George went back to work as a dentist, she could spend every day with Eva and Anne, helping out, being a part of their lives. Abby and Jack could try and stop her all they wanted. They could try and convince Sara that she was on the wrong course, but already, in her mind, Sara knew where she was going.

In her mind, she was on the subway. She was on the bus at Waverley Square riding into Waltham. She was getting off at Trapelo Road and walking three blocks to Warwick Avenue, heading up the flagstone path to George and Eva's light-filled home with a big grassy backyard. The neighbors had seen her there so many times, they knew her by name. A few might even wave and say hello. She could go into their house and know where everything was without even looking. She could make herself at home. As soon as she walked through the front door, Eva would smile. All Sara would have to do was look at Eva and she could feel loved and needed and appreciated. She could feel she had made the right choice. Eva was telling her the truth. No matter what anyone said.

Already, she was there.

chapter

three

The week Eva and George brought Anne home, they threw a welcome-home party. They hired the best caterer in town, a bull-doggish woman the *Boston Globe* had praised for the miraculous things she could do with a piece of salmon. There was a parade of people, Eva's best friend Christine, friends from work, neighbors and relatives. George's father, Harry, came up from Arizona, tan as a walnut, laden with presents, planning on staying only a few days because he was having the kitchen redone in his condo.

"Look at this one," Harry said. He rubbed two fingers in front of the baby's face, making a noise like someone calling a pet. *"Chi-chi-chi,"* he said.

"Dad," George said. "She's a baby, not a bird." His father gave a goofy grin, raised his hands, and then turned and headed for the Thai marinated chicken wings.

"My father's going to be a help," said George dryly, watching his father pile his plate.

"Well, thank goodness for friends," Eva said. Watching George's father made her miss her own parents, dead ten years now. She smoothed down the yellow dress Anne wore. How her parents would have loved all this. Well, she thought, they say you either want to give or protect your child from the kind of childhood you yourself had had, and Eva wanted to give Anne a childhood like her own. Happy. Filled with love.

"Eva! You look beautiful!" Nora, their next-door neighbor touched Eva's arm. "Eva!" someone else called and Eva turned to show off Anne.

They had planned to just have the party for a few hours, had even printed the times out on the invitations, but two hours passed and then three, and by six, Eva's eyes weren't focusing. Her house was noisy and confused, and her back and feet hurt. She was sure that since she hadn't carried the baby herself, she wouldn't need rest, wouldn't feel as overwhelmed, but to her surprise she found herself scheming about how fast she could politely shoo everyone away, thinking how much she wanted to get back into her nightgown and just be alone with the baby and with George.

The doorbell rang. Who would be coming this late? "Ai-yi-yi," Eva said.

"I'll get it," George said, his smile broadening. He stepped outside to welcome people in, the pink balloons he had tied to the railing dancing around him.

People crowded around Anne, which worried Eva. She watched for runny noses, for coughs, for people getting too close. The baby didn't seem to mind. Anne was placid and quiet, lying in a bassinet in the living room. She moved her fingers, like baby Braille.

"I have to hold this dumpling!" a neighbor said, reaching for Anne.

"Wash your hands," Eva ordered. The neighbor rolled her eyes, but Eva didn't care.

Eva lifted Anne up and felt the baby's wet diaper against her arm, looked up at her friend Christine and laughed. "Changing time. Again. Like a little leaky faucet."

"Let me take care of that diaper," Christine said.

"You already did two," Eva said. "I've been waiting a long time for diapers." She carried Anne away with a flourish. She made her smile bright.

But as soon as she brought Anne into the other room and set her on the white changing table, her confidence faded. The baby kicked and flailed her arms and moved so much Eva was afraid she might fall off the table. "Stop, stop," Eva tried to soothe, grabbing a diaper, keeping one hand on Anne who gazed solemnly up at her. Babies were supposed to have blue eyes, like chips of sky, but Anne's eyes were this eerie grey. Her hair was this rusty color. Sara's hair. Looking away, Eva got busy searching for the wipes.

The phone rang. "George!" she called, and the phone rang again, and she lifted Anne up and went into the other room, plucking up the receiver.

"Eva, it's Sara." Sara called every day, and usually Eva was happy to talk. All she had to do was look at Sara, and she'd want to hug the girl and take care of her. But now, the baby was squirming, and she could hear a guest calling for her. "The house is filled with company," Eva said. She thought suddenly of the letter she had first written Sara. *"There's nothing we like better than to be surrounded by people!"* Ha, she thought.

"Company? What company?" Sara said.

"Just friends. Relatives. You know." Anne squirmed harder. "Oh, I've got to go—"

"Wait—" said Sara.

"I'll talk to you later," Eva promised, "I want to talk to you—" and then Anne suddenly peed down the side of Eva's dress and Eva had to hang up.

She changed Anne first, going back into her room, pulling out a clean diaper. She held both of Anne's legs up and gently hoisted her up, tugging the diaper under Anne's bottom, shutting it with Velcro. Anne blew a spit bubble and batted her hands.

"Now me," Eva said, and went to change her dress, laying the baby in the center of her bed where she could keep an eye on her.

When the baby had first been placed into her arms, Eva had wanted her so much, she was afraid if she moved too quickly, the baby might disappear. She was used to the waiting, the hungriness of her want, but the having was something different, something almost equally terrifying, because now she knew just what she might lose.

All that first night they had brought Anne home, she and George hadn't been able to sleep. George had hooked up a monitor so they could hear any sound from the nursery, and every time there was even a hiccup, they both sat up in bed. "She's fine," George said. He sank back down, throwing one arm about Eva, but Eva couldn't help tensing, as if something were about to happen that would be out of their control, and finally, she swung her legs out of the bed and went into the nursery. Anne was sleeping so still that Eva put her hand by Anne's mouth, just to feel a sip of warm breath against her palm.

She knew she was just a tad anxious. Maybe because she was older and hadn't been around babies much. Maybe because getting this baby seemed like such a miracle, a last chance, that she felt she had to be extra vigilant. Before Anne had even been born, she and George had bought a library of books on baby care. They had taken a class at the Y, bathing a plastic doll, changing its diapers. They had read so many books on adoption, Eva could recite them. She knew all the pros and cons, how it was important to remember that mothering was what you did, not who you were.

Eva slid out of her pee-stained dress and slipped on another one. Anne made a sound and fussed. "What is it now?" Eva said, bending to pick her up again, patting her back.

She brought the baby back into the living room, just as George snapped a picture, making her and the baby both blink. Eva saw rings of light. Already on the mantel were framed photographs of Eva holding Anne, there was George lifting Anne up, a goofy smile spread across his face. And there was George, Eva, and Sara, who was so pregnant she was holding on to them for support. Nora picked up the photo and studied it.

"That girl. She's not coming here today, is she?" Nora's voice sounded accusatory.

"She'll be over later this week."

"God."

"God what?" Eva said. "Sara's a darling."

"I'm sure she is. It's just the things I read in the papers. It's a wonder anyone adopts at all. The courts just always seem to favor the biological parents."

"Now wait a minute," interrupted Christine. "Lane Prager has two adorable adopted kids! And the birth mother is just great. Newspapers love those horror stories."

"You know the father?"

"He's out of the picture," Eva said. "All they have to do is serve him with papers."

"I'd be nervous," Nora said. "The stories I hear—"

"Nora," Christine warned.

"It will all work out," Eva said firmly.

Eva could smile now, but for a long time she hadn't been so sure adoption would work out for them. Eva had always yearned for a child, but she had married late, when she was forty, and to her surprise, George, her sweet, tender, loving George, absolutely did not care if he had kids. Eva was the one smiling at babies in restaurants, while George reached for the menu. Eva had to stand close to little ones so she could practically inhale them, while George smiled and cracked silly knock-knock jokes at a distance, and after a few minutes of contact, he had had enough. And while George came to her classroom, dressed up as Mr. Tooth, talking to the kids about brushing, while he laughed and let them climb on his lap, it was Eva his eyes were glued on. He had thought he was so lucky to have found her, that for him, trying for a child too was just greedy. "You're my everything," he told Eva when she first expressed her wish for a child. And too, what about their age? "Do we have the energy?" George had asked her. "When our kid is in college, we'll be doddering old fools. When our grandkid is in diapers, we will be, too."

Eva refused to listen. She pointed out all the people who had kids later in life. Men in their sixties. Women in their late forties! All you had to do was go to the park and see the older mothers and dads to know how common it was. When she started to cry, George sat beside her and held her hand. "All right," George said slowly. "Why not?"

Her yearnings though were the only thing that grew inside of her. She bought ovulation kits, tried IVF and embryo transplants, and still, nothing happened, and each time, she grew more and more heartsick. "Well, we tried," George said, but Eva shook her head. "I think we should adopt," she told him.

She knew he was ambivalent. He came with her to the adoption lawyer, but the first few meetings, he didn't ask any questions, even though she touched his sleeve expectantly. "What do you think, George?" she blurted and he patted her knee. "Do adoptive parents ever change their minds about adopting?" he asked, and she started.

"No, no, that's an excellent question," the lawyer told them. "Of course they do. A child can be born with problems you didn't foresee. Finances can change."

"You wouldn't really change your mind, would you, after we brought a baby home?" Eva asked George in the car.

"I was just asking a question," he said. "Nothing's even happened yet." He leaned across the seat and kissed her. "Come on," he said. "I didn't mean to get you upset."

It was Eva's idea to go with open adoption. It seemed like the best for the child, the best for everyone. She hadn't been teaching for so many years not to know how important identity issues were with kids. "Sure, that makes sense," George agreed.

They made up their adoption scrapbook together, pasting in colored photographs of the two of them holding hands in the country, and then in the city and at the beach. Photos of their home and the bright, sunny room that would be the baby's. They wrote the letter, and got the 800 number, and placed their ad in twenty different little papers: LOVING COUPLE WANTS TO ADORE YOUR BABY. CALL 1–800–555–7799. But to her surprise, no one called, not even a wrong number. "Why aren't they picking us?" Eva asked George, astonished. "What's wrong with us? I'd pick us!"

Finally, a week or so later, to Eva's great relief, the calls began. The birth mothers didn't want to speak to George at all ("Well, they've all had bad experiences with men," the agency told them) and the few times Eva tried to get George on the phone, sure his warmth and wit would melt any unease, the birth mothers hung up. But worse, the birth mothers who called didn't seem to like Eva.

"You go to church?" one birth mother had asked her.

"We're Jewish."

"Would you convert?" And when Eva waffled, the woman sighed. "Forget it."

"You're a teacher?" one birth mother asked, disapprovingly. "So you won't be at home for the baby?"

Every plus about them Eva thought of, a birth mother saw as a minus. When she said she loved movies, one girl complained, "Kids need sunshine." When she said they lived in a semi-urban area, a birth mother protested, "Then there's no place for a kid to play." Every time Eva got off the phone, she felt overwhelmed. And none of the birth mothers ever called back. "Maybe we aren't doing the right thing," George suggested, "maybe we should fudge a little," but Eva was adamant. "No fudging," she said.

Eva began to despair of ever finding the right one. She began to feel like Miss Haversham, lost in her ragged white wedding gown, waiting and waiting for something that everyone else knew was never going to happen. But what worried her more was George, who didn't seem distressed at all. "What happens happens," he told her. "Either way I'll be happy."

She couldn't tell him how that seemed the worst answer of all to her.

All the waiting made Eva feel as if she had lived her whole life wrong, that her possibilities were sifting out of an hourglass. George kissed her shoulder. "So would it be the worst thing in the world if we didn't have a child?" George asked her, and all he had to do was look at her to know her feelings.

And then Sara had called.

Eva had loved their talks, had loved it that Sara talked with George, that George seemed to like Sara, too. "She's smart, that one," George said approvingly. And she had loved Sara on sight, such a dreamy-eyed girl, healthy, from a good home, with an IQ off the charts. Gorgeous red hair. A mouth that had a darling little slant to it. Meeting Sara's parents was another story. They sat so close to Sara on the couch, they looked like bookends. And as soon as Eva had mentioned a really open adoption, Jack had practically spilled his coffee. "Open is one thing, no doors is another," Jack said. Sara didn't speak much and finally, impulsively, Eva jumped up. "Come on, Sara," she said. "Let me give you a tour. George can talk to your parents." She held out her hand and Sara took it, and it was then Eva saw the bitten nails painted red and it touched her so much she wanted to reach over and take both Sara's hands in her own and warm them.

In the den, Sara picked up Eva's copy of *Wuthering Heights*. "I love the Brontës."

"Me, too," said Eva. She folded Sara's hands over the Brontë. "Borrow it."

And then Sara began coming over, more and more, and each time she did, she borrowed another book, returning it in such pristine shape that if she didn't talk about them so excitedly with Eva, Eva wouldn't even think she had read them. "I can lend you books, too, if you like," Sara offered.

"Oh, I'd love it," Eva said, and after that Sara began bringing books over to her, memoirs and novels and once a book about the color red that was so fascinating Eva sat up all night reading, her delight like sunlight splashed in the room. "I love this book," she told George, but what she really meant was she loved Sara.

Make friends, the adoption agency had urged them, get the birth mother to like you, and Eva had, and it had been ridiculously easy. And ridiculously fun to have another person to do things with. Another person she truly liked. "Our family's getting bigger," she told George, exultant.

Of course, there were times she worried. One night, when she and George were taking a walk in the neighborhood, using flashlights to show their way, Eva blurted, "Do you think we're the only people she's considering?"

"I don't know. I guess we could ask," George said.

"I'm afraid to hear the answer. What if she is? What if we're second choice? What if she's not going to choose us at all?" A door slammed shut and Eva shone her light at it.

"Well, we're still taking calls, right?"

"What calls? We haven't had a new one in weeks." Eva glanced at the neighborhood. Her eyes were already adjusted to the dark and she shut her flashlight off. "I want this so much it's making me crazy. Doesn't it make you crazy, too?"

George shrugged. "She's been pushed into things enough. Let's just let her be."

But Eva couldn't let anything be. The next day, she went into town and bought a beautiful blue box. In it, she put all the initial flurry of exchanges. The letters and photos. And she shared the box with Sara. "You saved all my letters?" Sara asked.

"Every one," Eva said, sifting through the box. She showed Sara the first letter Sara had sent them, the copy she had made of her and George's response. There was Eva's wedding picture, and then another picture of Sara and Eva and George in the backyard. Eva glanced at Sara, who was frowning. "Is something wrong?" Eva asked.

Sara shook her head. "Why are you saving everything?"

"Maybe it will be a scrapbook for the baby," Eva said.

"Maybe," Sara said, and Eva winced because *maybe* could also mean *no*.

Eva didn't tell Sara that sometimes, when she felt most unsure, when she worried that every time the phone rang it might be Sara telling them she had chosen someone else, Eva would get down that blue box. She'd reread all of Sara's letters, she'd study the photographs, as if each one might be a talisman keeping their covenant.

One day, when Eva and Sara were just sitting out back on the chaise lounges, sipping iced tea, Sara talked about what it would be like to recuperate from giving birth, how it would feel to go back to school in the fall, and how anxious that made her. She talked about Danny, too, how much she had loved him, and how he had hurt her. Eva had to admit it was hard to listen to that because the girl was in such pain, it was hard to make the appropriate supportive noises about Danny getting back in touch when what she most hoped was that he'd disappear forever. But then, as Sara cried, all she could think about was how much this young girl was hurting, how awful a thing it must be to be sixteen and pregnant and abandoned to boot. She got up from her chair and leaned over and wrapped both arms about Sara and rocked her. Sara looked up at Eva, blinking. "My parents think I'm a fool for loving someone like that. They think I made the biggest mistake of my life," Sara said.

"It's never a mistake to love," Eva said.

"The baby's a mistake."

"Oh, my God, absolutely not! How could you even think such a thing," said Eva, rubbing Sara's back. "This baby's a miracle." Impulsively, Eva kissed Sara's hair. It smelled of maple and vanilla. "And you are, too. You're the miracle in our life."

"I am? Really, you think that?" Sara sat up, rubbing at her eyes, snuffling, so that Eva dug in her pocket for a clean tissue and handed it to her.

"Every day I think that. I love having you here. I hope you love being here, too."

Blowing her nose noisily, Sara looked off into the distance. "I do," she said. "I really do." She grew suddenly calm again. "I've decided something," Sara said.

"What is it, honey?" said Eva alarmed, and Sara reached for her purse. For a moment, Eva wasn't sure what she was doing and then Sara dug in her wallet and brought out a crumpled photo and handed it to Eva. It was Sara, in an Indian-print summer dress, standing next to a boy with brown hair, the two of them laughing.

"It this Danny?" Eva asked and Sara nodded. Eva tried to study the boy's eyes, to see what he might be capable of, but no matter where she placed the picture, he wasn't looking at her, but always at Sara, like one of those pictures with the eyes cut out that they always had in horror films. Eva handed the photo back and Sara waved her hand.

"You keep it," Sara said. "For the blue box."

"The box?"

"So the baby will know who its father was."

"Sara?" Eva said. The air about her seemed to grow lighter.

"I think you should be my baby's parents," Sara said, and wept harder.

And that had been that. Sara began coming over every day. She helped Eva cook dinner, she played checkers with George. They all talked on the phone every night, they took so many pictures that the blue box began to bulge with them, and although Eva meant to get a scrapbook, she waited, superstitious, she kept filling up the blue box with more and more photos and letters. "After the baby is born, I'll figure it out," she told George.

Although Eva was dying to come, Abby wouldn't allow Eva to go with them to the doctor's appointments. Sara gave Eva copies of all her sonograms, pictures Eva pasted into an album and couldn't help peeking at. Eva learned to read Sara like a barometer, tracking her progress by the glow in her cheeks, the swell and ripple of her belly, even by the new way she was walking. "Tell me what it feels like," Eva kept asking her.

One day, Eva was lying on the couch, foot to foot with Sara. George was making dinner that night and Eva could hear him chopping vegetables and meat for stew, the thwack of the cleaver against the cutting board. "Ugh, I feel so bloated," Sara complained, and Eva rested her hand on her own flat belly. Absently, she stroked it.

"My parents won't touch my belly," Sara said.

"Can I?" Eva asked, and when Sara nodded, Eva put one hand over Sara's belly. She felt a sudden snap under her fingers, making her draw back her hand in amazement. "Baby kicked," Sara said. She took Eva's hand and put it back on her belly. "You can listen if you want. The baby makes noises."

Tentatively, Eva rested her head along Sara's belly. There it was, that whooshing sound, and she bolted upright. "George!" she called. "George! Come now! Quick!"

"What's wrong?" George rushed in.

Eva grabbed for his hand. "Listen," she urged.

Gingerly, he crouched down. He rested his head. "Oh, my God," he said, delighted.

Eva put her hand back on Sara's belly and suddenly Sara's belly seemed to roll toward her fingers. "Oh!" she said, astonished, lifting her hand, and the roll stopped. "The baby's communicating with me!"

"What's the baby saying?" Sara asked.

Eva grinned and looked at George. "That it's never been so happy in its entire life."

Oh, but she was the one who was so happy. Every time Sara walked into the room, Eva's baby was walking into the room, too. But it wasn't just that. Sometimes it seemed to Eva that Sara was the only one besides herself who was so bonded to the idea of open adoption. The only other one who was really in it together with her. Everyone else got so cautious it made her crazy. As if they couldn't celebrate with her until it was a done deal! She couldn't stop talking to George about feeling the baby kick, but she knew her George, she knew he was happy mostly because she was happy, that his big love was her. Even Christine—her best friend!—was hesitant when Eva told her, when she tried to explain how sometimes, eerie as it was, she felt as if she and Sara were connected on a deeper level than anyone could imagine. How amazing it was that they could talk for hours. How wonderful that they truly liked and respected each other, that they considered each other family. "Sara is great," she told Christine, "and the baby! The baby's a real presence. It's like we're Pyramus and Thisbe," she said excitedly. "I swear we're talking! I touched one side of Sara's belly and the baby came rolling toward me!"

"Did you hear what you said? Pyramus and Thisbe. Sara's the wall," Christine said.

"No, no, she's not the wall! There's no wall! We love Sara," Eva said excitedly. "We couldn't have asked for a more perfect situation, a more perfect girl." She looked around the kitchen, imagining where she'd dry the baby bottles, where she'd put a high chair.

And then, Eva had seen the baby being born, standing there, gripping Sara's hand so tightly it was as if the experience were being transfused right into Eva's veins. She had sweated along with Sara. When Sara screamed, Eva screamed and gripped her hand harder.

And now Anne was here, right in this house. Now people were crowded around them, and now, glory be, they were finally beginning to leave.

"You call if you need anything," Nora said. "Remember, I'm right next door."

Christine hugged her. "You're going to be a natural! You must be so thrilled!"

"Of course she's thrilled," someone said. "Look at that smile."

"Let me do those dishes," Nora said, gathering plates.

"Don't be silly, you're here to visit, not to work," Eva said.

Nora put the plates down. "They say when you have a newborn, you should go to the doctor so he can give you tranquilizers!" She laughed.

Eva's smile began to feel pasted to her face.

"Are you springing for a baby nurse?" Nora asked.

"Nah. We want to do it all ourselves. And Sara will be here."

"Sara? The birth mom? You're kidding, right?"

You sound like Jack and Abby, Eva thought. "A baby needs all the love possible," Eva said evenly. "And Sara's a part of our family."

There was a silence. "How nice," said Nora.

Lynne Matson, who had six cats and lived down the block, touched

Eva's arm. "Listen, I know exactly what to get the baby. One of those red and black and white mobiles they say stimulates their mind. I just wanted to wait before I bought it. To make sure everything was going to be fine. Who needs to deal with returns, right?" Lynne said.

Eva's smile tightened. She bet any gift from Lynne would be covered with cat hair.

"Best of luck to all of you," Lynne said, and headed for the door, waving.

When the house was empty again, Eva peered anxiously into Anne's bassinet. She couldn't help feeling that this baby was somehow on loan.

"Let her snooze," George said. "She's had a busy day."

George and Eva began to clean up, collecting the dishes, putting the gifts on the table to open the next day, when they weren't so tired. "I should have let Nora help," she told George, and he shrugged. "Next time," he told her.

Eva stretched. Who could imagine that such a tiny little thing would generate so many diapers, so many wipes? Every five minutes it seemed she was reaching for a drool cloth. Every ten minutes she had to change the baby's clothes—or her own because Anne had spit up on her. And every two hours, Anne ate, which meant scrubbing and boiling and drying bottles. Already Eva's whole body ached.

She wanted to be held. She heard George clattering in the kitchen, and she suddenly thought of all the times he used to surprise her, showing up at her school to take her to lunch and driving her to a fancy hotel instead. They'd make love the whole lunch hour, and she'd come back to school flushed and happy, her hair a little awry, and an hour later she'd be starving because she had never gotten around to eating. Their old life, before Anne, pulsed inside her. They hadn't made love once since they had brought her home.

She rubbed her neck, lifted up her hair as if to cool herself, and even though George was a room away, she felt a flare of desire so strong, it nearly toppled her over.

Eva stopped straightening the living room. Everything could wait. She went to the bedroom and put on a new sheer black nightgown. She stood in front of the mirror, admiring it. One of her friends had told her that after she had had her son Reggie, she hadn't wanted sex for a year. "Hemorrhoids! Sore, leaky breasts!" her friend had joked.

Eva had a baby now, but she hadn't given birth. Her hormones were intact, her desire spiking. She brushed her hair and daubed perfume on all her pulse points. She felt as if electric current were shimmering off her. She left her feet bare and padded to the kitchen to find George. The room was empty. Everything was cleared up. "George?" she said.

She checked the kitchen, and then she saw Anne's door was ajar. She touched the door with a fingertip, opening it more. Anne was sleeping, her rosy little mouth an O. George was in the rocker, half dozing, too.

"Hey," he said with a sleepy smile. He touched her nightgown. "Look at you."

She smiled back at him. He hinged up on his elbows and then got up. She trailed two fingers up along his spine, so he turned and draped his arm about her. She didn't know what it was about him—but all she had to do was look at him and she wanted him. He led her to their room, falling with her onto the bed. She touched the constellation of freckles along his shoulder. He cupped her face in his hands. He pulled off her nightgown, his shirt, his pants, letting them all puddle to the floor. He shut his eyes. He was just about to kiss her when Anne suddenly cried, a newborn mewl that made Eva think of one of Lynne's cats, and then the moment died. Anne's cries grew louder, more frantic, and they both bolted up, grabbing their robes, their slippers kicked under the bed, and rushed to tend her.

"I'll get the bottle," George said, and then Eva lifted Anne up and sat in the rocker with her. Anne's eyes squinched tightly shut, her mouth opened like a drawstring purse. There was that mewl again.

"Nineteen eighty-seven. A very good year," George said, coming into the room, presenting the bottle. Latching on, Anne sucked greedily, her small legs kicking against Eva's.

"Who's a hungry girl?" George said.

Anne fell asleep eating, and Eva gently put her back in the crib.

Eva went into the bathroom to wash her hands, to splash cool water on her face. She came into the nursery and there, in the rocker, was George, one hand slung on the crib, the other in his lap, his eyes rolling with dreams, sleeping.

"Come back to bed," she whispered. His lids fluttered and opened. He stood heavily, and slung one arm about her shoulder and then yawned. She got him into their bed, and as soon as his head hit the pillow, he was snoring faintly. Eva took George's hand in hers. I'm so lucky, she thought. She had George, and Anne. She was looking forward to seeing Sara. And then she shut her eyes, and she slept, too.

For Eva, falling in love with the baby was almost like falling in love with a mate. There was the first stage, that giddy infatuation and euphoria, where everything Anne did was delightful and incredible. Look at how she grabbed Eva's finger and held on fast! Look how she was trying to lift her head just so she could follow Eva's every move! It killed Eva with pleasure, it made her want to move around the room, taking extra steps just so she could see the baby's response. Eva walked out of Anne's room so the baby could nap, and two seconds later, she went back in. Leaning over the crib, she inhaled Anne's scent: powder and roses. She touched the silky skin, the bunny toes, and then she crept from the room.

But then there were the day-to-day adjustments to this new presence, and the mountains of diaper changes and spit-ups didn't make it any easier. Eva boiled bottles in the kitchen and then ran downstairs to throw in laundry and got back upstairs just in time to put the breakfast dishes in the dishwasher. She was just about to go downstairs and put the clothes in the dryer when Anne woke up, and the mewling cry that had seemed so impossibly delicious a week before now made Eva shut her eyes. She grabbed a bottle from the fridge and ran it under the hot water to warm it. Anne's cries went up a decibel.

"Here's Mommy," she said, entering Anne's room. Anne's face was scrunched tight as a purse. Her hands balled into angry fists, and when Eva picked her up, Anne's whole body stiffened, as if it were Eva's fault that Anne had to wait. She fed her, and then lifted her up to change her. "There, a nice clean diaper," Eva said, and then, just as she was about to fasten the tabs, Anne peed over the diaper.

"God!" Eva breathed, and Anne waggled her arms and legs. "Stay still," Eva ordered. Her temper frayed. Grabbing for another diaper, she heard the jangle of the phone in the other room. It might be school and she needed to talk to them, to ask about her class for next year. It might be George. She picked Anne up to go get the phone, and it abruptly stopped ringing. How did anyone ever have time to do anything? She thought of the mothers at the preschool, how the nonworking mothers were just as harried as the working ones, how sometimes the only difference was that the working mothers were better dressed, and that instead of a sloppy ponytail, they had a really good haircut.

She fastened Anne's diaper and Anne suddenly yawned. "Sleepy again?" Eva said. She felt guilty. She shouldn't have snapped. Anne was just a baby, what was the matter with her? She put Anne back in her crib and went to finish the laundry. She boiled bottles, and then went to check on Anne, who was awake in her crib, not making a sound.

Anne was now so quiet, it was eerie. Eva picked her up and made parabolas on her little back. "Sleeping?" Eva asked, and started to set Anne down in the crib, and as soon as she did, Anne's eyes flew wide open. "Don't have anything to say?" Eva whispered. She watched the tiny chest rise and fall and rise up again.

"A quiet baby! Count yourself lucky!" Christine advised when Eva called to give her the daily report. "You can work. You can read."

"Of course I can," Eva agreed, starting to feel a little better. When she got off the phone, she decided to work on her lesson plans for the next year. She set Anne in the bassinet beside the table and she started fiddling with ideas. But Anne was so silent, that instead of helping Eva to concentrate, it took her focus away. "Hey," Eva said, and Anne gazed up at her with enormous eyes. "What are you thinking?" Eva asked. Anne yawned, her lids fluttered, and then Eva bounded up and turned on the radio. She had heard music was good for babies, that it helped them with their speech, and she, for one, couldn't wait for Anne to start talking. She leaned over to Anne. "So what do you think, should we go to the park, see some people?" Eva asked. "Are you getting a little stir-crazy, like me?" She suddenly thought of Sara and missed her; it'd be wonderful to have her company in the house again, her help. Anne studied her toes, ignoring Eva. She got Anne's jacket, she filled some bottles. Already, thinking about getting out, she felt a little lighter, and then as soon as she reached to put the jacket on Anne, she heard a pattering against the window, and when she looked up, she saw the rain, and the heaviness came back.

That night, Anne woke them at three, an hour before her normal feeding. Eva turned to George, who was sleeping so soundly an atom bomb wouldn't have woken him. "George," she said, shaking his shoulders, but he still slept, and she swung her legs over the bed to go and get the bottle.

She held the baby and fed her, humming something under her throat. Anne sucked more greedily, her eyes squinched shut. Anne drained the bottle and Eva set it down, standing, the baby in her arms. A slant of moon came in through the blinds. Eva looked down at Anne and was startled to see the baby watching her with grave slate eyes. "What?" Eva whispered. "Tell me." And then Anne put her small baby hand on the side of Eva's face, like a conversation, and something fluttered through Eva's stomach, and no matter how late it was, and how tired she was, she stayed right where she was, swaying the baby in her arms, as if Anne might be a dream that would disappear in the cool light of morning.

chapter

four

It was morning, twelve days since she had given birth, and the day Sara was due to go to Eva and George's. She was trying to stay in bed until after her parents left. Already, she had been up since five, grabbing for her summer reading, *The Mill on the Floss,* trying to get lost in it the way she usually was, but today it wasn't working. Maggie Tulliver whispered at her, but she couldn't hear. She missed the baby too much. She missed George and Eva, and even though every day she had called, first from the hospital and then from home, it wasn't the same. "Just have to change Anne," Eva said, her voice rushing. "Just have to give the baby a bath. I'll call as soon as I can," George promised.

She could smell her mother's coffee, the slightly burnt toast her father loved and Abby always scraped. She could hear her father's voice, but not what he was saying.

Sara couldn't stay in bed anymore. Leaping up, she grabbed her blue robe and headed for the bathroom, locking the door. She turned the water on full force, as hot as it would go. The mirrors had to be fogged over before she'd undress. She couldn't bear to look at her belly, at the stretch marks like white webs. Her breasts shrunk down to nothing.

She stepped into the shower. The hot water hit her like a punishment. She grabbed the soap and washed, staring up at the tiles, the door, any- where but her body. Danny never could stop looking. He used to say her skin reminded him of apricots, that her being so sleek, so small-boned, was sexier than the lushest model. He used to wrap her hair around his hand like a skein of yarn, and then he'd draw her gently against him. She sighed just as he drew a breath in. "I inhale, you exhale," he said.

What would he think now if he saw her body? She tilted her head toward the water, so it coursed down her like rivers. What would he think now if he saw Anne? Would he say, "I made a terrible mistake," the same way she sometimes did? Even now, she still couldn't help harboring hope that Danny would come back. He still had to sign papers saying he knew there would be a hearing giving up his rights, which wouldn't be until six months from now. A lot could happen in six months, couldn't it? He could still find her.

Or she could find him if she only knew how.

She had thought about that the day George and Eva had taken Anne home from the hospital. She had been holding the baby tight in her arms. The baby seemed tinier than anything she could have imagined. Chubby legs folded in like commas. The baby's face didn't look anything like Danny's, but Anne was the only part of Danny that was still hers. The moment Eva lifted the baby away from her, the whole room got darker. It didn't matter what she had felt before, or promised, it all seemed like a terrible mistake and Sara suddenly wanted time to stop.

"Wait!" she cried, and Eva smiled, one hand protectively over the baby's head. "We'll see you soon," George promised. *Stay with me,* she wanted to tell them. *Don't go.* And then they had left and Sara had lain in the white hospital bed, staring at the walls, her arms suddenly so empty she couldn't imagine anything could ever fill them.

Sara bent to the spigots, making the water hotter. Then she sat down in the tub, the spray pouring over her, and she thought about the baby, and about Danny.

Danny Slade.

Sara had met Danny over a year ago, a bright sunny May day when she was fifteen. Like everyone else, she had spring fever. All that week Sara hadn't been able to concentrate. She meant to go to the library, and instead found herself at a shopping mall, drawn to all the filmy dresses, the blouses made of cheap, shiny material. She had spent days trying to finish a paper at home, but the scent of the roses came in from the open window and drove her crazy, and when she got up and shut her window, their perfume grew even more powerful. It was more than spring fever, she told herself. This was possession.

She was in the science lab, measuring chemicals into a test tube for a project she was doing. She was the only one in the lab besides the science teacher, a middle-aged woman who insisted all the students call her Dr. Kubin, and who wore a white lab coat every day as if any moment she might be called to perform surgery. Dr. Kubin was saying something to Sara, but Sara felt drugged from the weather, and Dr. Kubin's voice seemed muffled.

"Should I ask you a third time?" Dr. Kubin snapped.

"Ask me what?"

Dr. Kubin sighed. "Again, Sara? Those test tubes aren't clean." Dr. Kubin tapped one of the tubes, and Sara shut her eyes until there was a loud, sudden crash.

Sara's eyes flew open. Her books were now on the floor, and there was Dr. Kubin, her hands on her hips. "Now, do I have your attention?" Dr. Kubin said acidly.

"I'm sorry—" Sara bent to retrieve the books, but Dr. Kubin kicked them out of her way with the toe of her pump. "Get out of my lab," she said.

Sara needed to finish this project. It was the kind of thing that would be a real plus on her resume. And it was her project, her baby.

"Dr. Kubin?" Sara said, but Dr. Kubin ignored her and sat down at another computer, pulling up Sara's program. "Dr. Kubin?" Sara repeated, and Dr. Kubin waved her hand, as if she were shooing a fly, and Sara grabbed her books and ran out of the room, fighting tears, and there, leaning against a building, smoking, was Danny Slade.

She knew him. Walk past the principal's office and there was Danny Slade. Be late to school, and there was Danny Slade, outside, smoking, taking his time, so beautiful you could die just looking at him. He always wore the same musky patchouli oil, so strong that sometimes you could walk into an empty corridor, and you'd know he had just left it. She knew the stories about him. That except for Danny, his family was superreligious and conservative, and that Danny was the black sheep, a boy who was smart enough, but didn't give a damn about school, a boy who actually said things like "God is dead" in class and didn't flinch when he was sent to the principal for it. A boy whose father had died in some scandalous accident that Danny wouldn't talk about, which made it all the more mysterious. "I want him," the girls stage-whispered when they saw him, and even though Danny could have had any one of them, he kept to himself and that made them all want him more. He had long, glossy dark hair and strange eyes, bright and green as a traffic go signal, and now they were staring at her, as if he recognized her from somewhere a long time ago. That look worked its way into her bones. "Sara," he said.

She was startled he even knew her name. He glanced at her books, taking another drag of his cigarette, lowering his head so his hair fell into his eyes. "You're always reading," he said. She thought he was making fun of her, the way some of the kids at school did. Every time report cards came out, someone would always jeer at her, "What'd you get, all As again?" as if being smart were a terrible disease you might never recover from. Every time her name or the name of another honors student was announced on the PA system for winning an award, there would be snickers. Eyes would roll.

"Don't ruin those beautiful eyes," Danny said. His voice was so soft, so kind, that she knew he wasn't making fun of her and she burst into tears.

She tried to stop crying, but she couldn't move, couldn't take her eyes off his face. She was sure he was going to walk away, to leave her. He seemed the kind of boy who couldn't stand tears, who couldn't stand trouble not of his own making.

He threw his cigarette into the dirt, grinding it with his heel, and then came so close to her that her heart knocked against her ribs. He touched her arm as delicately as if she were a piece of fine china. "Want to do something besides read?" he said.

It was a question, but it got inside of her, like a command.

She followed him. She was too upset still to talk, but he didn't seem to mind. He did all the talking. "Detention. Smoking in class," he said. "What was your crime?"

"Daydreaming," she said, and he raised one brow.

"We both had bad days, then," he said. She followed him to a fence, and when he climbed over, she climbed over, too, right into a lushly green backyard with a shimmering blue pool. "It's warm today. Want to swim?" he asked.

"I don't have a suit."

He grinned at her, shucking off his T-shirt. He was lean and angular, with a faint scar on his stomach, and as soon as she saw it, she wanted to touch it. He took off his leather belt and she froze. She was thin as a soda straw, the last of the girls in her class to wear a bra, and even then she barely filled it out. No way was she going to take off her clothes, especially in front of Danny Slade. She looked around for the gate, then she heard a sudden splash, and there was Danny, in the pool in his jeans, waving lazily at her. "It's hot. Your dress will dry," he told her, and then she dove in, too, her dress billowing up about her, and as soon as the water hit her, she felt the whole bad day washed from her.

"Better?" he said. They swam a little, her dress fluting out about her legs, like a pour of milk, his blue jeans turning black and heavy with water, and then they sat on the edge of the pool. He lifted up his dry T-shirt and slowly wiped the water from her face with it, and she felt a shiver of pleasure so keen, she had to shut her eyes. Her thin cotton dress dripped about her, her hair sluiced back. "You're lucky to have a pool," she said.

He laughed. "I wish. This pool isn't mine!"

"It isn't?" She looked around. "Whose is it then?"

"Beats me. The only thing I know about these people is they leave the house at noon and don't come back until after midnight and they're a little nuts. The only time they drain their pool is winter." He leaned toward her conspiratorially. "I've been coming here every hot day. If you're careful, no one even knows you're here."

He walked her back to her block and by the time they got there her dress was nearly dry. And then he turned to her. "See? I made you feel better, didn't I?"

"I feel great."

"Let me tell you a secret. You start feeling bad again, you think about the pool."

"Deal," she said, though she knew it wouldn't be the pool that'd claim her thoughts. He leaned toward her and wrapped one of her ringlets about his finger. She didn't mind. Her hair was the one true gift her mother gave her. It set her apart, made her special, and it made other girls look at her with something close to yearning, so they'd keep trying perms and bottled color in imitation of her. "I like your hair," he said. "It's so wild."

She sat perfectly still, suddenly a little frightened. "But I'm not," she said.

He let her hair go, studying her. "You're different than I thought you'd be," he said.

"What do you mean?"

"You look at me when I talk to you. You really look."

"You're different, too."

"Really? How?"

She thought for a moment. "You look, too."

His smile spread. "I would have thought everyone was always looking at you, that you'd have a million boyfriends."

"Not even one," she said, flushing.

"Well," he said, as if he were considering something, and then he waved at her, and walked away. "See you," he said.

Electrified, she couldn't move until he was out of sight. Then she ran into her house, racing for the phone, calling her friend Judy. "Guess where I've been," she said.

The whole time Sara was telling her, Judy kept sucking in a breath. "You and Danny Slade?" Judy said, amazed. "Are you on drugs?"

"He's nice. Really nice."

Judy was silent again for a minute. "If you don't tell me every detail, I'll hurt you."

"There won't be any more details," Sara said. A cavern opened up inside of her, and she felt the enormity of that loss.

"You just be careful," Judy said.

That night, Sara woke up, remembering the way Danny had stroked her face with his shirt. She got up from bed and got her dress and held it to her face, breathing in the chlorine smell. She went to the mirror and

brushed her hair until it snapped with light, gazing into her own eyes, trying to see what Danny had seen there.

The next day, when she came out of school, she felt a charge in the air,
and there was Danny Slade again, waiting for her, looking at her with as
much astonishment as she looked at him. "I didn't expect you here," Sara
said, and he shook his head.

"That makes two of us," he said. "What is it about you? This is the first
time I've ever waited for a girl. The first time I've ever wanted to."

They began to see each other. Every day after school, he took her
someplace different. Sometimes swimming. Sometimes to a diner where
they sat and dunked their fries into ketchup and wrote their names on the
white plate. They sat talking when Sara should have been studying, talking
when she should have been at her computer, and when she talked, he
didn't take his eyes from her. He acted as if nothing were more important
than what she was saying, even if it was just, "Pass the salt, please." When
she got home, with her books spread about her, she couldn't see anything
on the page except for his face.

"What are you dreaming about?" Abby asked curiously, but Sara
couldn't tell her, Sara didn't want to share Danny or anything about him
with anyone, least of all her parents, who didn't want her dating, who'd
end it. "Concentrate on studying," Abby said, and Sara thought how Danny
took books from her hands, kissing her fingers. "When do you think
you're going to need to know calculus?" Danny asked her. "Where's all
this schooling going to get you?" He never asked her anything about
school, and when she mentioned something, he interrupted her. "I just like
being with you," he said, and hearing something like that seemed like the
most astonishing fact she could ever learn.

"I want to be a therapist," she told Danny. "I want to help people with
their feelings."

He leaned his forehead against hers. "Help me with mine," he said in a
low voice and then he laced his fingers together with hers and kissed her so
gently that for one moment she wasn't certain their lips had even met.

But the more he was with her, the more questions he began to ask.
What was it like growing up in a house where you were the only child,

where your parents doted on you? What was she learning in school and what was it like taking all these special courses, knowing your future was wide open, that you were special?

"It doesn't feel wide open," Sara said. "It feels like a path I can't deviate from if I know what's good for me. And I don't feel special." Just that day, her history teacher had told her that her thesis idea was a dime a dozen, and that if Sara wanted to stand out, she had better think on it a little harder. "I feel like I'm drowning," Sara said.

Danny took her hand, turning it over so he was looking at her palm. "Then I'll be your lifeline," he said.

He began to buy her presents. Beaded bracelets she never took off. Magnets in the shape of planets. Tortoiseshell barrettes for her hair. And once, a book of short stories by Kafka, inscribed: "*This is for you, Danny.*" She looked at the book, and then at him, surprised.

"Is something wrong?" he asked. "You don't like Kafka?"

"No, no, I do. I just—I thought you weren't interested in books—"

"I'm interested in you—in what you're interested in. And I know who Kafka is," he said, wounded. "I'm not stupid." He opened the book, showing her where he had underlined certain parts for her: Gregor Samsa awakening to find himself a giant insect. And one line jumping out at her: "*There was a time when I went every day into a church since a girl I was in love with knelt there in prayer for half an hour in the evening and I was able to look at her in peace.*" A girl I was in love with! She snuck a cautious glance at him, and there he was smiling at her. The fact that he had given her this book, that he had written in it, touched her so much, she clutched the book to her chest.

She read the book so much she had it memorized. She carried it everywhere with her. She was reading it one night in the living room when her mother passed by and nodded at Sara approvingly. "Oh, Kafka! That's one author I haven't read yet," her mother said. "Maybe I should read it, too, when you're done with it. You sure seem to love it."

Sara held the book tighter. "I do love it," she said, though what she meant was she loved him. She loved Danny. That night, she tucked the book deep in one of her drawers, burying it protectively under some sweaters, and when her mother asked about the book again, Sara said she had lost it at school. "I'll order a copy," her mother said.

"What is going on with you?" Robin complained when Sara broke a study date. "I'm going to have to study with someone else," Robin warned, "and I'm not going to miss another movie because of you," and all Sara could think was, good, it was one less thing cutting into her time with Danny. She canceled so many plans with Judy that Judy finally refused to make any plans with her at all. "Spur of the moment or nothing," Judy said. Her friends used to call her at night to talk; but her phone was silent now, and the one time she called Robin, the conversation was tense and stilted. "I feel like I don't know you anymore," Robin said, and Sara had to agree with her, because she knew she wasn't herself any longer. She was someone better when she was with Danny.

"Why are you with him?" her friends asked.

"Why's he with you?" one of the tough, vocational girls asked Sara, planting herself in Sara's path. She gave Sara a quick, measuring look. "No accounting for taste."

And Sara, too, asked Danny, over and over, as if he had the key to some secret, "Why me?" She tried to deconstruct their relationship, the way she might if she were a therapist. Pheromones, she thought, that chemical scent that zinged from one person to another, attracting you so much it could change the way you acted. She thought he was going to say, because he thought she was beautiful, or because she was different from his other girlfriends, but instead he just shrugged. "I feel like I've always known you," he said. "People say that no one knows why someone loves someone, but that's bullshit. You know. Deep inside of you, right in the first few seconds you meet." He took a piece of her hair, a curl, and swung it. "You and me, we'll always be connected."

She started. *Love.* He had said *love.* And he began saying it more and more.

They had been seeing each other every day for a few weeks when he took her to his house. It was in a rundown section of town, the lawns scrubby looking, the houses in need of paint. "This is it," he said, and he gave her a funny look.

"You have a bigger lawn than we do," she said finally, and he smiled.

"No one's here," he told her.

Inside was cramped and dark, and she struggled to adjust her eyes to the dim light. She trailed her hand along the ugly brown couch by the wall. The carpet was worn and grey with a mysterious reddish stain that made her want to look anywhere but at it. Her eyes flew to the big wooden cross on the wall, to the ashtrays filled with cigarette butts.

"Home sweet home," said Danny dryly.

Sara's words knotted in her throat. She didn't know what to say about this place, but she didn't want to lie to Danny. A photograph caught her eye. A woman, lean and pretty in a printed dress, her hair curling about her face. "She's beautiful—" Sara said, grateful for something she actually liked in here. She leaned closer, hoping to find something more to exclaim about it, and then she saw the hard, lonely cast to the woman's mouth, a bitterness that made her step back as if she had been slapped.

"My mother," Danny said. "My dad left when I was five. Ran off with a waitress and then, a month later, he died."

Sara lowered her eyes. "I know about the accident."

"He and his new honey died coming home from Niagara Falls. Both of them drunk. Did you know that part?" Danny's shoulders were so hunched, she wanted to touch them.

"I'm sorry."

"We keep that part in the family. Our dirty little secret."

"I won't tell."

"I know. I trust you. It's just that it was so hard for us, for so long." He told her that his mother didn't believe in women working, but what else could she do, left like that? "The church gave her a job. Office work. Money. First pick of all the clothes people left off for charity." Danny made a face. "First time I wore a wool sweater to class, someone else pointed and said, 'Hey, that was mine.' I took it off and never wore it or any of those church clothes again. My older brother Mike got a job to help out. He took over." Danny told Sara that Mike had been running the house since he was eight, just like he was the man of it. Laying down the law, taking care of all the bills, controlling all the money, doling it out to Danny depending on what kind of mood he was in, which was always a crappy one.

"My mother thought he was God's gift and I was the Devil's," Danny said bitterly. "Still does. And so does he. Both of them think if I just went to church, I'd straighten out." He shook his head. "My brother's working in Texas now, selling cars, picking the tumbleweeds out of his teeth. But he might as well still be here, hovering over us like some ghost. He sends home money, he calls to check up on me, and even from a distance, he still can yell. The good son. Mr. Goddamn Perfect."

"You're the perfect one," Sara said. Tentatively she moved toward him. If she didn't touch him now, she was sure she would die. She touched his arm and a jolt of heat flew through her fingers. She swore he felt it, too, because he turned to her, surprised.

"My family—" he said quietly. "I told my mother about you, but she acted like she didn't believe someone like you could like someone like me."

She tried to swallow and couldn't. *I more than like you,* she thought, but she couldn't say it. His gaze pinned her in place, made her breath into little shallow clips. "I'd like to meet your mother," she said, and her voice sounded strange and faraway to her.

"You would?" he said. "Really?"

Sara glanced back at the photo, at the woman's hard line of a mouth, and thought, what would she say to Danny's mother? How could she feel comfortable under that gaze? "I'd love to," she said, and Danny glanced at his watch. "Let's do it, then. She ought to be here in half an hour," he said. He was suddenly giddy, like a little kid, smoothing back his hair, tucking in his shirt, making Sara wish for a dress instead of her black T-shirt and shorts.

They waited around that day for Danny's mother. They sat on the couch kissing, talking, and every time a car drove past, Danny pulled away and looked up at the window expectantly, and Sara rushed to comb her ringlets with her fingers. "False alarm," Danny said. The phone rang once, and Danny jumped up, grabbing for it, his face bright. He cocked his head, listening. "Mike," he said finally. She heard his voice, rising and falling. "Mom told you? Want to talk to her?" he said, and he sounded different to Sara. New. Hopeful. And then she saw a pulse working in his face and his eyes grew stormy. "You never change," he said bitterly and hung up the phone, and when it toppled from its cradle, he slammed it down again, so hard the whole phone fell off the table.

"What did he say?" she asked. "He didn't want to talk to me?" And Danny just stood up, shaking his arms as if he were dislodging all that rage. "Danny, talk to me," she said. "I know you're mad." And then he looked at her, blinking, as if he were deciding something, and then he moved to her and kissed her. "Who cares what he thinks?" Danny said. "Who the god-damn fuck cares about any of them but us?"

"Well, my parents will be crazy about you," Sara said impulsively.

"You want me to meet your folks?" He looked at her, surprised, and then she felt surprised, too, because she knew what such a meeting might cost her.

"Of course I do," she insisted, hoping he'd forget. But when she saw him the next day, he instantly asked her, "When can I meet your folks? When's the day?"

She felt a skip of panic and tried to compose herself, breathing in deep. How bad could it be? Sara thought. Maybe she was underestimating her parents. Maybe they'd be glad she had someone loving her, glad she had wanted to introduce them.

"How about Friday?" Danny asked. Sara tried to think. Friday, Abby was cheeriest because her workweek was over. Jack was home early. She told herself that you couldn't pretend you knew how things would turn out, because really, hadn't Danny surprised her? Couldn't her parents surprise her, too? When they saw how happy he made her, maybe they wouldn't harp about who his parents were or ask how her studies were suffering, maybe they wouldn't insist she was too young to date. "Friday," she told him, and he grinned and grabbed her for a kiss.

All week she worried. Should she prepare her parents? Should she warn Danny how they might really react? When Abby was forming patties for burgers, Sara cleared her throat. "Mom—" she started and then Abby turned, expectant, and the words dried up in Sara's mouth. "Can I help?" Sara blurted and Abby handed her a greasy pattie of beef.

Danny had dressed specially for the occasion, in his good jeans, a checked shirt he had ironed by smoothing it on the couch overnight. His hair was raked into furrows and slicked back so it didn't look so long. "I'm a little nervous," he admitted. "I need something to hang on to," and he had slung one arm about her shoulders. "They'll love you," she said, but she averted her gaze. He didn't know she hadn't told them about him, that he was coming, and she felt sick with her own lie. A white lie, she reminded herself. The kind you told to protect someone you loved.

Her parents were sitting on the front porch, and they stood when they saw him, confused. Sara gripped Danny's hand. "This is Danny Slade," she said, then she took a long breath. "My boyfriend."

"Your what?" Sara felt Jack staring.

"Well," said Abby, pleasantly, and Sara saw her mother's eyes dart to the pack of cigarettes poking out of Danny's pocket.

"Oh, they're menthol, is that okay?" Danny said, whipping out the pack, offering them with a flourish. "Please. Take as many as you like." He flushed, embarrassed.

"We don't smoke," Jack said.

"Oh. Like Sara," Danny said, lighting a cigarette and taking a slow drag. He tapped ashes onto the grass. "Well, good for you," he said. "That's very smart."

"Are you in Sara's classes?" Abby said and Danny glanced at the ground.

"Wish I were," he said. Sara gave his hand a squeeze. He straightened and gave them friendly, hopeful looks. "I'm studying small engines," he said.

Abby's face hardened. There was an awkward silence. Danny's gaze flickered and lowered. Then he drew himself up. "Well, I'd better be going. It was nice to meet you," Danny said. And then he turned to Sara and looped one arm about her waist and tugged her to him. He kissed her full and gently on the mouth, and then let her go, so that she stumbled, off balance.

She heard about it as soon as he was out of sight.

"What's the matter with you, bringing a boy here? You're too young," Jack said.

"I knew you'd say that," Sara said. "I'm not too young."

"Why'd he leave so fast?" Abby said. "What's he got to hide?"

"He was hurt. Anybody could see you made up your minds not to like him as soon as you saw him. You didn't even invite him in."

"Was that a way to dress to make a good impression on us?" Abby asked. "Did you see those boots?" she said to Jack. "It looked like he had spurs on them. Did you see how tight his pants were? And what was he doing kissing you like that in front of us?"

"You don't know him."

"Oh, yes, I do," Abby said. "Trust me, I know all about that type of boy and he's not the one for you. And you should be studying, not dating."

"I knew you'd say that, too," Sara said.

"You're much too young—" Jack repeated, but Sara was gone.

Sara stormed upstairs to her room, slamming her door. She grabbed for her headphones and blasted her music. Her parents didn't have a clue. Her mother thought you could go through your whole life doing nothing but studying, and her father would be happy if she was his little girl until she was eighty.

She yanked off the headphones and flung them to the floor. She wouldn't stop seeing Danny. Her room was closing in on her. She sat on the bed and bolted up again because the bedspread felt raw and scratchy on her bare legs. She tugged her hair into a tail and then set it free again. Nothing felt right. Nothing. At least nothing here.

She had to see Danny. All he had to do was touch her forehead and everything inside of her relaxed. All he had to do was look at her and she felt calm. She grabbed for the phone and called Danny, but no one answered. Think, think, she told herself, and then, heart skittering, she went downstairs, grabbing up her book bag.

Her parents were sitting in the living room, drinking coffee, and as soon as she came into the room they looked up at her. She struggled to look calm, relaxed. "Is it okay if I go study at Judy's?" Sara said. She held up her book bag. "I have a history exam this week."

Abby set her teacup down and then repositioned it on the saucer.

"You can call Judy if you don't believe me. If you don't trust me," Sara said.

Her parents exchanged glances. "Of course we trust you," Abby said.

Jack glanced at his watch. "You be home by ten."

"Ten! That's hardly any time at all!" Sara felt panic taking root, sprouting. She bit down on her lower lip. Calm, she told herself. Calm.

"Ten," Jack repeated.

* * *

She ran to Judy's, knocking on the door, and as soon as Judy opened it, Judy's expression changed. "Look what the cat dragged in," Judy said. "I haven't been able to see you for weeks now and you just show up?"

Sara's head was swimming. "I need to use the phone," she said.

"That's why you come to see me, to use my phone?"

"Please, Judy," Sara begged. "Please."

Judy studied her and her face softened. "You look kind of funny. Are you okay?"

"I just need the phone," Sara said. She didn't care that Judy was dogging her steps, that her curiosity was like a fierce little animal, nipping at her heels.

This time, Danny answered, and as soon as she heard his voice, she gripped the receiver even harder. "Danny—" she blurted, and Judy folded her arms, frowning. Sara cupped the receiver closer. "My parents won't let me see you. I can't even call you from my house. I'm at Judy's—"

"They can't do that," he said. "I won't let them do that."

"They can make it really hard for us to see each other. I don't know what to do."

"I do," he said. He told her not to worry. He told her he'd see her tomorrow, first thing at school, right by the wire fence where they always met. He'd see her at lunch, and last period and after school right up until she had to go home again. He knew just what to do, and she shouldn't worry, not for a moment. "No one can separate us," he told her. "We're the same person." Sara's breathing slowed. The weight about her ribs lifted. She hung up the phone and Judy made a face. "Danny Slade?" Judy said evenly and Sara nodded.

"Are you sure you know what you're doing?" Judy asked.

Preoccupied, Sara headed for the door. "I have to go."

"I'm trying to talk to you here! I'm trying to help!" Judy said, grabbing for Sara's arm, but Sara was already out the door, out into the cool, clear night, and when she left Judy's house that night, she left more than Judy behind. She left her old life, too.

She learned quickly how to come up with excuses. The flush on her face was blush she was using. "Why do young girls think they need makeup?" Jack protested. She hid the new slinky dress she had bought under a baggy shirt so Abby wouldn't ask questions, and any gift Danny bought her, she told her parents she had bought herself. She had a whole roster of excuses for stealing out of the house. Studying always worked. Sessions at the library.

It was even easier in the summer, when she was taking special classes at Harvard, when she could blame the subways, the buses, for always coming home late. Maybe she couldn't drive, but she went into the garage and dug out her old three-speed green Schwinn and rode to wherever he was. At the abandoned day camp. Behind the Thrift-T-Mart. "I'm glad you're being smart about all this," Abby told her one evening when Sara was doing her homework at the kitchen table, just waiting for her parents to go to sleep so she could sneak out her window and find Danny. "I'm glad you came to your senses," Abby said, and all Sara could think was that because of Danny, her senses were all the more intense. Colors shimmered. Sound pulsed. Her heart grew in size.

And then school started up again and they had a whole new routine. They'd see each other before classes. During lunch when she'd run outside to meet him. At odd times during the day. She was in calculus class one day, taking a pop quiz, when she sensed Danny's presence, a charge in the air. The test was so easy she could do it in her sleep, but she couldn't concentrate anymore. She heard Danny's whisper, just behind her, making her turn around. *Sara. Sara. I'm here,* he whispered. She looked at the numbers and she smelled him—laundry soap and cigarettes, making her so dizzy she got up from her seat, as if she were sleepwalking. Drawn, she walked to the window, and there he was, like an apparition, and as soon as she saw him, she felt wings beating inside of her.

"Miss Rothman!" the teacher said sharply, pointing to Sara's seat. Sara turned from the teacher back to the window, and Danny was gone.

The first time they made love she was in Danny's room, getting ready to bolt out of there, because she had a paper due the next day that she hadn't even started. "I've got to go," she said, but she couldn't move from his bed. He grinned at her and came so close his nose almost touched hers. His breath was warm, smoky from cigarettes. She inhaled at the place where his neck touched his shoulders. "You smell so good," she said.

"Stay," he said, and slid a hand along the front of her shirt. He shut his eyes, shivering.

"Be right back," he said, and then he ran upstairs, and when he came back, he had a pink satin sheet in his arms and a small bottle. He unfurled the sheet, spreading it on the floor so the folds rippled with light. "Mike gave it to my mother for her birthday," he said. He lowered her down so that when she looked up she saw a painting of a deer on the wall, another small silver cross, a Jesus looking down at her. Then he took the bottle and opened it and she smelled his scent. He daubed the tip of the bottle along her shoulder. "Now you smell like me," he said, and when she smiled, he told her she could take the bottle home. She could always wear it. "I will," she promised.

He undid her blouse a button at a time, gazing at her in admiration. "I have never seen anything like you in my life."

He kissed her stomach, her knees, knobby as teacups, her feet, her hair. She had never had a real boyfriend before. She wasn't quite sure what to do, where to put her hands, her legs, her mouth. "Wait," she said. He stopped what he was doing. He looked cool, unconcerned, but even lying beside him, she could feel how his skin radiated heat. And then he kissed her neck, her face, her fingers, and then she forgot to stay his hands, to protest. Instead, she shut her eyes. She arched her back, and moved toward him. She memorized the slope of his neck, the downy hairs on his arms. "Is this all right?" he whispered, and she didn't know what to say, she didn't know what anything was supposed to feel like, how it was supposed to fit, or if she was any good at it, and it suddenly seemed like the most important thing in the world that she was. "Wait—" he whispered. "Are you on the pill?" When she shook her head, he reached over her to his night table and fumbled in a drawer. "Shit," he said. "Shit, shit—" and then she pulled him back to the bed, back to her. She kissed his mouth, his neck, the slope of his shoulder, wanting to put every part of him right inside of her. "It'll be all right," he whispered, his voice hoarse. "It'll be all right—" And he moved closer toward her, and all she heard was the rasp of his breathing.

They were both slick with sweat. And when he pushed himself inside of her, she felt the strangest shock of recognition, as if this moment were something she had been trying to remember, and suddenly, here it was. And when he cried out, her eyes flew open. She watched his face, the pulse beating behind his lids, and when he slid from her, she felt a sadness so overpowering, she could have cried. *Come back,* she wanted to say.

Her body felt as if he had marked her somehow. She sat up, resting on her elbows. Now even his room looked different to her. Colors were brighter, the air had a heavier feel to it. "Sara?" he said. She rolled toward him and as soon as her belly touched his again, she shivered. She would have inhaled him if she could. "You okay?" he asked. She looked up, rolling to her other side, her face away from him. There was a starry stain of blood on the pink sheet and she touched it gingerly. "Oh God! Your mother's sheet—" she said. "She'll kill me. She'll kill us."

He leaned over to her, brushing her hair from her face, taking her hand from the sheet. He threw one end of the sheet over the stain so you couldn't see it. "Sara?" he said, and it was as if he had a sheen about him, like a kind of suntan oil, glossy and inviting. She sat up. She smoothed the sheet, she tried to fix the pillows. Her mind raced, thinking about the paper she had to do, the way her grades were slipping, and then Danny pulled her back down beside him. "You don't have to do anything. Just be here," he said. "I'll never be with anyone else but you. I'll never want to." She lifted up one hand and put it against Danny's face. "Mine," she said.

They began spending more and more time in Danny's room. He opened his drawer. "Look," he said shyly, and she looked down and saw the five kinds of condoms he had bought: red and blue and ribbed, all with names so ridiculous she sputtered with laughter. Bareback Rider. Intense. Wild Thing. In the supermarket, all he had to do was trace a line down her back, and her whole body felt a flutter and she would turn and kiss him. She wouldn't be able to stop. "Kids, get a room," someone muttered, walking past them, and all Sara could think was, *I wish we could. I wish we could get a whole country.*

He took her places she didn't even know existed. A Japanese mall at the far end of town, a supermarket where every item was either in Japanese or translated incorrectly. Sara plucked up a sponge, delighted, because it was called Clean Life Please. She bought Danny a tea towel that said "From the Kitchen of Buxom Beauties."

He showed her how to tune an engine, sneaking her into the vocational school, patient when she flubbed it. "Soon as I get a car, I'll teach you to drive," he said. He showed her the maps he saved. California, Alaska, the paper soft because he had opened and closed them back up so many times.

"You don't need much money to live a good life in Alaska," Danny said.

"Is that where you're going when school's over?" Sara asked. She didn't want to look at the maps anymore.

"I'm going where you're going," he said and folded the maps shut.

They talked quietly about the future, planning it out. The house they'd live in, by the water, with a backyard. His auto body shop nearby, and her psychologist office on the top floor. The dog they would have, a big rangy mutt that would sleep at the foot of their bed. "You're the first thing I haven't somehow fucked up in my life," he told her. "The first thing I've ever gotten right."

That night, when she was alone in bed, she imagined Danny there beside her, and she got so restless, she bolted up from bed and went to the kitchen for ice, rolling it across her arms and legs, trying to cool some of the heat down. She came back upstairs and sat at the window, willing him to come get her. If he showed, she vowed she'd climb out her window to be with him. She swore she'd let him into her room. She reached for her phone and told herself if he didn't answer on the first ring, she'd hang up.

"Hello?" His voice was soft, heavy with sleep.

"Come and get me," she whispered.

She felt him before she saw him. Then she heard pebbles rattling at the window. Stealthily, she opened the window and slid outside, grabbing on to the maple tree she had grown up climbing, shimmying down in her nightgown, her toes curling on the dewy grass. The neighborhood was dark. A cat yowled in the distance. And then the two of them lowered to the damp grass. Wordlessly, she slid off her nightgown, she unbuttoned his shirt and lifted up her mouth to his.

Later, when she finally came back in, she fell into a sleep so deep she felt drugged. When Abby came in the morning to wake Sara for school, there were bits of grass on the sheet, and the hem of her nightgown was muddy, and Abby, racing to leave for work herself, didn't notice. "There's my beautiful daughter," Jack said, walking past her room.

Sara ran off for school, stopping at the patch of grass where she and Danny had been the night before. In the hazy morning light, it seemed almost magical, and she crouched, raising one hand over the grass, and she still felt its heat.

She didn't think anything of it when she missed one period, but when she missed the next one, she told Danny. "It's just nerves. You can't be pregnant," he said. "We used condoms."

"Condoms don't always work. What if I am? What are we going to do?"

He shook his head. "It's an impossibility. Please, please don't look like that! Would I let something like that happen?"

She couldn't help it though. Every time she saw him, she wrapped herself under his arm, trying to convince herself that everything was the same, everything was fine. But his touch felt different on her skin, as if there were a whole extra layer between them. His eyes, when he looked at her, seemed as though they were seeing her through a screen. *It's nothing,* she told herself.

There were lots of reasons for missing a period, Sara knew. The stress of sneaking around. The dizziness of love. When her belly started to get rounder, her bra too tight, when she began to feel queasy, she blamed it on all the nervous eating she was doing. And then when she missed her third period in a row, she started to get scared. She shucked off all her clothes and stood in front of her mirror, staring at her changed silhouette, her hands on her belly. Swallowing she put her clothes back on, she kept her eyes shut. You could give yourself sore throats and headaches and asthma just by the power of your thought. Hadn't she read about hysterical pregnancies? Women whose bellies and breasts grew tender and swollen with nothing but air? Hadn't she read how the mind could create all sorts of false symptoms for the body? She breathed deep. Danny hadn't seemed to notice anything different; he hadn't commented. *I'm fine,* she told herself, *I'm fine.*

Still, the next day, before Abby got home, she called Planned Parenthood, but as soon as a woman answered, she hung up. Fool, she berated herself. Idiot. She dialed again, determined. Knowledge was power. Better to know now what she might be facing than to bury it away. This time a different woman answered, but as soon as Sara mentioned she hadn't had her period in three months, the woman wanted her to come in for an appointment right away, and panicked, Sara hung up again.

What was she going to do? She couldn't call back, not now, not after she had made a fool of herself. She couldn't tell her parents, and if she called Danny, he'd just tell her not to worry again. She sat down and then stood up and sat down again. Pregnancy kits. She'd go and buy one.

She walked a mile to the Thrift-T-Mart on the side of town where she knew no one, and looked at the pregnancy kits. Every one of them had a picture of a smiling woman, or a couple, locking eyes as if they shared a great and wonderful secret. Where were the girls who were all alone and so scared they could barely breathe? Where were the terrified expressions? The panic? Sara squinted at the price. Ten dollars. That was expensive. She'd have to cut back on things she wanted this week. She peered at the directions on the back and chose the one that seemed easiest—just a quick pee and a blue cross would appear. She didn't look at the girl who rang it up, who put it into a brown paper bag. She told herself she'd tell

Danny after she found out; it would be something they could joke about. *Can you imagine my face when I saw the line wasn't there,* she could say. *I whooped so loudly, the girl in the next stall must have thought I was crazy.*

She carried it around in her purse for two days before she could work up the courage.

Last period. Honors history. She could be late, no one would notice. She waited until the halls were empty and then she slipped into the girls' bathroom. Two girls she didn't know were standing by the mirrors, leaning over the sinks, layering on mascara, peering at their reflections. "More?" one girl said, handing a mascara to her friend, and Sara went into a stall. She carefully opened the book, she peed on the long white tube. Three minutes. She'd have to wait three minutes.

"Fuck him," said one of the girls. "He thinks with his dick."

Sara flushed the toilet so the girls wouldn't wonder what she was doing in there, and glanced at the tube. She stood there, terrified, her back against the stall. Three minutes, the package said, but already the line was turning into a brilliant blue cross.

She didn't know what to do, but she had all these thoughts in her head. She had to find Danny. He'd help her. She counted back the months. One and one make two, he said, but now one and one made three and all there was to do about it was to either have it or not have it, and either solution sounded like the worst thing in the world to her.

The girls' voices faded and then were gone.

She couldn't leave the tube here. It seemed too personal, too damning, so she tucked it into her pocket. She couldn't bear the thought of going to her history class, so instead, she ran to find Danny, standing outside his class until he came out, pulling him outside. And then she told him, and the moment she did, his joy at seeing her faded. He took two steps back from her. "How do you know?" he asked.

"I know." She felt the tube, still in her pocket.

"You can take care of it, can't you?" he said. He pushed back his hair with his hand, over and over, as if he were sweating.

She blinked at him. "Maybe it's too late," she said.

"No," he said, stunned. "Don't say that. That can't be right. I've heard of girls further along. You can fix it."

Sycamore
Speedway

Nicholas Thompson

"Shouldn't we talk about this?" she said. His mouth seesawed. If she didn't know him so well, she'd say he was about to cry.

"We just did," he said.

"What's wrong? Are you mad at me?"

"I'm mad at myself." He leaned toward her and kissed her, but his kiss felt different to her, and she couldn't pinpoint how. She needed to kiss his mouth again, but when she moved toward him, he turned from her. "Danny," she said, and he started walking away. "Danny!" she said louder. Her hands flew to her mouth, and he pushed open the front door to the school and disappeared, and as he did, she realized that other than that last hasty kiss, he hadn't touched her once, not the whole time they had been talking.

She couldn't move, not even when Robin walked by, and seeing her, Sara realized that more than anything what she wanted right now was a friend to talk to. She used to talk to Robin for hours. They used to confide in each other, but now Robin's glance skimmed right over her as if Sara weren't even there, making Sara feel a sudden chill. Well, Robin wasn't her friend anymore. Judy hadn't spoken to her since the day Sara had run to her house to use the phone. The one friend she counted on more than anything was the one who moments before had just walked away from her and wasn't looking back.

He stopped coming to school. The days got colder and darker and more wintry. She kept going over and over in her mind all the things he had said to her about how they'd always be together, she kept seeing the way he couldn't walk down the street beside her without taking her hand, or touching her face, without some part of their bodies connecting. And no matter how she tried, she couldn't understand what had happened, how and why he had changed and what might bring him back to her.

At night, a noise made her bolt awake. *It's him,* she thought, but when she went to the window, there was nothing there but all the closed doors, the blank windows of the neighborhood. "*I'm not mad at you,*" he had told her. She repeated it over and over to herself like a mantra.

"Did anyone call?" she kept asking Abby. "Did anyone come by for me?" and even after Abby assured her that no one had, Sara stared at the phone and the door, stricken.

She tried to prepare. She got as far as a clinic and then grabbed some pamphlets about abortion and fled before the nurse could ask her name. She stood out on the sidewalk reading. How could she afford this? "*We recommend someone come with you,*" the pamphlet said, but who would that be? Who could she dare to tell what was going on, let alone ask to help her?

At the end of the week, she couldn't stand it anymore, she waited until last period and then she ran to his house, around to the side where his window was, and she bent and threw stones and no one answered. Then she rang the bell and no one answered there, either, and she stood on the stoop and tore a piece of paper from her notebook and wrote him a letter. *Danny, please. We can be happy. Please just talk to me about the baby. I love you and I know you love me. Sara.*

She folded it up. She looked around for something she could use as an envelope, finally making one out of another piece of paper. She wrote his name on the front, addressing it like a letter. She marked it "Personal" and slid it through the slot, and then she went home, and all that day, she waited for him to call her, and when he didn't, she called his house. To her surprise a woman answered, "Yes?" The voice was tired.

"It's Sara."

The woman was silent.

"Please, is Danny there? It's really important I speak with him."

"Who is this again?"

"It's Sara."

"Sara who?" the woman asked, and Sara felt stung.

"Danny's girlfriend." It felt funny to say it. *It's true,* she told herself. *I swear it's true.*

"Danny's girlfriend," the woman said, more wearily. "Well, Danny's gone."

"What do you mean, he's gone?" Sara wrapped the cord tightly around her hand.

"Gone," the woman said. "I don't know where. He took half his things with him."

The cord around Sara's hand tightened. "No, that's not possible——" she said.

"Well, he's gone."

"Please, if he calls, will you tell him to call Sara? Will you tell him it's important?"

"Sure," the woman said. "Sure, I'll tell him," and then she hung up.

Sara told herself his mother was wrong. Danny wouldn't leave her, not for good. Maybe he had just run off someplace to think, and any moment, he would be back.

Every time the phone rang in her house, she jumped up, but her parents always got to it first, and it was never for her. She ran to the mailman before he even got to their house. She hadn't heard from Danny in three weeks, even though she called his house every day, never getting anything more than a busy signal, or a line that rang and rang. How could he have changed so quickly? She felt torn in two. One jagged half. She tried to keep busy. She threw herself into her schoolwork again, trying not to think.

He'll come back, she told herself.

She waited one more week, and then another. She didn't care that it was freezing out. Every day she walked home from school, taking the long way, so she could go by Danny's house, but it was always quiet, and empty, not even a flutter behind the curtains. Every day, she half-expected Danny to show up at school, to have an explanation for her, and every day, that chance seemed less and less likely. She spent forty dollars taking out an ad in the back of *The Village Voice,* a paper she knew Danny read. "*Danny, call Sara. Important.*" The ad ran two weeks but he never called.

He'll come back, she told herself. *He won't leave me.* Sara began to wear baggy sweaters as long as dresses, to layer things and joke about eating everything in sight even though she barely could manage crackers. Under her sweaters, she held her skirts together with safety pins, and by then the morning sickness became afternoon sickness.

She was at the cafeteria, eating alone, when she heard someone say his name. "Slade," a boy said, and Sara got up and walked over. The boy grinned at her.

"Where's Danny?" Sara asked.

He leaned back in his chair, his whole body at an angle. "Last I heard, California," he smirked. His eyes rolled up and down her body. "But baby, I'm right *here*," he said.

A wave of nausea roiled through Sara, and she barely made it to the girls' room, throwing up in the toilet.

She tried not to watch the calendar, not to keep track of all the time passing by her. Not until she was outside one day, so warm she took off her jacket, did she notice the day was cloudless and cool, hinting of spring. And only a fool, Sara realized, would think there was any reason to hang on to hope any longer. That day, when she got home from school, because there was nothing else to do now, she called Planned Parenthood asking about abortions. She'd beg her friends' forgiveness and borrow money; she'd plead for one of them to come with her, swearing secrecy. She would even ask Danny's mother if she had to. That was how desperate she had become. "How far along are you?" the clinic asked.

Sara wet her lips. "Almost five months," she said, and her voice sounded so far away to her, like a little girl's.

"You should have come to see us sooner," the woman said. Her voice was soft, sympathetic. "You should still come in, but we can't talk about abortions. It's too late."

Panicking, Sara hung up the phone. She grabbed it up again, but there was just a dial tone. The sympathetic woman was gone, and even if she called back, who knew who would answer the phone, and what did it matter if the information was going to be the same? What was she going to do now? What would happen to her? She paced the living room, and then another wave of nausea hit her and she ran to the bathroom to throw up. She was still in there when she heard Abby's key in the door. "Honey, are you home?" Abby called. Her mother's voice was bright, full of bells, and Sara couldn't help it. She began crying and crying, hunched over the toilet, her head in her hands so she wouldn't have to face her mother. Her nose ran, her eyes pooled. She wanted to turn herself inside out. She wanted to grab the baby and fling it from her. She wanted to be anyone but herself, anywhere but here in this bathroom waiting for her mother to find her.

Abby knocked on the door. "Honey, what's going on?" Abby said, and opened the door Sara had forgotten to lock, and as soon as she saw Sara, the swelling belly Sara had been hiding under big clothes, Abby's hands darted up. "Oh Jesus," Abby said.

"Mommy," Sara said, a name she hadn't called her mother since she was ten, and then she looked up and saw that Abby was crying, and it made her so ashamed, so terrified of what might come next, that she hid her head, she curled herself up into a ball.

There were days of terrible fights, of accusations. How could Sara be so stupid? How could she have waited so long? Did she want to ruin her life? "What do you think is going to happen now?" Abby demanded. "What kind of a future are you going to have?"

She thought her father would shout more, but instead he sat sorrowfully on the couch, shaking his head, looking as if he had aged a thousand years in just the time it took her to tell him. He kept repeating, "I could kill that boy," but Sara knew what he meant was: *I could kill you.* "And he better not ever come back around here again if he knows what's what," Jack said. Sara put her hands over her ears, afraid that if her father kept saying that, it would come true, Danny would never come back, not to the house, not to her.

"He's gone," Sara said, bursting into tears. She sat down, too, crying, and then she felt her mother beside her, her mother's hand stroking her back, soothing her hair. "Good," Abby said vehemently. "I'm glad he's gone. We'll handle this without him."

"We'll figure this out," her father said, and when Sara dared to look at him, he was looking out the window, and not at her.

They sat at the dinner table in silence, no one really eating. After dinner, she went to her room and shut the door. She lay in bed with her eyes wide open, her hands clasped across her chest as if she were praying, and listened to her parents talking late into the night. "Why didn't we know?" Abby asked Jack. "How could we be so blind?"

"Don't you remember that girl who gave birth in the stall at her prom?" Jack said. "It was in all the papers. A good student. From a good family. Her parents didn't know."

"Oh God, our poor baby," Abby said. "When I think of that young unspoiled body getting all blown out of shape—she's too young! She's just too young! She's a baby having a baby! No one should even think of having a child until they're thirty, until they've got everything already in place!"

"Abby. Don't do this."

"Pregnancy should be beautiful, like some badge of honor, but every time I look at her all I see is everyone's failure. Was it my fault? Was it yours? Her school's?"

"It doesn't matter whose fault it is. Maybe it's no one's fault, maybe it's God's. It doesn't matter. It's done."

Their voices rose and fell and then were still. Sara's eyes stayed open.

The next day, while Sara stayed around the house, unsure what to do, Abby went out by herself and came back that afternoon with a huge bag of books. Sara was used to her mother's stash—books on business management or medicine or sometimes the classics, anything that Abby thought might help her better herself. "It's to keep up with you," Abby said.

Abby set the bag down, but her usual delight in a book purchase was gone. "Take a look at some of these," she said, lifting books out, handing a few to Sara. *Adoption: The Right Choice. The Adoption Sourcebook. The Birth Mother's Handbook.*

Stung, Sara put the book down. "It's always better to educate yourself," Abby said quietly. She pulled out a notebook and some Post-its and held them up. "We're all in this together," Abby said, handing them to Sara.

All that afternoon, Abby sat reading. Her forehead creased, her focus strained. The pages were littered with yellow Post-its sticking out of the pages. When Jack came home, he leafed through one of the books rapidly. "Gently!" Abby said, and Jack looked down.

"I ripped a page," he said, astonished, putting the book down.

The books found their way all over the house. In the bathroom with a page turned back. In the kitchen by the bread box, Post-its crowding the pages. Sara avoided them, too paralyzed to touch even a cover, too afraid if she did, she might help to set something in motion she could never stop.

It was Abby who found the adoption agency, who took Sara over there with her. It was Abby who got Sara a good doctor and drove her to all her appointments.

Sara went to school and kept to herself. Never had she felt so lonely or so scared. She ate lunch in one of the empty classrooms, she avoided the halls, and when everyone else took gym, she used her doctor's note to stay in the library. "What's with you?" some of the kids asked, and when Sara was silent, they shrugged and turned away.

Business as usual, Abby kept saying. One day, Abby and Jack took off work to drive Sara to Harvard for her college interview, just as if there weren't a single thing to keep her from going. They sat outside during her interview while Sara tried to remember to keep the boxy jacket she had borrowed from Abby buttoned, to lean forward so you couldn't tell she was pregnant. "Well, you certainly are impressive," the interviewer said, and Sara curled her fingers into her palm. *He should only know how impressive,* she thought, *because really, how many knocked-up kids did Harvard interview?*

Afterward, her parents walked with her on the tour, though she already knew the campus. Two other girls and four boys. And two of the boys kept looking at her, smiling, flirting. "If we both get in, I'm taking you to Schrafts," one boy said.

She couldn't imagine having ice cream with any other boy, couldn't imagine wanting to, but that was her old life, and as everyone kept urging her, she had to move on. "Only if it's chocolate," she said, and the boy's smile grew.

"I live just in Newton," he said, and then suddenly, Sara felt that edgy sensation that Danny was just behind a building, just around a bend, that he was whispering something to her, and all she had to do was find the right place to stand and then she'd hear him. She tried to shake it off. She knew it was just another one of her Danny mirages, that she could think she saw him all she wanted, her mouth could form his name a million times, and it wouldn't change anything. She looked to her left quickly: someone's father.

She forced herself to turn to the boy, to smile. "Newton's cool," she told him.

One day Abby came home with big drawstring pants and oversized shirts because Sara needed something to wear. "Try it on so I'll know what fits,"

Abby said, and when Sara came out with the pants pulling against her swelling belly, Abby looked stricken.

"I'm so sorry, Mom," Sara said, and Abby waved her hand.

"Anything you don't want, I'll take back myself," Abby said slowly.

One night, when Sara was sleeping, she heard a noise at the window, and for a moment, she thought Danny was back. She sat up, so happy and relieved she could have cried, and then she saw her father's back, his arms moving behind her shades. He was checking the locks on the window. Then he turned, and she half shut her eyes. He was moving in the dark toward her. He placed one hand on her hair, just for a moment, and then she heard the creak of her rocking chair, she heard him crying and she opened her eyes. Then he got up and left the room, quietly closing the door, and she wept a little, too.

Now, in the shower, that day seemed like lifetimes ago. Now Sara didn't hear anything at her window anymore except the wind or the rain or an occasional cat. If she was awake nights, it was because she was doing the reading for school this fall. Every time she finished a book, she crossed it off the list.

The water in the shower was turning cold. Sara stood, shutting off the spigots, getting out. The house was noisy. She heard a strange voice. She dressed quickly, in the same baggy clothes she had worn through her pregnancy, and then she went downstairs, and there was Jack and a man Sara had never seen before, but all Sara had to do was see the desperate look in the man's eyes, and the two big brown paper bags overstuffed with receipts to know this was a client. Usually Jack saw them at the office, but the desperate ones, the ones who did their taxes last minute, the ones who got audited, always came to the house, laden with bags of paperwork and ledgers, and sometimes a gift for Jack. A bottle of wine. Packaged candies. Once, a bolt of silk from a man who owned a fabric store. "It's the mom-and-pop stores that are truly appreciative," Jack always said. "I'd rather deal with them than the big corporations anytime. Them I take good care of."

"You got to help me with this," the man said, "I know I should have kept better records, I know, but this audit—"

"We'll pull it together in time, Donald," Jack soothed. He led the man to a couch and had him sit. He took the bags and gently put them on the side of the couch, where the client couldn't focus on them.

Donald looked up and suddenly saw Sara. "Oh, hello," he said, smiling.

"My daughter, Sara," Jack said. "Sara, Donald Weston."

"Your dad's saving my skin," Donald said to Sara. He gave Jack a look of real devotion. "Best accountant in the world. He can make sense of anything." He lifted up the paper bags. "Even these. You're a lucky girl to have such a smart dad."

Sara was sure her father was going to make some remark, that yes, she was lucky, or yes, he was indeed the smartest accountant in all of Boston, or what he usually always said, yes, but my daughter's much smarter than I am. Instead, he gave Donald a funny smile, and then looked at his hands for a moment. "Well," he said finally, "we'd better get back to work."

Sara excused herself and went into the kitchen.

Abby was sitting at the table, a book open in front of her, a mug of chocolate in her hand. Her hair was shored back with one of the tortoise-shell barrettes Danny had given Sara. "Where'd you get that?" Sara asked, her voice chipping.

Abby's hand touched the barrette. "Oh, I found it in the bathroom—what, you don't want me borrowing it?"

"It's mine."

Abby started to say something and then shrugged, and took the barrette out of her hair and handed it to Sara. Sara couldn't bear to put the barrette in her own hair, but she tucked it into her pocket.

"Interesting book," Abby said, thumping a finger onto a page. When she looked down at the page, she saw one of her summer reading books. F. Scott Fitzgerald, *The Great Gatsby*.

"Mom," Sara said, tapping her mother on the shoulder. "Mom," she said louder.

Abby looked up, her eyes bright.

"It's amazing, this book," Abby said. "Would you believe I never read it?"

Sara looked down at the book. Of all her reading, that had been the hardest to get through. She had felt so sorry for Gatsby, for all he couldn't let go of.

"By the time it's fall, I'll be as well-read as you are," Abby said.

Abby casually brushed a flurry of crumbs from her green dress and looked at Sara.

Sara had scrubbed her face clean. She had pulled back her wet hair with a plastic headband. She had always had a young face, had always looked as if she were in the wrong class, and now, she knew she must look all of twelve years old. Well. Twelve years old with stretch marks. Twelve years old with breasts that only recently stopped leaking milk.

"I thought you'd sleep later," Abby said.

"I couldn't sleep."

"So," Abby said casually. "What are your plans for today?"

Sara looked awkwardly around the kitchen. They had set a place for her. There was a muffin sitting on a plate. A glass of juice.

"Want to join the Y? Start swimming? Get yourself in shape?" Abby took a bite of egg. "Why don't you call your friends? I bet they'd love to hear from you."

"My friends?"

"What about that nice Judy Potter? What about Robin Opaline?" Abby persisted.

Sara tightened her mouth. That nice Judy Potter had told her not to bother calling anymore. The last she had heard about Robin Opaline was that Robin was telling everyone what an idiot Sara was.

"You still have time this summer to take a class if you'd like. Or get a summer job."

"I have plans for the summer."

She could feel the mood changing. The air grew tight around her, scratchy like a too-small woolen coat. Abby sighed.

"Why are you doing this?" Abby asked.

"Do we have to talk about this?" Sara said. "This was all settled."

"I want to talk about it," Abby said. "It's just crazy. We just want you to move on with your life. You need to be doing something with people your own age. You need to be out there instead of dwelling on what's happened—" Abby said. "Look. Honey. We'd like you to get some counseling. I have a few names of people who are supposed to be very good, very helpful. We'll all go."

"I'll be home for dinner."

"Sara!" Abby called, but Sara was already out the door, out into the bright, shimmering heat of the morning. She couldn't hear them anymore. They couldn't stop her. She'd always find a way, the same way she had found ways to be with Danny.

A mosquito kamikazed by her head and she slapped it away. A few neighbors were getting into cars, in dark suits or work dresses in dull prints. They were carrying cups of coffee, balancing pastries in a napkin. Everyone looked hot and preoccupied and pressed for time, but still they looked at her. Bill Tinker, who sometimes played golf with her father, who hadn't said two words to her the whole time she was pregnant, nodded at her. "Morning," he said. She felt like running over to him, but then he got in his car and started it up. She saw Judy's mother and Sara held up her hand to wave. Judy's mother gave Sara a clammy stare and Sara pulled her hand down and thrust it deep in her pocket. After that, Sara kept her eyes front. She kept walking, all the way to the bus stop.

Forty minutes later, Sara stood in front of Eva and George's house.

She had loved this house the moment she had first come here, very pregnant, and very scared. Her hair had been carefully brushed, held back with a silver clip. But now, she couldn't help but feel anxious.

This was the first time Sara had been here not pregnant with Anne.

The house was a white ranch, with a big sloping backyard, dotted with dandelions, shaded by two big maples. It was a rambling, comfortable house.

Sara climbed the four brick steps to the front door. She lifted up the brass knocker, sipped in a long, slow breath, and then knocked.

"Hang on—" Eva's voice was muffled, and then the door opened and there was Eva, in a flowery dress, her hair wound on top of her head, her face flushed and happy. She was holding Anne, and as soon as Sara saw the baby, she felt a flood of yearning so strong she thought she might faint. She reached out her hands and Anne, stormy, screamed.

Eva stepped back. "She was good all morning." Eva swayed Anne, trying to calm her down. "She must miss her daddy." She motioned Sara inside, and then she yawned, flustered. "I'm really, really, really glad you're here."

Sara couldn't take her eyes off the baby. She hadn't seen the baby in what seemed ages, and already both Eva and Anne looked different to her. All she could think about was what she had missed, what had happened without her. "I'll take her," she said.

"No, it's all right." Anne struggled in Eva's arms. Eva led them deeper into the house. The house felt alive around Sara. There were the big windows she loved, covered with only the thinnest antique lace curtains floating over them so the rooms were flooded with light. There was the antique sofa and chairs, old and comfortable and nicked, there were the Oriental rugs faded where the sun hit them. But now there were piles of laundry breeding on chairs. Now there were dishes stacked in the sink. Everywhere Sara looked there were purple bags of disposable diapers. There were all sorts of things she had never seen before, a playpen and two different strollers, toys and blankets, and there, beside the picture of Eva and George and herself when she was nine months pregnant, was a photo of Eva and George and the baby, alone.

Sara looked away from the photo and then back again, as if by some miracle she had made a mistake, as if she'd look back and see her own picture there, where it belonged. But no. There was the new photo and all Sara could think was that she had stepped into a strange, alien universe and she wasn't sure the atmosphere was good for her to breathe.

Sara glanced at Eva, who was turned away from her, and then she took the photo with herself in it, and put it prominently up front.

"Come on," Eva said. She led Sara into Anne's room.

Anne burped loudly and a rivulet of creamy foam dribbled across Eva's bare shoulder. "Oh, you know what—please, would you? Just until I clean this up?" As soon as Eva fit the baby into Sara's arms, she felt as if she'd never let go. Anne abruptly stopped wailing. Then the baby studied Sara.

"Well, would you look at that," Eva said, stunned. She reached for a tissue in her dress and swabbed at her shoulder. Anne's whole body loosened and relaxed. Anne gummed the edge of Sara's shirt. She yawned and flexed open her tiny, balled fists into fingers.

Sara didn't dare to move. "I think she likes me."

Eva gave a half-smile. "I'll take her," she said. Eva lowered the baby into the crib. Sara touched a small white plastic attachment clipped to the railing. Another new thing she didn't know anything about. "What's this?" she asked.

"Turn it on," Eva said. "The switch is in the back."

Sara's fingers found the switch. The attachment hummed, vibrating the crib. "It's supposed to get babies to sleep," Eva said. "Like driving in a car. Consumer Reports said it's the best thing."

"When Anne was kicking inside of me, I used to get her to sleep by playing music. I'd put the earphones on my belly," Sara said. "She liked Tom Jones. The Beatles. She even liked my father's old Herman's Hermits albums. Maybe I could bring them over."

Eva took Sara's hand and rested it on the crib vibrator, and then Sara felt that buzz, too, deep in her bones, the same way Anne must. She lifted up her hand. It still buzzed.

"Look at that. She's sleeping," Eva said, looking down into the crib. "Didn't I tell you? Now I can take a quick shower. Oh, I'm so glad you're here. So very glad."

"I would have watched her," Sara said, "I could have rocked her." But Eva was moving from the room, holding the door, waiting for Sara to follow.

"I'm just going to get a drink, want something?" Sara said, and Eva shook her head.

"Oh, honey, there's all sorts of things in the fridge because people are coming over. Don't take the stuff in the pitchers, okay? And if you're hungry later, just ask me."

"You want me to ask you?" Sara's mind felt jumbled. She never had to ask. "Our house is your house," they told her.

"Things are just so crazy now," Eva said.

"I can help—" Sara started to say, but Eva was moving past Sara, opening the linen cabinet, reaching for a plush green towel.

*   *   *

Sara was too keyed up to sit still. She wandered the house. When she was pregnant, Eva and George wouldn't let her lift a finger, even though she told them it was good for her to be active, though the truth was she just wanted to be so busy, she wouldn't think about what was happening to her. Eva had cooked her huge, elaborate, healthy meals. Grilled vegetables and different kinds of veggie burgers. George was always popping into the car to pick up whatever it was she had a yen for. Chocolate ice cream. Ginger tea. Soft slippers in size six because her feet hurt. Every day George would tell her: *You are the best. What can we do for you? How can we make you happy?* Eva and George acted delighted all the time to do the littlest thing for her. They looked at her as if they couldn't believe their good fortune, when really, she was the one who was grateful.

"They're doing that because they want something from you," Jack had told her. "And once they have it, mark my words, you won't be who they want anymore."

"You're not there. You don't see how they treat me," Sara had said. She twisted the ring George and Eva had given her. She had been doing that so much lately that she was beginning to get a raw spot on her finger.

"Oh honey, we don't have to be there to know what's what," Abby said.

Well, Sara was there, right here and now in George and Eva's house, and she still remembered what it had all felt like, and the horrible thing was it didn't really feel like that anymore and she wasn't sure what to do about it. Sara sat and clicked on the TV and watched a few minutes of a game show, peppy music blaring. "Name the one thing that isn't an animal: man, the elephant, a beetle," a toothy announcer asked, and the contestant, a man wearing glasses, scratched his head and said, "Man?"

"Wrong, they're all animals!" the announcer shouted happily, and the studio audience roared with laughter. The man flushed and made a silly face, as if he knew that that had been the answer all along and he had just been trying to fool everyone, to be funny.

Sara shut the set off. She should have brought some of her reading for school. Instead, she picked up a *Parenting* magazine with a laughing baby on the cover and leafed through it. It was all marked up in red pen, the same way Sara used to highlight her books. Pages were folded back or torn out, and tucked in one fold was a card for a parenting class. It reminded her of Abby's adoption books. She put the magazine down. Why did you have to learn parenting? Wasn't it something you just knew instinctively?

Eva was still in the shower. Sara could hear the water, could hear Eva talking to herself. "I get my best thoughts and ideas in the shower," Eva had once told Sara.

Sara trailed about the house. There was a new throw rug in the den, some blue and red braided thing that looked handmade. A bright green playpen sat in the corner. Wandering into the kitchen, she opened the refrigerator. There used to be fresh fruit and cut-up veggies, things she could grab and eat, but everything was now in covered tubs. On the wall was a sampler: HOME SWEET HOME. Home, Sara thought. She didn't feel at home, not with everything so changed. She didn't feel like family or even like a guest.

Digging in her purse, she pulled out a notebook. Maybe she'd make a list for herself of things to bring over. Things she wouldn't have to bother Eva about. The crackers she liked. Diet Cokes. She opened a page.

You sleep on your back, she wrote. *You look so different each time I see you, but I'd still know you anywhere.* She thought of the blue box Eva had, stuffed with letters and pictures and photographs, all things that were going to be an album for the baby. Well, she could make her own baby journal for Anne, if she wanted.

She couldn't help it anymore, she went into Anne's room.

Anne snored slightly. Her face was damp. Sara moved in closer and she felt a ping deep inside of her, like the twisting of a sharp wire. Her hand floated toward the baby, who stretched and moved toward her fingers, and Sara drew her hand back.

She thought suddenly of all those Girls in Trouble stories of her mother's. The last story Abby had told her had been about a girl who had made the mistake of looking at her baby after it was born. She had seen the baby was deformed and the nuns told her God was punishing her and her baby both. She would never forget the sight of her baby, and her baby would have to live with being deformed.

"Can you imagine saying such a thing?" Abby had asked. "The very cruelty!"

Sara looked down at Anne. Perfect. Her baby was perfect. And here she was, alone with her child, in this big, quiet house and she felt so happy.

Sara pulled the light blanket up over Anne. It was white, printed with hopping yellow rabbits. She knew Anne when she was carrying her. She knew Anne liked to bunch up along her left side, that Anne hiccoughed every time Sara drank soda. She knew Anne now, too, more every minute she was with her. She brought her face close to Anne's and hummed something low and deep, and she swore Anne sighed. "You like that, don't you?" she said.

She kept one hand on the baby's bare chubby leg. She looked up at the wall, at the *Sesame Street* calendar Eva had hung up. Big Bird waving. A few days had big red *X*s. Pediatrician appointment. One-month anniversary with a big exclamation point after it. At the bottom of the calendar were two minicalendars of the next two months. August. Then September. Sara looked away from the calendar. September. Then school.

Anne fussed and Sara bent and picked her up. Anne gummed the edge of Sara's blouse and Sara placed one hand gently on the baby's head.

"Hey." Eva suddenly stood in the doorway, a bottle in her hand. She was in a blue dress Sara had never seen before, and strappy blue shoes. Her wet hair was held back by a black velvet headband. Energy seemed to bounce off her skin, which was flushed and damp. "What are you two up to?" Coming closer, Eva reached for Anne's fingers. "Thank you Sara for taking over so I could shower."

"It's okay."

"What would I do without you?" she said, and for a moment, Sara wasn't sure whether Eva had been talking about her, or Anne.

Even though she wasn't so sure of her place now, Sara came over to George and Eva's every day. Eva seemed glad to see Sara and Sara made sure to make herself useful. Eva and George had a cleaning lady, but even so, there was almost always laundry to fold and put away, and Sara did that, even though Eva never once asked her to. "What a help you are!" Eva kept saying, and Sara had to admit she was just as surprised because all she ever heard from Abby was how she couldn't do anything right. At home, the few times she tried to make dinner, the fish burned, the vegetables got overcooked, but here, the dinners were so delicious, everyone asked for seconds. At home, her room was messy, but here she liked order. She could straighten up the chaos in the time it took Eva to shower and dress. And most important of all, most surprising, she could somehow look at the baby and know what Anne needed, like a secret spring welling up from deep ground. "She's hungry," Sara said, when Eva started tugging at the baby's diaper.

"She can't be, I just fed her—" Eva said, but when Anne kept crying, Sara went ahead and fixed her a bottle. "I told you I fed her," Eva said, but Sara held the bottle out to the baby, and Anne hungrily grabbed for it, her mouth greedily working at the nipple. When later in the day, Anne started fussing, Eva put on music and began to talk to Anne. "What do you think about macaroni and cheese for lunch?" she said. "With, say, a nice tossed salad, dressing on the side?" Anne flailed her arms.

Sara lifted Anne up and sat with her, rocking her, and Anne suddenly calmed. Thrilled with her triumph, Sara beamed. "Pretty good, right?" she said to Eva excitedly. She felt flush with power, but Eva had this strange new look on her face that made Sara uneasy.

"How did you know to do that?" Eva asked quietly.

"I didn't. I just did it. I thought it would work."

"I guess I'm a little anxious," Eva said finally. "It's so new to me."

"It's new to me, too," Sara said, but Eva didn't respond.

Sara got into the habit of just sitting with Anne, and she began, like Eva, to talk to the baby. She didn't tell Eva, but she swore the baby understood her, that Anne was communicating just in the way she fluttered her fingers, the way her gaze changed. "I know," Sara said to Anne. "I feel just the same way." She told Anne what she did the evenings when she wasn't with her, and once, when Eva was taking a bath, Sara dared to tell the baby about Danny. "He's your father," she whispered. "We were in love and I know he would love you." Anne stared solemnly up at Sara. "He loved tinkering with cars. He loved swimming. He could talk and talk for hours." Sara's breathing slowed. "He just got scared, that's all. It doesn't mean he doesn't love you." She moved her finger, making circles in the air. Anne's eyes followed Sara's finger. She made sounds as if she were going to speak back. "It doesn't mean he doesn't love us," Sara whispered.

One night, they all took a drive. George and Eva sat very close together. Sara sat beside the baby in the backseat. The little plush car seat was turned, facing the back. *I'm the only one who can see your face,* she thought. She held one hand on the infant seat even though it was bolted in tight. Anne's eyes were glued to hers.

"So, everything okay at home?" George said, and Sara started. She glanced over at his reflection in the rearview mirror, trying to gauge what was going on, if there was something she didn't know. Anne's slate-colored eyes followed Sara. George's voice was soft, considerate. He looked at her with real concern. How could anyone be that nice to her, that kind? Eva was so lucky. Eva told her that she had fallen in love with George the first week she had met him. "Big, bald, goofy-looking. I wouldn't have looked at him twice," Eva said. "But the day after our first date, I got sick and he sent me over soup and sci-fi videos. He left a lullaby on my answering machine."

"Your parents giving you trouble?" Eva said.

"I don't know. Sometimes." She shrugged, embarrassed.

Eva cleared her throat. "Ever hear from Danny?" she said.

"Not yet," Sara said slowly. She saw Eva and George lock eyes and she sank down lower in the seat. All anyone had to do was mention his name and she yearned for him.

"It would be good to find him," Eva said. "Just so he knows what's going on here," she added quickly.

"Do you know where he might be?" George said.

There was that fishtailing in her stomach, as if she had swallowed live minnows and there wasn't enough water for them to swim. They flopped around in her stomach, gasping for air. "Please. Can we not talk about this?" Sara said.

"Oh, of course," said Eva quickly, and Sara saw the way Eva glanced at George.

"Well," George said finally. "When you get upset, go into yourself. That's my advice. Or better yet, you get out. Take a walk, a drive."

"I don't know how to drive." *"I'd teach you if I had a car,"* Danny had told her.

"What?" He gave her a look of mock alarm, then he glanced over at Eva. "Did you hear that, Eva? Why, that's a travesty. That's un-American. A teenage girl not driving."

"My parents wouldn't let me touch their car."

"You didn't take driver's ed?"

"The math teacher taught it! He told me to keep looking at the side of the road to keep the car straight, to put my foot on the gas like a sponge—"

"Like a what?" Eva laughed.

"And then he pulled over and told me that some people weren't meant to drive, and maybe I was one of them." She looked out at the traffic ruefully, at all the young kids driving. "And my parents agreed."

George snorted. "That's the most ridiculous thing I've ever heard."

He looked at his watch and then grinned. He made a right and then a left, until they were in a big, empty schoolyard. There was a huge blacktop playground. A few benches under leafy trees. "Oh, Anne will love that," Sara said.

He got out of the car. Eva got out and started unbuckling the baby from the seat. Eva lifted Anne up and held her in her arms. "We'll see you guys later," Eva said.

Sara got out of the car.

"Back in you go," George told her, opening up the front door. She was still. "Come on, get behind the wheel," he told her. "I'll be right beside you. There's nothing here you can hurt. I love this car. It's a dream to drive."

"You'd teach me to drive?"

"At your service," George said in a courtly voice.

Excitement snapped on inside of her. She couldn't wait to get in the car, to scoot behind the wheel, grabbing it, four o'clock, just the way the driving instructor had told her. "No, no, not like that," George said gently, and repositioned her hands.

She wasn't very good, but it didn't matter to her. The car jerked and pulled. "Whoops," she said, but he didn't seem concerned. He sat calmly beside her while every cell in her seemed to be flying out to space. He didn't lean in close every time she made a turn. He didn't even press his foot into an imaginary brake on his side of the car. "You'll get it," he said kindly. He made her drive around and around. He showed her how to park and U-turn and go in reverse, and then she finally relaxed. She leaned over the wheel, putting on a bit of speed. She turned the car this way and that.

"See? Now you can go anywhere. You don't have to depend on your parents or Eva or me. It's freedom."

But Sara wasn't thinking of freedom. Wide open spaces didn't interest her. Instead, she wanted this small circle to grow smaller, tighter, closer. Instead, all she could think about was the feel of the car speeding beneath her, the glide of the blacktop. All she could imagine was the incredible fact that George loved his car and he had let her drive it. She felt the warm night. She and George and Eva and the baby were all family.

She turned the wheel again and George beside her disappeared. She imagined she was older, driving in this car, and the person beside her was Anne, a sturdy little girl with Sara's hair tucked into two braids. Maybe the two of them were going to Anne's kindergarten play or out to Brigham's for hot fudge sundaes. The two of them would be singing along to the radio, laughing, or telling goofy jokes. Maybe they were even dressed alike, in jeans and black T-shirts, in high-top sneakers. The two of them would get out of the car and all anyone had to do was look at them and know they were mother and daughter. Everyone would see how much they loved each other.

"Good job!" George said, and Sara's reverie dislodged. Instantly, she was bumped back beside him in the car again. Eva and Anne were back outside, waiting patiently for the car to stop so they could get back in.

After a while, Abby and Jack stopped asking Sara where she was going, when she might be back. They didn't ask her how her day was when she returned. Instead, Jack kept to himself. Instead, Abby left college catalogs on Sara's dresser. She kept the Help Wanteds on the table, dead center, where Sara couldn't miss them, and a few times she had circled things in bright purple ink. Intern. Library helper. Tutor for grade-school kids. Sara, walking by, swept the catalogs into her top drawer. Her hand dusted the Help Wanteds onto the floor. Instead, the books she read were recipe books so she could cook dinner with Eva. She went to the bookstore, but the books she gravitated to weren't the ones Eva picked up like party nuts, *The Wise Parent, The Good Baby.* And the one title that made Sara laugh, *What Every Baby Knows,* as if every baby had a secret and it was an adult's job to tell you what it was. Sara picked up *Charlotte's Web,* a book she had loved all through her girlhood. She grabbed for bright colorful books Anne could touch.

It was two in the afternoon and already George was irritated. Cora, his office manager, was out sick. She had overbooked and now he had a root canal in room one, and an abscess in room two, both cranky and miserable and demanding his attention. Teresa, his hygienist, had told him that morning that she was quitting with only a week's notice. "What I really want to do is write," she said.

He had too many patients for one day, and for the last few nights he hadn't been getting any sleep at all. The baby was two months old now, and she still woke every two hours, like a little alarm clock, her wails splitting the night. They both stumbled up, grabbing for their robes, shuffling their feet into their slippers. Eva padded to the kitchen to warm the bottle, and he stood over her crib, watching her.

He couldn't get over Anne. "You with a kid?" one of his friends had said to George when he had mentioned they were adopting. He could hardly have imagined it, either. He liked and appreciated kids well enough, loved going into the schools to talk to them, to have them clamber up on his lap, imprinting his cheek with sticky kisses. But he loved leaving them, too. Loved being fancy-free enough to go to movies whenever he wanted, and theater, and good restaurants, and have all that child bounce and joy be a memory he could retrieve happily whenever he wanted. And Eva. He wanted Eva all to himself. He'd be lying if he didn't think that a child might change his relationship with Eva. "You have a child, you lose your partner," someone had told him once, and George worried over it. He loved Eva, he couldn't bear to be the cause of her unhappiness, and maybe he had agreed to children not just because he wanted her to be happy, but because not to agree might be a way of losing her, too.

When they had first brought the baby home, there was so much noise and commotion, and he and Eva were so sleep-deprived, that he had looked forward to going back to work, to getting away from all the diapers and feedings, to being back in a circle of adults. But once at work, to his surprise, he couldn't stop thinking about Anne. He could be making amalgam for a filling and the shape would suddenly remind him of a toy she had. He'd be walking on the street and he'd see a stroller and his breath would skip. He was filling a tooth when he heard a baby cry and he had to stop for a moment, leaving his patient, to go into the waiting room where a woman and a baby sat, the two of them smiling. "New patient," she said, but he couldn't unlock his eyes from the baby.

Last night, he was drawn into Anne's room as if she had cast a spell on him. He slipped in, just for a look, he told himself, and then, before he knew it, he sat for hours beside her crib, and just watching her sleep seemed the most miraculous thing in the world to him. It tickled him how small she was. How she blew bubbles in her sleep, how her tiny fingers curled. How all he had to do was look at her and be filled with feelings that even the most basic thing—eating, sleeping, wetting her diapers—seemed amazing to him now.

He spent as much time with her as he could. Imagine that, a tiny baby and he missed her, she flooded his thoughts. He came home for lunch, he tried to schedule appointments no later than four so he could get home early to see her, and a few times he called Eva. "Put her on the phone," he said, and Eva laughed and went to get Anne and he listened, just for a few minutes, to her breathy sighs and burbles.

"You ought to get a load of the look on your face," his hygienist told him, walking by, her arms laden with files. She laughed. "It's just wonderful," she told him.

He was in love and he knew it.

He had to admit Eva was a little better with the baby than he was. And why not? Hadn't he come to her class and stood outside, leaning in the doorway, watching her with her kids, their faces turned to her like little daisies to a sun. He had seen her with her friends' babies, how good she was, how gentle, how the babies all seemed to adore her. But he could learn. He could catch up.

And seeing Eva with the baby did something to him he never expected. He had come into the house last night to find the two of them asleep on the couch and he was flooded with emotion. "Eva," he said softly and she roused, blinking up at him, and suddenly he wanted her so much, it made him dizzy. Walking toward her, he bent and kissed her full on the mouth, he stroked back her hair.

"I love you," she said.

"I love us," he told her.

Now, he checked his watch. He'd never get out of here in time.

"Doctor."

He finished the root canal and gave the abscess patient novocaine. "Be right back," he said, trying to sound cheerful. The patient glared at him. "I promise," he said.

He passed the waiting room. Six patients, leafing through magazines, shifting position. They looked up at him expectantly. One put down her magazine and leaned forward. "Soon, Mrs. Lido," he lied. Soon, baloney. He went into Cora's little office. He picked up the phone and called Eva and as soon as he heard her voice, bright and lustrous as a piece of silver, he felt soothed.

"I can't come home for lunch today," he apologized. "But I'll get out of here early."

"Well, okay," she said. "Anyway, Sara's here."

He glanced at the clock. "Really? Again? I thought you and Anne were going to go out to see your friend Christine later—"

"Sara came by."

"Shouldn't she be home? Or with her friends?"

"Doctor," someone called.

"Look, I've got to go. Love you. Love our baby. See you at dinner," he said.

At four, he was finished, an hour earlier than he had hoped. His last patient had been another emergency, a woman who had come in with her bridge still attached to a bright red taffy apple she hadn't been able to resist biting. She left with a temporary and a list of foods she shouldn't eat. He'd have to place an ad for another hygienist. He wished he could place an ad for a clone. Most dentists worked solo, and he had never wanted to be in a partnership, but maybe it might help things. He wouldn't have to work so hard, such long hours. But of course the question was, who would be the partner? You had to be careful with things like that. The only person he could think of was his old friend Tom from dental school, who lived in Florida and was always trying to get him to move down there. "Blue skies, sandy beaches," Tom urged, but George hadn't really wanted to move.

George shut the office. He drove home, stopping to pick up fresh flowers from the Korean greengrocer, a box of chocolates he knew Eva would love. All he wanted was to eat dinner and lie in bed with Eva, the baby between them, a blissful oasis of family.

He didn't know what he had thought would happen, but with Sara there, the whole dynamic had changed. Yesterday, when he had come home, Sara had been there cooking in the kitchen with Eva. He hadn't been able to get a word in edgewise, but Eva had looked so happy that he had let it go. He had gone in to see Anne, lifting her up out of her crib. He had wanted a moment with her, quiet time, just the two of them in the rocker. The baby smelled so delicious, like powder and vanilla, and he held her tiny hand, admiring the little nails, the peachy skin. "Let Daddy tell you about his day," he started to say and then the door opened and Sara burst in with a bottle and the mood was spoiled.

"I'll feed her," he said, and took the bottle, warm in his hand. Sara sat on the bed and he felt a flicker of annoyance. He liked Sara, but really, couldn't she just leave him alone with his own baby for a minute? "We'll be fine," he told her, and Sara hesitantly stood up. "See you in a while," he told her. "Oh, could you just shut the door?"

"The door?" She blinked at him. He nodded and she shut it.

But he could still hear her, right outside, laughing and talking about something, Eva's voice a counterpoint. Even with the door closed, he still felt her presence, and it suddenly felt too near to him, like clothing that was a size too small. And even after she had left, two hours after dinner, she was still there, too.

*   *   *

He opened the door. The house smelled spicy with garlic and he was suddenly ravenous. There was music, something soft and bluesy. He felt giddy with happiness. The bad day swept away from him. Eva had always been able to do that for him, from the first day he had met her, when she had been the last of his patients after a particularly bad day. Her eyes were big and sparkling as mica, and while every patient that day had sat glumly or complained that he was hurting them, Eva was bubbling. Every time he took an instrument from her mouth, she talked to him, as if she remembered something more she had to say, and he found himself talking back, unable to stop, and six months later, they were married.

"Anybody home?" he called. He looked for a space to put the paper down. He smelled his wife's vanilla perfume, and then, like an undertone, he caught a whiff of something else. The damned smoky-smelling scent Sara wore. It clung to everything. He headed for the kitchen, tripping over something. He leaned down and picked it up. Sara's hairbrush. Right there on the floor. Last week he had found her sweater in the bathroom, pulled over a rod as if it were a towel. She was everywhere, all over the house, and he suddenly began to feel a little cramped.

He started taking off his coat, pushing the hangers to the side to make himself room. "Hey, you."

There was Eva, in a pale blue dress. "Hey, you, yourself," he said. Her feet were bare, her hair tumbled down her back. She looked so beautiful, so luminous, he forgot he had ever been annoyed today. He reached for her.

"Anne's sleeping," she said, and he bent to kiss her neck. He started unbuttoning her dress, to kiss her throat, her shoulders. "Hey," she said, "wait—"

"Let the dinner burn," he said, in his best Barry White voice, and then he heard something. He looked up, his mouth on Eva's skin, and there was Sara, in an apron, in oven mitts, smiling. "I made dinner for all of us," Sara said.

*   *   *

Sara got her coat after dinner. She was almost at the door, ready to leave, when he remembered. "Wait," he said, and she turned. "Don't forget your other things." He walked around the living room. He felt suddenly grumpy, he felt crowded in, as if there were too many people in an elevator. He hadn't minded Sara's being over every day when she was pregnant—no, that, in fact, had made him feel better, as if the fact of her being over so often might bond her to them more, and it had made Eva happier, too. He hadn't thought he would mind Sara being here after the baby was born, but now—her presence made him a little anxious. He wouldn't even mind if Sara came a few days a week, or called all the time, but being here, a presence, every day? He plucked up Sara's sweater, her comb, her tube of mascara, and handed them to her. "Wait. There's a book in the kitchen. Let me just go fetch it," he said.

"I can get it tomorrow," Sara said, but he waved a hand. "No, no, it's easy enough to do it now," George said.

He put everything in a brown paper bag for her. "That's everything, right?"

"I'll see you tomorrow," Sara said.

When Sara left, George watched her from the window, and he didn't know why, but it bothered him the way she stopped at the end of the block, the way she turned and looked back at the house. He heard Eva in the kitchen, the whistle of the kettle.

He walked into the kitchen. Eva was wiping the counter with a damp sponge. "She's here too much," George said.

Eva shrugged. She wouldn't look him in the eye. "We said she could be here whenever she wanted."

"I know, but did you think she'd be here every day? Didn't you think it would taper off, the way the agency said?"

Eva started wiping the table.

"Look, she's a nice girl, but doesn't it bother you, the way she's here all the time?" George asked. "Wouldn't you like time alone with the baby?"

Eva stopped wiping the table.

"Is something wrong?"

She looked away from him, and then Anne started to cry and she went into the baby's room and he followed her. Bending, she lifted Anne up; she moved in an awkward dance and Anne wailed louder. He touched her shoulder and she whipped around. Anne's face was tight with rage.

"Eva?"

Tense, she handed the baby to him.

"There you go," he said. He rocked Anne, he did his own sort of awkward dance until the baby quieted a little. "Look at this face," he said, holding the baby up for Eva to see, and then he leaned toward her and kissed her. "And look at this one," he said.

Eva burst into tears.

He looked up at her, stunned. He held Anne, gently rubbing her back.

"Eva, what is it? What's going on?"

She hesitated. She rubbed her nose. "It's just sometimes being a mother is overwhelming, that's all. Sara helps out."

"Is that all it is?" he said, relieved. "We'll hire you help. Or we can get Anne into one of those fancy day cares. Just a few hours a day, so you can have a little space."

Eva was still. Her breathing calmed a little. George glanced around the room, at the big Disney calendar they had bought for the baby, and suddenly perked up. "School's starting soon. Sara won't even be able to be here as much. You'll see. You'll be alone here with Anne, and you'll have some time for yourself, too, and Sara and you will work it out together."

"You think?" said Eva, and then George kissed her. "I know," he said. "Trust me."

chapter

five

Sara stood in front of the school. Jefferson High. Three floors of red brick, ringed by woods. A big American flag waving at her like a crazy hand out front. She glanced at her watch, the third time in five minutes. Quarter to nine. Last year, she made a point to get to school by eight at the latest, sometimes even by seven. She was always rushing, eyes glued to her watch, worried she'd fall behind. Jack had even offered to drive her this morning, but she had walked instead, dragging her steps, stopping and starting like a rusty car, just to draw the time out. She couldn't go slowly enough.

The buses were long gone. The parking lot, filled with cars, was eerily quiet. Even the kids who usually hung around until the last possible minute, flirting, smoking in their cars, were inside. Sara was alone, in a new short black jersey dress and black tights, her book bag slung over her shoulder. Her parents had been so happy she was going back to school that Abby had given Sara her Filene's charge card. "Buy out the store," Abby said.

They had made such a fuss about her that morning. Abby prepared a special waffle breakfast and they all sat down together, though Sara was so anxious she barely could manage a sip of juice. Jack beamed at Sara. "Senior year!" he said. "You'll see all your friends. There'll be all those activities. You'll feel so much better!" he said, but Sara knew what he meant was he hoped she wouldn't have time to go over to Eva and George's.

She had brushed her hair that morning until her hand ached. It was less curly now, the color dulled, which surprised her, and when she gathered it into a ponytail, she noticed, to her shock, it had thinned. "That happens with pregnancy, sometimes," Abby told her, and it made Sara a little sad, as if she had lost an important piece of herself. She had applied makeup and then washed it off and applied it again. A line of black rimming her eyes. A wash of pink on her cheeks. She felt so old, why didn't she look it?

She heard the warning bell from inside and her bones seemed to soften and turn liquid. Attendance was already taken. In a few more minutes, another bell would ring, and kids would be swarming from home room toward their first class.

Sara forced herself to climb the cement steps. She pushed open the big red door. As soon as she stepped inside, she felt ill. There was the same scuffed black linoleum, the cork bulletin boards fluttering with notices no one ever paid attention to, the blue lockers lining the walls. There was that school smell, her old life, the one she had loved.

This was nothing like being sixteen again. This was not where she had left off.

She walked past her locker and touched it, the metal cool against the heat of her fingers, but it didn't feel familiar, and unnerved, she touched it again, as if for luck. Sara breathed hard. And then the bell rang, making her jump, and kids poured out into the hall and she didn't have to think at all. All she had to do was get to her next class.

She bolted ahead, wishing she could be invisible. "Sara—" she thought she heard, her name, snaking toward her. There was a group of kids standing by the elevator and when she passed by, one girl, someone Sara had never seen before, pointed right at her. "That's *her*," the girl said, and the others huddled around. Sara walked faster, her head down. *They know*, Sara thought. Robin must have told.

All that day no one really talked to her. She felt people watching her; every once in a while she'd see a familiar face—Robin, Judy, kids she knew from her honors classes, but they met her eyes and then, embarrassed, they looked away again, and she was too anxious to push a connection. No one ever stopped. Instead, she heard snatches of talk. *"Knocked up. How clueless can you get?"* Every word hurt her, and after a while, she stopped smiling, she stopped trying to find a friendly face or be friendly herself. She pretended she didn't care, that it was fine to walk the halls all by herself, it was terrific to have all this quiet about her, because look how well she could study now.

She was getting a book out of her locker when a hand reached out and slammed her door shut. She turned, and there was a boy she didn't know, with rough-cut blond hair and icy green eyes, his arm still stretched out on the locker, keeping her pinned where she was. Behind him, she saw another group of boys, watching, nudging one another, giving her knowing grins. "You and me, hooking up Friday night," the boy said, his voice low. "All night."

She stared at him. He was standing too close, leaching the air from around her. "No," she said, and then he slowly, deliberately, lifted up his arm and freed her. He stepped away, still watching her, muttering under his breath, loud enough for her to hear, for the crowd of boys to hear, too—*cunt*—before he casually walked away.

Her mouth trembled, but she wouldn't let him see how he had hurt her. She wouldn't let any of them see. She forced her head up, and started walking, down the corridor, to the other end of the school, the boys' laughter a trail behind her.

All that day, she took her time getting to and leaving her classes, fiddling with her books so that by the time she got to the hall there were only a few kids, rushing to another class, not having time to stare at Sara anymore. At lunch, she found an empty room to eat in. In gym, she hid in the exercise room, curling up on one of the machines, while everyone else played tennis, and when class was over and she went to change out of her uniform, she found her clothes on the floor by her gym locker were tied in knots.

But if the kids were cruel, her teachers were surprisingly kind, and somehow their kindness made her feel even worse, more separated from the kids around her. Carl Morgan, her art teacher, set down a circle of clay in front of her. "Go ahead, pound," he said quietly. "You should see how many tables I've broken myself." She hit the clay halfheartedly. "It won't always be this hard," he said simply. When she turned around, he had vanished. *You don't have to leave me alone,* she wanted to cry, but he had.

Mademoiselle Antoine, her French teacher, praised Sara effusively when she conjugated a simple verb. Mr. Reynolds, her calculus teacher, didn't know what to say to her, so he didn't say anything at all, not until she was leaving his class. "Nice to have you back, Miss Rothman," he said, and Sara, surprised and grateful, turned to him, but he was already moving away, already talking to someone else. And Mr. Tillman, her honors English teacher, snapped at her the way he always did, but to Sara it was welcome. It felt like everything might be the same. "Did you do your summer reading?" he asked her, and she perked up because, oh yes, she most certainly had. She thought of her pile of books by her bed, how all she had to do was look at how high they were and feel comforted, because time spent with every book meant less time spent in her real, waking life. She thought of the careful notes she had made. She thought of Abby, sitting at the kitchen table, swept up in Sara's books. Reading had saved both of them, Sara thought.

"Which book affected you most?" Mr. Tillman asked, and then suddenly, Sara's mind felt whitewashed. Blank. She couldn't remember a single title. She tried to think back, to remember a cover, or words on the page, but the more she tried to visualize, the more her thoughts stalled. "Um—" she said.

Kids turned around in their seats, staring at her, some of them grinning.

"I—" she said.

"Well, what were you doing then?" he snapped, and someone snickered, and then a few other people laughed, and Sara felt her face heat with shame, and she suddenly bolted to her feet. "Miss Rothman!" Mr. Tillman said, but she was already out the door, down the corridor, and then she was running, her shoes smacking on the linoleum, not stopping until she was at the far end of the school, at the bank of pay phones there.

She dug out a quarter, she dialed, and as soon as she heard Eva's voice, the tightness inside of her loosened. "Eva—" she said. "I just had to talk to you."

She could hear Anne crying in the background, she could hear a clatter of pots.

"Sara, hang on—" Eva interrupted. Sara heard Eva talking to someone. "Okay, I'm back. Now calm down, take it slow," Eva said, her voice soft, sympathetic.

"It's so awful here! No one's really talking to me!"

"The what? Wait, wait—Sara, it's going to be okay. Listen, the dishwasher repairman is here. I'm sorry, honey, I've got to go. We'll talk later. I promise."

"Wait!" Sara said. "Wait!"

"Sara, I have to go—you're crying, the baby's crying—"

Dial tone. Sara couldn't let go of the phone. She held on, and in the dead quiet of the hallway, she took deep, shaking breaths. Calm, she told herself. Calm. She glanced at her watch. It was two. She had one more class to get through. She hung up the receiver. She started back to her class and then two girls rounded the corner and both of them stared at Sara so hard, she was pinned in place.

"So how's Danny, Sara?" one of the girls asked. Sara started. How did this girl know her name? And even worse, how did she know Danny?

"I fucked him, too. We all did."

The other girl laughed, watching Sara, taking her measure.

"We both know that's a lie," Sara said.

"Oh, we do?" The girls laughed and nudged each other.

For a moment, Sara wavered. Then she turned, and instead of walking to her class, she walked out the front door. *It's not true,* she told herself. And even if it was true, well then, it was true before they were Danny and Sara, and any time before that didn't count. Outside the air was clear and blue. There wasn't much traffic on the streets, and the only person she saw was an elderly man with a shock of white hair, walking a big, woollylooking dog. Sara headed for Eva's and as soon as she rang the bell, as soon as she saw Eva, it was like oxygen. She felt so relieved that she burst into tears, and for a long while, Eva did nothing but hold her.

*　*　*

Afterward, she felt better. Eva gave her a cool cloth to wash her face, some extra tissues for her nose. Her nose prickled. "The house smells like lemons," Sara said.

"We have a woman who comes in mornings. You wouldn't believe what a help she is! She cleans, does laundry. She even helped me bathe Anne."

"I could do that," Sara said slowly.

"Don't be silly, you're not a maid," Eva said. "I just have to make a few phone calls. Why don't you take it easy and when Anne wakes we can take her to the park."

"Okay, I'll just study in the other room, then." Sara sat on the couch. She pulled out her notebook. She had history reading to do, and a paper to write, too. She opened the history book and started reading about World War II when she heard Anne whimper. Sara jumped up and went to check, but when she opened the door, Anne was sleeping.

Sara sat back down and picked up the history book again. She read a few pages and then began scribbling notes, but she kept thinking she heard Anne. She couldn't get lost in that place where she needed to be to study, fully focused, oblivious to everything but her work. Plus, she was hungry. "Eva, you want something to eat?" she called, getting up. She could study at home tonight.

"On the phone in the bedroom," Eva called. "And not hungry." Sara went in the kitchen and opened the refrigerator. She didn't want to make a big deal out of eating if Eva wasn't eating, too, so she picked at what was there, peeling open tinfoil and taking a bit of coffee cake, breaking off a chunk of cheese. She poured herself a glass of milk, saving time by drinking it standing in front of the refrigerator.

"Eva?" she called.

"I said in a minute——" Eva said, and then she came in the kitchen. She picked up a rag and stooped to the floor, where Sara saw drips of milk, a pattern of crumbs. "Oh, I'd get that——" Sara said, but Eva shook her head.

"I already did."

Anne began crying from the other room, and Eva rubbed her eyes with the flat of her hand. "Oh, she's up again."

"I'm sorry," Sara said. "I'll clean up." She reached for Eva's hand, she wanted to touch her, but Eva was moving past her like quicksilver, disappearing around a corner.

All that afternoon, Sara felt as if she were trailing Eva. Every time she tried to talk to Eva, Eva had something she needed to do. She was diapering Anne, preoccupied, and when Sara reached out an arm to help, Eva said simply, "I can manage." Sara wanted to feel useful. She wanted to be with Eva and Anne, and she wanted to do her history reading, and by six, she had really done none of those things. Instead, she had to go home.

Timing was everything. She usually got in before her parents did, so that by the time they put their key in the lock, she was on the couch studying. "How was school?" Abby always asked. "How's my girl?" Jack wanted to know. Neither one of them ever asked if she was at Eva and George's. They never asked about Anne or commented on the photo of Anne she had tucked in her mirror, that small, perfect baby face looking out at her.

That evening, right after dinner, she went to her room to work. Her books spread across her desk, her computer hummed on, she tried to read. The words swam in front of her eyes. She stood up and stretched and then sat down again, and tried to read, but she couldn't get past the first paragraph. There was that strange static in her head again.

Coffee. What she needed was coffee. Strong and black and thick. She couldn't fall behind, wouldn't let herself. She went to the kitchen and made herself a pot of inky coffee, then carried it back to her room. She sipped until she felt a little buzzed, and then she made the light brighter and hunkered down to do her work.

"Sara?"

Sara awoke, drifting up from her dream, squinting at the light and at Abby who was in a flowery robe, her face glistening with cream. "It's late, get to sleep now," Abby said.

Sara stood up, her legs wobbly. Her head still felt thick. Outside it was dark, and she glanced at the clock. Twelve-thirty. She had fallen asleep at her desk, and now there was a crick in her neck. "I didn't finish my reading—" Sara said, but Abby shook her head adamantly. "Finish in the morning, then," Abby said. "Get to bed now."

Sara waited until Abby left. She shut off her overhead light, and then sat at her desk waiting until all the other lights in the house went off, until she heard Abby's door shut, her father's deep, sonorous snores. Then she clicked the light on again. An extra hour would do it. She could finish and then she'd be fine.

The alarm rang and she jolted awake. Stretching, she padded onto the floor. This wasn't that bad. She wasn't that tired, even with a lesser amount of sleep.

One week of school passed, then another, and gradually, after a month, she began to feel like her old self. Oh, maybe her jeans were looser now, her T-shirts more baggy, and her hair less wild, the color faded, but she was still first at the board figuring out a complicated math equation in first period, still first to hand in homework. "That's the Sara we know and love," her teacher said, making her blush. She was old news now. People had stopped staring at her, and when she overheard a bit of gossip, it was now about a boy who had broken his leg in a motorcycle accident, about a girl who was seen having dinner with the history teacher.

In third-period history class, she felt her lids drooping. Propping her head in her hands, she tried to concentrate, but the teacher's voice was hypnotic and droning. She shut her eyes for just a moment, and then someone was shaking her, the bell for next period was blasting, and she was rousing up from a deep, steady sleep.

Sara tried readjusting everything, playing with how she used her time. One month, she stopped eating lunch so she could try to do her work at lunchtime, but then she was too hungry to concentrate. Another month, she set the alarm an hour early so she could get up and study, but she fell asleep in history class again and the teacher sent her to the principal's office with a note. "Sleeping is one thing," the teacher said. "Snoring is another." At Eva's, she tried to stay awake so she could talk with Eva, so she could help with Anne, but half the time, she'd fall asleep, waking with a start to find herself on Eva's couch, a blanket thrown over her, and the person Eva was animatedly talking to was on the other end of the phone. Dazed, she tried to shake off her drowsiness.

"You don't have to come over every day," Eva said gently. "Stay home and sleep."

"Of course I have to come every day," Sara said. "I'd miss you too much."

"Go home. Sleep. We'll see you tomorrow."

Sara went home and busied herself with schoolwork, falling asleep at her desk. The next day, when she got to Eva's, Eva was just coming back into the house, Anne in a baby carrier, her hands full of grocery bags. "Oh, you should have called—" Eva said. "Today turned out to be impossible. I have so much to do, and Anne's out of sorts."

"I tried to call," Sara said.

Eva glanced at the car and then back at Sara. "Okay, honey, come on inside."

Inside, Eva put Anne in her rocking carrier and started unloading groceries. "I can't figure out how to do everything—" Sara said. "School and Anne and coming here—"

Eva put three packages of pasta high up on a shelf. "Why do you have to do everything?" she said. Bending, she lifted up another bag and handed it to Sara. "Can you be a love and help me with this?"

Sara took the bag. "What do you mean? What are you saying?"

Eva nodded at the bag. "Perishables," Eva said. "I'm saying if you have a paper due, you should do it at home. I'm saying if you need to talk to me, you can call me on the phone, you don't always have to be over here."

"Call you! That's not the same—"

"But sometimes I'm busy—"

"And that's why I'm here. I can help—"

Eva glanced at the bag. "The ice cream," she said, reaching over to the bag and taking out the pint herself. "Don't want it to melt." She put it in the freezer and then reached into another bag for a package of cereal. "Can you believe how time flies? Five months old. Solid-food time," Eva said, her face lightening.

They talked only a little after that. The phone kept ringing, and it was always a call Eva needed to take. "I'm sorry, Sara," she apologized, but as soon as she got off the phone, it rang again. Sara felt like every step she took was in Eva's way. Sara sat at the dining room table, opened her books, but the words shimmied on the page, her hand wouldn't hold her pen. Finally, she just put her schoolwork away and went to see Anne.

"Look at you," she said, lifting up the baby. Anne had spit up over her romper. "Yow. Let me give you a bath." she said.

She didn't think twice about it. She had helped Eva bathe the baby before. Filling the tub, she tested the water with her elbow the way Eva did, she set up the nonskid baby seat and put Anne, squirming and naked, into it. She couldn't get close enough to the baby. The day Anne had been born, the doctor had put her on Sara's belly, skin to skin, the way all the books she had ever read had suggested, but then her baby had been whisked away from her by Eva. There had always been barriers. Even bathing Anne with Eva, Sara had had to step back, to give Eva the room Eva always said she needed. Eva's elbows were always slicing the air. Bending, Sara floated her hand in the water, and the baby kicked and splashed water on Sara's dress. "Hey, you soaked me," Sara said. Anne smiled and then Sara slid off her dress and got into the tub with Anne, splashing water on the floor. It was the most natural thing in the world. Chortling, the baby slapped her hands in the water. Sara grabbed for the baby's hands and nuzzled them. She rubbed her nose against Anne's, making the baby laugh even louder. "Ah, isn't this better?" she said. She couldn't believe how wonderful it felt to be in the tub with Anne. How silky Anne's skin felt, how delicious she smelled, like plums, Sara thought, or fresh green grapes. She lifted Anne up out of the baby seat and put her in her lap. Wrapping her arms about the baby, Sara hummed, rocking them both in the water. Bliss. This was bliss.

"Sara?" She heard Eva. Footsteps coming closer.

"Giving Anne her bath," Sara called. She slapped gently at the water, making waves, and Anne squealed happily, trying to slap the water with her own baby hands. She held Anne tight because everyone knew babies could drown in just inches of water.

Sara was gently washing Anne when the door opened. "Oh, what a help this is—" Eva started to say and then she saw the two of them naked in the tub, and her mouth dropped open, and as soon as Sara saw Eva's expression, she knew she had done something wrong. Something flickered in her belly and grew until she felt covered in shame, and she hunched over, hiding her breasts with her free hand, keeping the other about Anne.

"Oh, my God, what are you doing?" Eva's voice rose. "Where are your clothes?" Her eyes widened. "And she's not supposed to be out of the baby bath seat! The tub is too slippery!" Bending, Eva grabbed Anne up, drawing the wet baby against her. Water dripped down Eva's dress, and Anne squirmed. Eva grabbed for a towel, one foot skidding on the soapy floor, and she grabbed onto the towel rack to right herself.

"I'll clean the floor—" Sara said and Eva cut her off.

"Don't you ever do that again," Eva said, her voice sharp, and Sara drew back, stung. When she dared to look up at Eva, at the baby bundled in the towel, Eva was looking at Sara as if she no longer knew her.

"Come out of that tub," Eva said, and then she strode from the bathroom.

Sara dressed. She was shaking so badly it was hard to mop the floor with the towel, harder to put on the same damp dress she had been wearing. Eva had never been angry with her like this, or disapproving, especially over something Sara had meant to be helpful. Didn't all the baby books Eva had talk about bathing with your baby? Wasn't it the most natural thing in the world? By the time she shored up enough courage to walk into the living room, George was just getting home, pulling his key out of the lock. "Sara, still here?" he said pleasantly. "Your hair's wet."

Sara touched the ends of her hair. She wanted more than anything to say something to George, to have him comfort her, tell her it was all right, but she was afraid.

"How about since I have my coat on, I give you a lift home?" He looked around for Eva. "I'll just be a moment."

She heard him in the kitchen, talking to Eva. She heard Anne babbling. Their voices carried. *"Getting tired of this,"* she heard. *"Not a moment to myself. Needy. More work for me. Bath. I can't take care of two babies."*

And then George's voice. *"You shouldn't have to."*

And then, George walked out, frowning, Eva carrying the baby behind him, and Sara flinched, waiting for him to say something, for Eva to yell at her, but instead they were silent, and it made her more uncomfortable. Weren't they going to talk about this? Clear the air? And if they didn't, how would things ever get back to normal?

George cleared his throat. "Sara—" he began.

"All I did was bathe with the baby," she blurted. "I thought it would be easier."

"It's inappropriate," George said.

"Why? I wasn't doing anything but bathing her." She searched Eva's face.

"We don't want you naked in a tub with the baby," Eva said.

"Naked! It was innocent! All of it was innocent!" She looked at Eva. "It's better for her! You shouldn't be so nervous about it!"

"Nervous! Of course I'm nervous! Babies can drown in three inches of water! She has a bath seat! You have to be careful!"

"I was careful!"

"Look," George said firmly. "The fact is we don't want it happening again. The matter's closed. Now, let's get you home."

As soon as they got in the car, he turned on the radio. He stared straight ahead, but even though he didn't say anything, Sara felt the tension in the car. Hunching, she wrapped both arms about her body, the same way she had in the tub. There were a million things she could say, a million ways she could defend herself. *I carried the baby inside me for nine months in water, what's the difference in being in a tub with her?* But no matter what she thought to say, she kept seeing the way Eva had looked at her when Eva had first come into the bathroom. She kept feeling the same flush of shame, the first time she had ever felt such an emotion in Eva's presence. All the words Sara wanted to say were locked in her throat. "Good night now," George said curtly, and as soon as she was on the sidewalk, he pulled away.

*   *   *

Sara stayed home from Eva's the next day, and then the next, but the day after, as soon as school was over, she rode her bike to Eva's. Two days had passed. Surely they couldn't still be so angry with her. Surely they might laugh about it, or at least not talk about it any longer. In any case, she had learned one thing not to do there, and she would have to deal with her anxiety about what else they might consider wrong about her.

It had been a horrible day. That morning, she had woken from a dream about Danny. He was at home, trying to call her, but something was wrong with his hand. Swinging her legs out of bed, Sara rushed to the phone, dialing his number, but no one answered. Why hadn't he tried to contact her? Why hadn't there even been a postcard or a call? She daubed herself with the patchouli oil he had given her, hoping it might signal him to her.

By the time she reached Eva and George's house, she was panting. Her legs were rubber, jittering when she stood on them. She ran up to the house, ringing the bell, but no one came to open it for her.

She pressed her ear against the door. The house was quiet.

Sara looked around the neighborhood. The street was so still, it seemed to hum. What if something were wrong inside the house? Eva was so tired these days, what if she had fallen down the stairs? Sara looked around. Nothing's wrong. Nothing's wrong. But still she kept seeing Eva sick. She kept imagining all the terrible things that could happen. She had studied chaos theory. One little move affected all else. A butterfly flapped its wings in Africa and the next thing you knew, the stock market collapsed in Japan.

It wouldn't hurt to check, to be careful. People kept extra keys sometimes. She checked the black mailbox, under the rubber welcome mat, under a potted plant. She was about to give up when she noticed a grey rock by the begonias. Sara went down the stairs and crouched and as soon as she touched the rock, she smiled. Rubber. Fake. As soon as she picked it up, it rattled and then a key, small and brass, fell out into her hands.

She hesitated. This had to be wrong, this had to be worse than taking an innocent bath with the baby. She started to put the key back and then an image shone in her mind. Eva hurt, tumbled at the bottom of the rickety cellar stairs. The baby crying and hungry in her crib. What if she left and something had happened? What if she didn't check?

The key flipped through her fingers. She told herself she'd go in for only a minute. Just to rest before she headed back home. Just to make sure everything was all right. Sara put the key in the lock, looking behind her. The street was empty.

Sara turned the key. She let herself in and then shut the door behind her, her heart knocking so loudly she wouldn't have been surprised if the whole neighborhood heard it.

She licked her lips. "Eva?" she called. The house was quiet. She did a quick tour, even opening up the basement door and looking downstairs. "Hello?" she said.

She came back upstairs into the kitchen. She could leave now and no one would even know she had been here. She could call later, pretend she had been home all the time.

What was the matter with her? What kind of a girl was she to break in? She walked to Anne's room and stood inside of it. There was a new oak rocker in the corner she hadn't seen before. There was a stuffed white bear with a blue ribbon.

This isn't your house. This isn't your baby. It was a drumbeat inside of her. Her good mood slid off her like a coat. She went back into the kitchen to get a drink and there on the refrigerator was a notice. "Sunny Skies Day Care." Sara stared, stunned. A whole list of what to pack along with Anne. Bottles, diapers, wipes, food.

When had Eva and George put the baby in day care? And why? Sara didn't want that for her baby. She'd rather quit school and take care of Anne herself than have her baby with strangers in one of those places.

She sat frozen on the kitchen chair, unsure what to do. Then she got up and walked outside. The street was empty. She could hear kids shouting but she couldn't see them. She could hear the crack of a bat against a ball. She wondered if Eva or George would know she had been there. It felt like a risk as dangerous as telling someone you loved them when you weren't sure how they felt about you. She closed the door and locked it. She bent to tuck the key under the rock, but at the last moment, her fingers curled tight about the key, warming the metal, and then she slid the key into her pocket, instead.

It was ten at night. George was driving, Eva in the seat beside him, Anne asleep in back. Eva was feeling woozy from the wine. They had spent a whole lovely evening with Christine and Christine's new boyfriend, Mark, a math professor at Tufts. Mark was funny and handsome and he couldn't take his eyes off Christine—or Anne. He insisted on taking the baby from George and settling her on his lap, and when Anne fell asleep, he couldn't stop marveling. "Give me this baby to raise," he said, making them all laugh.

"She's getting so big," Christine marveled.

"Five months. And next month, we go to court," Eva said. She didn't tell Christine how even though it was just a formality, a sort of official stamp to the adoption, she felt scared.

"Piece of cake," said George, putting one arm on Eva's leg. "No worries."

"I want to come back to work soon," Eva said, "maybe the afternoon session."

"Sara's working out, then?" Christine said.

"Day care," Eva said, feeling a twinge of guilt. When Sara was pregnant, Eva hadn't been able to get enough of the girl, had wanted her over there every day, but now that the baby was here, everything was different. Every time she turned a corner in the house, there was Sara. Every time the phone rang, it was Sara. She began to think that maybe an open adoption could be too open, that maybe it was time to establish some limits. Especially the way things were going, how Sara was getting needier and needier. And then, of course, there was the bath incident.

"Well, good for you!" Christine said.

Mark teased a finger along her shoulder and Christine rested her head against him. The look he gave her was so charged, Eva suddenly felt like a voyeur. "We should get going," she said, nudging George, just as Christine's hand found Mark's knee.

Anne fell asleep again as soon as they got her in the car seat. "Well, that was quite an evening," George said, turning down onto their street. "We'll put the bunny rabbit to bed and hang out." He tapped a finger along her nose. "We didn't even get to the dessert."

"I want you for dessert," she said.

George laughed, pulling the car into the driveway.

"It was great to see Christine," Eva said. "Her new man's pretty nice, too, isn't he?"

"Yup. And I hate to say it, but it's been nice not having Sara around today." George looked encouragingly at her. "Don't you think? You were so great with the baby tonight. And you seem much more relaxed."

"It's the wine." Eva got out of the car and stretched, the night clear and cool around her. "And the day care," she admitted. Three hours three times a week. Just enough so Eva could get everything done, so she could read, or start thinking up new lesson plans for when she went back to work. The day care center was big and bright and sunny, with two young teachers, and as soon as she had set Anne down on the floor, Anne had reached happily for one of the colored blocks. It made all the difference. It had made Eva feel competent, like she had done something right with Anne. Like she could be a great mother.

Eva bent and got the baby. Anne stirred in her arms and then fell back asleep again.

She opened the door. The house smelled of something.

"What's that funny smell?" George said, stepping into the house.

Eva took two steps into the room and then stopped. She tilted her face up and breathed deeply, trying to figure out what was so familiar. Then she turned and locked eyes with George.

"Patchouli," she said. "It's what Sara wears."

"Sara? I thought she wasn't here today."

Eva shook her head. "She wasn't."

George was quiet for a moment. "How'd she get in?"

He looked at Eva again, and then Eva handed the baby to him and went to the front door, running her hand along the lock, frowning.

"What?" George said, but Eva was going down the stairs, crouching by the flowers. She picked up the rubber rock and lifted it.

She shook the rock, but nothing jangled inside of it. There was no sound, and Eva felt something snapping off and on inside of her like a light. She felt Sara behind her, just out of sight, so close, she stood up abruptly. She looked back at George. "We told her our house is your house," Eva said.

"But it isn't," George said. "It never really was."

"I'll talk to her," Eva said. "I'll get the key back." And then she put the rubber rock in her pocket, and her fingers curled around it tight.

chapter

six

Eva thought it'd be easier to talk to Sara on neutral ground, away from the house, so she made reservations for Saturday at La Vita Spaghetti, in Cambridge. "Let's have lunch," Eva said.

"Good. I need to talk to you, too," Sara said, and Eva felt a flicker of unease.

When Eva told George about the lunch, George had asked if she wanted him to be there, too. "I can be bad cop and you can be good cop," he offered. She shook her head. It was all her fault. She had let this happen by encouraging Sara to be so close, to be so much a part of the family, and now she'd have to straighten it out.

"Should Abby and Jack be there?" George asked.

Eva hadn't wanted to call them, but she didn't really want to have this lunch, either.

"Just call," George told her. "Maybe they'll want to be at the lunch."

"I wish." Eva called Abby at work, trying not to sound as if any of this might be Abby's or Jack's fault. "She broke in," Eva said. "I thought we should talk about it."

"She broke in?" Abby was hushed for a moment. "But I thought she wasn't coming over that much anymore. She's been so busy with school and studying and—"

"She's over every day. And she was over when we weren't. You didn't know?"

"I don't understand—are you saying she stole something?"

"No, but she can't come in when we aren't there. I'm calling because she's your daughter."

"She's my daughter when she's done something wrong?"

"I didn't say that."

"You didn't have to." Abby cleared her throat. "It's easy to be the hero to someone else's kid, isn't it?" Abby said quietly. "You don't have to grab her arm and stop her from running in front of a car and then stand there feeling horrible because she accuses you of hurting her. You don't have to yell at her to make her bed and study and then think up proper punishments for when she doesn't do those things. She probably doesn't break your heart the way she does ours, sometimes."

"Abby—she does break our hearts—"

"No," Abby interrupted. "You think we like being the bad guys here? Well, now it's your turn. No, she hasn't told us. We never thought she should be over there so much, so often. You did. And now she did something wrong to you, something you don't like? We'll deal with it. But you deal with it, too." Abby hung up.

Eva was breathing so hard that she had to brace her arms against the counter.

La Vita Spaghetti was sunny and filled with potted green plants and red checked tablecloths. Sara was already seated, dressed up in a soft blue dress, her curls spilling over her shoulders. She looked so very young, and as soon as Eva saw her, all she felt was weary. "Sorry I'm late," Eva said, setting Anne down in the carrier beside the chair. Anne sneezed noisily. "Her eyes are crusty," Sara said, alarmed, but Eva waved a hand.

"She picked it up at day care. All the babies have it. The doctor said it was nothing."

"All the babies," Sara said, amazed. Instantly, a waiter appeared, setting down menus. Eva settled Anne onto her lap, giving her a pair of spoons to bang. "Could I get a high chair, please?" she asked the waiter, who nodded. "It's just three mornings a week to start," Eva said, turning back to Sara. "And day care is good for babies. They learn more quickly. They get socialized faster. They've done studies showing it."

"Studies say whatever you want them to. I took statistics. I know how it works."

"She's just fine," Eva insisted. "I'll have the ravioli," she told the waiter. "Iced tea."

"Oh, me, too," Sara said. "Why do you need to put her in day care? Anything you need to get done, you can do when I'm there."

"I'm going back to work," Eva said evenly.

"Already?"

"I love my job. And it'll only be half a day to start."

Sara's face brightened. "Can you work afternoons? I can take over then with Anne."

Eva dug into the baby bag for the jar of strained beets. She tried to compose herself a little better, so this wouldn't be so difficult. Dunking the spoon into the beets, she pointed the spoon to Anne's mouth, but Anne twisted and the beet smeared her cheek. Sara leaned over immediately, daubing beet from the baby's face with her napkin.

"I want to tell you something—" Eva started.

"Oh, me, too," Sara said, putting the dirty napkin back on her lap. "I've been thinking, I'm going to go to college right in Boston. I could watch Anne when you needed me."

Anne yelped and Eva turned to her. "Bah," Anne said, banging her hands on the table. The waiter appeared, setting down their plates, their iced teas.

"What do you think? Isn't that a good idea?" Sara said.

"Sara," Eva blurted. "Were you at the house the other day?"

Sara sipped at her iced tea, averting her eyes. "They put real peppermint in here."

"We smelled your patchouli oil. And the key was gone."

Sara bowed her head lower. She kept sipping her iced tea.

Eva held out her hand. "I want my key back."

Sara put the glass down. She looked up at Eva, her face innocent.

"I know you have it, Sara."

Sara stayed very still. "I was worried. I kept calling and there was no answer."

"Sara." Eva made her voice a warning. "I thought we didn't lie to each other."

Slowly, Sara reached for her purse and opened it. She put the key on the table. "I just thought it would be a help. That if something happened—"

"Listen. Maybe we should talk about what's going on here. Rethink it a little."

"Rethink what?"

"Sara, we always wanted this to be open. We always wanted you to have as much contact with Anne as you wanted. But, I guess—we were too idealistic. We thought the contact would lessen, that you'd go on and have your own life, and we'd have ours."

"But how can we do that—"

Eva floundered. "It feels sometimes like you're living at the house with us."

"No, no, I'm not living there."

Eva sighed, exasperated. "Yes you are! You come over as soon as school is out! You stay until we kick you out! We never have a moment to ourselves!"

"I spend a lot of time with you, but I'm not living there."

"But you'd like to."

"I like to spend time with you and time with my baby."

Eva put her fork down. She felt light-headed. Anne twisted in the high chair and dropped a spoon onto the floor with a loud clang. "My baby," Eva said. "It's my baby."

Sara blinked at her. "It's—it's an open adoption. It's—it's our baby."

"Bah, ba, bah!" Anne shrieked and then, when Eva and Sara turned to her, Anne laughed out loud. Eva tickled the baby's cheek and then looked back at Sara.

"Sara, no. We adopted Anne. We didn't adopt you." Eva saw Sara flinch and she hesitated. "Not that you aren't a wonderful young girl—"

she said. "Honey. The end of the month is the court date. Maybe—I think we can draft a new agreement and present it. If you want. Get things in writing. Maybe we should sit down with the adoption agency, get a little help here in making things as clear as we can get them."

"I don't understand what you're saying to me. What new agreement?"

"I'm saying that you should have your *own* life, not ours. Don't you want to get ready for college? Don't you want to date?"

Anne clattered her spoon on the high chair and Eva, eyes still on Sara, held her hand over Anne's to soften the blows.

"I am going to go to college," Sara said. "No one said I wasn't. And date who? The boys who make sucking noises when I walk past them?"

"Sara, honey, spending all this time with us isn't good for anyone, not even you, but you're too young to see that now. That's all I'm saying."

"No, no, it's good for Anne. It's good for me."

"Look, what if—what if you start coming over less often, oh, say, once a week?"

"Once a week!"

"Well, let's just try it," Eva repeated. "Call first, so you don't get there to find we're gone. I don't want you coming all the way out there for nothing."

"For nothing? It's not for nothing—" Sara whispered.

Eva tried to brighten her tone. "We'll all go out then. What do you think?"

Sara looked down at her food, picking at it. Eva felt drained. The only one having a good time at all was the baby, who was busy grinning at every diner who looked her way.

The waiter swept over to the table. "Anything else, ladies?" he said. He nodded at the baby. "I'm in love with this one here," he said. He looked at Sara and then back at the baby. "You know, your sister looks like you!"

"Oh, she's not my—" Sara said.

"Check, please," Eva said and reached for her purse. Sara grew more and more still, and Anne grew more boisterous, and when Eva took the spoon away from her, Anne banged her hands on the high-chair tray.

"She's usually so quiet—" Eva said, pulling on her coat, pulling Anne up and putting her into the carrier. The baby babbled and Eva half-smiled.

"She's excited to see me," Sara said, and Eva stopped, looking from the baby to Sara and back again, at the way Anne couldn't take her eyes off Sara. Eva tickled Anne's chin, and the baby's eyes flew delightedly toward her. "There's my big girl!" Eva said.

Eva drove Sara home. "Tomorrow?" Sara said hopefully.

"I'll call you," Eva said.

Sara stood on the sidewalk, wavering. "I don't want Anne in day care."

Eva pushed back her hair. "I'll call you," she said, "I will," and then she drove off, and Sara got smaller and smaller in her mirror until she wasn't there at all.

Back at home after the lunch, the house was so quiet that Eva missed all the noise Sara brought with her. She brushed the thought away, and then by afternoon, the baby was out of sorts and noisy enough for a whole army. Anne fussed when Eva changed her diaper. She refused her oatmeal, turning her face away, and when Eva put her in her carrier, she batted irritatedly at her toys and then began to cry. "What is it?" Eva said. She tried dancing with the baby to music, but that only made Anne stiffen. She tried taking a drive, but Anne screamed in the car, she screamed when Eva tried to stop at a park and set her on the grass, and finally, overwhelmed, Eva brought her home. Anne kept fussing, kept flailing her arms. Eva was nearly at her wit's end, in the kitchen, Anne screaming, when the phone rang. She let it. The machine kicked on and there was Sara's voice. "Hi, I was just checking—" and the baby quieted suddenly and Eva couldn't help it, she was in no mood. She snapped the answering machine off.

One day, Eva took Anne to the zoo. The next day, to the children's museum. Then to day care. And one lovely afternoon, the two of them spread out on Eva and George's bed and napped, sleeping until the phone jolted Eva awake. "Can I come over, just for a moment?" Sara said. "I miss Anne. I miss you."

"Not today." Eva stayed firm. She hung up the phone, then she turned to the baby. "It's just you and me, kid." The baby yawned.

All that afternoon, Eva was in heaven. She felt as if she had shed a heavy winter coat and now the cool spring was gently blowing on her skin.

She even felt more charitable toward Sara. They had had good times after all, but still, she didn't feel any impulse to call her the way she used to. Instead, she bathed Anne, and fed her, and then took her outside in her stroller, walking from the neighborhood to the park. "What a cute baby," someone said, peering into the carriage.

"My daughter's going to be a heartbreaker," Eva said. She couldn't stop saying it. She deliberately went into stores where she didn't need a thing just to say it again, to have people admire her baby. "Will you look at this baby!" a woman said. "Wendy, come here!" The two women crowded around, and then Eva came home and put Anne in her crib. "What a time we had," she said

She was doing the wash downstairs when she heard a noise. A window opening. A door. She ran upstairs, but the door was locked. The window sealed. She was putting Anne to bed and she saw something slip by her line of sight. A flash of blue cloth. "Sara," she warned and she walked out into the living room, the kitchen. The house clicked around her, silent and empty. She was grocery-shopping, Anne strapped to her chest, when she turned into the frozen foods section and there was a girl with hair red like a brush fire and she stopped. *How did you get here*—she started to say, and then the girl turned, and Eva saw she had bad skin and wasn't Sara at all. "Silly," Eva told herself.

It was afternoon and Sara was gliding on her bike. She was going crazy. She had been almost used to missing Danny, the consistent dull ache was familiar in its dimensions, but now that she missed Eva and Anne and George, too, one loss fed the other and missing Danny had grown in proportion, too. God, but she had to see Eva. Had to see the baby. And she knew she couldn't.

Sara pedaled faster, rounding the curves, trying to think of nothing but the ground she was covering. She hadn't talked to Eva and George in days, she barely said two words to her parents, who barely said two words back. She glided around a corner, and when she looked up, she found herself on Stanton Street. Danny's block.

It felt like forever since she had been here. There were the same houses she remembered, the pastel-painted Cape Cod, the ranch hidden by bushes. The kids' toys flung carelessly, a red and white jump rope, like a snake coiled on the grass.

There. Sara saw the house. Pale blue. Danny's house. She stopped pedaling, planting her feet on the sidewalk, her heart racing.

Danny's front door slapped open and a woman stepped out. Sara stared. The woman was tall and thin and shockingly lovely, with a curly cap of black hair and pale skin. She was holding a black down jacket closed about her, and when she bent to pick up the newspaper, tossed on the porch, a gold cross glinted at the base of her throat. She looked up and saw Sara. Her hand reached up to touch the cross.

Danny's mother, Sara thought. It had to be. Sara had never once met her, and here she was in the flesh, and she seemed nothing like how Sara had imagined her, nothing like the photograph she had seen.

"Are you lost?" Danny's mother said. Her voice was low and deep, but there was a sticky quality to it, like dried honey on a counter.

Sara shook her head. She wanted to, but she couldn't move. Danny's mother studied her, considering. "Do I know you?" she asked finally.

"I'm Sara."

Danny's mother came down the walk and over to Sara. She stuck out her hand to shake Sara's. Her nails were bitten and unpainted. "Frances," she said.

"I need to find Danny. It's really important. I'm his girlfriend."

Frances cocked her head, considering.

"I left him a note. Do you know if he got it?"

"I don't know anything. Anyway, he's not here right now."

"Please. You have to tell me where he is. Please."

"Why would I want to do that?" Frances said and then she peered closer at Sara. "Are you all right?"

Sara nodded.

"Well, that's good, then." Frances looked at the house. "I need to go now."

Frances started to turn, another silent person who wouldn't talk to her, and Sara couldn't help it. The words flew from her mouth. "Did you know we had a baby?" she blurted. "Did Danny tell you?"

Frances narrowed her eyes. "I knew all right," she said shortly.

"Do you want to see her?"

Frances started. "Like in person?" she said.

"She's living with another family. Not officially adopted. But I have a picture."

Frances stayed silent while Sara dug in her purse. She found the photo of Anne she loved, the one she always carried, the baby in a tiny yellow dress. Sara's hands shook.

"Isn't she beautiful?" Sara said. Frances studied the picture, and just for a moment, her mouth tightened, and then she handed the picture back to Sara.

"All babies are beautiful," Frances said flatly. "And if you think I can't imagine how you feel, you're wrong."

"Excuse me?"

"Look at you, young, pretty girl with all the doors in the world ready to open for you, and there you are wanting to slam them shut and put on the dead bolts."

"No, no, it's not that way. You don't understand."

"Oh, yes I do. Better than you think." Frances squinted at Sara. "There's nothing more terrible for a mother than losing her child. Doesn't matter how old they are or how it happens. Sometimes, you do things you might never have figured yourself doing. Impossible things. It's just what love does to you."

"Do you know where he is?" Sara blurted. She heard the begging in her voice. "I have to talk to him. Before it's too late."

"It's already too late, isn't it?"

"Please. Tell him I came by. Please."

"I'm doing you a favor, not telling you anything, and you don't even know it," Frances said. "You probably shouldn't come back here again," she said. And then she turned, tucking the paper under her arm, and walked back inside. Sara balanced on her bike, just for a moment, and then she bent her head, and began to ride as fast as she could.

As soon as she got to Eva's, before she even parked her bike, she heard the baby crying. Not the usual cat cries Anne made, but real wails, loud and ragged. Alarmed, Sara let her bike fall on the soft grass, and bounded up the steps.

Eva would be furious that she had come over, but she couldn't think about that now, not with the baby crying like that. Was something wrong? Maybe she would just come inside for a minute, make sure everything was okay and then leave. Maybe Eva would be in a better mood now, maybe she'd want Sara to come in and help, the way she used to. They should figure this out, the same way she would figure out a calculus problem. "Unsolvable," people would say, and Sara would go right ahead and solve it.

She didn't have the key anymore, so she knocked on the door, and when no one answered, she knocked again. "Eva?" she called.

She went around to the back of the house, where she saw the small window, half open, easy enough to shimmy up into.

As soon as she was inside the house, the baby's cries went up two decibels. *My God,* she thought. Where was Eva? Had something happened? She didn't care if Eva was mad she was here, she just wanted Eva to be okay, she wanted the baby to be okay. "Eva?" she called, and the baby cried louder. She rushed through the kitchen, past the hanging calendar. Every day had something written on it and she peered at it. "Lunch with Christine." "Meeting at school." "Mommy and Me Class." Every day was filled and not one day had space for her on it. She passed by the living room, automatically looking for the photograph of herself, big and pregnant, but it was gone from the mantel, removed, and when she saw the blank spot Sara felt as if she had been punched in the chest.

She stopped, and she could hear Eva downstairs, the noisy rattle of the dryer, the radio blaring, Eva singing the way people do when they're alone, belting out "Blue Bayou." *Jesus,* Sara thought. *My God. Didn't she hear Anne?*

The phone rang and Sara froze. The radio clicked off but instead of hearing Anne wailing, Eva picked up the phone. Sara stood there, amazed. "Oh, let me call you later," Eva said. "I can hardly hear myself think down here." And then in that moment of quiet, when Eva could have heard Anne, when she could have raced upstairs to tend her, when she could have seen Sara standing there in the kitchen where Sara wasn't supposed to be, Eva turned the radio back on, and then all the fear and tension Sara was feeling catapulted right into rage. Was Eva that oblivious?

Sara knew what to do now. She strode into the baby's room, and as soon as Anne saw her, Sara swore the baby's cries got lower. Anne gulped and sobbed and glued her eyes onto Sara and Sara ached with emotion. Sara picked Anne up, and hugged her close, and the baby's cries slowed to whimpers. Sara loved her. This was her baby and no one could take that away from her, no matter how they tried to separate the two of them, no matter how they tried to make her invisible. Especially someone who would stay downstairs singing and chatting on the phone while a baby cried.

I changed my mind, she thought. *You're my baby no matter what anyone says.*

She thought of Danny's mother, with her bitten nails, standing on the front lawn, telling Sara how she had lost her son. *Love can make you do impossible things,* Frances had said. Sara held Anne tighter. *I won't lose you,* she thought. *I'll never lose you.*

She held the baby in one arm and, with the other, grabbed the diaper bag and stuffed it with diapers and clothes. She was acutely aware now of Eva's singing, of the noisy banging of the dryer. She had to rush. She was sweating now, and her throat felt stapled shut, and she raced into the kitchen, jamming Similac and baby food into the bag, warm winter clothes. Then she bundled Anne into a hooded, fuzzy coat and carefully fit her into her baby carrier. "Shloo," said Anne and Sara said, "Shhh." The baby studied her, newly interested.

The dryer suddenly stopped and a pebble of panic formed in Sara's belly. Grabbing up the carrier, she rushed to the front door and flung it open, didn't even stop to close it, but strode out across the front lawn. She'd stop at the bank. Grab what money she had there. It wasn't much, but it would be enough to get them started. Her bike, well, it would just be another thing she was leaving behind, another thing she'd have to regret.

* * *

Eva came upstairs balancing two loads of clean wash. She was feeling so good, so impossibly good. Downstairs, while sorting wash, she had day-dreamed she and George were snorkeling in Hawaii. Maybe that's what they all needed. A little vacation. Someplace warm and lazy where all they had to do was bake on a beach and not think about anything more pressing than what suntan lotion to buy. Winter blues. That's all it was. She went to get the baby. Tomorrow was day care again, but today she thought she'd take Anne out; maybe she'd take her to see Christine, after all. Just talking to Christine that little bit on the phone had made her want to talk to her even more. Every day she had something new planned. She was getting out, feeling better. The whole world seemed to be opening up again. "Anna banana," she called, "Did you finish your nap?" One of the things everyone was telling her was so great was the way the baby slept, so deeply you could shoot off fireworks next door and she wouldn't rouse. It was good, Eva supposed, though sometimes, standing by the crib, watching her daughter in her still, long sleeps, Eva wondered why Anne wasn't more anxious to be awake, to get lively.

"Let's see if we can get you up," she called, and then she walked into the baby's room and saw the empty crib.

She felt confused and then scared, and then, almost like relief, she caught that damn scent, that musk, and then she felt anger. Of course. Oh goddammit. Of course. Sara. This was just the kind of thing that girl would do. Eva didn't have any idea how Sara had gotten in here, but she could just imagine. Maybe she made up an extra key knowing full well Eva would ask for it back. Maybe she came in through the window. That did it. "Sara!" Eva called, her voice rising.

She looked through the house. The kitchen, the den, the rooms in the back. "Sara!" And then Eva saw the carrier was gone. She'd kill her. She'd absolutely kill her. Sara probably took Anne to the park or out for a walk. How dare she!

Eva grabbed her keys and her coat and headed out the door and then she spotted Sara's bike. "Sara!" she shouted, but the neighborhood was empty. She got in her car and drove, around and around the neighborhood, to all Sara's old haunts. The schoolyard where there was a small swing set and a blacktop, the same blacktop where George had taught Sara to drive. The Star Market where Sara might have gone to get supplies. She couldn't find her, couldn't see the baby, and she began to feel angrier and angrier.

Eva drove back to the house. She was too furious to go back inside, so instead, she waited on the front porch for Sara to show up with some excuse. She simmered with rage, waiting, imagining Sara's explanation, the thin soft voice. The baby had needed air. The baby had needed diapers so she took her for a walk. She was doing Eva a favor. She was helping out. A million excuses. Eva stared at her watch. Six already. This was it. The final straw. She was boiling over now. She stood up and looked down the street, so empty not even a dog was lolling down it, and then her fury began to fade into fear, and by the time she went back inside to call George, she was panicking.

"It's all my fault!" she cried.

"How is it your fault? Is it against the law to do the laundry? To leave a window unlocked in your own house? Eva. Stay calm," he said. "I'm coming home."

But Eva's calm had dissolved. Where had Sara gone for so long? She stepped outside and knocked on Nora's door and asked if she had seen Sara that afternoon. She even called Abby's office, but Abby bristled when Eva told her Sara had taken the baby.

"Taken the baby! What are you talking about?" Abby said.

"She broke into the house!"

"The 'one big happy family' house?" Abby said. "What proof do you have that she would do such a thing! You're negligent, and you blame my daughter?" Abby hung up. *Negligent*, Eva thought, her fear growing. She was negligent and even Abby knew it.

She picked up the phone and called the police, and the moment they arrived at the scene, George pulled up in the drive.

There were two cops. One was stocky and older and the way he kept staring at Eva unnerved her. The other cop looked barely older than sixteen, which startled Eva. His face was dusted with freckles, his hair was boyishly cut, and his nails, she noticed, were chewed. "Start from the beginning," the sixteen-year-old-looking cop said, opening up a notebook, and Eva shook her head, as if she could just shake everything free.

"I see," said the cop, but Eva saw how he exchanged glances with the other cop.

"What?" she said.

He wrote something else down. "Nothing." He looked at her impassively. "Can you describe the girl?"

"There's a picture." George reached into his pocket and pulled out a shot of all of them, laughing up into the lens.

"You keep a picture in your pocket?" the cop asked, and Eva took George's hand.

"The baby had two different-colored socks on," Eva cried.

The cop raised one eyebrow at her.

"On purpose!" Eva cried. "She loves colors!"

"She just came in?" the cop said.

She turned to George. She clutched his arm. "I should have watched her better. I should have locked the windows." She swiped her hands across her eyes.

"Don't. You don't have to do this."

"I don't?" she asked. "Why don't I?"

Eva couldn't look at the cop. "Can I use your phone?" he said. "Do you have her parents' number?"

Eva nodded, dumbly. George went to get the number, to lead the cop to the phone.

All she could think of was that she had been doing laundry and the baby was gone.

It didn't take long for George and the cops to come back into the room. George shook his head. "I got the mother at work," the cop said. "She says Sara often goes off on her own, that Sara often left things over here." He frowned and scratched at his head. "Are you sure she took the baby?"

Eva gripped George's hand. It was too terrifying to think otherwise. "Yes," she said.

"Do you know where she might go?"

Eva shook her head. "She had a boyfriend, but he's gone."

The cop shut the notebook. "Well, she's a kid. How far can she get?" he said. Both cops got back into the car. Eva heard the skittery whine of their radio, the smooth way the car started up. She saw Nora peeking out from her front door, looking over. And then they were gone.

That night, George and Eva just lay in bed. Neither one of them could sleep. Eva crawled as close to George as she could and then, suddenly, he bolted up, frowning.

"What is it?" Eva asked.

"The cop never gave me the picture back," George said. "I forgot to ask."

"We'll call the station, get it back."

"He folded it in two."

Eva rubbed George's shoulders, at the tiny knots, and then suddenly she felt chilled.

"You don't think it's someone else who took Anne? You think it's Sara?" She couldn't help worrying it in her mind. She remembered a few years ago, when she was teaching, reading about this terrible thing. A single father and his best friend and their two young boys were at a Waltham ice-cream shop. A bright sunny day. A car had pulled up out of nowhere, a door had opened and a man had leaped out and had snatched one of the boys, had sped off in the car before anyone could move. The whole neighborhood went crazy. There were search parties. News reports. The father went on TV to plead and ended up sobbing so hard, the newscaster had had to take over. The boy was found two weeks later, in a mall, two cities away. He was dressed differently, in new, brightly colored clothes. His hair was dyed blond, and he wouldn't say who had taken him or why. "Well," the newscaster had said. "What matters is the boy is home safe."

It had bothered Eva, that story, that not knowing what had really happened. It bothered her so much that she and Christine had put together a Don't Talk to Strangers Program at the school. They had made the kids learn the song about remembering your name and address and going up to the kind policeman. They had playacted what to do if a stranger approached. "Bite strangers! Kick them!" Eva had shouted. "It's the one time you're allowed!" Christine had finally abandoned the program because it was making everyone more scared. Too many kids were flinching when relatives they hadn't seen tried to hug them, too many kids were screaming at their parents' friends, "You're not my mommy and daddy! Help!"

She wrapped George's arm about her. She asked again, "Do you think it's Sara?"

George rested his head against her shoulder. She could feel his breath tickling her skin. "Yes," he said heavily. "Yes, I do. It was her bike here, wasn't it?"

"Do you think Anne's all right?"

"She wouldn't hurt her own baby—" George said. He said it as if he were trying to reassure himself, but Eva bolted up in bed again.

"My baby!" Eva cried. "My baby!"

It was four in the morning and Sara and Anne were on a Greyhound bus. She hadn't slept at all, hadn't had a thing to eat, either. The seats were uncomfortable, bright red and crackling, and there was a jagged rip on the edge, as if someone had taken a bite of it. By then she had stopped thinking about Danny, about Eva or George or her parents. With every mile, another memory receded. She glanced at her watch. Another few hours and she'd feel even safer.

She had bought a ticket to Cleveland because it was the first bus that was leaving. Ten minutes later, she might have been on her way to Phoenix or Dallas. Santa Fe, she thought. She had paid for it with cash. The man didn't even blink when she asked for a ticket, and thank God he didn't make her pay for the baby. "She'll sit on my lap," Sara had said, but he had shrugged. "The bus is half-empty, anyway," he told her.

The window was smeary but still a ruler of yellow light shone through. She kept one hand protectively on the baby. The man an aisle up was snoring. The woman across from her was reading a magazine. "Hope that one's going to be quiet," she said pointedly.

Sara ignored her, fired with plans. She should have thought of this a long time ago. She was smart, she could make a new life. She could go to college anywhere, because as her guidance teacher was always telling her, any college would be thrilled to have her. The first thing she'd do when she got there was get a job, then a place for them to stay. It didn't have to be very big, just something with a little kitchenette, a single bedroom where they both could sleep. She opened her purse and touched her wallet. She had enough to last her two weeks and by then she'd have things in place. She just knew it.

She touched the baby's face, unzipping the fuzzy coat a little. She thought of all the things she would do. She wouldn't tell Anne she loved her and then renege on the promise. She wouldn't make Anne think she was family and always welcome, and then shut all the doors of her heart against her. She wouldn't make her feel that nothing about her was right or good or reasonable. And she wouldn't say a thing as foolish as "Wait until your father comes home."

The bus seemed to Sara to be stopping every few minutes, and then staying put for hours, not making good time at all. All these little towns she had never heard of, these grey-looking places. People trooped out of the bus and sometimes didn't come back. They were out of state when the woman who had been reading the magazine looked over at Sara again. "This baby's so good, not even making a peep! What's her name?"

"My baby's name is Priscilla," Sara said.

"Your baby! I thought you were a big sister. Or one of those au pairs. Pardon me for staring, but you look so young to be a mother!" the woman said.

"Oh, everyone says that," Sara said. "But I'm actually twenty-four."

"Well, aren't you the lucky one, then, looking so young."

At the next stop, the woman got off, patting Sara on the arm. "Good luck to you," the woman had said. Sara was exhausted, but she didn't dare sleep. Anne began fussing and she took her to the back to change her. As soon as she opened the door, she smelled disinfectant and pee. Her nose wrinkled. Anne cried. The bathroom was so tiny, she had to try and change Anne on the closed toilet seat, and even then, she barely had enough room to scooch down. When she stood up, her legs were jelly, and when she opened the door again, another person was waiting. "Took you long enough," the man said.

Back at her seat, Sara set Anne on her lap. The road sped by, and lulled, Anne slept. The sky was turning gold with light. In another hour, it would be morning.

While Anne slept, Sara opened her purse and got to work. It was too bad about her clothes, jeans and a sweater, her casual coat, but she still had things to work with. She put on lipstick and blush and curled her lashes dark. She took her hair and piled it up on her head with one of the barrettes Danny had given her, and then she studied herself in the mirror. There. Anyone looking at her would think she was at least twenty.

The bus suddenly slowed. The driver stood up. "Cleveland," he said.

Cleveland's air was clean and cold. She turned up the collar of her coat and wished for gloves. She wrapped both arms about Anne to try to keep her warmer. And there, right across the street, was a busy-looking restaurant called Tiffany's. "What a good omen," she told Anne, who blinked at her, yawned, and fell asleep in her arms.

As soon as they walked into Tiffany's, there was a blast of Christmas music, and a harried-looking waitress came toward them. "Two?" she said.

"I'm looking for a job actually," Sara said.

The waitress glanced at Anne, up and then down, a long, slow slide. "Nothing for you here," said the waitress and turned away.

In two hours, Sara went to four restaurants and two copy shops and no one would hire her. There was a hiring freeze, or they didn't think she had enough experience, and at the last place she had ventured into, a Rite-Aid drugstore, Anne had begun wailing so loudly, the manager had snapped, "Come back when you have a dress and a baby-sitter."

She bought a *Cleveland Plain Dealer* and leafed through it. Okay, so the want ads weren't all that promising, she could deal with that later. Maybe she had gone about it wrong, maybe the first thing they needed to do was find a place to stay.

She scanned the real estate ads. Eight hundred a month for a studio! Sixteen hundred for a one-bedroom! How could things cost that much?

She was almost about to put the paper away when she saw the ad on the bottom. A room. Ninety dollars a week. She could do that. Anne fussed in her lap. "Hang on," she told Anne and went to find a pay phone. "Hello?" she said breathlessly. "I'm calling about the room—"

"Ninety a week. First month, last month, and security."

Sara did the math. "All at once?" she said, incredulous.

"Where you from, the moon? Of course all at once."

Sara hung up the phone. Her arms hurt from carrying Anne. Her stomach growled. She felt like crying and then she drew herself up. No one said she had to stay in Cleveland. The farther out she got, the cheaper things would be. She started to think about a little cottage in the country, a bike with a baby seat in back.

She stopped at a grocer's and bought a ready-made peanut butter sandwich, some formula for Anne, and a bottle of water. Then she went back to the bus stop and bought a one-way ticket to Omaha.

As soon as she was seated, in the middle of the bus, she took down her hair, rubbing at her scalp, which hurt. She wiped off her makeup. Anne woke up and coughed.

In the back of the bus were three kids, giggling and carrying on so loudly she was afraid they'd wake Anne. She turned to look at them, narrowing her eyes. They were punching each other in the arm, laughing, waving at whoever was following the bus. Sara rolled her eyes, and then she saw what they were waving at and her heart beat so fast she felt lightheaded.

A cop car.

"Rest stop in five minutes," the driver called, turning on his blinker, and Sara felt her stomach plummet. The kids were still waving. The cop car was still following.

She slid down in her seat. She wouldn't get out. She and Anne would stay quietly in the bus and maybe it would be okay. If the cops were really following the bus, wouldn't they have pulled it over already? Wouldn't they have done a search?

Of course, she told herself. Don't get nuts. Of course.

The bus pulled into a parking lot, filled with cars and people. "Half an hour rest stop tops!" the driver said. "You're not here, I'm not waiting." He lumbered off the bus, and the passengers began to lift themselves up, to stretch. The waving kids jumped past Sara, laughing, knocking into each other, and then the bus was empty.

Terrified, she glanced outside. The cop car was parked, but no one was coming toward the bus or toward the driver. The two cops were walking toward the diner, laughing, their hips rolling with the weight of their guns. It's okay, she told herself, it's okay.

And then Anne began to wail, so loudly she was almost screaming, and alarmed, Sara tried to rock her, to calm her down. "It's okay," she said, trying to make her voice a promise. She rubbed Anne's back. She tried to readjust the baby on her lap and her fingers flew to Anne's bottom. Diaper. But it was dry. "It's okay," she murmured. "You must be hungry. Me, too."

She had a little bit of a chocolate drink left, but in settling Anne, she spilled some on the front of her sweater. "Oh bother," she said. Then she fed Anne the rest of the formula from her bag, but Anne still cried. "Let's see what else we have," Sara said, digging in her bag. She pulled out the peanut butter sandwich. Anne was eating solid food already. She knew Anne couldn't handle the bread, but the peanut butter was soft. She could feed it to Anne on the tip of her finger. Peanut butter was nourishing. High in protein.

The peanut butter smelled so good Sara was suddenly starving herself. Well, she'd feed Anne first, get her content, and then she'd eat the rest of the sandwich herself. Poking her finger into the sandwich, she held out some to Anne who sucked at it greedily, swallowing. "Delicious, right?" Sara said.

And then Anne coughed. Once, and then again, a strange little bark. Her small face pulled tighter, like a drawstring. Sara patted her on the back. "Take too much?" she said, and then Anne began to turn red and then to choke and everything in Sara froze.

She jolted up, still holding the baby. What were you supposed to do? All those books she had read and everything flew out of her head and all she could think about was how Anne's skin was turning from red to blue, how her choking was getting worse. She tried to hit her lightly on the back, but all it did was make the baby choke more. Terrified, Sara looked out the window for help. The cops were still inside. If they saw her, they'd ask her all sorts of questions. They'd make a call and she'd be arrested. They'd take Anne from her. No, no, she'd never let them separate her from her baby again. Never. "Anne," she begged, and then she saw how Anne's slate eyes were filmed, she felt how her skin was clammy and then Anne gasped for air, struggling in Sara's arms. "Anne!" Sara screamed. What were you supposed to do? Desperate, she thumped her across the back. Anne's eyes slid shut, she grew heavier in Sara's arms. "Anne!" Sara pleaded. Anne's chest heaved and clutched. And then Sara bolted out of the bus, gripping Anne, screaming and screaming for help.

She stumbled, hitting the pavement on her knees, struggling to hold Anne above her. "Help!" she shrieked. A woman who was leaning along the wall, smoking, flung down her cigarette and raced over. "She's choking!" Sara screamed and the woman grabbed Anne and popped her on her lap, thumping her expertly on her chest, and then Anne suddenly coughed and spit up a sticky bulb of peanut butter. The blue in her skin began fading, turning rose again, the gasping stopped and Anne began to whimper. Sara was so relieved, she burst into tears.

The woman stared at Sara. "Peanut butter?" she said, astonished.

"From my sandwich. I fed her the butter, not the bread," Sara said, reaching for the baby, but the woman stepped back from her, tightening her grip, suddenly angry.

"What kind of an idiot gives a baby peanut butter?" the woman said. "Babies choke on peanut butter! They're not supposed to have it until they're four! They get allergic reactions to it! Do you know what could have happened? Do you realize how lucky you are that I was here? She could have died!" Her eyes swept Sara, the skinned knees, the starry burst of chocolate she had spilled on her sweater. "God, you *kids*!" She said it as if it were a swear word, her voice escalating so that Anne's cries took on volume, too. "Where's the mother?" the woman said angrily.

"I'm the mother," Sara said, trying to keep her voice even. "Give me my baby." A few people were looking at them, pointing, talking to one another. "I'm not giving you shit," the woman snapped. Out of the corner of her eye, Sara saw the driver emerge from the diner, and then behind him the two cops, and both of them looked right at her.

Sara lunged, grabbing Anne from the woman and running.

She heard them coming after her. Feet pounding on the pavement. Angry voices shouting. "Stop! Stop right now!" And the whole time, Anne was shrieking, louder and louder, so that Sara couldn't think straight.

There ahead, was a turn. She could sprint across the field, rest, think what to do. And then an arm grabbed her in a steel grip. "I saved the baby!" Sara screamed, thinking of Eva, downstairs humming, not even hearing Anne wailing. "I saved her!" she repeated, and then she twisted, trying to tear herself free, and another cop pulled Anne from her arms and Sara couldn't tell who was crying louder, she or Anne. "You're all right now," one cop said, but he was looking at Anne, not at Sara, and then Sara lunged forward again, grabbing for her daughter, shouting, "I saved her!" and the other cop jerked her so roughly back, she spilled onto the ground into a hopeless ball of grief.

It was Saturday morning. Eva squinted at herself in the mirror. She looked faded, as if someone had rubbed at her with a gum eraser. Her hair felt sticky even though she had washed it that morning. She had worried and worried about losing Anne, but she had never thought it would end up like this.

She had woken in the middle of the night to find George's side of the bed empty. She had gone past Anne's room, which was dark, and she had suddenly seen George there, sitting in the dark, one arm resting on the crib, and as soon as she switched on the light, she saw how red his eyes were. She touched his shoulder and then he started to cry, something which always surprised and shocked her. "If we don't find her, I don't know what I'll do," he wept.

"Maybe we should call the news. Make an announcement, get people to help," Eva said. She thought of it. One of those faces on the news, weeping in front of millions, laying herself bare. *I'll do anything if you'll help me. Anything at all.*

George nodded. "I just want her back," he said. "I don't even care what happened or why. I just want the baby."

He got up and showered. Eva sat in the kitchen. She spent all her time worrying over what signs she had missed, why Sara had done such a thing. She worried what was happening now. Sara could be on her way to Danny. Sara could be doing drugs. Oh God, Sara and the baby could be dead. "Knowledge is power," she kept telling her class. "We know!" they clamored. "We're whiz kids!" With knowledge, you could close a door. Without it, all you had left was imagination. Stories you told yourself hoping they'd make you feel better. She thought of that poor man whose boy was snatched and then returned and no one knew why. She thought of all the days he'd have left wondering what had happened, each story he thought to tell himself more horrifying than the next.

She searched for aspirins, when the phone rang. Her hand stopped, paralyzed. The phone kept ringing. She ran into the hall and grabbed for the phone. "Hello—" Her voice sounded foreign to her. And then George came up behind her, smelling damp.

"What is it?" he asked.

Eva struggled for her voice. "They found them," she said. "Anne was choking and a woman saved her. They're flying them both back today. They said they should be at the Waltham police station by four."

"Thank God!" George hugged her fiercely. He kissed her mouth, her cheek, her hair.

Eva stepped back, nodding. "The police want to know if we intend to press charges."

George looked at Eva. "She took our baby," George said.

They were at the police station half an hour before the police brought back Sara. Cops were standing around, talking, shouting at a boy in handcuffs who was muttering to himself. A female cop was shouting at a woman who was rolling her eyes. "Where's my fucking phone call?" the woman snapped.

Everyone was talking at once, it seemed to Eva. And the place had an odd smell, like something terrible had just happened and it had been quickly cleaned up and now no one wanted to talk about it. The cop at the front desk stared impassively at them. Eva said her name, she told him why they were there, and his face softened, just for a moment. "Have a seat," he said, nodding toward the bench.

The bench was hard and uncomfortable, but Eva wouldn't move from it, not even when she had to pee. She sat, waiting, holding hands with George, refusing the cups of coffee the cops kept offering. Every time the door opened, Eva tensed and gripped George's hand tighter. She didn't know what she might do when she saw Sara, when she saw the baby. She didn't think she could be counted on to act rationally. Right now she wanted to kill her.

She was just about to give in, to go find a ladies' room, when the door swung wide open, and there was Sara, looking exhausted and defeated and scared. "God," George breathed. Sara looked all of twelve, a hole in her jeans, her coat stained, her hair all scrambled, and as soon as she saw Eva and George, she started to cry. And there behind her was a cop carrying Anne who was sleeping in his arms, and then Eva bolted to her feet. George's hand fell from hers. She stepped forward and walked toward Sara. "I have a right to my baby," Sara said in a low, defensive voice, and then something broke inside of Eva. Eva stepped forward another step and slapped Sara across the face.

Sara's hands flew to her face. She jumped back, horrified. A triangle of skin began to turn crimson on her cheek.

"Ma'am." The cop's voice had a warning edge to it, but Eva didn't give a damn.

"Give me my baby!" Eva reached for Anne. She blocked Sara out of her view, turning. Who knew what she might do to that girl? She rocked Anne. And then George was beside her, stroking Anne's face, her arms, her back, stroking Eva.

"George——" Sara said.

"Get her out of here," George said sharply. "Get her the hell away from us."

Eva could hear Sara cry, but she refused to look at her.

"Come with me," the cop said, and Eva heard Sara leaving, and then the room was quiet again, and Eva opened her eyes as another cop came in. "You want to press charges now?" he asked.

The cop took them into a room, sat them by the desk, and pulled out a sheet of paper. "What will happen to her?" Eva asked the cop. She suddenly saw Sara's young face, those small birdlike shoulder blades. "They wouldn't send her to jail, would they?"

The cop shrugged. "Depends. Girl like that, good home, good family. Probation. Community service. Maybe they'd want her to see a shrink." He tapped his fingers on the desk. "She could be out and about."

"File the charges," Eva said, holding Anne tighter. "And I want a restraining order."

For the first week the baby was home, Eva and George wouldn't let her out of their sight. George took his vacation early so he could stay at home. They brought Anne outside, they brought her shopping. Even though at five months she had just about outgrown the bassinet, they put her in it anyway, just so she could sleep by their bed.

Anne didn't seem any different to Eva, though sometimes Eva swore Anne looked around the room woefully, as if she were looking for someone. "She's not here," Eva whispered. "She's not going to be here. You're with me, kiddo."

They got the temporary restraining order almost immediately, but their lawyer told them it was good for only ten days, that a more permanent solution would take more time, which unnerved Eva. It was George's idea to call a locksmith, to put in new dead bolts on both the front and back doors. To get window locks put in every window, and an alarm system. "Now we're safe," he said, but Eva wasn't so sure.

Eva used to love this house, but now she could never stop feeling watched. She scrubbed the floors, scoured the walls, but it felt haunted by Sara. George would be talking to her, and she couldn't help it, her gaze would suddenly dart to a corner.

She was driving with Anne one day and the way the car seat faced to the back began to really bother her. "You okay back there, honey?" she called. The baby was silent. Eva slammed the car to a stop. Anything could happen at any time. Anne would vanish. Eva's neck snapped back. She got out of the car and yanked open the back door. She looked into the car seat over at Anne.

She kept replaying everything with Sara, how and why it might have gone wrong. In theory, open adoption sounded lovely, but with Sara, it had become a real nightmare. Her daughter was sleeping and safe, so why couldn't she relax? What was wrong with her?

George too looked more and more thoughtful. Every time the phone rang, he stiffened, the same way Eva did. He didn't relax until he knew it wasn't Sara. When the doorbell rang unexpectedly, he threw his napkin down, his face set. He strode to the front door, and then Eva heard his voice, low, measured, and when he came back, he looked sheepish. "Paperboy," he said. "We forgot to pay last week." He picked up his fork and stared down at his lamb chop.

"You okay?" Eva asked. She didn't have much of an appetite herself.

He suddenly pushed his plate away. "I wish we could just move," he said.

Eva looked up at him.

"I worry about you. I really do. I worry about us," George said. "I wish I could just move my practice far away. You could teach anywhere. We could all start again."

Eva reached for his hand and held it. "How could we do that? Eventually, don't we have to allow some sort of visitation with Sara?"

"You're asking me to do what's best for Sara?" He looked at her askance. "What happens if she gets over here somehow? What happens if we're not so lucky next time?"

Eva folded her arms tight about her body. "Next time," she said, horrified.

"She took Anne! I read in the paper the other day about this case. A woman gave up her baby, and two years later—four years!—she admitted she had lied about who the father was. And the father came back, he wanted the baby. And Eva, they gave the baby to the mother. The birth mother. The courts said her rights superseded theirs."

Eva's mouth went dry. "No, they didn't."

"Do you remember Baby Richard?" George said. "Four years old. Photos of him screaming, being torn from his adoptive parents' arms. And what about that case in Ann Arbor with the two-year-old girl? The birth mother came back, got the girl. Few years later, the adoptive parents divorced. So did the real ones. God knows how that little girl's life is going to turn out." He shook his head, defeated. "We can't go on like this."

The phone suddenly began to ring and ring and ring. Neither one of them moved.

"It's Sara," Sara's voice belled out. "Pick up! Please pick up!"

Eva looked at George. He stood up and yanked the phone cord from the wall.

The next day, George went back to work. "I'll try to make it half a day," he promised. Eva put the baby to bed when the doorbell rang, and she peered out, and then opened it.

Abby. In a pale green suit. A dark coat thrown over it. Her hair clipped back. Small gold hoops in her ears.

"Please," Abby said. "Please, may I come in and talk to you?"

She let Abby in, motioning her to the couch. "Anne's asleep," Eva said.

Abby looked down at her shoes, slim copper-colored high heels, and then back up at Eva. "Please. You already have a restraining order. She can't do anything. Please. Drop the charges. Don't prosecute Sara. Don't ruin her life more than she's already ruined it. She's smart. She could go to Harvard. She could do such great things."

"She stole our baby," Eva said stiffly. "She put her in danger! Can you imagine what might have happened?"

"But nothing did," Abby said. "Sara didn't take Anne to do evil. She's young, she didn't think. She made one mistake and, believe me, she's paying for it."

"Does she know you're here?" Eva said.

Abby shook her head.

"How is she?"

"I can hardly bear it. She lies in bed. She cries."

"She should cry."

"She'll be at college next year," Abby said. "She won't be anywhere near you." Abby leaned forward. "You can't prosecute her. Please. Don't ruin her life. I'm begging you. I'll do anything. I'll make sure she goes to school in another country if that's what it takes. She's my daughter! You can't imagine how we love her." Abby folded and unfolded her hands in her lap. "The same way Anne's your daughter and you love her."

"Don't compare the two," Eva said sharply.

Abby was silent for a moment. "Please," Abby said. "I'm begging you."

"I don't know," Eva said.

"Drop the charges," Abby pleaded. "I'll do anything. I love her. And you did, too, once. You know you did."

Eva stood up. She remembered how she and Sara had once laughed so hard over a movie they had both nearly wet their pants. She remembered sitting on the chaises outside with Sara, sipping lemonade and talking for hours, and Eva felt so comfortable, she could reach over and rest her hand on Sara's belly, and then Sara would rest her hand on Eva's. For a moment, she felt a raw pang, and then she heard Anne in the other room, and the pang vanished. Fairy tale, she thought. A fairy tale with an unhappy ending.

Eva led Abby to the door, opened it. The day felt chill, like any moment it might snow.

"You won't have to see Sara ever again," Abby said. "I promise."

And then Abby was gone, and Eva realized that the whole time she had been here, Abby hadn't asked to see the baby.

chapter

seven

It felt safer for Sara to be in her room. She lay on her bed, headphones clamped to her ears. She couldn't go to school until this was settled, but she filled out applications for early admissions to colleges in New York because her parents were pressuring her now to get away from the area, and every time she saw a required essay on "How have you changed this year?" she wanted to laugh, because how could she possibly write the truth?

That night, she ventured out of her room, just to the kitchen to get some water. Abby suddenly appeared, in her bright yellow nightgown, her red hair in curlers. "Just getting some water, myself," Abby said, filling her glass and then barely touching it before she dumped it out again. "Dry throat," Abby said, her fingers tapping her neck. Sara woke up in the middle of the night, padding to the bathroom, and before she even turned a corner, there was Jack, belting his flannel bathrobe, his brown hair askew. "Did you need something?" he asked. "What can I get you?"

They were watching her, and she knew it.

Her parents had stopped lecturing her. Finally. They used quiet, calm voices, which seemed worse, more ominous, than the harsh, angry tones they had used when they had first picked her up at the police station, the two of them rushing in like a winter storm.

There in that awful station, no one had to tell her then how alone she was. Eva and George and the baby had already left the station. She could feel it. By then, Sara couldn't have cried even if she had wanted to. She couldn't move from the hard wooden bench, even though her muscles ached. She had botched everything. She hadn't been able to get a job or a place to stay. She hadn't had enough money. She hadn't been able to save her own baby. That woman from the bus had cursed her, spitting out that Sara was a *kid,* a greenhorn who didn't have a clue how to act like an adult, and every time Sara remembered it, she knew that woman was right. All her chances were over, and Sara felt something breaking apart inside of her.

"What were you thinking? How could you do this?" her parents kept asking her.

"You think Harvard wants felons?" Abby said. "You think Yale does? You can't see them. You can't even go near them. You could be arrested, do you understand?"

They rode home in silence. Sara stared out the window, and at every turn she imagined how things could have turned out differently. If she had worn a dress. If she hadn't bought peanut butter. If she hadn't been a kid.

Abby twisted around to look at Sara. "Everything's going to be different now," Abby said quietly, and all those bright ifs Sara had been thinking fluttered away on wings.

All that week, Abby took off work and stayed at home, going out only to bring Sara's bike back. Every time she looked at Sara, her face was so sad, Sara wanted to die, but Abby didn't lecture her. She made mac and cheese that Sara barely picked at, and once she knocked on Sara's door. "I'm watching a wonderful old Bette Davis movie," Abby said. "Come watch it with me."

They both curled on the couch in the den, watching Bette's evil sister (who was really Bette in a dual role) steal the man she loved away from her. At the end, when the good Bette got her man back, Abby swiped a finger across her eyes. "Well," Abby said. "That was nice. I like a movie where everything turns out all right in the end."

"Her sister still drowned," Sara pointed out, but Abby waved a hand.

"She was evil. She had to drown to give her sister the happy life she deserved," Abby said. "Sometimes sacrifices are called for."

Sara picked at a tuft on one of the couch pillows. Abby pushed Sara's hands away.

"Love conquered all," Abby said, "everyone lived and learned."

Afternoons, Sara watched old movies with her mother, but mostly, she stayed in her room, reading. *Madame Bovary. Anna Karenina.* Women with ruined lives. Books she hoped might make her own plight seem less horrible to her, but as she got to the ends, she felt panicked. There was no escape for these women. Instead, there was a kiss of poison. Instead, there was a final leap in front of a train. Sara flung the books down.

She didn't eat, didn't even want to shower. *"You'll always be in our life,"* Eva and George had told her, and now they had a restraining order. At night, she couldn't sleep. She sat up and tried to read, but the words blurred on the page. One night, she heard noises in the house and she got up. Abby and Jack kept their bedroom door closed, but tonight it was open. The light was on. She crept by the room, leaning against the wall.

Abby was sitting up in bed, crying quietly. Jack, in his robe, was sitting beside her, rubbing her back, quietly talking to her. Sara tried to listen, moving a bit closer, and then she saw that Jack had his arms about Abby and was stroking her hair back, behind her ears. And then Abby lay down, and Jack covered her with the blanket, murmuring something so soft it was almost a lullaby. Then Jack walked toward the door, and shut it, and for a moment Sara saw his face, and he looked so sorrowful that she drew back.

In the morning, she came down to breakfast, not knowing what to expect. But there was Abby, already dressed, setting out vitamins for everyone, fixing breakfast. There was Jack, downing juice. "Did you sleep okay?" Abby asked cheerfully.

"Sort of." Sara hesitated. "Mom, I heard you crying last night."

Abby pulled at her collar. "Just tension. Don't they say it's healing to have a good cry? You ought to know that from all those *Psychology Todays* you used to love."

"No, you were really crying," Sara said.

"It's nothing for you to worry about——" Jack said.

"It's a hard time," Abby said quietly. "But it'll get better."

Sara did as Abby asked. She didn't try to call anymore, didn't try to see Eva or George or the baby, but it wasn't because she didn't want to. The truth was she was afraid, and not just about going to jail. What if she called and they hung up on her? What if she went by the house and they slammed the door on her? They couldn't shut her out from her own child, could they? *"Hope was the thing with feathers,"* Emily Dickinson said, and now Sara could feel those wings beating inside of her. If she couldn't have custody of her child, she could still see her, even if it was a supervised visit. And she could still see Eva and George.

Eva was sorting laundry, hoping the mindless work might soothe her, but instead, her nerves frayed even more. This was insane. She had to do something. Striding to the kitchen, she picked up the phone, and though she had promised herself she wouldn't, she called the adoption agency again. "Did you find the father? Did he sign?" Eva asked.

"We don't have the adoption surrender yet," Margaret admitted.

"What if you can't find him?"

"The courts can terminate his rights. But even after that, they'll still try to let him know, usually with one of those legal listings at the back of some newspapers."

"The back of the paper! Nobody reads those!" Eva said.

"Well, don't be so fast to think that's a good thing. It's a doorway for the father to enter later. He can say he didn't read the listing, he didn't know about any of it, that he wasn't being neglectful. And then you could still lose her, because no matter what, the courts always favor the biological parents."

"This can't be true all the time."

"A lot of adoptive parents consider offering an open adoption to the birth father. It's worth it rather than risking losing a child."

"Forget it. Absolutely not," Eva said. "Two people to worry about instead of one!"

"We'll find him. His rights will get terminated. You just enjoy your baby."

But Eva couldn't help worrying. She couldn't risk the adoption not being legal. Not with the way things had been going. She hung up the phone and then she did a truly stupid thing. She got out the phone book and looked up Danny's last name in the phone book and then dialed. Maybe he had come home. Maybe his mother knew where he was.

"Yes?" A man's voice.

"Is this Danny Slade?"

There was a clip of silence. "No, it's not. How can I help you?"

"Is Mrs. Slade there?"

"Hang on."

The phone clattered and then a woman's voice answered, dry with fatigue. "Yes?" she said.

"Mrs. Slade." Eva introduced herself casually, as if she were about to try and sell Frances some magazine subscriptions. "I'm looking for Danny. I was just checking whether he was aware that he needed to sign papers saying he knew about the adoption."

"Who do you think you are calling me?" said Mrs. Slade.

"I'm just looking out for everybody's best interests," Eva said.

"He doesn't want a baby. He's a baby himself. I already told the agency this."

"But to avoid any problems, he needs to sign the papers. Do you know where he is?" She hated the desperate way she sounded.

"My Danny doesn't want anything to do with that baby or that girl."

"Where is he?"

Frances cleared her throat. "Those papers will be signed. And you don't need to call here again. Ever."

Two days later, Margaret at the agency called. "The father signed the papers!" she said, exultant. "We're on our way!"

Eva fit her fingers into the rungs on the dial pad. "He did? You're sure?"

"Yup. The server told me. Signed without a fuss. The server caught him just as he was on his way out to catch a plane. Beefy blondish guy. The mother was there, too. And the server told me he was asking all sorts of questions about what would happen if he didn't show up at the hearing. That's usually a sign that the father isn't going to show, which is very good for us. The courts take no-show to mean no interest."

Eva's fingers released from the dial pad. One of the numbers moved a little and for a moment she heard the dial. "So I can stop worrying, right?"

"For now."

Eva hung up the phone. She should be thrilled, but the more she thought about it, the more unsettled she became, like she was a glass of champagne and every bubble was going flat. Beefy and blondish guy, Margaret had said. Eva went to the closet where the big blue box was, filled with the initial correspondence she had had with Sara. She never even looked at it anymore. Opening it, she riffled through the contents. Letters. Photos. A notebook she opened that seemed to be a baby journal Sara had started. It all seemed like such a long time ago. And then Eva pulled up a photo of Danny, the one she had been looking for, and she didn't have to study it very hard to see that Danny's hair was dark like the richest milk chocolate, that he was thin as a whippet. Her pulse speeded up. She rifled through the pictures, digging deep to the bottom of the box. And then she pulled out another photo. Danny again, standing with one arm slung about an older woman in a bright orange dress, and on the other side of her, his arm around her, too, was a boy two heads taller than either one of them. A big boy. A blond. *Oh Jesus. Danny had a brother.*

Reeling, Eva reached for the phone to call George. When the hygienist said he was busy, Eva said she didn't care. "Get him," she ordered, and when George got on the phone, she talked so fast, she was out of breath.

"I don't think Danny signed," she said. "I think his brother answered when I called the house—"

"Eva, you didn't—tell me you didn't."

"I never spoke to Danny. His mother never told me where he was. Or even if he was here in town."

"Maybe he was out. Maybe she didn't want him talking to you. You don't know for sure Danny didn't sign. The server could have confused him with someone else he served that day. And if something was wrong, it would be the family that was in error. Not us. And there's still the hearing.

If he didn't sign, let him show up. We won't lose her," George said quietly. "I won't let that happen."

The clock in the kitchen ticked loudly. Outside, Eva heard a squeal of tires.

"We won't lose Anne," George repeated. "The papers are signed."

One night, on the sixth day Sara had been at home, Abby and Jack came into her room and sat on her bed and for the first time, seeing the expressions on their faces, she felt afraid. She sat up, suddenly dizzy. Her fingers pleated the chenille spread on her bed.

Alarmed, she imagined all sorts of terrible things. She had to go to prison. Or they were sending her away, to a boarding school, or to live with some relative she had never met before. She could bear anything as long as they told her she could see Anne again.

And then Abby suddenly gave a long, slow smile. Jack's expression lightened. Her parents looked at each other and then back at her.

"The charges were dropped, honey," Abby said.

"They dropped them? Really?" Sara felt the colors in the room growing lighter.

"But not the restraining order," Abby said. "You aren't to go see them. You aren't to go anywhere near them. Do you understand?"

Sara was motionless. "For now," Sara said.

"No, not for now. From now on."

"No." Sara shook her head. "They're just mad still. That's all. They just need more time. They'll see me, we'll talk. I'll—I'll apologize. I'll do anything." She stood up.

"Sara," said Jack. "Do you understand what you did, how terrible it was, how lucky you are that they aren't pressing charges against you? If you call them now, if you go to see them, you could be in trouble again. Big trouble. You could be arrested."

She nodded. Her mouth felt suddenly dry, as if she had swallowed construction paper.

"Well, I can see them at the adoption hearing then," Sara said, glancing at the kitchen calendar. "That's just two more days."

"I wouldn't think of going," Abby said sharply.

"But that's different! I have a right to go to that. Margaret told me I could go."

"Oh, honey, but why would you even want to?" Jack said.

"It's still my baby. Even if I don't get to raise her."

"Sara. Let's just say it's the end of a bad time," Jack said, patting her shoulder awkwardly. "Now it's time for everyone to get on with their lives. Think about college. Think about all the wonderful things that can happen for you."

"You can go back to school, you can just forget this all happened. This wasn't in the papers. No one need even know," Abby said.

"I know that it happened," Sara said.

"Now," Jack said. "What do you say this grounding is over and we all go out to dinner? I'd love to try that new Thai place."

"Oh, me, too!" Abby's voice was bright.

"I'm not hungry," Sara said.

Two days later, the day of the court hearing, Sara got up early. She put on the blue cashmere sweater Abby had bought her for college interviews. She slid on a dark skirt and pinned her hair back with Danny's barrette. When she came downstairs, Abby was in jeans, drinking coffee with Jack, and she started when she saw Sara.

"Please tell me you're not dressed up for the reason I think," Abby said quietly.

Sara drew herself up. She knew they would give her a hard time. "I have a right to be there," she said quietly.

"No. You don't. You can't go," Abby said. "I know you want to, but you're in trouble. And if you go, you could be in more trouble. No one wants you there."

Sara's eyes flashed. "I have a right!" she repeated.

"What do you think is going to happen?" Jack said. "That they'll give you Anne?"

Sara wavered. "I could get visitation!"

"Sara! After what happened? You were lucky they didn't press charges!"

"Danny could show up!"

"Now?" Jack said. "If we have to stay here to keep you from going, we will."

Sara started to storm from the room when Abby grabbed at her arm. Jerking back, Sara banged her head against the cabinet. Her hands flew to her head. The bump didn't hurt, but she couldn't stop holding her head. Abby and Jack both jumped up, their faces concerned. "Are you hurt?" Jack asked. "Are you okay?"

As soon as Abby touched her, Sara started shaking. "Everything's going to be okay now," Abby said gently, "you'll see." And then Sara began to shake harder.

All that day, Sara stayed in her room. She kept waiting for a last-minute phone call, a reprieve like the ones she saw in Abby's old movies where the governor would call the prison right before the switch on the electric chair was pulled. She kept imagining Danny showing up, wild, searching every seat for her, as he stormed into the courtroom calling her name, crying, "Stop! I don't give permission!" Or Eva and George coming to their senses, thinking, What have we done? How can we do this to Sara?

By evening, she gave up. No one had to tell her what had happened. She knew it, felt it deep inside her, like a jagged chink in her heart. Final. The adoption was final and it was her fault. She pulled her pillow over her head.

All that week, her parents acted as if everything were fine, over and done with. They left her alone in her room, and Abby took to bringing Sara trays of food she barely touched. And then, a week later, she went back to school, but she was sleepwalking, going crazy, unable to bear not seeing Anne. Everyone was always telling her how smart she was—surely she could find a way out of this. So what if Anne was adopted, couldn't she still see her? Couldn't she beg George and Eva, stand outside their house until they acknowledged her? She felt a bright flare of hope.

She was already in trouble. What difference did it make if she risked even more?

By the time she biked to George and Eva's house, she felt numb from the cold, her breath felt siphoned from her lungs. Her heart felt as if any moment it might pound a hole through her ribs and her legs ached. She passed the rusty wire fence, the house with four Siamese cats. She rounded the corner, trying to practice what she might say, how she might act. "I'm sorry," she'd say. *I cannot bear this,* she'd think.

She didn't see the car in the driveway. She rode closer, and there, in the center of the front yard was a square white sign with red letters. FOR SALE. Sara froze on her bike. She rubbed her eyes, sure she must be hallucinating. FOR SALE, it said.

She looked at the house again, as if she might have been thrown into a different universe where nothing made sense. No, it was the same. Number 62. She threw the bike down on the grass and ran to the front door, and as soon as she gripped the handle, it opened.

The house was empty. The floors had been waxed and cleaned, the walls were all freshly painted white and it smelled of lemon Pledge. If you didn't know better, you couldn't even tell that a family had ever lived here. Stunned, she stepped deeper into the house. She heard voices, footsteps coming up from the basement into the kitchen. She followed the sound, walking into the kitchen where a strange woman in a red suit was talking to a couple who were holding hands. They all stopped talking and looked at Sara.

"Can I help you?" the strange woman said.

"Where's Eva and George?"

The woman frowned at Sara. The couple looked puzzled.

"Eva and George. The people who live here," Sara said.

"The couple who *used* to live here, you mean?" the strange woman said. "Well, clearly, they've moved."

Sara felt everything suddenly go upside down. "They moved? So quickly?"

"Oh, movers can do anything these days," the strange woman said.

She nodded at the couple. "Remind me to give you some good names, if you're interested. I know one place that can pack you up and get you out in twenty-four hours!"

"When did they move? Where did they go?" Sara asked.

"I can't say I know," the strange woman said. She straightened, brushing something invisible off her suit. "But you really shouldn't be here, dear."

"Are you sure they're not here?" Sara's mouth was dry.

The woman spread her hands and gave a little laugh. "Really. I don't know anything about them. Would you make sure the front door is closed when you leave?" She smiled at Sara. "If you'll excuse us," she said pointedly, and Sara finally left.

Sara rode into town to the adoption lawyer. She hadn't been in this office since Abby had brought her over, back when she was pregnant. "You don't have an appointment?" the secretary asked incredulously.

Sara was only sitting in the waiting room for ten minutes when Margaret strode out. "Sara," Margaret said calmly. "Come on in."

Sara sat opposite Margaret in her office. "They left!" Sara cried.

Margaret frowned. "They left? Who left?"

"George and Eva! The house is for sale."

Margaret was quiet for a minute. "That's highly unusual."

"Can they do that?" Sara cried. "What? Why are you looking at me like that?"

"Sara, maybe they should have told me, but they aren't required to. And they didn't have to tell you."

"What do you mean, they didn't have to?"

Margaret sighed. "Didn't I warn you to think about all of this carefully? Didn't I tell you there were no guarantees?"

"Where? Where are they?"

"The adoption hearing was held, Sara. It's a done deal. I told you before that open adoptions are enforceable only in Oregon. Right now that's just the way it is. I can try to find them. But my advice is to take this as a blessing. Get on with your life. Be a kid."

A kid. She didn't even know what that felt like anymore. Sara leaned forward. "They took the baby! I didn't even get a chance to say goodbye! How could they do that!"

"Listen to me. You signed papers giving up Anne. The father signed papers. Open adoption isn't enforceable here. And the hearing's over."

"Danny signed? Danny was here? No one told me that!" Sara looked at Margaret with amazement. "It can't be true. I would have known it if he was here, I would have felt it—"

"He signed," said Margaret. "He terminated his rights. And so did you. And you did something else. You kidnapped the baby. The courts won't look kindly on that. You don't have a job. You're a minor. No husband or parents on your side. There was a restraining order. That's going to put a big damper on visitation. And Sara, it's their baby to take. You know that. Don't tell me you didn't always know that."

"I don't know anything!" Sara cried.

She got back on her bike. She didn't feel her body pedaling. She was halfway down the street when she heard a low, keening noise that startled her until she realized it was coming from her. She sobbed so hard, she could barely see, and by the time she got back to her block, her eyes were nearly swollen shut.

She went inside her house. "Mom!" she called, her voice thick. "Mommy!"

Abby came into the room, a book in her hand, and as soon as she saw Sara, she stopped. "Oh my God, what happened?" Abby said, alarmed.

"Did you know?" Sara demanded.

"Know what?" Abby said.

"That Danny was here! That he signed papers! That George and Eva left! That the house is for sale!" Sara started to cry. "I did something wrong, but so did they!"

"They moved?" Abby said, stunned. "I didn't think they'd do something like that—"

Abby wrapped one arm about Sara, holding her so tightly Sara couldn't move. "Forget about those awful people," Abby said. "It's going to be good now, I promise. It's over."

Sara wrenched free. Her mind swam. Things bobbed to the surface and pushed down again. There was nothing to grab on to. "It will never be good!" she cried. "Never!" Sara bolted to her room, slamming the door, flinging herself on her bed.

Danny. She saw his face. A million times she had imagined him calling her, begging her forgiveness. She had imagined him coming to the house, to the school. How was it possible for him to be in the same town as she was and not come to see her?

She thought of this article she had read recently, just a piece in one of the old magazines Abby brought home from the dental office where she worked. It was about a special home for birth mothers. Of course it had caught her eye. Of course she had read it. It was completely unlike the Girls in Trouble home Abby always talked about. This home had only six girls, and they lived in an old colonial house in Georgia, coming and going as they pleased, all waiting for their babies to be born. The scrapbooks, the letters from prospective parents all came to the house and the birth mothers pored over them. Instead of being shunned, these girls were treated like royalty. They had so many couples desperate for their babies that they could choose or reject an adoptive family on the basis of whether or not they liked the color of the family dog, on whether or not the backyard pool was kidney shaped or oval. "We get to choose, that's the important thing," one of the birth mothers said. "That makes all the difference." But then there was one birth mother who decided at the last minute to keep her baby, and as soon as she gave birth, she was whisked instantly out of the home. She didn't even get to say goodbye to the friends she had made there. "We didn't want her decision infecting the other mothers," the head of the house said. *Infecting.* That was the word Sara remembered. As if the girl herself were a disease for wanting her own baby. A disease that had to be knocked out.

There was a knock on her door. "Sara?" Abby said.

Sara put the pillow over her head. "Go away!" she screamed, and then Abby did.

* * *

How could people just disappear? Sara wondered. She didn't have money for a detective or a lawyer and she couldn't ask her parents. Even if she somehow, miraculously, were able to find them, how could she make them listen to her? Her only hope was that they would start to miss her somehow, that they would contact her.

The mail came and Sara jumped, rushing through the envelopes, yearning to see Eva's familiar scrawl. *"We made a mistake. We'll be home soon."* Or better yet, *"Here's a ticket for you to come and live with us."* She tried to imagine where they might be, but all she could remember was Eva telling her a funny story about how she had burned on the beach in Hawaii and didn't love tropical climates, and George had chimed in that he didn't love cities. That had left her no clues, no way to follow them.

"The baby will fade from your memory," Abby had said, trying to be kind. But her mother was wrong. Anne didn't fade. She took on life and presence. Four o'clock and Sara thought, Anne has a bath now. Six and she was getting formula. And at night, when Sara slept, she imagined Anne sleeping too, the two of them like unmoored ships, veering dangerously toward the sharpest rocks, and all she could think was: *I can't protect you.* She woke feeling Anne in the bed beside her. There was a small indentation in the sheet, and when she placed her hand on it, it was so warm, she rested her cheek against it.

She made bargains with God. *Let me just see Anne one more time and I will never ask for anything ever again.* And sometimes: *Let me die.* She watched for signs. A fork in the road meant Eva would call. A bird flying overhead meant George would.

"Could you do some errands for me?" Abby asked, handing Sara a list. Sara knew there were no errands to run, that Abby just wanted her to get outside, doing something useful, something physical. She glanced at the list. Butter, milk, eggs, cream. Pick up dry cleaning. Pick up shoes from cobblers. She went and came back and felt the same.

One afternoon, she climbed up on the roof to sit, the way she used to when she was a kid. Way up, the new vantage point had always calmed her, as though she truly were seeing things from a different perspective. This time though it didn't seem to matter whether she sat or stood or did anything at all. Her pain felt too big; nothing could calm it. She walked to the edge of the roof, staring impassively down at the long drop below, her toes inched over the ledge, and then she looked across the block, and there, in the house across the way, was Mrs. Thomas, one of the neighbors, frowning warningly, shaking her finger back and forth at Sara: no, no, no. *She thinks I'm going to jump,* Sara thought. And then Sara slowly looked down, at the long drop to the hard cement below, and she felt suddenly dizzy. *What's the matter with me?* She pulled herself back, she stepped inside her house again, and, hands shaking, locked the window tight.

Sara didn't think she'd last through the year. She lay awake nights staring into the darkness. She pushed food around on her plate. She lost so much weight she began wearing baggy clothing again, but now to hide her skinniness instead of her girth. She forced herself to make an effort, to find a reason to go on living, to feel anything but this rawness. She played her music at stun level. She put hot sauce in all her food until it burned her throat, and if it hurt, well, at least she was feeling something. In school, she studied until her sight blurred, and if sometimes thoughts of Anne sifted through her mind, or of Danny, she turned a page and studied harder.

Her history teacher held her paper up. "You all should strive for such scholarship," he said.

Her teachers were happy with her again. Her parents smiled every time they caught sight of her. Be a kid, Margaret had told her, but she didn't know what that was supposed to feel like anymore. She was too much a kid to care for her own child, but she wasn't kid enough to fit into school, not anymore, no matter how much she tried.

Last week, in the cafeteria, two girls from her math class had plunked their trays down next to hers and started talking as if they were old friends. Sara tried to follow their conversation, but she couldn't relate to anything they were talking about. Boys. Clothes. Cars. "My mother grounded me for smoking," one girl said, "I could just die." Sara sipped her juice. *My parents grounded me for kidnapping my baby. I could die, too.*

The girls lost interest and left, and then Robin Opaline, her old friend, came over and sat beside Sara. "I need a new lab partner," Robin started to say, and then she stared down at her burger. "Oh shit, I just miss you," Robin said. "I'm sorry all this happened."

Sara filled with relief, cool as a splash of water. "Me, too," she said, and then she didn't know what else to say, because she wasn't sure how much Robin wanted to know, and also, she was afraid she might cry. Instead, Sara pushed her fries toward Robin, and when Robin took a handful, Sara felt as if some agreement had been struck, as if things would be all right between them.

"So, I heard from Berkeley," Robin said, and then her smile spread across her face. "Accepted," she said, and she leaned over and hugged Sara. "What about you?"

"Nothing yet," Sara said.

"Wouldn't it be cool if we ended up in the same place? The way we used to talk about?" Robin asked.

"Sure," Sara said. "It would be great." She tried to look enthusiastic, to feel a bright nudge of hope. *College,* Sara thought. She tried to imagine herself in school, but every time she thought of being at school in Boston, the way she had planned, her breath stopped. Her stomach rolled. What would she do if she didn't get into Columbia? How could she stay in the same area when Anne and Danny were gone?

Robin talked nonstop, telling Sara all the things that had happened that Sara had missed. How Robin had gone out with a boy named Paul for a while and then had broken up with him when she discovered he was cheating on her. How Robin's dream was to live in Europe after college. Sara struggled to concentrate. She was surprised how easy it was to smile at Robin's stories, how simple a thing it was to act as if everything in your world was all right. It was easy to crowd everything you couldn't bear away from you.

When the lunch bell rang, Robin touched Sara's hand, making her jump. "Hey, this was fun," Robin said. "Maybe I'll call you later. We could see a movie. Like old times."

"Sure. Like old times. I'll call you," Sara said.

* * *

That night, when she came home, Abby was setting up an elaborate new chessboard made of glass. "Chess is great for concentrating the mind," her mother said. "I bought books and everything." She stood, surveying the board, moving a few of the glass pieces about. "Oh, learn to so we can both play," Abby urged, and Sara sat down and made herself study it, immersing herself in it the way she would any other new subject, memorizing the pieces and how they moved, looking at the range of possibilities.

For weeks, every night, she and her mother played game after game until Sara felt vaguely hypnotized by the procession of roving bishops and tricky knights, by the way a lowly pawn could form an impenetrable shield or be promoted to queen, transformed into something so powerful it ruled the board. Her father came in sometimes and watched them, or he brought in cookies for them to chew while they considered moves.

"Checkmate," Sara said, moving her rook down the file opposite her mother's king.

"She's getting so good!" Abby marveled to Jack. "Third game she's won in a row!"

Sara stretched her arms over her head. "It's fun," she admitted. Abby started to clear the pieces, and Sara reached out her hand to stop her. "One more game," she said.

Behavioral therapy, Sara thought, setting up the pieces, lingering on the queen. Act like a winner and you might be one. Act like you're fine, and the brain rewires, and then you don't even have to understand the reason for it, you are fine. Exercise like crazy so the endorphins flow, brewing a chemical feast of good feeling.

"I'm going to have to learn just to keep up with you two," Jack said.

The next morning, on a Saturday when the sky was so blue it looked painted, Sara couldn't bear to be in the empty house another second. Abby and Jack were out shopping and wouldn't be home until later. Sara called Robin and got the machine.

Sara's legs jittered with energy. She got up and laced on her running shoes and ran for half an hour through the neighborhoods. She panted. She felt as if her past were nipping at her heels, and so she ran faster. She took in more air. Chess moves played out in her mind. See yourself as the pieces, one of the instructional books had advised and she struggled to feel like the queen, all-powerful, able to move in any direction she pleased. Her legs stretched, covering more ground. A collie dog barked and ran at her and then ran away. *I'm okay,* she told herself. *I'm okay.*

She came home, bathed in sweat, her hair damp, her heart pounding. And when she came inside the house, there on the floor by the door were three acceptances to colleges: Brandeis. Harvard. No, no, she couldn't stay here. She'd die if she had to. Hands shaking, she ripped open the last one. Columbia. And they accepted her.

For the first time in a long while, despite her sorrow, she felt excited. Here she was with her whole life still ahead of her, and soon, she'd be packing off to college, going off to a new place where nothing would remind her of what she had lost.

Her parents couldn't do enough for her. The house seemed almost giddy. "Nothing but good things from now on," her mother told her. It was early, there was plenty of time, but Sara couldn't wait. Abby took her shopping, for more clothes than she'd ever need, for a new CD player and a PC. Jack bought her a key ring with a flashlight attached to it and a big bottle of pepper spray. "Daddy—" she said.

"Just taking care of my baby girl," he said.

That night, for the first time since Eva and George and Anne had disappeared, Sara slept until morning. She dreamed she was running outside and it was snowing, a blizzard of flakes, but the air was warm like spring, and when she looked up at the sky, she saw that the flakes were really millions of white butterflies, brushing against her skin.

chapter

eight

George and Eva had a yearly lease on a cozy little two-bedroom in Boca Raton until they could find something more permanent. The day they moved in, exhausted from unpacking, dusty and rumpled, they took the baby and sat outside for a bit on the front porch. Six o'clock and it was still so sticky that Eva's clothes felt pasted on. Anne fussed in George's lap, blowing spit bubbles. Cicadas clicked and buzzed among the palms. Eva was about to suggest they go back inside, when a woman bounded over to the house, startling Eva, so her hand flew to George's shoulder. He held the baby tighter, but the woman lifted up a wicker basket. "Welcome to the neighborhood," she said gaily.

The woman stuck out her hand and pumped Eva's. "Hazel Reardon," she said, pointing to a green house down the block. She was tall and blond with a brown-sugar tan; she looked cool and sparkly as a fizzy drink. And then she took one look at Anne's hair and looked at Eva and George. "Where'd she get the red corkscrews!" Hazel said.

"From me," Eva blurted before she could stop herself.

Hazel looked surprised. "No! Your hair is stick straight! And who's your colorist?"

"Oh no. I meant she gets it from my side of the family. Recessive gene."

George watched Eva, but he didn't contradict her. He didn't say one thing about it until late in the evening, long after Hazel had gone, when they were in bed, Anne beside them, sleeping in her bassinet. George rubbed Eva's back. "Anne's ours," he said.

"Of course, she is," Eva said. "It's just—I can't help worrying."

His fingers stroked a knot at the back of her neck. "Come on. We're far away."

"But we're not off the planet. Dentists are licensed. All anyone has to do is go to the library, do a little research. We're not that hard to find."

"For a kid we are. And you're talking about a sheltered kid whose parents want her as far away from us as we do. A kid in trouble," George said. "No one knows where we are, not even the adoption lawyer. And we have the courts on our side."

"Do we?" Eva said quietly. "Do we really have the law on our side?"

George took Eva's hand and held it, stroking his thumb across her wrist. "We have Anne," he said finally. "And that's all that matters."

"I don't even know what's fair anymore. All I know is I love Anne." She rubbed at her forehead. "Do we ever have to tell her? That she's adopted? I know we talked about this, how important it is, but—" Eva looked pained. "Would it be the worst thing in the world if we didn't? If we just were able to forget everything terrible that happened?"

George lay down, pulling Eva toward him, holding her close, as if he were protecting her. "I don't think I even know that anymore, either," he said.

Every time the phone rang, Eva flinched. Every time the doorbell rang, she thought about running out the back door. She could only imagine how Sara felt now, and the one big mystery was what, if anything, Sara would or could do about it. All you had to do was listen to the news to know that you never knew how adoption cases would turn out. What if Sara contacted some organization and convinced them that she had been too young to know what was going on? What if the organization hunted her and George? And what if Abby and Jack changed their minds, suddenly yearning to be grandparents? She had read about cases like that. Grandparents' rights. What if Danny suddenly reappeared?

"You've got to relax," George told her. "We have a whole new life here."

For George, staying relaxed meant focusing on how lucky they really were. They had Anne! They had a new home, a fresh start, and he, thank God, had found a job. When he had first told Eva he wanted to leave Boston, he hadn't really thought it was possible. At his age, you didn't just give up a whole practice, start again, did you? You didn't run like you were some criminal—which they weren't, were they? But in Boston, he kept tensing every time the doorbell rang, every time he saw a flash of red. He and Eva were always looking over their shoulder, always bolting awake at night to make sure Anne was still there, still safe. How could the idea of relocating not seem like a good idea? He and Eva quietly talked it over, and he began putting out feelers, scanning the ads in the professional journals. And just the mere fact of looking for a new position made him feel so hopeful, that he began to search even harder.

Selling his Boston practice hadn't been all that difficult—he had a colleague who was happy to take it on, no questions asked, not even where George was going. But finding new work quickly wasn't so easy. He combed papers all over the country. He was used to working solo—preferred it—but you couldn't just move to a brand-new place and expect patients to come to your door. You needed referrals, and time, two things George didn't have.

He was going through his old address books, struggling to find contacts, when he came across Tom. Of course. Tom. His old friend from dental school, the guy who every once in a while would call to shoot the breeze, to try and convince George to move down to Florida and go into practice with him. And there had been no reason to until now.

George called Tom, breathing deeply, trying his best to hide his desperation. "Hey, remember that offer about a partnership? That still good?"

George swallowed hard. If Tom said no, who knew where they'd end up? "Tom?" George said. "I'd take the brunt of the patients. I'm just in need of a change."

There was that silence again, and then Tom said. "Buddy, you must be psychic because I was just about to put an ad in the paper selling my practice."

"You were? No kidding?"

Tom laughed. "I'm getting married. Peggy, my hygienist. Her dad's got a little seafood restaurant in the Keys and we're going to be partners. Buy my practice and you don't have to worry about a wedding present."

George had laughed out loud, so gleefully that Eva moved closer to him, resting one hand on his arm. "Great," he said. "This is just terrific. Good luck to you!" George hung up the phone, his smile splitting wide across his face.

God, was it a great job! The office was so close, George didn't have to fight traffic to get to it. Instead, he bought a red ten-speed bike and rode it over, a ten-minute ride lined with palm trees and brilliant flowers. He could smell new-mown lawns and the spark and tang of citrus. He loved the feel of the sun on his scalp, and the cool, delicious breeze he could generate when he coasted down a hill. Delighted, he tilted his head up.

Tom had left him a whole cheerful suite of rooms in an adobe building surrounded by cactus. Everything was in good shape: the sleek leather couches and chairs, the huge aquarium, the freshly painted walls filled with photographs of the beaches that had lured Tom away, but the first thing George did was to change everything, to make it his own.

He hired a new hygienist named Sally, a new office manager, Barb, and both were bright, capable women who said they could start immediately. He took a weekend and painted Tom's pale blue walls a sunny yellow. He got rid of the aquarium, and the heavy leather furniture was replaced with soft, comfortable cloth. A small color TV fit in the waiting room, along with a small fridge for iced herb tea. And because dentists were sometimes accused of being humorless schlubs, he hung funny antique advertisements about teeth. A bride with her hand over her mouth saying, "Jilted because my teeth were telltale yellow!" A man shaking his head: "Did bad breath cost me my job?"

The first patients, coming in, looked a little confused. Where was Tom's braided rug? Where was Elaine, the office manager they knew and loved? And he could tell by their expressions that even though Tom had promised to prep his patients about George, they were thinking: who was he and what would he do to their teeth and would it hurt?

"Well, hello and welcome," George said warmly, holding out his hand, opening up his smile. He knew he had to court Tom's patients, he had to make them so comfortable, so happy, that not only would they keep coming to him, they'd bring him referrals.

"Stella Merton," said the woman doubtfully. "Boy, everything's so changed." She squinted at George. "You use laughing gas like Tom?"

"Novocaine," he said, and she frowned. "You won't feel a thing. I promise."

She made a sound in her throat. "I certainly hope not." She stared at one of the antique ads. George hesitated, watching her, and then she burst out laughing. She sat in the cloth chair and patted the armrest. "Comfortable," she decided.

Before he even started on her, he talked with her, asking her about her family, her job, even if she had any pets, and the whole time she was talking to him, she gave him sidelong glances. "Okay," he said finally, "let's have a look at your pearly whites."

Stella Merton's teeth were a mess. The gums were starting to recede, there were multiple cavities and a nasty-looking abscess forming under a molar. George sighed. This woman was forty years old and told George she had just gotten married and her husband insisted she go to the dentist more often. "Who am I to refuse him anything?" she said happily. She glanced at the picture of Eva and Anne and him. "You're married. You know what I mean," she said knowingly, and George thought of Eva, how tense she still was, how he'd do anything to make her more relaxed.

"I certainly do," he said, and Stella Merton smiled.

He was so gentle with her that he didn't even see her wince, and when he was finished, she was smiling. "Painless!" she said.

George took the bib off. "Your husband must be very special," he said, but what he was thinking was he must be love-drunk or anesthetized to be able to kiss a mouth like Stella's. What kind of a dentist had Tom been not to have taken care of this sooner? He handed Stella a new bright green toothbrush. "Let's book three more appointments to get your teeth in shape," George said. "We'll see how it goes from there."

The next time Mrs. Merton came in, for a follow-up, he handed her a CD of the White Album. "You said you liked the Beatles," he reminded her.

"Oh!" she said, startled and pleased.

He remembered one patient was a vet and so he put out *Cat Fancy* on his table of magazines. He had a knitting magazine for a woman who made sweaters. And as soon as he found out one patient, Frank Corcoran, was a chef at Chamingo's, a local restaurant, he and Eva made reservations. The chicken was a little overdone, the beans mushy, but they cleaned their plates, and he had the waitress send their compliments after the meal. Frank himself came out, in a white chef's hat. "You know," he said, pleased, "in all the years I saw Tom, he never once came to the restaurant. Always said he was too busy."

Two weeks later, George had his first referral.

A year after they had moved, they finally found a home, a two-story with a wraparound porch, the yard lined with orange trees, and after they moved in, they had made a few friends. The Scots, a couple across the street who were both accountants. "Do your taxes for you!" Ellen Scot said, laughing. The Mermans, an older, retired couple who lived next door and were always gardening. "Fresh strawberries," Paul Merman, the husband, said, coming over with a batch.

You couldn't always be looking over your shoulder, couldn't always tense up the way Eva had last week in the diner when she had felt a woman staring so intently at Anne that it made her uneasy. She had nearly bolted up out of her seat, grabbing Anne, when the woman smiled pleasantly. "I just had to tell you how gorgeous your daughter is!" the woman said. "I've never seen red spirally curls like that! And those grey eyes!"

Eva had smiled weakly, but when she took Anne home, she brushed her daughter's red curls until they flattened a little. She pulled them back with a ducky barrette. Instantly, the curls sprang up. Against the white of the barrette, Anne's hair looked even redder.

Anne turned two. And then there were newer, more immediate things to worry about. Anne was quiet as a box of tissues, which made Eva wonder if something was wrong. Even as a baby, she hadn't cried much when her diapers were wet. Now, she could sit for hours with crayons or blocks or simply dreaming. "She should be making sounds at least," Eva said. She and George began to talk more to Anne, just as if she were a little adult, hoping to kick-start Anne's speech. They left the radio on all day to talk shows, they blared the TV, so a constant patter of speech surrounded Anne like a soothing blanket, but Anne ignored all of it, concentrating instead on her colored blocks. Her hands kneaded the soft heads of her stuffed animals, and she stayed happily mute. In the park, surrounded by other babbling children, Anne did little more than smile and laugh, making Eva more worried than ever. "Ah, it's the quiet ones you have to watch out for," other mothers in the park told her, and Eva tried not to stiffen.

Worried, Eva approached the pediatrician, but he waved his hand. "Kids develop at different rates," he said. "I had one patient who didn't say anything until he was three!" He snapped his fingers with a flourish. "Stop worrying. She'll talk when she's ready and then she'll probably talk so much you'll yearn for this quiet."

She drove home, Anne in the backseat, and every time Eva looked in the rearview mirror to check on her, Anne was staring dreamily out the window. Eva felt unsettled. She turned the radio on and began singing loudly. "Come on, honey, make some noise with Mommy!" she urged. She turned around to look at Anne, just for a moment. Was that possible, that her daughter's slate eyes were now bottle green, or was it just the light? She knew eye color, hair color could change. Maybe all that red would darken into a nice brown, transforming Anne, making her look like a whole different girl. Eva squinted, and then another car bumped into them, jolting her. Anne's mouth was a startled O and Eva hurriedly unhooked her seat belt and stretched over the seat, checking Anne's arms, her chubby legs, all the time murmuring, "You're all right, honey."

The car bumped again. "Damn!" Eva cursed, turning back around. She'd have to stop now, exchange licenses.

"Hang on, honey," Eva said, digging into her purse.

"Mommy!"

Eva turned around, stunned. Anne blinked at her. "What did you say—" Eva whispered. Eva saw the woman from the other car coming around to talk to her, but she wouldn't take her eyes off her daughter. "Say it again," she begged.

"Mommy!" Anne said and squealed with laughter, and then Eva laughed, too, which made Anne jump in her car seat. Eva laughed even harder, so that when the other woman bent to her window, she must have thought Eva was crazy.

One word, though, didn't open any floodgates. Slowly, gradually, Anne began to speak, always in individual words, like chips of chocolate on ice cream, sweet, perking your appetite, and frustrating you, too, because what you really wanted was the ice cream. Mommy, daddy, ball, book, crayons, I love you. "She's not fluent yet," Eva said to George. She ruffled word flash cards in one hand and held one up. A big red circle. "Ball," she said, and George lowered her hand.

"Come on, everything doesn't have to be a lesson." He tickled Anne who laughed and wrapped herself about his legs.

"I'm not making it a lesson! I'm trying to help."

"If all she ever said was *Daddy,* I'd be in seventh heaven forever," George said.

He held out his arms and Anne squealed and let go of his legs, leaping up toward George with a ferocity Eva couldn't help but yearn over. "She likes you better," she said.

"I'm here less, that's all it is," George said. "I'm the Great God Daddy."

Anne's whole body seemed lit up. George roughhoused with her, swinging her and tickling her, and Anne didn't grow quiet until George set her back down again.

When Anne turned three, they started her in the Happy Life Day Care. Eva found work herself as a kindergarten teacher at Northeast Elementary School. Immediately her days were filled with lesson plans and projects, with kids and parents and school meetings. She made friends with Miriam, the other kindergarten teacher, and the two of them sometimes stopped off for coffee before they each went home to their families. Anne seemed happy, George loved his job, and she was back teaching again, with fifteen noisy little voices clamoring around her, and she could never get enough of it.

The first time Eva brought Anne to day care, half of the other babies were crying, straining for their mothers, but Anne plunked herself down in front of some blocks and began to play. "No separation anxiety there," said the teacher.

"I'm the one with the anxiety," Eva said, trying to smile.

"Oh, now, she's going to be just fine," the teacher soothed.

And she was fine. When Eva came to pick her up that evening, Anne did cry, but it was because Eva wanted her to come home. "She's tired," Eva said out loud and tried to hold her daughter close, even as Anne scrambled to reach the block area. "Mommy!" she cried. "Down! Down!" Eva smiled and held her tighter.

Eva felt her life was split in two. She went to her class and her kids clamored around her. They climbed in her lap, they reached for her hand, when they drew pictures, they drew Eva's face, they filled the paper with Eva's blond hair. "This is you!" they cried, pointing. "You're on my paper!" She knew exactly how to draw a child out. She'd crouch to their eye level so she wouldn't seem overpowering. She'd modulate her voice so it was softer, more gentle. She put books into the hands of shy children and drew them out. She gave active kids jump ropes to play with that channeled their energy. "I love you, Miss Eva!" Every day, she heard it. And then she came home to her quiet little girl, and when she crouched down to Anne's level, Anne took a step back. When Eva handed Anne books or crayons, Anne would sometimes look overwhelmed. Anne could sit in her room for hours coloring, playing with her dolls, and as soon as Eva stepped into the room, Anne would look flustered and Eva couldn't figure out why.

"How'd you luck out with such a quiet girl?" Miriam asked her.

"I wish she'd be more outgoing."

"Because you are?" Miriam asked. "Who says your kids are like you? My daughter Brigette's so different from me I sometimes thought the hospital had switched babies on us. She loves sports, loves roughhousing, and all I want to do is play dolls with her or shop. What are you going to do? They're their own people right from the start. All you can do is nurture who they already are."

Or nurture what you'd like for them to be, Eva thought.

When Anne turned five, the same age as Eva's students, Eva decided to bring her to her kindergarten class. "I want to show her off," Eva said, but the truth was, she wanted to show herself off to her daughter. She dressed up in a rainbow-striped skirt and long beaded earrings. Then she put Anne in a new dress, green as her eyes, and she tidied Anne's red hair into pigtails, tied with a ribbon. "What color?" she asked, and when Anne said yellow, Eva grinned. "Ah, my favorite color!" Eva said, pleased.

"Wish I could be there," George said.

"Just us girls," Eva told him.

The whole ride to the school, Eva kept telling Anne all the wonders that she'd find in Eva's classroom: music and instruments and art supplies! A cooking center where they could make butter! A dress-up center where they could play theater! "Guess what I have planned today!" Eva told Anne excitedly. "A nature walk!"

"A nature walk!" Anne's eyes shone.

As soon as Eva walked into the room, the children rushed toward her, clamoring. "Miss Eva! Miss Eva!" Fifteen voices were all talking at once.

Anne hesitated and then shyly leaned along the wall, lowering her eyes. Billy grabbed at Eva's hands and Anne sprinted forward, tugging them away so roughly Billy cried.

"Anne!" Eva said, surprised. "That's not nice!"

Anne's hands darted back to her sides. Her lower lip trembled. "Why're you crying?" Eva asked, crouching down. "Billy's the one who was startled." Anne shook her head.

"Come meet everyone." Eva sprang up again, like a rubber band. "This is my daughter, Anne!" Eva said. She tugged at Anne's hand, but Anne hid behind her.

The kids were excited, restless, churning like a tide, but Eva knew what to do. She clapped her hands, one, two, three, her signal for them to gather ·round. And then, outside, it began to pour. "The nature walk!" Anne cried.

Eva stared at the gloomy day. Great, she thought, and then an idea prickled into her mind. "Well, maybe we can have fun anyway," Eva said.

"How can we do that?"

"You'll see," Eva said.

"What are you going to do?" Anne asked, her eyes bright.

"You wait and see," Eva whispered. "Your mommy can make magic."

While the children played at the activity centers, Eva got out the blanket and spread it on the floor with the picnic basket. She went next door and borrowed the microwave they used for cooking. There was a package of hot dogs in the fridge and they could nuke them. She got all kinds of summertime songs for the boom box to play for the kids. "We're having a summer picnic!" Eva announced.

"But it's raining," Billy said.

"Not inside it isn't," Eva said. "Come on, now, everyone line up behind me, hands on the person in front of you."

The kids scrambled into a line. Anne lagged in the corner. "Anne, honey, come on!" Eva urged, but Anne shook her head. "Well, join in anytime," Eva said.

They all sang "Day-O," marching around the room, making so much noise, the next-door teacher came by, leaning in the doorway, laughing. "You are one teacher!" she said, but Eva, looking at her Anne sitting alone, couldn't help feeling that she had failed.

All afternoon, Eva tried to engage her daughter. When Eva handed out blue and green and yellow streamers for the kids to swirl in the air, pretending they were waves at the beach, Anne waved hers around limply.

"Come on, honey!" Eva urged, and Anne waved her streamer harder and when it snagged on something and ripped, she looked stunned. "Never mind!" Eva said, but Anne sat on the floor.

When the first of the parents arrived to pick up the kids, Eva was playing Frisbee with a group of them, and none of the kids wanted to leave. "Can't we stay?" they pleaded.

Gradually, Eva's hold loosened. The Frisbees fell, the streamers slid to the floor, the kids ran to their mothers, their grandmothers, their nannies.

"See you tomorrow," Eva called to John and Jack and Harry and Emma, and in the end, it was just Eva and Anne in the chaos of the room.

Eva knelt down by Anne. Both of Anne's pigtails were undone and Eva smoothed them back. "Did you have fun today?" she asked.

"A lot," Anne said.

"What was the best part?"

Anne was quiet for a moment, surveying the room. "The books?" she asked.

"Honey, I'm not looking for a right answer," Eva persisted. "You don't have to try and please me. I just want to know what you liked. The picnic? The streamers?"

"The books," she said, and despite her best efforts, Eva deflated.

"Well, good," Eva said quickly. "I'm glad you had a good time." Anne shot her an anxious look and then bowed her head. "What is it?" Eva asked. "Are you crying again?"

"Do you like them better than you like me?" Anne whispered and Eva felt something splintering inside of her heart. "How could you even dream such a thing?" Eva asked. "Who's my girl?" she said. "Who's my absolute favorite, most loved girl?"

"I love you, Mommy," Anne said, and Eva bent and held her until Anne pulled away.

By third grade, Anne's teachers were writing on her report card, "She doesn't apply herself. She's off in her own world dreaming."

Anne was always reading, always telling stories. At dinner she told George and Eva that she had seen a lion in the neighborhood but she had fed it cookies and it went home. "Oh, a cookie-loving lion," George said. "My favorite kind."

On the way to school, Anne told Eva that she thought she was growing angel wings under her dress. "Don't fly away on us," Eva said, grabbing hold of Anne's hand.

When Eva took Anne to the park or the make-your-own pottery place or the pizza parlor, she saw other children in groups, their mothers hovering nearby. "Would you like to make a play-date with someone?" she asked Anne, and Anne shrugged and picked at a scab on her knee until Eva swatted her hand away.

"She needs friends," Eva told George. "Maybe we should just call some of the other mothers and arrange something."

"You can't force friendships," George said. "And I don't think we should push her. You wait. She'll have plenty of friends soon enough."

Eva only felt a little better when Anne came home one day and announced she had a new best friend at school. "Darnelle," she said proudly. For weeks, all Anne talked about was this other little girl Darnelle. Darnelle could sing songs backward. Darnelle knew how to speak French. Eva was thrilled that Anne had found a friend. "Invite Darnelle over," Eva suggested. "We can make cookies together. Or make our own Play-Doh."

Anne shrugged. Eva kept nudging her to call and finally Anne burst into tears. "We aren't friends anymore. Darnelle hit me."

"She hit you?" Eva said, shocked.

Eva didn't tell Anne that she called her teacher, that she wanted to find out who this Darnelle thought she was. "Darnelle?" Anne's teacher said to Eva. "Who's Darnelle? There's no girl in our class with that name."

"Why didn't you tell us the truth?" Eva asked Anne. "Darnelle wasn't real."

"She was to me," Anne said.

She needs real friends, Eva kept thinking, even as Anne began playing by herself again. She'd race across the backyard, head thrown back. She jumped rope singing to herself or rode her bike, and she liked to write stories, too, filling up the brightly colored notebooks Eva gave her. Eva tried to coax a look, but Anne held the pad to her chest.

"It's private," Anne said.

"Why can't we see? I know I'll love anything you do."

"You promise?" Anne asked.

"I don't have to promise, I *know*. What's the story?"

"Oh, let her alone," George said. He winked at Anne, who laughed. "Our little Greta Garbo. 'I vant to be a-lone,'" he said and tickled her.

Eva personally hated to be alone. She had always loved big groups and lots of noise, which was one reason why Eva loved teaching preschool. She was thrilled when Anne found girls she liked to be with, real flesh-and-blood friends that Eva liked, too. Anne had first met Flor and June in third grade, two new girls in her class. She came home solemnly asking if she could have them over. "Are you kidding?" Eva said.

The girls came the next day, scrambling up her walk, two bright-faced little girls in brown pigtails and stretchy-waist jeans. They came the next day, too, making Eva's house a habit, making themselves at home, pouring their own juice, turning the TV on and off. Eva was always on the phone with their mothers, assuring them she'd get the girls home on time, asking could the girls stay for dinner, could the girls sleep over with Anne? Eva grew to expect them, to buy extra juice and cookies so there would always be enough on hand. She was always bandaging their bumps and scrapes, drying their tears and doling out hugs. Sometimes she interrupted their play to ask if they'd like to test-drive a project she was going to try out with her class: making bread from scratch! "Of course, the project is for much younger kids, but I could use the expertise of a few ten-year-olds," she said. The girls giggled, pleased. They were happy enough to get messy in the kitchen with Eva. She gave them each one of her T-shirts to put over their clothes so they wouldn't get too dirty. She helped them tie their hair back and showed them how to pound the dough with their hands, how to shape it. She turned to rinse a glass.

"What are you doing? You big silly!" Flor cried, and Eva turned, glass in hand, and saw Anne pushing both elbows into the dough, the same way Sara had when Eva had taught her how to make bread, and for a moment, seeing that gesture, those red curls, it was like seeing a ghost. Eva felt catapulted back in time, when she hadn't been able to wait for Sara to come to the house, when she couldn't speak a paragraph without Sara being in it, and she suddenly missed Sara, only this time, the anger was gone, and now there was only a confusion of yearning and guilt and grief. "Pull your hair back so you don't get dough in it," Eva said to Anne.

"You're spilling water!" June called to Eva and Eva, confused, tilted the glass upright. She walked over to Anne and took her arms. "Not like that," she said, steadying her voice. "Use your hands. Warm the dough with their heat. See? The way I'm doing?"

"Ow!" Anne looked at her, astonished.

"Oh, honey, I'm sorry——" Eva said. Anne looked down at the dough, but not at Eva. Slowly, she started to knead it, and then Eva turned away to finish the dishes.

They were all laughing, and then Anne left the room, and ten minutes later, Flor said, "Where's Anne?"

They found her in the backyard, sitting on a swing.

"Anne, you big dodo," said Flor, "get your butt in here."

"You said *butt,*" June said, delighted. Then she turned to Anne. "Are you in a mood?"

"I just wanted to be outside for a while," Anne said, sliding off the swing.

Eva looked at the other girls, how their faces fell and then recomposed, and then she felt a sudden kinship. *I know how you feel,* she wanted to tell them.

Inside, Eva spread out colored paper and handed out crayons.

"I wish you were my mother," Flor said, grabbing for a bright green crayon.

"No, I wish, you were *my* mother," June said.

"She's *my* mom," Anne said quickly. "My mommy."

"Can we come live here?" said June.

"You can visit," Anne said.

One day, walking by, Eva heard the girls telling stories to each other. She leaned against the wall and listened to one story, and then another, the girls interrupting each other excitedly, adding details, asking questions. The stories were centered around one girl named Betsy, a girl much like them. Betsy had adventures at camp with a big spanking machine. Betsy was at boarding school with a mean headmistress. The thing that disturbed Eva was that Betsy was an orphan.

She walked into the room. "Great stories, girls," she said.

"We've been working hard," Flor said. "We're all writing our own stories, but we talk about what the story's going to be before we write it."

June held up a purple crayon importantly. "And we're *illustrating* them."

"What happened to Betsy's parents?" Eva asked.

"They died," Anne said simply. "That's it. *Kerplunk.*"

Unnerved, Eva looked at Flor and June. "In your stories, too? The parents died?"

"Oh yes," said June. "That's the way we do it. All the same."

"But how does this girl live?" Eva asked.

"Her parents were millionaires and she gets the money."

"But she has to have a guardian, someone looking over her, doesn't she?"

Flor and June looked suddenly worried. "Maybe she's adopted," June said, and Eva grew still, but Anne shook her head. "She's not adopted. She's a millionaire," Anne said.

Eva went into the other room and sat down, stroking at her temples. Orphans. Adoptions. At the school this year, in another class, there was one mother with two adopted Chinese kids, and every Sunday she sent them to Chinese school so they could know and understand their own heritage. There was another mother who had an adopted boy whose birth mother came to see him every year and stayed in the house. "She's a member of the family," the woman had said. "We love her to pieces!"

She and George never talked about Sara anymore. They never discussed if they'd tell Anne about her birth mother or when, and when Eva thought about it, she grew frightened. She got up and went to Anne and held her as if she might contain her in her arms forever. God help her, but the answer to that question of telling was always *not yet.*

She heard Anne sobbing. Alarmed, she got up and ran into the other room. Flor and June were murmuring over Anne, rubbing her back, stroking her hair. "What happened? What is it?" Eva cried.

"The headmistress is dead," said Flor.

"The who?"

"The headmistress. From our stories. We killed her off."

Eva knelt down beside Anne. "It's only a story," Eva said, and Anne wrenched away from her. "Honey—" said Eva. Seeing her daughter so upset made her upset, too. "I'm so sorry," she said, reaching out to hold Anne, who cried louder.

"Okay, okay, the headmistress doesn't die," Flor blurted. "Let's have her just get sick and then recover and she loses her memory and is a nice person. Anne, it's just a *story*."

Anne snuffled and looked up and then a little smile spread across Anne's face. "And we can draw her in a pretty new dress," she said.

It ruffled Eva that the girls could comfort Anne when she herself couldn't, but she told herself that the important thing was that Anne had been comforted, that she had stopped crying. And she liked those girls. She was sorry when they went home.

"Come back anytime," she told them.

"Come back! Come back!" Anne waved so hard she had to support one hand with the other. "Please come back!"

The house felt newly quiet. Eva cleaned up the crayons.

"You look like a princess, Mommy," Anne blurted, and Eva looked over at her.

"I do?"

"Like in one of my stories. Like the headmistress."

"The headmistress? I thought she was evil!"

"No, no, she's nice!"

Eva bent and kissed Anne, lightly, barely a butterfly brush. "Want to help me make dinner?" she asked Anne, but Anne shook her head. "I want to work on my story," she said. "I want to make sure the headmistress doesn't die."

Eva started. "Honey, I thought you all wrote her back alive."

"But what if she doesn't stay that way?"

"She will, honey."

When George got home, Anne didn't run out to greet him the way she usually did. "Hey, I miss that!" he said. They went to find out what was wrong, and there, in the den, curled in a chair, sleeping, scribbled pages all around her, was Anne. "Let's get this bunny rabbit to bed," George said. He gently picked her up and they settled her under the covers. "Sweet dreams, princess," George said.

That night, long after Eva and George were asleep, Anne woke with a nightmare. "Mommy!" she screamed. "Mommy!"

Startled, Eva threw back the covers. George roused, blinking. "She always calls for you," Eva said. "Go back to sleep—it's okay." He burrowed under the covers.

She dashed into Anne's room. Anne was sitting up, sweating, her hair damp, clutching the sheets. "Mommy!" she cried.

"It's okay," Eva soothed. "I'm here. I'm here."

She stroked back Anne's hair and kissed her forehead. "Don't go," Anne whispered, grabbing Eva's hand. "There's a monster in here."

Eva lay down on the bed beside her daughter. "There's no monster," Eva promised.

"Go look," Anne urged.

Eva turned on the lights. She looked under the bed and behind the dresser. She looked in the closet and opened every drawer. "No monsters," she promised, and then she put her hand on the door.

"Mommy, don't go!" Anne said, sitting up, alarmed.

"You want me to stay?" Eva asked, coming over to the bed and sitting. Anne threw her arm about Eva. "You won't die, will you?"

"Honey, no," Eva said, shocked. "I'm right here. I'll never leave you, don't you know that?" She smoothed one hand over Anne's hair, she drew her close. The story, she thought. That silly story about the headmistress had upset her.

The bed was just a twin, too narrow for the two of them. Eva wasn't tired, there were lesson plans she had to do, but there was nothing in the world that would have compelled her to move. In minutes, Anne was asleep, one hand resting on Eva's shoulder. Eva lay there beside her, keeping still, so as not to dislodge Anne's hand from her shoulder.

chapter

nine

During Sara's first year in New York, everyone thought she was doing great. Her parents couldn't brag enough about her. Jack hung a Columbia school banner in his office; Abby insisted on wearing a Columbia sweatshirt to their beach club. "Columbia!" they repeated, as if they couldn't believe their good fortune.

Sometimes, Sara couldn't believe it, either. For the first time in her life, everyone around her was as smart as she was—if not smarter. Every A was a badge of honor rather than shame. And she loved New York City. In SoHo a tourist asked about museums and she knew what to tell him. The waitresses at her local diner knew her by name. *I'm part of something,* she thought happily. *I belong here.*

In New York, too, Sara began to date. She immediately got herself on the pill, and she tried her best to be careful about whom she slept with, and if nothing ever took, she told herself, well, she just needed to give herself time for that to happen, too. There was Doug, who grew quieter and quieter on their dates until, one night, he interrupted a story she was telling him with an exasperated sigh. "Do you always have to talk?" he asked. There was a history major named Paul who decided to go back to his old girlfriend. And just last week she had stopped seeing an artist named Robert because he had run his finger over her stretch marks in bed, making her instantly freeze. She hadn't known what to do, what to say, and then he had said, critically, "It's hard to believe a skinny minnie like you was once a heifer."

"Why do you even like that type?" one of her friends asked Sara about Robert, but Sara knew it wasn't that she was drawn to a type as much as she was desperately trying to escape one. She thought that if she dated men as different from Danny as she could find, she would stop yearning for Danny, would stop seeing him in her dreams, whispering her name. It was like the habituation tinnitus patients sometimes did, using a new sound to blot out the old one, until the old one disappeared.

If only it would work. The day she stopped seeing Paul, she came back to her dorm and caught a scent of something so strong she had to brace her hand along the door. Patchouli oil. What Danny and she had both worn. What she didn't wear anymore. Sara jammed her key into her lock and quickly went into her room, shutting the door.

She grabbed for the phone, calling home, feeling like a little kid needing approval. No matter what she told her parents now, they were enthusiastic. She could have said she bought canned tuna on sale at D'Agostino's and her mother would kvell for hours about what a smart girl Sara was. How thrifty. How adult. "I stayed in all day," she told them.

"Great! You got studying done!" Abby said. "Nothing wrong with that."

Sara tugged on the phone cord. She swore she still smelled the patchouli. "Mom—" she blurted. "Does any mail ever come to the house for me?"

"I know what you're talking about," Abby said. "And if it had I would have thrown it right out. Those people were evil. And that boy was responsible for a lot of pain."

"It wasn't all his fault."

"You're doing all right now. He's probably pumping gas. You wait. The right man will come along for you. But you get your degree first. Stop thinking about the past. There's nothing you can do about it except make yourself more miserable."

Sara bit the edge of a nail. "I know," she said.

"Nothing but wonderful things from now on for our little girl," her father told her.

"Well, it's wonderful, but it's hard——" she started to say, and he interrupted her.

"Just stop at *wonderful*," he said sagely. "That's all we want to hear."

"You're in a whole new place," Abby told her. "And you're a whole new person."

Sara grew her hair longer, from her shoulders to just past her breasts, using colorful shoelaces or bandanas as headbands. She pierced her ears, and wore large complicated-looking earrings. While scouring the Village, she found a pair of hot-pink cowboy boots for just ten dollars and she wore them everywhere and with everything. In high school, she had worn mostly black or drab colors, but now she dressed in flamboyant gauze skirts and embroidered peasant tops, and when she looked at herself in the mirror, she saw the whole new person Abby had mentioned. Holding her skirts out wide, smiling at herself, she bowed with a flourish.

She told no one what had happened in her past. Not friends, not the occasional men she saw, and not the therapist she saw, a gently probing older woman named Kaysen. "If you bring things to the surface, they lose their power," Kaysen told her, but Sara knew that that was what happened in an ideal world, in theory but not in practice, that sometimes bringing things to the surface gave them a wingspan you might never clip. "The way to get free of pain is to dive down into it. To acknowledge it," Kaysen said. Kaysen had cropped grey hair and vivid blue eyes, and her earrings were always tiny, glittering studs, like the eyes of an animal. "Dive," Kaysen advised, but Sara knew that to dive was dangerous until you knew you could swim.

The day Anne turned two, Sara bolted awake, blinking at the morning light. She didn't have to glance at the Women in Science calendar she had on her wall to know what day today was, and how it would make her feel. The only recourse was to get busy, to crowd her day with so much activity time might speed up, and the day might pass.

Her legs swung out from the bed in an arc. Her hand reached for the small white phone and she called one friend after another, but they were away or doing something with boyfriends or simply not at home, and in the end, she grabbed her jacket and went out herself. She wasn't sure where she was going, so she ended up walking and walking, down to the nineties, past the fifties, not feeling jelly-legged until she reached Macy's on Thirty-fourth, and then she went inside. Maybe she could treat herself to something, even if it was just a pair of tights in a striking color. Maybe afterward, she'd treat herself to a movie.

Macy's had rearranged the store again. The red carpeting was now blue and there were flowers everywhere. A woman tried to spritz her with perfume and Sara waved her hand and went up the escalator. "Hosiery?" Sara asked a clerk, who pointed to the corner.

Sara walked past men's shirts, past ladies' shoes, and suddenly, she found herself in the baby section. Rows of little dresses, little corduroy pants in pastel colors. Stuffed plush bears and tigers. They all hit her like a shock. For a moment, she couldn't move. Shoppers brushed past her. A salesgirl gave her a pointed, inquisitive look. "May I help you?" she said, and Sara politely shook her head no. Leave, she told herself, go outside to a movie, to a restaurant, see some friends, but instead, her hands were drawn to the clothing, her fingers found the fur on the stuffed toys and couldn't stop patting it. Two years old, she thought. Her baby was two years old. Was Anne having a party with hats and a real cake? Were there relatives crowded round? What did Anne look like now, would Sara recognize her, and what did she *sound* like? What words was she forming: *truck, bunny, Mommy.* Her heart opened and shut like a door.

Sara felt like she was hypnotized. She grabbed the first dress on the rack, a blue gingham, and walked with it to the counter. She couldn't make herself put it back. "What a darling dress!" the saleswoman chirped and rang up the dress. "Gift wrap?" she asked, and when Sara just stood there, the salesgirl tenderly folded the dress into a box and wrapped it. As soon as she reached for the gift, Sara's hands started shaking.

She walked away, tightening her grip. The bag swung, so big and cumbersome it knocked against her legs. *I didn't forget you,* Sara thought. *I never forgot.*

By the time she got home, she knew she was being stupid. What had she been thinking? What was she going to do with the dress? She had no money to hire a detective, and even if she did, she knew no one would give Anne to her. She had no job yet. And she had broken the law. She sat, staring at the package. Throw that thing out, Abby would tell her. Now, none of that, Jack would say. Instead, she tucked it back into her closet, behind her winter boots. Then she grabbed her things and went out to a movie.

I'll never do that again, she told herself, but she couldn't seem to help it. On Anne's third birthday, she reminded herself that she wasn't going to do anything foolish again. Remember how blue she had felt coming home with a gift she'd never be able to give Anne? She planned out her day, all activities that would place her nowhere near a store: dates with friends, studying, and then, on her way to a movie, she passed a store window filled with toys and she felt pulled to go in, and by the time she came out, she had another wrapped gift for her daughter, a blue velvet teddy bear with a pink ribbon around its neck.

It became a habit, a private joke that wasn't funny. For Anne's fourth birthday, she bought her a paint set. *Four years old,* she thought. What four-year-old would go to her now? She had read once that babies could pick out their mothers from a crowded room just by their scent, but Anne was no baby anymore. She could pass her daughter on the street and they would be strangers.

She always felt the same desperation, the same grief. How was she better than the case studies she read about in her psychology classes? The girls who cut themselves to release the pressure they felt building up inside of them, the girls who starved and vomited to have some control? She wouldn't do this anymore. She couldn't. And if she couldn't throw Anne's gifts out, she could at least keep them out of sight in her closet.

She finished school, and started grad school, still at Columbia. Sara was in her second year, majoring in clinical psychology, when she started interning as a counselor, sharing a tiny office in the same building as Kaysen, her therapist. Students got the people who couldn't afford the real therapists, who came in off the street and paid sliding scale. A lot of the people came once and that was it, so Sara had no idea whom she helped and whom she didn't, though she liked to imagine people didn't come back because she had taken away some of their pain for them, because she was good at her job. Her hair reached to the middle of her back now, and for work, she tied it in a knot. She traded in her big earrings for small studs, polished her shoes so they gleamed, and bought herself a few good dresses. It didn't matter if the clothes weren't really her, it was even better that they weren't because it wasn't good for patients to know too much about you, to get too invested or distracted. Therapy was all about them, not you.

"You've got it all together, don't you," one patient accused, looking at Sara up and down. "Bet you never even get a run in your hose, do you?"

Sara smiled serenely. "Why would you think that?" she asked.

Sometimes, though, it was harder than she had thought, listening to peoples' problems, keeping her distance. "Don't get involved," Kaysen told her. But how could you help it? Yesterday, a teenage boy had burst into tears because his girlfriend had left him, and it was all Sara could do not to scoot over to him and put her arms around him in comfort. The day before a woman came in terrified because she had just had a biopsy and was afraid it was terminal. Her pain was so palpable, Sara started to hug her own body, until she caught sight of the woman watching her, alarmed, and then Sara put her hands casually to rest on her knees, and the woman relaxed.

In any case, people really didn't want to be told what to do. Sara's job had more to do with what she didn't say, with how she listened or asked questions that would make clients keep talking. Half the time what was the most effective was simply mirroring back what people said to her, making them feel they had been heard, that their sorrow had been seen and validated, if not solved. "You'll make a fine therapist," Kaysen assured Sara.

One day, a woman named Nicole came in. It was Sara's last appointment of the day.

Nicole couldn't have been much older than Sara, and she was in jeans and a white sweater, her blond hair cropped like a boy's, and the first thing Sara noticed were her hands, the nails bitten raw. Boyfriend, Sara thought. Parental problem. She liked to guess, to see if her instincts were sharp. As soon as Nicole sat down, in the straight-backed chair instead of the comfortable one, Sara made a note on her pad. She waited to see if Nicole would make eye contact with her, and then, staring into her lap, Nicole sobbed.

Sara stayed calm, serene. "Tell me how I can help," she said.

"My baby died," wept Nicole, and Sara felt a sudden fissure inside of her, like a crack in thin ice. She sat up straighter.

Nicole talked nonstop for nearly the whole session, about how beautiful her baby girl Clare had been, how everyone said so, how she couldn't walk down the street without people stopping in admiration. She talked about how she and her husband used to stay up nights just watching Clare sleep, and on one night, when they hadn't, Clare had died of SIDS. Nicole stopped talking for a moment. She tilted her head as if she were listening to something. "I see her everywhere," Nicole said. "Can you imagine what that's like?"

Sara was beside herself, but she fought to look calm. She willed her voice to be measured, in control. "Tell me how you're handling this," she said. She asked about Nicole's support systems, she recommended a group of other mothers who had lost children. She talked about grief being a roller coaster, and then the session was over.

"I can't forgive myself," Nicole said, balling Kleenex into tiny fists on her lap. "I see her! I keep seeing her!"

"You didn't cause this. No one did. Sometimes things just happen." Something flickered along the wall and Sara glanced over. There, just for a second, Sara saw the ghost baby, too, in the corner, stretching, starting to stand. Startled, Sara blinked and the baby disappeared. "It's not your fault," she repeated.

Nicole didn't take her eyes from Sara. Drawing in a breath, she stood heavily and then noisily blew her nose. "You believe that, don't you?" Nicole said in wonder.

"I do."

Nicole swiped at her eyes and took in another deep, measured breath. "Then thank you," she said, swiping at her eyes. "This helped. I think it helped."

Sara stood up and nodded. "Good," she said. She felt like a fraud. She knew that Nicole might feel better now, but what would happen that night, when Nicole was back in her home, when everything suddenly reminded her again of all she had lost?

"Can I come back? If I come back, can I get you again?"

Sara's stomach tightened. "Of course," she said, but she couldn't meet Nicole's eyes. Sara walked Nicole to the door, opening it and closing it in one graceful move. She waited until she heard the whoosh of the elevator outside and then Sara felt the crack in the ice around her growing. She grabbed her coat and her bag and left the office. "Don't take on other peoples' problems," Kaysen had said. "It's countertransference."

She headed for the ladies' room and threw her purse on the orange couch by the wall. She stared at herself in the mirror, and suddenly, nothing looked right to her. Not her smooth hair, not the chic earrings or the sleek dark dress she had on, and then she yanked out the knot in her hair, so her curls sprang across her back. She unhooked her earrings and flung them in her purse, and then she turned the spigots on full force, splashing water onto her face.

Sara kept seeing Nicole's hunched shoulders. She kept remembering the way Nicole had kept her hands protectively on her belly the whole time she was in Sara's office. She heard Nicole's voice, saying, *"My baby died. I'll never see my baby again."*

Sara walked, automatically veering right, then left, until she was at Kaysen's office. She didn't have an appointment, didn't even know what she expected might happen, but she knocked on the door and Kaysen answered. "Sara," she said, surprised, and then Sara's whole body began to shake.

She couldn't seem to stop. She covered her face with her hands, and then she felt Kaysen's hands, warm and dry, guiding her forward. "Come inside," Kaysen said.

"Are you okay?" Kaysen's voice was soft. She was seated across from Sara, settled in the black leather chair. Sara wrapped her arms about her body. "My client's baby died."

Kaysen was silent. "Did something else happen today?" she asked finally. "Something with you and not a client?"

"I had a baby when I was sixteen," Sara whispered.

Kaysen leaned forward.

"I gave her up," Sara said. "An open adoption. But before I gave her up, I fell in love with her, with the family, too." She couldn't stop the tears now, couldn't stop the words, either. "I fucked up. I ruined everything. I don't even know where the family is anymore."

"You were young, you couldn't know from fucking up."

Sara's laugh sounded harsh. "But I did. I did fuck up in ways you can't imagine."

"What ways?"

"I lost my baby. I lost the family. I can't even really go back to Boston anymore."

Kaysen shook her head. "You never would have come this far if you had kept a baby. You wouldn't have been able to go to school, to have a life. Think about what is. Not what isn't. You could think of what you did, giving your daughter up, as very loving."

Sara grabbed for a tissue and then balled it into her lap. Her eyes were tight and dry.

"It's okay to cry, Sara. You can cry about this."

"No, no, I can't. If I do, I'm afraid I won't ever stop."

"Surely you know a thing like this takes time. Think of Odysseus. He had to go down into hell to emerge with new knowledge. Now so do you."

"Odysseus is a myth. And I've already been to hell, thanks."

"Sara—it was important that you tell me this. I'm glad you told me."

"I don't know if I am," Sara said. She felt Kaysen's eyes on her.

"I think we should start seeing each other twice a week," Kaysen said.

The room seemed filled with Danny's scent, with the baby, with a thousand memories she wanted to forget, and she leaped up. "I'm sorry— I have to go, I have to get out of here—" she said, and then she was out of Kaysen's office. Then she was out on the street, gulping in air, telling herself over and over that everything was going to be all right, that this was just a derailment and that's all and before she knew it, everything would be back on track again, racing toward a new destination.

*   *   *

Sara tried to bury herself in her work, but the next few sessions she had with clients, she couldn't listen to their issues without feeling her own pain reverberating deep inside of her. "Me, too," she kept thinking. "Me, too." She struggled for control, for detachment, and then when Nicole called to schedule another appointment, Sara put her off. "I'll get back to you," she promised.

That day, Sara went to the dean's office and got a leave of absence from school. She told herself it was just until she built herself back up again. Maybe when she was stronger she could deal with this, she could sit in an office with Kaysen and dissect her past, she could help her clients, but right now all she wanted was to feel better, to feel things were possible, not to dive deeper into a pain so bottomless it threatened to drown her.

She called Kaysen's office when she knew Kaysen wouldn't be there. She waited for the record beep, her throat dry. "I need to take a break from therapy," Sara said. "I know you're going to want to talk about this, but I just can't. I'm sorry." She rested her head against the receiver. "I know you tried to help me."

That night, she was making pasta, a salsa CD was blaring, when the phone rang. She stopped cooking, listening intently.

"Sara," said Kaysen's voice. "You have to come in and talk about this. I can't stop you from leaving, but we do need closure." *I've closed already,* Sara thought.

"Call me," Kaysen said, her voice stern. "Sara, call me."

All that week, Sara tried to figure out what she could say to Kaysen. Finally, she simply called, relieved when the machine clicked on. "I'm not coming back," she repeated. "I'm sorry. I can't even talk to you about it, and I'm sorry about that, too, but please don't call me again. I'll call if and when I'm ever ready." And then she quickly hung up. She lay flat on her couch, her arms over her eyes. Already, she missed Kaysen. She used to love the feeling she got when she'd go to Kaysen's all knotted up inside, and after a half hour of talking, the knot would slowly loosen. Her breath would flow and she'd feel more hopeful. She used to love the way Kaysen leaned forward as if every word Sara said was important, and even though she knew it was all part of the training, that no one really had the answers for another person, and that part of a therapist's job was to look like she really cared, sometimes, she truly believed that Kaysen had cared about her. Well. Sometimes you could make yourself believe anything if it made you happy. And sometimes you couldn't.

That night, she called her parents to tell them she was taking a leave.

"This isn't the right thing to do," Abby said. "Can't you just take off a week?"

"Come home," Jack said. "I'll make calls so you can work here. Or take classes."

"Yes, take the classes. Don't go backward—" Abby warned.

"No, no." Sara swallowed. "Going home would be backward. I'm staying here."

"But why?" Jack said. "We can take care of you here. How will you pay your rent? How will you live? A young girl alone in the city!"

"I'm twenty-four. I'll work. And I'll be fine."

"Why won't you let us help you?" Abby asked. "We're your parents. It's only natural."

Sara thought of her parents taking over when she was pregnant, taking over after she was banned from seeing Eva and George, and something twisted deep inside of her. She took a deeper breath. "Listen, I appreciate your offer but I just can't take you up on it. I have to work things out on my own. I just have to."

"Oh honey, it just breaks my heart to hear that." Jack sighed and for a moment Sara imagined herself getting smaller and smaller until she could scramble up on her father's lap, the way she used to when she was a little girl. He used to tell her the story of Rapunzel, making his voice high for the princess, and gravelly for the wicked witch, and when the story was over, she half-believed he was the one who had saved the day, that he was the one who could do anything, not the prince. And then she thought: *Red light, Danger.* She wasn't a little girl anymore. And Rapunzel was a fairy story, told to put Rapunzel and her prince in the best light. Who knew what the witch's version of events might be, how she might have put Rapunzel in a tower not to imprison her, but to keep her close and safe? "I don't mean to hurt either one of you," Sara said, "but I know what I have to do."

* * *

Sara had to find work fast. She could stay in student housing until the end of the following month and she had enough savings for a deposit and the first month's rent. She riffled through the employment section, and finally, she found a job opening as a junior copywriter at Madame, on Forty-ninth Street and Sixth. The McGraw-Hill Building.

The president of the company was a tall, stark-looking woman named Yvonne. "Full-fashioned clothing for the fabulously full-figured," Yvonne recited, and when Sara started to smile, Yvonne's mouth narrowed, and Sara's smile retracted. Yvonne turned Sara over to the vice president, a man named Hal Viceroy. He was young, with sandy, choppily cut hair. He sat across from her at his desk, snapping his striped suspenders, and his eyes were flat and blue as pond water. "What makes you think you can write ads?" he asked.

"Try me," Sara said. She tried not to flinch every time he snapped his suspenders.

Hal nodded in a way that made her sure he was about to dismiss her. She started to stand, when he extended his hand to her. "Okay, then, we will," he said. "The salary's not much to write home about, either. So, can you start today?"

Hal walked her past rows of open cubicles to the back, where he finally stopped. "Mona's on extended sick leave," he told her. There was half a desk, a small computer, a chair, and an empty bulletin board. Sara sat. She could barely turn around. Her knees bumped the top of the desk. Her feet stubbed against a grey wastebasket already crammed with paper. "I'll bring you some work, you see what you can finish by the end of the day, and we'll take it from there," he told her. Sara looked across the aisle. There was another cubicle, and another in front of it, but no one was there.

He brought her pages of layouts, scribbled with red corrections. She was done by three, printing everything out, attaching the new layouts to the old ones, and brought the work in to Hal. He frowned at her, annoyed. His mouth twitched. "What's the problem?"

"There's no problem. I finished."

"You finished?"

She nodded. Her stomach growled. Her mouth pooled with saliva. She was starving.

"You did it all? Every correction?" He tapped one of the pages. "You did this here—'Take a Good Long Look' for the long dress?"

"I thought it sounded better," she said.

"Uh-huh."

He looked over at his clock. "It's three."

"It took me time getting used to the computer. I'll be faster tomorrow."

Hal leafed through the rest of her layouts. " 'Bohemian Wrapsody' for the tied Indian-print skirts," he said, and then he shook his head. "Okay, you can go," he said.

"Go?" Sara said, confused. "I spell-checked. Did I do something wrong?"

He lifted his head. "I didn't think you'd finish half of it, let alone get it all done. And I like this copy." He still wasn't smiling. "Maybe we'll make you a copy chief."

With steady work, she could afford an apartment, a shoebox-sized studio in Chelsea that she found advertised on a kiosk and took sight unseen because they weren't asking for a damage deposit, or for first and last month's rent. The apartment was all painted beige, and it had a funny smell, like something had died behind one of the walls, but Sara felt hopeful she could take care of that with cleanser and a good scrubbing. The bathtub was in the kitchen, covered by a plank of wood, forming a table, but Sara was sure she could make it charming. She painted the apartment soft white, the bathtub light blue. She bought a small sleep sofa on sale and a table. Two place settings in a cheery cobalt. The apartment wasn't much, but it was hers and she liked coming home to it, liked having a door she was the only one who held the key to. "My home," she said, patting the walls.

* * *

Sara, Walkman clamped to her head, Mozart soaring in her ears, happily typed. Her fingers, nails bit to the nubs, sped, primed from all those years of term papers, of so much pressure to excel that she couldn't afford to waste a second. There were stacks of paper beside her, yards and yards of catalog copy that she had to finish by this afternoon, the pages of corrections continually plunked into her In box. Spelling errors. Size mistakes. She looked at a picture of a laughing woman in a pair of cheap, synthetic jeans, her sunny blond hair thrown over one shoulder, her teeth a blizzard of white. *"Pure jeanius,"* she wrote. *"Leaner, cleaner, these are the new rhythms in blues."* The faster she typed, the better she liked it. The heady rhythm of the keys soothed her.

Sara was one of thirty people crammed into grey cubicles, arranged in rows that took up the whole nineteenth floor. "Welcome to McGraw-Hell," one woman said to Sara. The space had high white walls and polished wood floors like a gym's, and sealed windows ("so no one can jump out and end their misery," was the joke). It was sweltering in summer because the building's air-conditioning never worked properly, drafty and cold in the winter, and the same stale air seemed to circulate so that every time someone got a flu, it traveled up through the floors, and it infected everyone. It was a fairly new company, and even though no one other than employees ever came onto the floor, even though the catalog shoots were all held elsewhere, everyone was still expected to dress fashionably. Writing about clothing all day made Sara feel like the saleswoman in the Godiva shop up the block from her office, who couldn't even look at chocolates when she was finished working. When Sara woke up, she grabbed for what was clean, what didn't need ironing, what was closest, and if there was a designer name attached to any of her clothing, it was usually Gap.

The employees were mostly women, and all thin as swizzle sticks, with fussed-over hair and makeup, but Madame catered to women who were so over the usual plus sizes that they had real difficulties finding anything to fit them in the stores, and even if they could find something, it usually had all the style of a paper bag. The Madame woman, according to a profile Sara herself had recently written, was educated and style conscious. She held a good job, and was married or had a steady boyfriend who thought she looked great and sexy just the way she was, and who in fact approved of the larger woman's own unique beauty. The Madame woman had size 55 hips and a 40-inch bust, but the models for the catalog were only slightly overweight, which made even the synthetic fabrics Madame used look chic. Madame got lots of adoring letters from their customers, and only a rare letter complaining about the models, but every time there was one, Sara brought it to her boss. "Why can't we use real-sized models?" she asked, fanning the letter. "Why can't we celebrate size?"

"We're selling fantasy," Sara's boss told her. "Fantasy sells."

She knew it. She went back to her desk, crumpling the letter into a ball, tossing it into the trash. They loved Sara at Madame because they thought she understood the client, but what Sara understood was the yearning to accept who you were coupled with the yearning to be someone else. What she wrote to was that desire to believe anything that might make you feel better, the need not to see what might be painful to you.

Sara could name a line of clothing in five minutes instead of the two weeks it usually took everyone else, she could write an entire spring catalog in three days when it might take others a month, and she was the fastest typist anyone had ever seen. She didn't take half-hour breaks or go with groups to the ladies' room, lolling on the snazzy red leather couch in there, gossiping and reapplying makeup. She didn't make more than a few personal phone calls to her friends a day. Instead, she mainly stayed at her desk, working so intently you could call her name and she wouldn't hear you. You could tap her on the shoulder and she would start, not even realizing you were there watching her.

Six months after she got the job, on a hazy spring day, Sara's parents came to visit. They hadn't been thrilled by her new job or the sound of her new apartment, but she was sure when they saw it, when they saw the work she was doing, they'd be happy. She spent the whole morning scouring the apartment, buying fresh flowers. She casually left some catalogs around, the high-fashion ones that she had written all herself, the *Vogue* that had her ad in it for the Stretch Your Imagination campaign.

At ten, the buzzer rang. She buzzed them in and opened her door wide. She heard Jack complaining before he was even halfway up the third flight of stairs. She heard Abby panting, making jokes, and then there were her parents, looking just the same. Both of them had arms full of packages that they immediately set down.

Sara hugged her parents hard. "What do you think?" she asked happily.

They stared incredulously around. "The bathtub is in the kitchen," Abby murmured, trailing one hand along the plank covering it. "What kind of nonsense is that?"

Jack pointed to Sara's closet. "The bedroom's here?" he asked, opening the door to Sara's clothes and then quickly shutting it, his face closed, defeated. "What do they charge for a place like this?" Jack walked around Sara's apartment, as if he were measuring it. Foot for foot. He turned to Sara, amazed. "This floor has a slant."

"That's part of its charm—" Sara said, and Abby threw up her hands.

"I love my apartment," Sara said firmly. "I'm very happy."

Abby got busy, taking things out of the bags. Shampoo, soap, potholders. A set of sheets and a comforter. "All things you need," Abby insisted. "Maybe I should have mailed them earlier but I wanted to bring them myself, help you set up."

"Thank you, but I have those things," Sara said quietly. "And I am set up."

"Not the right kinds of things, I'll bet. And I'd put that table by the window, honey, not where you have it. You'll get better light." Abby started to move the table over. "No, no, I like it there," Sara protested, and Abby smiled, and kept pushing the table, and Sara gave up.

Jack sat down on the edge of Sara's futon, wincing when it made a creaking noise. "I admit I'm a little concerned here."

"You don't have to be."

"I'm your father. I'll always be concerned." He rubbed the bridge of his nose. "I thought you were happy at school. I thought things were working out."

"I'm happy," she said. She lifted up the catalog to show them. "Look, I did this whole catalog!" she said. "Everyone at Madame's loved it." Abby winced, but Jack tilted his head, reaching for the catalog. "Every page is mine," Sara said.

Jack leafed through it in silence and then set it down. Sara cleared her throat. "How about if we get something to eat?" she said finally.

They went to Da Silvano's in the Village. Sara had been saving to treat her parents, wanting to show them just how all right she really was. The restaurant was pretty, and as soon as they walked in, Jack looked more like himself, his eyes bright, his head aloft.

"Well, this is nice," he said, nodding at the gleaming silverware, the white tablecloths. After a glass of wine, he put his hand on Abby's, he leaned over and kissed her cheek.

Sara tried to eat slowly, because she knew she wouldn't be eating like this again, she could never afford to, and she wanted to remember every bite.

She was relieved her parents didn't talk about her during the meal. Instead, Jack told Sara he had a new client, a fashion designer who worked only in fluorescent colors and couldn't understand why her business wasn't booming. Abby talked about her work, too, about a little girl whose teeth came in black because her parents were feeding her all the bread and butter and sugar she could eat. She talked about the new neighbors who had four poodles. And she told Sara she was reading the collected works of B. F. Skinner. "So I can talk about your work with you," Abby said.

"I'm not in school anymore, Mom."

"But you will be. You'll go back."

"My work is copywriting."

"Maybe for now. But not forever." The busboy came to clear the table when they were finished. Jack sat back. Abby beamed.

"I really like my job," Sara said pointedly.

"Well, I really liked being a hygienist, too, when I first started," Abby said. "And then by the time I stopped loving it, I was too tired to go back to dental school."

"No," Sara said. "You're wrong about me."

"Are you still rebelling against us?" Abby said. "Is this what this is?"

Sara blinked. "Rebelling?" She shook her head. "I'm not sixteen. This is my job, Mom. This is my life. I'm doing the best that I can."

Abby carefully blotted her mouth. "I want you to do better."

In all, Sara's parents stayed only three days. They didn't do much, mostly ate at different places, or walked around, and when they left, Sara felt both relieved and yearning for them to stay.

Sara went inside her apartment. Her parents hadn't taken home any of the catalogs she had written, hadn't even looked at them. Sara sat down and leafed through one. There was a corduroy coat. "Sheared Genius." Everyone at work had gone crazy over it. It made her grin remembering how much fun she'd had thinking it up. She sat quietly, looking through the catalog, admiring her work, until she was tired enough to sleep.

After the first visit, Abby began to call her more often, every Friday, wanting to know how Sara was doing. They talked for a while and then Sara would always ask for her father, and he would always somehow be out. "Why doesn't he call me?" Sara asked.

"He hasn't called?" Abby said. "Why, that's terrible."

"Is he there? Can I speak to him now?"

"He's visiting a new client. He'll call tonight," Abby said.

And then Sara would get off the phone and stay in that night, not go to a movie, and still the phone wouldn't ring.

Finally, one day, she called him at his office. "Daddy," she said, and there was that silence again.

"Hi, sweetie," he said. "Can I call you back?"

"No. You never call me back."

She heard his sigh.

"Are you mad at me? Are you disappointed?" she asked.

"Honey, no. Of course not."

"Did I do something wrong?"

She could hear the hum of the wires. "Dad, tell me the truth."

"I'm glad you have a job," he said. "I'm happy you have friends. I just feel—" He didn't say anything for a moment. "I feel that I've failed you somehow. That I didn't do my job as a father."

"Dad. You didn't fail me."

"I never wanted lots of kids. Just one so I could do it really right. One I could concentrate on, give all my time and devotion to. I saw how the other fathers were, how they came home too tired to throw a ball with their kids, how it was always the mothers you saw at the PTA, at the zoo. Never a father. And that's important, especially for a girl. They've done studies on how it affects self-confidence, did you know that?"

"I've read them."

"Remember how I came on your class trips, how I was the only dad?"

"Yes." Sara remembered the zoo. The circus. The swan boats. A sea of skirts and just one pair of pants, her father, sitting beside her on a narrow open boat with a painted swan head and back feathers. She was so proud she could have died. He showed her how to crack the peanut shells before she threw the nuts to the hungry ducks. He hummed "The Men in My Little Girl's Life" to make her giggle.

"I want you to go back to school. I want you to have a real profession. A decent apartment. I want you to start dating nice men and get married, find someone who'll take care of you."

"I take care of myself."

"I feel like you're not living your real life. The life you were meant to have. I don't want you waking up at forty finding you missed your chances."

"I'm happy, I told you. I don't ask myself how I'll feel at forty."

"Well, maybe you should." In the background, Sara heard other voices. "Look, I have to go. But I'll call you. And I love you. You're my—" He hesitated. "My baby girl."

She held the phone tighter. "I love you, too," she said finally.

Abby began to write to Sara. She sent Sara stories about how Sara's old friend Judy was studying to be a cardiologist. Robin was now the youngest full professor Stanford had ever had. She sent Sara college catalogs. School and loan applications. She sent love. "From me and your father," Abby promised.

Sara didn't go back to school that year. Nor the next year or even two years after that. She still missed Kaysen, but sitting in Kaysen's office and talking seemed to belong to a whole other life, one that she couldn't return to. Although she half-expected to run into Kaysen, she never did. The people she would have run into from her classes moved on to graduate schools in other states, and her friends stopped asking her when she was going back; they accepted her life the way it was. And so did Sara.

In the spring, Madame gave her a huge raise and she found a bigger apartment on West Twenty-fourth Street. She was busily packing for her move, digging out her shoes from the back of her closet, when she came across all the years of gifts she had bought for Anne.

She sat down on the wood floor, unable to move. She rested her chin against one of the packages, swallowing hard. She hadn't bought gifts for her daughter in a long while. What was her daughter doing now? What kind of a voice did she have? Did she like to sing? Did she dance? Did she have any memory at all of Sara? Would George and Eva ever tell Anne about Sara or had they erased her from their lives? If Anne somehow walked right in front of Sara, would Sara even recognize her now, or would Anne be like one of those computer-aged pictures you sometimes saw on the back of a milk carton? *"The longer you wait, the harder it is,"* Abby had said.

Jolting to her feet, Sara got herself a glass of water, gulping it down. She couldn't bear it. Kaysen was wrong. Dive into the pain, Kaysen kept telling her. Sara had told that to her own patients when she had had them. But it was wrong advice. It was dangerous, because you didn't necessarily find buried treasure when you dove. You could dive so deep embolisms formed. You could bring something back up with you from the depths, thinking it would fade away in the light of day, but instead, it would gain

new life, transforming, and you'd find yourself drowning, even on the dri-
est land, and there'd be nothing to save you. And time didn't heal you.
That was the big lie. Time stretched so that some days pain was far from
you, and other days it was close as your own heartbeat. The best you could
hope for when it came to pain were scars, healing so you could get used to
them. And even then you had to do everything you possibly could not to
reopen the scars, not to make them fresh again, because then you might
bleed and bleed and never stop.

Ten years had passed since she had last seen Anne. You had to know
when it was time to let go, and how you did it was up to you. One of her
patients wrote the name of an ex-boyfriend on a piece of paper and
burned it. Another, suffering when her husband left her for her best
friend, told Sara that the only thing that had helped her was to have a ceremony for her lost marriage, saying a little prayer, releasing a clear helium
balloon into the sky, and as soon as the balloon disappeared into the sky,
she had felt better. She hadn't wanted to consider those stories when she
had been told them, hadn't wanted to think what they might mean to her.
These are my patients, not me, she had thought.

Sara got a big black garbage bag from a cabinet and tenderly laid the
presents inside. She wouldn't take these gifts with her to her new apartment. And she couldn't leave them here, caught like ghosts, whispering
their secrets to the next tenant.

Sara dragged the bag to Saint Mary's on the Upper West Side.

It was her favorite church. Big and stately, with two angels carved into
the cornices, and a heavy wood door. There was a small marquee as if the
church were a theater and every week they posted the sermon, which
always made Sara grin. *"God's rap is music to our ears. If you want to run the
race, why not walk with Jesus?"* Sara hesitated and glanced around. The church
was empty. No one on the street was paying attention to her. She climbed
the steps and set the bag down. She dug out the card she had written. *"Please
help these gifts find good homes."* Like abandoned babies, she thought. Like
something out of Abby's Girls in Trouble stories, only this time, it wasn't a

story at all, it was her real life and she was scripting her own ending.

She stood on the steps. It was a clear, cool night, and the sky was sprigged with stars. She touched the bag, just for a second. And then she turned, and without looking back, she began the walk back home.

chapter

ten

Sara was walking home from work, layouts and catalogs tucked in her bag. It was still light and she was taking her time, traveling out of her way so she could go up to Central Park first before she started back downtown, needing a fix of greenery. As soon as she got into the park, she felt better. Bikes whizzed past her, and the soft smattering of sound hit her like light dappling a window. She breathed deep, trying to relax, to get herself in the right frame of mind before she had to go back to her apartment and work. All that morning Hal had been on her case, yelling at her because she hadn't come up with a new name yet for the not-so-best-selling Grecian Swimdress, a homely, girdled bathing suit with a skirt draping to the knees. "You think a new name is going to make it sell better?" Sara asked. "Why can't we just make a decent, pretty swimsuit to sell? This suit looks like we're punishing these women for wanting to go to the beach."

Hal gave her fish eyes. "You and your new campaign had better be in my office by Monday morning," he warned.

She passed an old couple on a bench, holding hands, talking, and yearning clenched her stomach. She slowed her steps. What did you have to know to make something that miraculous last through your life? She glanced back at the couple. The man rested his head on the woman's shoulder, and the woman sighed with pleasure, like a cat in the sun.

Sara kept walking. Better to think about swim dresses.

Sometimes ideas came to her right away, zinging into her mind, and other times, such as now, it was like pawing through sludge for a dark brown jewel you had lost. Everything she thought of sounded absolutely wrong. Mermaidens. Dives. She laughed at herself.

She should go home, should start her work for Madame, but she couldn't tear herself away yet. She kept watching and then she was in front of the kids' playground. She leaned on the fence. A little girl was playing with a balloon. NO ADULT ALLOWED IN WITHOUT A CHILD. She stepped back, retracting her hand from the gate. She sat down on a bench and suddenly, despite herself, she felt shaken. She told herself she was just tired, just overworked, and then she covered her face with her hands.

"Hey, are you okay?"

She looked up. A man was standing there, in jeans and sneakers.

"I'm fine——" she said.

"You don't sound fine," he said doubtfully. "Your voice is quavering."

She stood up. The concern on his face made her embarrassed. "I'm fine," she said.

"Are you sure?"

She nodded. Kids squealed from the playground. The balloon bobbed. "Yeah." She slung her purse on her shoulder. "I'd better get going."

"Okay if I walk you a little? Just to make sure you're okay?"

She glanced up at him. "I don't know you——"

"Well, I'm Scott. Scott Fields," he said.

"Sara," she said, and then she joined him.

While they walked, she sneaked glances at him. She liked his straight nose, and his long black hair, liked the way you couldn't tell what color his eyes were because they kept changing in the light, from green to brown to hazel.

"So," he said, looking at her suddenly, as if he were trying to read her. "Student?"

She shook her head. To her surprise, she heard Abby's voice whispering in her ear: "Tell people you're a writer and stop at that," and for the first time, Sara felt shamed by her job. Well, Abby wasn't here, and Scott was, and Sara dug into her bag and pulled out one of her catalogs. A woman poised in white flowing trousers. "Wear the Pants," the headline said. "Making Fashion into a Plus."

They stopped walking and he looked at the catalog. "Madame!" he said.

"You know the catalog?" Sara said, surprised.

He leafed through the pages. "Sure do," he said, "my mother's bible." And then he looked at her quizzically. "Wait," he said, confused. "You're a plus-sized model?"

"No, no, I write the copy!"

"You're kidding!" he said, delighted. "Wait until I tell my mother! She'll go nuts!"

"It's fun," she admitted. She glanced at his shirt. "The white stuff," she laughed.

"Do my sneakers."

"Set the pace with stepped-up styling that sneaks up on you."

He laughed, glancing down at his shoes. "Did you always want to do that, to write?"

She shrugged. "I was the only little girl who wanted to be a shrink. Guess that was one of those dreams I gave up."

"No, no, you didn't," he insisted. "I mean, in a way you still are a shrink. That catalog does more for my mother than a bottle of Valium. She looks forward to it. And I bet a lot of other women do, too." He helped her put the catalog back in her bag.

Sara smiled. He was nice, this guy. She was starting to like him.

"Teacher?" she guessed, looking at him.

"Architect. I'm lucky because I'm a designer. Business is so bad now that half the architects I went to school with are driving cabs. I was the fool who held out for what I loved," he said. He molded the air as he talked, as if he were shaping clay, and she couldn't help but notice how large and graceful his hands were. "But you don't go into architecture for the money." He wanted to have his own firm, he told her, and eventually, he wanted to design his own house, build it from the bottom brick up. "Most of the architects I know like modern, so I guess I'm a throwback. I like all those old features, the wraparound porches that keep you cooler summers, that let you get some feel of outside when it rains. It's crazy to throw out the past just because it's the past, don't you think?"

They came to the subway. People were pouring down into it, jostling their way up onto the street. In ten minutes, she'd be home. "Well . . ." She fumbled for words.

"Would you have dinner with me?" Scott asked.

Her smile spread across her face. She tried to think about her schedule, to reach into her purse and dig out a pen or a scrap of paper. "Almost got a pen," she said. He touched her hand, and then she felt a jolt of heat and looked up at him, startled.

"No. I mean right now," he said. "Let's have dinner now."

They went to a Mexican place he knew in the West Village, a little hole in the wall that he said was his favorite place in the world. The restaurant had bright striped Mexican blankets on the walls and margaritas the size of soup bowls, and the two waitresses were young and cheerful and dressed in T-shirts and jeans.

Sara folded herself onto the tiny chair, her knees knocking against Scott's, but she didn't take them away because she felt that same jolt of heat again. She couldn't concentrate on the menu and, in the end, ordered the same chicken tamales Scott did.

Scott was telling her about growing up an only child in a Santa Fe suburb. He told her how his mother used to scribble sayings from the Bible on the napkins she packed in his lunch box every day. "Almost every one of them was frightening. I remember finding 'God has cast me into the mire,' and she just loved 'Fret not yourself because of the wicked.' She used that one a couple of times. I always felt she was trying to tell me something but all she'd say was, 'That's between you and God.' That was her way to get me to head for church and pray for answers." He grinned. "It was my way to head for the local movie theater. To me, double features were very, very holy."

Sara laughed. The waitress set down the tamales. "Very hot plates," she warned.

Sara hadn't eaten all day. She loved Mexican food, but the way this food was prepared tasted different from any Mexican food she had had before. Each dish was more fiery than the next, and her mouth began to feel raw, her stomach was in a tangle. She took a big, enthusiastic bite, and instantly her mouth felt in flames.

"These are my favorites," Scott said and Sara nodded. "Wonderful," she managed to get out, and she grabbed for her water and finished it in a gulp.

"Are you all right?" Scott said. He handed her his water. "Have more."

She nodded and sipped, moving her tongue experimentally. She bet she had burned a layer of skin off the roof of her mouth.

"Okay now? Good. Now tell me about you."

"About me?" She played with her fork. "What do you want to know?"

"Oh—everything."

She took another long, slow sip of water. Her mouth cooled, her stomach settled a little, and she started to talk.

She told Scott about growing up in Boston, about her parents. She told him how her father was an accountant, and how he had once bought her a real cash register for her birthday to teach her math, stocking it with ten dollars' worth of real money. "He thought it would teach me the value of money, and it sure did. I learned that ice cream cost a dollar, that three dollars could buy you more than enough chocolate to make yourself feel sick, and that you could empty a whole cash register in two weeks without even trying."

Scott's smile widened and he put one hand casually on the table, and all Sara could think was that she could move her hand an inch and she'd be touching his.

"I've been making you talk and your food's getting cold," Scott apologized. "You eat, and I'll be right back."

He left the table and she saw him head for the restrooms at the back of the restaurant. The restaurant was noisy with people. Sara's plate was still filled with food and all of it was so fuel-injected with jalapeños that she thought she'd spontaneously combust if she took another bite. She didn't want to hurt Scott's feelings since he was so enthusiastic about this place. She tried to arrange the food on her plate so it looked as though she had eaten more, pushing it to the side the way she did when she was a kid, but even so, her plate still looked loaded. Sneaking a glance around for Scott, she quickly spooned the food into her napkin, folding it over into a ball. Then she crossed her knife and fork on her plate and there, suddenly, was Scott. She put one hand to her stomach. "This was so delicious," she said, and Scott smiled. "Didn't I tell you?" he said, and then he caught the waitress's attention, making a check mark in the air for the bill.

Outside was muggy, the air thick as a woolen coat. Scott walked her home, but he didn't take her hand or touch her again, and the one time she touched his shoulder, he kept looking straight ahead. She wasn't sure what had happened to make him suddenly seem to like her less, but the closer they got to her apartment, the quieter he got, which made Sara want to talk more. They passed the Chelsea Cinema and she told him she had seen three movies there last night. She looked up at the marquee. "Oh, new movies are up!" she said. She felt fake as painted pennies. "Have you seen the new DeNiro?" she persisted.

He looked up at the marquee and then at her. "I hear that's great," he said, "I love DeNiro," but he didn't ask her if she wanted to see it. Instead, he pointed to a building across the street. "I like Chelsea because it's got these great old buildings," he said. "Look at that stonework, that nice brick detailing. Who does work like that today?"

She didn't know what to do at her door, whether to invite him up, or say good night, but she didn't have to. He thrust out his hand and took hers. He smiled warmly. His palm was dry, his grip as steady as if he were shaking the postman's hand. "Thanks for coming to dinner," he said pleasantly, and then, before she could say anything, or scribble down her phone number for him, he turned and started walking the other way.

Her apartment was eerily quiet. No one was shouting or stomping or doing anything that would reverberate through her walls. Her answering machine blinked with messages. A woman at work named Jennifer. Kate. A man someone had given her name to, clearing his throat. "Would you like to come to dinner with me, say next Friday at eight?" he asked, pausing as if any moment she might pick up the phone and answer.

She sat down at the table and tried to work, but she kept thinking about Scott. She didn't have to replay the good-night scene to know when a man wasn't interested. He hadn't even asked her last name. Forget it, she told herself. She glanced at the clock. There would be other men, other hearts that would make hers beat a little faster. Work, she told herself, think about Madame's bathing suits.

The next morning, Sara was on her way to the greengrocer's for supplies—pretzels and cheese and juice—planning to do nothing but hole up in her apartment and work.

Her block was busy with people, and most of them seemed stunned by the heat. A turtle walked along the edge of the sidewalk, urged on by two children. A man turned on his boom box and salsa blared, making Sara wince and cross the street.

Jesus, this street, she thought. What she'd give for a serene little country house, for cool breezes and blue lake water. "Sara!" someone called.

She turned, and there, standing in the doorway of Healthy Chelsea, a tall glass of something gold and frosty looking in his hand, smiling out at her in delight, was Scott.

"What are you doing here?" she said, hoping he'd say he was here because of her, but he just shrugged.

"Checking on a building, stopping for juice." He held it up so she could see and then he looked closer at her and grinned, took his napkin and wiped at her nose.

"You got some ink there," he said. "What are you up to?"

"Taking a walk."

He checked his watch. "Can I come?"

She didn't have a clue where they were going, and he didn't really seem to know, either, but in any case, she didn't care. Even in her platform sneakers, he was a head taller than she, and she liked the way he seemed to measure his steps with hers, as if he had asked her to dance. She could have walked forever, jet-propelled. She kept looking at him out of the corner of her eye, marveling that he was here, beside her again. He asked her a million questions. How was work? Had she seen any movies?

Read any books he should know about? They were strolling, but every-thing felt in fast-forward. The pavement was uneven, and she stumbled, but he grabbed her hand to steady her. "All right now?" he said, and she nodded, and when they continued walking, he kept her hand in his.

She began to try and steer him someplace, to the diner she liked on Eighteenth Street, to the bookstore with the great café. She pointed to the Joyce Theater and he nodded happily. "I love that place," he told her. "Last week, my friend Mona and I saw Mark Morris there."

Sara's heart tumbled in her chest. She smiled evenly and said nothing. They walked around and around for a while, and were heading back to her apartment.

When they got there, he came to a complete stop, then he let go of her hand and grew silent. She wasn't ready for him to walk away from her. She tried to imagine what it might feel like to touch his chest, to place his hand against her cheek. Heat rose inside of her.

"I have iced tea," she blurted. "Would you like some?"

He hesitated, considering. "No," he said. And then, "All right."

She led him upstairs. As soon as she opened the door, Scott was study-ing her floor-to-ceiling windows, so tall she had had to get blinds custom made for them. He pulled the blinds up. "Great windows," he said. "Bet you get a whole lot of light in here." He traced a hand along the panes.

He sat on her couch, and she switched on her air conditioner and brought him some iced tea. She felt as if she were in a kind of trance, being pulled toward him. As soon as she put the tea on the table, he reached over and touched one of her ringlets before he abruptly let his hand fall back into his lap.

"I should get going," Scott said. She sat down beside him and put her hand on his face, and when he didn't move, she took her hand away, shamed. "I'm sorry—I thought—"

"What?"

"Are you married?"

"What? No!" he laughed, but she stayed serious.

"I'm not good at reading people sometimes," she said. Her shoulders rose and she rested her hands in her lap, hesitating. "I like you," she admit-ted. "Are we just friends? Am I not your type?"

"Sara," he said, looking down at his hands. "I guess I need to tell you something."

She was certain he could hear the sick rolling in her stomach. Whenever someone told you they needed to tell you something, it was usually something you didn't really want to hear.

"There was this woman," he said, carefully. "Wren. We were going to get married last year, then a week before the wedding she told me she was in love with someone else."

"Oh no."

He rubbed Sara's thumb. "I saw the wedding announcement six months ago. I still can't figure it out. We were always together. When had she even had time to meet anyone else, let alone fall in love with him?" He pulled Sara's hand up and kissed it. "When I met you, I didn't know what to do, because I liked you instantly. I couldn't figure out how to protect myself and still see you, so I've been trying to play it cool."

Outside, a siren whined. "Do you still love her?" Sara rested her chin on her knees.

"I've still got my wounds. She called me once to ask if I'd renovate their loft in Soho. I couldn't do it." He sighed. "What about you? Any secrets I should know?"

Sara looked away.

"Should I have not told you? Did I blow it?" Scott asked.

"There's no reason to tell anyone," Abby had said. *"As soon as people know, they'll look at you differently. They'll think different thoughts about you."* Sara shook the image off.

"Come on, I showed you mine, you show me yours," Scott coaxed.

She couldn't look at him while she was telling him about Anne and George and Eva, about Danny. Instead, she looked at her toes, at the square of light by the far window. She had told this story to herself so many times that it felt as if someone else were telling it now. When she dared look at him, he was so silent, she began to be afraid of what he must think of her. "I'm sorry," she said. "I shouldn't have told you."

"I'm not going anywhere, Sara," he said quietly. "I'm glad you told me. And I'm so sorry." And then he reached for her hair again, and he pulled her to him, kissing her full on the mouth. She put her arms about his neck and leaned toward him. She liked the way he smelled, like wood. She licked his shoulder and found she liked the way he tasted, too, salty and warm, and then he held her tighter, and they rolled onto the floor.

She slid out of her clothes, and then he touched her again, and her lids floated shut.

Afterward, lying there, his eyes on her, she felt suddenly self-conscious. Her stomach had flattened long ago, and her stretch marks were faint, silvery webs you wouldn't notice unless you looked as intently at her as Scott was doing. She shifted position away from him. She glanced at Scott. If he said anything at all to her, she knew she'd feel undone. He was looking at her now as if he were memorizing her. She reached for her blouse and his hand stopped her. "No, don't. I love to look at you," he marveled.

She was so warm that her hair lay damply on her body. "I'm a little chilly."

"I'll warm you, then." He leaned closer to her and gently rubbed her hands, her legs, the tips of her toes, and she felt her body relaxing, so she scooted closer to him, finally taking his arms and wrapping them about her.

"I wasn't sure you liked me this way," she said happily.

"I liked you the second I saw you sitting on the bench. I liked you even more when I saw you hide your food in your napkin."

She flushed. "You saw that!" she said, and he grinned.

"I just wanted to take things really slow. Then I realized I couldn't."

She lay beside him, his arms about her. "We'll sleep just like this," he told her.

He called her two days later to go to the movies, and then the next week to see a play. And once, at the movies, as soon as the lights went out, he gave her a gentle nudge and fit a plastic champagne glass in her hand and slowly, carefully, poured her some wine from a tiny bottle he had snuck in. She got used to seeing him two or three times a week and sometimes he just showed up. One night, she was bounding out of her apartment, a book she was reading in one hand, and she banged right into a group of tough-looking street kids. She stopped short, but they weren't interested in her. Instead, they were scowling at Scott, who was crouched down, snapping picture after picture of the building next to hers, oblivious. "What the fuck you doin', man," a guy in loose, baggy jeans shouted. Scott took one more shot, stood upright, and then he spotted Sara, and his whole face filled with light, and he snapped a shot of her, standing there, mouth open, dumbfounded.

They walked. "What's the book?" he asked. Danny had always picked up the books Sara was reading and wanted to read them, too. "It's all about Paris," she told Scott, handing him the book. He glanced at it and then handed it back to her. "Want to read it when I'm done?" she asked, and he shrugged. "I guess," he said.

They went to his apartment on West Eighteenth, a roomy one-bedroom, with big windows. She finished the book that night, and left it on his nightstand, and two weeks later, when it was still there, she brought it back home.

It was Friday and Scott was showing a client the construction site for the client's new house, and Sara was tagging along. The client's name was Harry Morgan and he was middle-aged and disgruntled and kept thrusting his hands in his pockets, and the more excited Scott got, the more Harry's mouth formed a line.

It was just one huge space right now. A few walls had already been built, some ceilings. Scott strode across the floor, beaming, as if he were showing off his child. "Bedroom," he said, waving his hands. "Kitchen here. Skylight. Gorgeous skylight so the room's always bright."

"Skylights are expensive."

"You'll save on electricity, I'm telling you," Scott said.

She saw the tender way Scott touched a beam, how he talked about the fireplace as if it were the most marvelous thing in the world. "I'll crack the tiles in the bathroom to give them texture," he said, ignoring the way Harry was shaking his head no.

"Oak door," Scott said, pointing to the entrance.

"Aluminum," said Harry. "I mean it."

That night, Scott put in the oak door himself. When Harry saw the finished section the next day, his jaw dropped open. "If you don't like it, I'll take it off," Scott said, but Harry shook his head adamantly. "I've never seen anything so goddamn beautiful in my life," the client said. He looked at Sara. "He that persuasive with you?" he asked.

"Always," she said.

But as elated as Scott was about most of his projects, she saw him in a funk over others. He came over one evening an hour late because he had been arguing with a client, a production company. "They're threatening not to pay me," he said.

"They can't do that!"

"Happens all the time." He had designed an office for this production company, he had had months of meetings with them, he had been on top of everything, from the conceptional design to the schematics to the design development. "I was just wiped out from overseeing the construction every day, from dealing with the permits, but when it was finished, it all seemed worth it. I just loved the space. But my client took one look and said it was like dating a beautiful girl and finding out she's wearing dirty underwear." Scott stood up and began pacing. "The closets weren't big enough for him. He didn't like the high ceilings because he said it would cost more than they wanted to heat them. 'Form has got to follow function,' he said. Like I don't know that. Like any architect doesn't know that. But beauty counts, too." He threw up his hands.

"This was a great job. I could use it to get more, and he won't let me in to photograph it. I'd sneak in when he wasn't there, but even security knows my face."

Sara suddenly laughed.

"What?" he said. "This is serious."

"They don't know my face," she said. "I'll do it for you."

She wore a jacket with pockets, a camera tucked into one of them. "I spy," she said.

"If anyone asks, say you're looking for Meyers' Candies," Scott told her. "It's the previous tenant. I'll be waiting around the corner."

Scott waited for her a block away, and she strode into the building, walking as if she belonged there, as if she had done this a hundred times before. She swung her arms, she kept her head up. A security guard in a blue uniform was dozing over his newspaper and he gazed up at her. Sara averted her eyes and riffled in her purse. "Oh, great, I forgot my ID card again!" she said. "Can you believe it?"

He drummed fingers on the table, considering. "I only have to run upstairs and get something, I'll be right down—" Sara said. "I'm so sorry, I don't mean to be a pain to you."

The guard considered her and then he pushed a paper toward her. "Sign," he said, and she did, in a big loopy scrawl, Betty Lou Leverbrothers.

She rode the elevator up two floors, and as soon as she saw the glass doors, she took the camera out. Her pulse was beating in her throat and she was sweating, so her shirt felt pasted to her back. No one was in the office, and each step she took echoed.

Scott was right, this place was beautiful. One curving wall separated the space, a high ceiling made it feel light and airy, and for the first time she understood what he meant by the quality of a space. She felt good in this room. Whisking out the camera, she began snapping away. She was almost to her last picture when a voice behind her said, "Do you need help?" and Sara quickly hid the camera in her pocket. A man in a dark suit was frowning at her. "What are you doing? Did I see you taking pictures?"

"Are you Mr. Meyers?" she blurted and his frown deepened. "Meyers' Candies?"

"Why, they moved," he said, folding his arms, puzzling over her. His eyes slid over her. "Who are you?" he asked, and then Sara backed out.

"Wait!" he called, coming toward her, but Sara was running, past the elevator to the stairwell. Two flights and she took the steps two at a time the whole way down. When she got to the first floor, she was panting so hard, the guard looked at her with concern. "Told you I'd be just a minute. I can't thank you enough," she said, and he smiled at her.

"It's okay, Ms. Leverbrothers," he said.

She ran outside to Scott, who was pacing anxiously by the next building. She dug out the camera and placed it in his hands. "Evidence!" she said
gleefully.

He looked at her, delighted.

"Why are you looking at me like that?"

"You're really as happy about this as I am."

"Of course I am. Why wouldn't I be? You and me—we're like the
united front."

Grabbing her, he kissed her full on the mouth.

She woke in the middle of the night. She had been dreaming she was
building a house herself, and suddenly, everywhere she looked there were
secret compartments. She blinked and there he was, sitting up, watching
her, a funny smile playing on his mouth. "What happened?" she said, rubbing the sleep from her eyes.

"You were singing in your sleep," he said. "I never knew anyone who
did that."

She laughed. "What was I singing?"

He hummed a bar or two, something jazzy she couldn't recognize.

"Was I in tune?"

His face grew grave.

"What's wrong?" she said. He picked up a section of her hair and let it
fall through his fingers. "Is this too fast?" she asked hesitantly. "Is it because
of what I told you? Do you need to press the pause button for a while?"

"I love you," he said.

chapter

eleven

They started looking for a place to live together, traipsing about the city. They saw brownstones in Brooklyn Heights and Park Slope. They looked in Hoboken and Jersey City and Manhattan. They saw a beautiful old two-bedroom on West Eighty-eighth Street, four large rooms, wood floors, and big, bright windows, but it wasn't until they got outside the building again that Scott shook his head. "What's wrong with it?" Sara said, mystified.

"It's not the apartment. I can't move into this building. It's ugly. Look how mottled those bricks are. You can tell they were painted, that someone sandblasted the paint off."

Dumbfounded, Sara looked at the building. She traced her hand along the rough red bricks. She studied the black door, the row of cement steps. It all looked okay to her. "But who cares about the building?"

"I do. It's part of the whole space."

"Architects," she teased, but she turned around and looked at the building again. Would she have even noticed the flaw if he hadn't pointed it out? "You're sure?"

"We'll find something. It's got to be just perfect."

They also began going to realtors, who were usually brisk young women, pushing expensive spaces at them. "You like lofts?" one realtor asked. "I can show you a loft to die for right in SoHo. Great block, too."

Scott grew quiet. Wren, Sara thought, the one who had jilted him, lived in SoHo.

"We'll be in touch," he told the realtor.

Outside, Sara took his arm. "I thought you were over Wren," she said.

"Of course I am," Scott said, but he wouldn't meet her eyes.

Sara hesitated. She tugged at his sleeve. "Hey," she said. "Remember that old joke about New York? It's so big that you can live on the same block as your ex for years and never once run into each other." She smiled hopefully.

"It has nothing to do with Wren," he said.

"I met someone," Sara told her parents on the phone.

"Is he good enough for you?" Jack asked.

"Better than I deserve," Sara said.

"Well, I'm just saying. Never be with anyone you couldn't imagine yourself being able to live without," Jack said. "That'll get you through any rough patches."

"Good advice," said Abby briskly. "And just remember, honey, the past is the past."

"What's that supposed to mean? Don't you think we tell each other everything?"

"Good Lord," Abby said. "Is that going to make you happy?"

Well, Sara was more than happy. Elated, she couldn't believe her good fortune. Scott sent her a dozen yellow roses at work for her twenty-eighth birthday. He left sweet notes under her pillow and in the brown bag lunch she carried to work. *"You are a treat. I love you."* They met each other's parents, both sets beaming with sunny approval. And lately, he had begun looking at buildings differently. He didn't talk so much about the structure of the windows, or the way the design let in light or hid it, anymore. Instead, he talked about whether Sara would like to live in that neighborhood, if she wanted a doorman or not. Sara took his hand and kissed it. "I'd live anywhere with you," she said.

But the thing was, after a year, they were still living out of each other's places. Her clothes were in his closet, her shoes under his bed, her name on his answering machine. After a while, Sara would stop at her place only for clean clothes or a book she might need, because most of her things were at Scott's. Oh, they still looked for a place to live, but Scott always managed to find some mistake in the building that couldn't be fixed without way too much effort or expense. The windows weren't big enough, the floor had a tiny slant. Sara got used to walking into places she found wonderful, only to have Scott knock them out of the running. It became almost a joke, something they'd tease each other about. Five years and they still hadn't found the right place. "Why don't you two just get married?" Abby asked when she phoned. "What are you waiting for?"

"The right moment," Sara said with a half-smile.

"So we don't share a space yet, so what?" Scott said when Sara told him what Abby had said. "We spend more time together than most married people. And we're twice as happy as any couple I know."

He nudged her toward him. "Oh, yes we are," he said and kissed her forehead.

It was Friday and she was taking antibiotics for a respiratory infection. She was also expecting her period, which, because she was on the pill, usually came like clockwork. It didn't come Friday, or Saturday, or all that week, and when it was Monday, she began to feel a little light-headed, but she chalked it up to not eating, and popped her antibiotic. Four more to go and then she'd be done. But it wasn't until she was eating a cheese sandwich at a local restaurant that she started to feel queasy.

Half-dazed, she moved past the coffee bar, past the fried foods bar, to the bin of red apples and blue plums, to the whole grain muffins wrapped in cellophane. She stopped, bracing her hands on the counter. What was this feeling? It felt like moths trapped inside of her, crazy to get out.

"Lady——" someone said, and she moved forward, headed for the phone in the corner.

"I feel so nauseous," she told the doctor.

"Well, antibiotics can do that," he said.

"Maybe I'm just premenstrual," she said hopefully. "It's always worse when my period is late."

"It's late? How late?"

One of the moths in Sara's belly careened past her ribs. "A week, but I'm on the pill!"

"Well, antibiotics can affect the pill, though it's not likely. You may want to double up on your birth control, just to be safe."

"Antibiotics can affect the pill?" she said. "Why didn't you tell me that when you prescribed them?"

He cleared his throat. "It seldom happens. But call me next week," he said.

All that day, she couldn't concentrate, couldn't tell how she really felt about this. Being pregnant at sixteen was one thing, being pregnant when you were an adult, with a job and a man who loved you, was another. Did she want to do this? Would it feel like redemption, a second chance; or would it remind her instead of everything she had lost?

Stop, she told herself. It was probably nothing. Her period wasn't even all that late for her to be getting so worked up. Walking down the hall, she absently put one hand on her stomach when someone passing said, "Bellyache, Sara?" and she put her hand down.

She walked home, trying to calm herself, to steady her nerves. She peeked at the windows of all the shops, catching glimpses of fancy silk shirts, leather boots, every item idly turning in her mind, turning to copy. *Leather weather,* she thought. *Stay tuned for the leather report.* She was about to cross the street, to cut over to Fifth Avenue, when her stomach roiled and she felt a dry heave. Walking over to the nearest shop window, she pressed her fingertips against the glass and squinched her eyes shut until it passed. *What if,* she thought. *Oh God, what if.* She opened her eyes and saw a row of yellow handbags.

The doctor was wrong. It didn't feel too early for her. When she was sixteen and pregnant, she had glossed over her symptoms, had refused to notice what was happening to her body, but she wouldn't make that mistake again. Sara straightened and headed for the nearest Rite-Aid. She went to the aisle where they had the pregnancy testing kits, the ones that would tell you twenty-four hours after your period hadn't made its appearance. Two women came and stood beside her, both of them laughing. "Oh, I hope, I hope, I hope," said one of the women, clutching one of the kits to her chest.

Sara bought a kit, and went to Macy's, to the fourth-floor bathroom, where the blowers were so loud you might think no one else was around. *Please,* she thought. *Oh please.* She hoisted her skirt and peed on the tube and three minutes later, there it was, a blue line so faint she wasn't sure what it might mean. She stared at the package, trying to compare, but all she could discern was that it was a line and, as such, it meant something. Clutching the tube, she walked out of Macy's and to Scott's.

She heard the music before she put the key in the door, Scott's voice belting out "Good Day Sunshine" with the Beatles, slightly off-key, full of enthusiasm. When she opened the door, she saw him in the kitchen, cutting up salad greens. "Hey, sweetie," he said to her and she anxiously smiled.

"You look green about the gills," he said. "You okay?" He picked up an uncut carrot and chomped, his teeth even and white as a rabbit's. "You can tell a lot about a man from his teeth," George used to tell Sara, but he never told her exactly what that was.

"You want to lie down until dinner's ready?" Scott asked.

"I think I'm pregnant," she whispered.

He stopped chewing and put the carrot down. "You're on the pill."

She shook her head. "The doctor said antibiotics can screw things up."

"Well, that's nice of him to tell us that now," Scott said. "Isn't that something he should have told us before he put you on those horse pills?"

Her legs buckled and she hinged down in one of the chairs. "I bought a kit. I took the test. There was a blue line."

He pulled out another chair and sat facing her. "Are you sure?"

"What will we do?" she asked quietly.

"Well, we'll take care of it, of course."

"Of course?" Her voice sounded rougher than she expected. She suddenly thought of those billboards she used to see when she was pregnant with Anne. There was always a picture of a baby, six months big and rosy with health. *"Kill her today it's murder. Kill her yesterday it's abortion."* *Give her away, it's death,* Sara thought.

"I thought you were prochoice—"

"I am, but—"

"But what? You wouldn't want an abortion after what happened to you the last time you got pregnant?"

"Why does one thing have anything to do with the other?" she said. "It's not the same thing. I'm not sixteen. I have a job. We're a couple."

"What are you saying?"

Her mouth was so dry she couldn't believe words could form in it. "Would it be the worst thing in the world if we had a child?" *If we kept it, if we raised it,* she thought.

He looked at her, perplexed. "Sara, yes. It would. Kids shouldn't be accidents. They should be planned and loved."

Sara drew back. "Who says it wouldn't be loved!"

Scott grabbed at her hands, making her focus on his face. "My parents didn't plan for me. They used to have these great pictures of the two of them, holding hands, kissing, dancing in the moonlight, and I can't remember them ever even touching, the whole time I lived in that house, and when I asked my mother about it, she started telling me how she had me six months after the wedding, and then all the dancing stopped."

"It doesn't have to be that way."

He held her face in his hands. "I love you. I'm not ready for kids now. I admit it. I'm selfish and I don't want to share you with anyone. Not yet. Tell me that's not so terrible."

"Of course that's not so terrible—but I can't help feeling what I feel! I can't help it. And sometimes things just happen, and you have to be open to them—"

"I don't want any of it to be the way it was for you before. Something you make the best of." He leaned forward to kiss her. "Anyway, those kits aren't infallible. Wait a bit, then call the doctor, and we'll see."

"But what if I *am* pregnant—" she said, but he was ignoring her now, bending to kiss her, and she lowered her head so he was kissing her hair instead of her mouth.

All that week, she saw pregnant women everywhere. In the supermarket, a hugely pregnant woman wandered with her cart in front of Sara, and no matter what aisle Sara turned down there she was, making Sara so frustrated, she finally abandoned her cart and fled the store. At lunch, Sara sat opposite a woman grimacing over her cottage cheese. "Calcium," she said. "When this baby's born, I'm never eating cottage cheese again." At work, the dresses she was writing about were so full of fabric, Yvonne joked they should call them "the new maternity." Every five minutes Sara went to the ladies' room to check her panties for blood, and every time there was none, she braced her hands against the cool of the sink and tried to think what she felt.

She and Scott had stopped talking about it, as if a light had switched off. But they didn't have to talk for her to know how he felt. He walked gingerly around her as if the slightest word might send something off in her. At night, she tried to cuddle against him, wanting comfort, but he patted her shoulder in a fatherly way. "When you're feeling better," he told her and then turned over away from her, and in minutes she heard his faint snore, while she stayed awake, staring up at the ceiling.

That night, Sara woke at four in the morning. Outside, a car honked. Someone screamed, "Lydia! I love you, Lydia!" Blue morning light poured into the room, but when she looked at the clock, she saw it was nearly four. Scott snored and turned in bed, pulling the blanket with him, lifting it up over the sheet, just enough so Sara, squinting in the dim light, could see the line of blood streaked on the sheet.

She started to cry. How stupid she had been to dare to imagine she could have been pregnant, that she could be so lucky. She grabbed for a tissue, waking Scott. Alarmed, he wrapped himself about her. "What is it?" he asked. "What's happened?"

"I got my period," she said, and he whooped and hugged her, "Thank God!" he exulted, and then he saw her face and his own fell. "Oh, I'm so sorry, so sorry, honey." Wrapping her in his arms, he rocked her, he soothed, but all she could feel was his relief, rising up off him like a wave of heat, and all she could wonder about was how anybody could ever feel this empty, this absolutely alone.

She threw herself back into her work, coming up with two hundred names for a new line of cosmetics for Madame, a name they wanted to sound Italian but not really be Italian. "Fienello," she said out loud. "Plississamo." She did the catalog for the spring line of shoes, which went over so well, that later, they let her do the one for the fall boots. The babies she had seen on the street, sprouting like seedlings, the expectant mothers, vanished as suddenly as they had appeared, and all she saw now were the well-heeled working women, the snazzy polished shoes of the young and dating and working. She joined the gym down the street so that nights, when Scott was working, she grabbed for her sweats and went to the track, running off her tension until she was bathed in sweat and felt more hopeful.

One night, when she was in bed, she reached for Scott, she stroked his belly, wanting him, and he kept sleeping. Rubbing against him, like a cat, she whispered his name. She saw his head lift from the pillow.

"Oh, sweetie, I'm so tired," he said. "Tomorrow." He groaned, yawning, ruffling her hair affectionately. "I promise."

She cuddled against him, wanting to be cradled in his arms as they slept, the way they usually did. "Can I have a bit more room?" he said, rolling from her so her hand slipped off his shoulder.

"Has something happened to us?" she asked. "Is it because of the pregnancy scare?"

He turned around to look at her. "You think needing more room in bed means I don't love you?" he said. He kissed her so tenderly she forgot she had ever felt slighted. Desire flared in her belly, but when she stroked his face, he was already sleeping.

The next morning, when they were walking to breakfast, she found herself looking at all the other couples who were holding hands, who were walking close together, and she felt empty, yearning, and reached for his hand, which he held for a few seconds and then let go. "I love you," she said, and he nodded happily at her. He craned his head to look at a building. "You love me?" she asked him, and he suddenly frowned. "What's going on with you now? Why do you have to ask me this all the time?" he said. "Of course I love you. Don't you know that? I'm comfortable with you. I don't have to always paw you to show it." It was her turn to get silent. *Paw,* she thought. Like an animal. Paw.

But the more comfortable he became, the more he didn't seem to see her. On their walks, he zoomed ahead, cutting across traffic, leaving her stranded on the other side. "Hey!" she shouted. He looked at her, surprised. "How'd you get all the way over there?" he called. She reached for his hand and grabbed it.

It was Monday and Sara was back home in her parents' living room, her heels propped up on the coffee table. It was a spur-of-the-moment visit, a few days because Scott had had to go upstate to try and talk some people into putting more windows into a prison he was designing. "These guys need more light," Scott had said. Three days without Scott, and every nerve inside of her was longing for him, pulling like little magnets.

At night, she bunched up the pillow, like a body beside her, flinging her arm about it, drawing it close. She knew it was impossible, but she was so used to having him by her that she kept thinking she heard him coming up the walk, moving in the kitchen, just out of her sight. Sara stood up, so restless she couldn't stand being in her own skin.

A bowl of fruit sat on the dining room table. There was raisin bread from the bakery, but she was still feeling stuffed from the blinis she had had last night at the Russian restaurant Abby and Jack had taken her to. She had talked about Scott all through dinner.

"Well, he seems wonderful," Abby had said, lifting her wineglass and clicking it against Jack's, and then against Sara's. But her voice sounded flat, and Sara could tell that Abby was thinking that even the dearest man wasn't the same as a graduate degree.

And then, to Sara's surprise, Jack had reached across the table and taken her hand in the two of his. "I hope he's taking good care of you," he said.

That night, Sara had picked up the phone and called Scott at his hotel. His machine had answered after two rings, but she still left a message, the same one she had for the last two days. "God, do I miss you."

She wished Scott would call her back because the day was stretching out in front of her like a plain white sheet. She plopped on the couch and read two magazines. She finished a novel she had brought, about a man whose amnesia saves him from grieving his dead wife, then she got herself a bowl of red grapes and sat and watched *Blade Runner* on cable. The gorgeous android Sean Young wouldn't believe she wasn't human. "I have photos!" she insisted, taking them from a drawer, showing Harrison Ford all these terrific color pictures of her and her mother, a woman who had died ten years ago. She told him how she still missed her mother's warmth and good humor, and all Harrison Ford could do was repeat, "The photos were doctored. They were created. Those moments never happened," while Sean Young stared uncomprehendingly at him.

Sara shut the movie off, resting her head in her hands. She had come here because she felt as if she were mourning something. A pregnancy that wasn't a pregnancy. Could you turn off your pain if you discovered the situation that caused it wasn't the way you had thought it had been? She had read once that the brain didn't even know the difference between what was real and what was imagined, that that was how hypnosis worked. Tell someone they were encased in ice and it could be 104 degrees outside and that person would shiver. Tell someone allergic to cats that a Persian was sitting on his lap and that person would sneeze. "Think of the happy things," Abby used to tell Sara when she woke frightened from a dream filled with monsters. "Think about the beach." Crowd one thought out with another because there were a thousand realities you could engage in, a thousand possibilities you could choose to believe.

Sara prowled the house restlessly. Her parents wouldn't be back for a while. Scott was out. She picked up the phone book and leafed through it, and then she saw the old names: her old friend Robin! She dialed but a strange voice answered. "No Robin here," he said.

Back when she lived here, when she felt like this, she used to walk for miles until she tired the anxiety out of her. She used to ride her bike from her house into Boston and back again. Her whole body yearned to move, so she went to get her old bike from the garage, and as soon as she was pedaling, she felt something start to uncurl deep within her.

Her breath evened. The wind scooted past her and she lifted her face happily into it. It was a glorious spring day and she didn't know where she was headed, but it didn't matter. Winding in and out of the neighborhoods, she stopped thinking altogether, gliding, her feet popped out from the pedals, her arms straight up like "look ma no hands." She laughed, giddy with pleasure, and then, without even meaning to, there she was in Danny's old neighborhood. Her breath stopped and a wave of longing nearly doubled her over.

People had it so wrong about missing. "It's like a pie," her mother had once told her. "The pie is your whole life, the pieces are the pain, and after a while, each piece gets smaller and smaller, and then you have your whole life back." Her mother was so wrong. Maybe the pieces grew smaller, but your hunger for them didn't, it was always there, real and immediate, like breathing, necessary and something you couldn't control or stop, even if you wanted to. And like a pie, your past was something you were always hungry for.

She was rounding the corner. The day was heating up, the air growing golden with sun. Mosquitoes hummed about her. She took the tour. It comforted her to feel like a stranger here, to see that the blue house down the block was now white, that the woman who had kept twenty cats was gone, that even the school had been revamped. Different. Everything was different. Each new store, each strange face, she saw buoyed her.

Every once in a while, when she came home, she rode past Danny's block. Sometimes she thought she did it to see if he was there. Or if Frances, his mother was. Other times, she thought she was testing herself, seeing if she could do it and not feel anything about it one way or another, and then she'd know she was really healed. No one had ever been home, though sometimes there was a car in the driveway, a blue Honda, and then a dark green Ford, and each time she had felt unsettled. No, she wasn't over this.

Her legs pedaled harder.

And then she turned the corner again and she saw his house, the third one in, painted yellow now, and there standing in front of it was Danny and he wasn't alone. A woman was there, in a loose dress, her back to Sara, her hair yellow as a stick of butter, cropped close to her head. The woman lifted up a hand, smoothing the collar of Danny's shirt. She leaned forward and said something to Danny, laughing, and then he burst into laughter, too. His whole body seemed to light up.

Never had Sara expected to see him again. She hadn't allowed herself to imagine it.

It seemed like the most foolish thing she had ever done in her life, coming to this neighborhood again. She could turn around and pretend a million things, including that this was not happening, that she had never seen it. She could get to the nearest phone and call Scott and have all this zap right out of her life, and then the blonde turned and started lazily walking back toward the house, and Danny turned his whole body to watch her. The front door slapped shut, and Danny looked away from the blond woman, right at Sara, and the way he was looking at her froze her in place. The same way he had looked at her the day she had first met him.

"Sara?" He breathed her name and she rode closer.

His face was more weathered, as if he had been in the sun too long, and his hair was shorter, but looking at him, she felt electric current, and it was all she could do not to lay her head against his shoulder, the way she used to, and imagine that all those years between them had never taken place.

"My God. What are you doing here?" Danny said.

"Visiting. Same as you, probably, right?"

He gave her a long slow look. "Look at you. You look exactly the same."

She flushed, and dipped her head, and then looked back at him. He lifted his hand to brush her hair from her face, and then she saw the wedding band, so thick it was a wonder he could bend his finger. "You got married," she said.

He looked down at his ring, as if just seeing it gave him a jolt of pleasure. "Three years this month," he said. "I still can't believe my luck." He rolled the band about his finger. "Charlotte's like you a little," he said.

"How?" As soon as she said it, she wanted to bite the words back, but he was smiling. "Oh, I don't know," he said. "She's smart. She makes me think I can be better than I am." He stopped rolling the ring. "After meeting her, I got into a training program at a bank. Regional manager now. In Pittsburgh." His grin widened. "You must be a shrink, the way you always wanted."

"Copywriter."

He laughed. "Sara! You're making me laugh."

"No, I'm not joking, Danny. I work for a catalog company. I do writing for them."

"You can't fool me." He kept his eyes on her. "You married?"

Scott flickered in her mind. "There's someone."

"I'm glad." His face lit up. "Look at the two of us, standing here talking just like no time has passed at all. We should have dinner. Really talk. Are you here for a while?"

She tried to speak and her throat felt as if it were closing up on her.

He took another step closer to her. She could hear his watch ticking. And then she smelled something. Lime aftershave and it made her think of the patchouli he used to wear, a smell so intoxicating she'd dribble it on her clothes so she'd feel she was wearing him.

She couldn't stand it. "Danny," she said abruptly. "You just disappeared on me."

"So did you," he said slowly.

"No, I didn't. I never would have—" She blinked at him. "I was pregnant and you left."

Danny looked pained. "I fucked up. I didn't know what else to do."

"You could have stayed—you could have helped me—"

"I didn't know how! I didn't have any money. I knew I couldn't ask my family. I knew yours would hate me, and all I kept thinking was that you'd end up hating me, too. And every time I looked at you, you were so scared and unhappy, that I just saw my own failure hammering me in the face."

"So you just left."

"I was a kid. I panicked. I was torn inside out with missing you and I finally came back. I didn't care anymore what would happen. I just wanted to be with you. But you were already gone."

"What are you talking about? I wasn't gone."

"Sara, you were. I came back because I was going crazy, because I didn't care about anything but you. I was going to figure something out for us, and then my mother told me how you had come to the house."

"No, I didn't come. I called. She said you were gone."

Danny shook his head. "She told me how furious you were with me, how you never wanted to see me again."

"What?" Sara said, astonished. "I never said that!"

"She told me how you said you hated me and wouldn't forgive me. She said you wrote me a letter so nasty, she ripped it up rather than give it to me."

"She told you what? That's not what happened! I told you I loved you in that letter!"

He frowned. "Sara, I couldn't believe her. But I called your house, over and over, and your parents wouldn't let me talk with you, they said you were too upset right now. I came to your house in the middle of the night, the way I used to. I even threw stones at your window, but you didn't come to open it. And then one night I heard your window slam shut, I saw the curtains tugged closed."

"I never would have done that! I must not have been there that night!" Sara said. She tried to think where she had been all those nights that she didn't see Danny outside her window, didn't sense him the way she always had. Had he come for her the nights her mother had talked her into going out for a Dairy Queen? Was it when she was sprawled on her bed with the headphones on, trying to tune her life out?

"My father must have slammed the window shut," she said finally, but Danny shook his head.

"Your father said you did. He came out. He said he was calling the cops. He said you were home and wouldn't see me, that you hated me and that if I cared about you, I'd leave you alone." He looked at her, pained. "He said you deserved better than me."

"Danny!"

"My mother was treating me like I was the gum on the bottom of her shoe. All she said was how it would never work anyway, a smart girl from a good family and a shit like me. How I could never give you any of the things you'd need, how I'd never be rich or smart enough for you."

"That's so ridiculous! I never thought that! I looked for you everywhere! Why didn't you come back to school? You could have seen me, you could have talked to me!"

"I *did* go to school, Sara. I tried to find you. I looked everywhere and finally some girl told me you were taking the day off, going to a college interview at Harvard. Sara, I hitched into Cambridge, I showed up on the campus and walked around looking for you. I was ready to just grab you and take off!"

"I didn't see you—" she started to say, and then she stopped. She remembered that one day when she had felt him nearby, the way she always did, like a current in the air, and she had turned and it was only someone's father.

"I saw you. Standing in a group of kids, all of them so—so—privileged looking. So—so well fed. Well dressed. And one of them flirting with you, making you smile. All I could think about was everyone telling me you deserved better, my own family telling me how it could never work—you so smart and me barely passing. And then your group went into a building, and I came after them, and this security guard came over to me, and asked what I was doing there. Like he knew I didn't belong on that campus. And he was right."

"Danny—"

"It was like every door slamming shut on me. I just took off. This time for good. I drifted from place to place, taking on jobs just to have enough money to survive. Every once in a while I'd think, fuck it, who cares if you're in college and I'm not, and I'd send a letter to your house, or I'd call you, just to hear your voice, but I never got you. You never wrote back. Finally, I just tried to put it all out of my mind. And I couldn't. Not for a long, long time."

Sara stared. "I did come to your house once, Danny, months after you had left. Frances still didn't know where you were."

"What are you talking about? She knew," Danny said, startled. "Of course she knew. She was sending me money when she could."

"I don't understand. But then you came home again—you still didn't try to see me."

"I didn't come home."

"Danny. You were home. I know you were home. You signed the papers."

He frowned. "What papers?"

"The papers. The agency served you with papers to sign. You had to say you knew the baby was being put up for adoption, that you knew there would be a hearing. Not showing up for the hearing meant you didn't want the baby, that you wouldn't fight the adoption."

Danny looked suddenly dazed. He stepped back from Sara. "What are you talking about? What adoption? What papers? You had an abortion. My mother told me. That day you came to the house furious with me, blaming me, all upset because you had had one."

"I never had an abortion. It was too late. And I never blamed you."

A door slapped open at the house next door and a taffy-colored dog bounded out.

"We had a baby?"

"A girl."

"What?" He stepped back from her, stunned. "What are you telling me? We have a little girl?" He stood back from her, looking at her as if he didn't know her.

Sara swiped at her nose, at her eyes. "I would have gone anywhere with you," Sara said. "I would have done anything," she said, and then she remembered. Danny's mother standing outside, telling her she knew what it was like to lose a child, what you had to do to protect the ones you loved, and suddenly she felt sick.

"Oh God, Sara. You let someone else have our kid?"

She swallowed, feeling suddenly dizzy. "What was I supposed to do? You were gone! I was only sixteen!"

"A kid! I wouldn't have let anyone else have my kid—never, never. I wouldn't have deserted my child like my old man did with me and my brother. I wouldn't have deserted you if I had known you still loved me, if I had known you had the kid. Never, no matter what. How could you not have known that?"

There it was, the pulse in his face, the one he used to get when he was angry. His eyes were so black she couldn't see the pupils. He was so furious at her, she drew back.

"The papers were signed!" she said. "They told me the papers were signed."

"I never signed any papers. I never knew about any hearing."

"But someone did! The server has to ask for ID, go by a picture. Something, anything. And the server had to sign his name, too, right by yours."

"So maybe the server screwed up. Maybe he signed them himself. Who knows? All I know is I didn't sign any papers. It wasn't me. I didn't know anything about this, Sara." He stared past her. "I can't believe it. A baby."

"Maybe you didn't sign your rights away." She looked toward the house. "Ask your mother about this. Maybe she knows something. She was here, wasn't she? I'll ask her."

His eyes narrowed. His shoulders grew straight. He suddenly looked different to her, as if he were traveling far away from her and nothing she could ever do would let her catch up. "This isn't the time—it isn't the place—"

"Someone signed! Maybe your brother signed—"

"My brother was living in Texas—"

"Well, maybe he came to visit—maybe he thought he was helping— couldn't you ask him?"

"My brother was killed five years ago in a car accident in Alaska. It just about destroyed my mother."

"It destroyed your mother?" Sara said faintly. She looked toward the house, and he grabbed her arm. "My wife's in there!" Danny cried. "I told you this wasn't the time!"

"Your wife! You never told her?"

"Of course I never told her. I was a mess when she met me, but I didn't want her to have to worry about this. I couldn't let myself think about it anymore, either. It hurt too much. It almost destroyed me, Sara." He looked toward the house and then back at Sara. He looked suddenly older to her.

She freed her arm from his hands. "Danny, the baby was so beautiful, so perfect. You would have been so amazed to see her. She had these full lips. She had these slate-colored eyes and red hair, Danny, and this rippling laugh—"

"Sara, stop—" Danny said, pained.

"Her name's Anne, Danny. She'd be sixteen now. Can you imagine?"

"Sara, stop! It was a long time ago. What difference can it make now?"

"Because I could have gotten my daughter back! Because it's fraud!"

"So what! So it's another bum rap! There's nothing we can do about it now."

"We could go find her."

Danny started to walk away and then whipped back around. "Find her? What are you talking about? Find her and do what? I have Charlotte, I have a job. Charlotte's pregnant, Sara. I've finally done something right. My mother adores her, and because of that, she adores me, too. They go to church together when we're in town! And Sara, you know what, sometimes I even go, too. Charlotte knows I'm not a believer, but she likes having me there. It's a little thing, it makes her happy, what does it cost me?"

"It costs," said Sara, pained. "Look at you pacing. Why can't you admit you're angry about this, too? You're angry! I know you are!"

"And where's anger going to get me?" Danny asked. "I have a *wife*. I'm a good man and for the first time I don't have to prove anything, I don't have to be anything different. I have a place in the community, can you believe it? Me, the rebel? I like feeling that people are proud of me, that they look up to me. Why would I want to ever stop feeling like that? Please. I can't tell Charlotte I lied. I can't make her feel she can't trust me."

"It's not just in the past—"

"Our kid is what sixteen? If she's got any of my genes, she's already thinking about hitting the road, making her own trouble, hating her parents' guts because they're trying to keep her down. Why would I want a share of that?"

"Because she's your kid—" Sara said. "You know there was never anybody but you," Sara repeated. Never had she felt more desperate. "And you know we could find her. Even if you didn't want to be her father, you could do it for me—" she said. "We made this child together. You could help me—"

"No—"

The front door slapped open and Sara looked up to see Danny's wife, Charlotte, slowly making her way back to them, and now that Sara could see her from the front, she saw how pregnant Charlotte was, and she saw, too, the way Charlotte looked at Danny, how her smile brightened, her eyes sparkled. "Hello, there," called Charlotte, and her voice was like a spell breaking over Danny. He turned toward Charlotte and then he turned back to Sara, as if he had remembered her, like an afterthought.

"No, Sara," he said firmly, his voice still low and hard. "It's the past. Drop it."

And then Charlotte was there beside them, in a cloud of perfume, all pineapple blond and pink, flushed skin, freckles sprigging her nose. She draped one arm about Danny and gave him a kiss on the side of his face, then she waved her pretty hands like a fan. "Woo, it's a hot one, isn't it?" she said. He grinned at her and then gave Sara a quick, warning glance. Charlotte put one hand on her belly. "Are you one of Danny's old friends?" Charlotte laughed, nodding her head at Sara, studying her. "We've been averaging one an hour since we got here."

One an hour. Which friends were those? When Sara had known Danny, he really hadn't had any friends. It had been just the two of them. "Us against the world," Danny had said, but now he grabbed for his wife's hand, now he refused to take his eyes off her.

"Are you staying for dinner?" Charlotte said. "We've got enough food to feed the whole state."

Danny interrupted. "Sara has to go," he said, not meeting Sara's eyes.

"Oh, now, that's a shame," Charlotte said. "Another time, then."

"Sure, another time," Danny repeated, as if she were no more important to him than the person who tossed the newspaper onto the front porch.

"Well, it was good to see you," Danny said. He clapped her on the shoulder, friendly, the way he might any buddy, but she felt the push in his hand. Her face was frozen, but she struggled to smile, to show he hadn't hurt her, and then she shook Charlotte's hand, and got back on her bike, and as she turned around to look at him, one more time, the last thing she saw was Danny kissing his wife, the way he used to kiss her, blatantly, right out in public so the whole world could see it, as if he were proving that neither she nor Anne nor anybody else had any claim on him but Charlotte. He put his hand on Charlotte's blossoming belly. He swayed her in a kind of dance. And Sara saw his knuckles were white, that he was holding on to Charlotte for dear life.

As she pedaled faster and faster, her breath came in puffs. Huh-huh-huh. How could he not want to help her? There was a spurt of speed and then she rode over a rock, she heard something pop, and then she was falling, crashing from the bike down onto the pavement, skinning her knees. She cried out in pain. *"All that stuff is in the past,"* Danny had said, and then she was crying more heavily, but not about her bruises, not about her bike, which she could see had a flat tire. *I miss you. All these years and I still miss you.*

She thought of a client she had had when she was studying to be a therapist. He was nearly fifty and recently divorced. He had tracked down his high school sweetheart, a girl he hadn't seen in thirty years, a girl everyone had told him was nothing more than puppy love, and within two months, they were married. "It was always meant to be," he said, and then he had gone on to talk about his anxiety at his job.

There was a woman who came to her, too. She was married to a wonderful man, but she still dreamed about her fiancé who had been killed in a car crash. "It's been ten years," the woman kept saying to Sara. "Why can't I get over it?"

Unfinished business. All of it. Why wouldn't she miss Danny?—because what she was really missing was all that possibility that had been between them, all that time cut short before they had a chance to see what might have happened if they had been allowed to be together. Maybe they would have been happy. Maybe she would have tired of him and moved on. Maybe he would have found he wasn't ready to be a father, let alone a husband, and they would have started fighting and not getting along. He might have not come home nights and then, when they had split, it would have been something they both would have welcomed. A sigh of relief. But they neither one of them got the chance to find out.

She walked the bike home. A few cars slowed as they passed her, a few voices catcalled. "Hey, you got some fries with that shake, honey?" And she kept crying. As soon as she got inside the house, she found her father at home, gathering up his briefcase.

"I thought I'd come home for lunch and surprise you, but you were gone," he said. "Now I have to get back to the office."

"Dad—" she said, her voice cracking.

"Honey, what's the matter? You look so terrible," he said.

"Danny never signed the papers. Someone forged his name."

"Danny? What are you talking about? What papers?"

"I was riding around past his neighborhood. He was there." She couldn't bear to tell the rest of it, to mention the wife he loved so much he'd tamp down his own anger just so he'd never risk her happiness, certainly not the way he had with Sara's. "He lives in Pittsburgh now. Did you know where he was?"

Jack's face grew slack. "So he lives in Pittsburgh," Jack said finally. "So he didn't sign the papers. What difference does it make now? You were sixteen. You were babies."

"You don't understand! You aren't listening! It means the adoption wasn't legal, it means Anne is mine—"

"Sara. That's ridiculous. Let it go."

"No. Never," Sara said. "Did you know about this?" She wiped her tears with the flat of her hand. "He said he came to the house and you and Mom threatened him! He said he sent me letters and called! Why didn't you tell me any of this?"

"You would have ruined your own life!"

"How do you know that?"

"I know! Believe me, I know!"

"It was my life to ruin!"

"Now you just wait a minute before you start shouting at me or accusing me of things," Jack said. "A father protects his kids, and that's just what I was doing! Why is that so terrible? Yes, he came to the house, like some wild thing, and yes, I told him to leave because he was acting so crazy. And you were in a state yourself. I didn't want you married and with a baby at sixteen and no future at all. Who stays married to their high school sweetheart? And you have a man who loves you now, you have a job you say you like. Things are good now, aren't they?"

"Things are unfinished!"

"You wait until you have experience. You'll see I was right."

"I loved him——" she said, and Jack held up his hand.

"Love," he said. "The love that counts is the love for your child."

Sara stopped. "Did you hear what you just said?"

But her father was buttoning his suit jacket, gathering his things to go back to work. "You'll see I was right," he repeated.

After her father left, Sara sat on the couch, trying to sort things out. Sara put both hands over her face. She couldn't let it go, no more than she could let go of her own heartbeat. She thought of Danny and Charlotte, bathed in light. She thought of Frances, in the house, not coming out.

Danny might not have thought he had helped her, but he had, by telling her he hadn't signed the papers. But Jesus, who had? And who had known about it? She thought of Eva and George, the way they had pulled back from her. Margaret. She thought of Margaret, the adoption lawyer at the agency. She could find her and see what had happened. Except Margaret hadn't exactly been on her side. But back then, Margaret hadn't known the adoption was fraudulent. Margaret had clearly fucked up—if anyone was at fault, surely it was an attorney who didn't know enough to get the right papers signed at the right time, an attorney who made a terrified kid feel as if she had no recourse in the world but to trust her. The agency would have to help her find them now.

But when she called, Margaret was no longer there. Instead, she spoke to a woman named Lorna Chase, who went to get Sara's file.

"What can we do for you?" Lorna Chase said, and then Sara began talking.

Lorna Chase sighed. "Well, this is very unfortunate, but as far as I can tell, this agency acted in good faith. It's not our job to get a handwriting analysis done, too."

"It wasn't his signature," Sara insisted. "It was fraud. My daughter was stolen from me."

"Stolen's a very strong word. And can you prove that? Will the father go to court and say it wasn't his signature?"

"I don't know——" Sara lied.

"Sara." Lorna Chase's voice was weary. "Don't think I don't sympathize, because I do. I really do. But your daughter would be a teenager now. What's to be gained by this? You'd have to take this to court, the birth father would have to testify, too. Maybe even the process server, if you could find him, which you probably couldn't. And even then, what are you going to do? Did you do anything Anne's whole first year to try and overturn the adoption? Did the birth father? Look, anyone can petition the court to hear anything, but whether you have a leg to stand on is another story. The person who should do something is the birth father, not you. And even then, the courts rule in the best interests of the child. Do you really think your daughter might want to leave the only family she's known? Do you really want to disrupt her life at this late stage with a court case? That's not in her best interests. The most you could hope for would be for the courts to order visits between the birth parents and the child."

"She's my daughter. If you don't know where they are, can you give me the Social Security number so I can look myself?" Sara pleaded. "Please."

"No can do. Against the law," Lorna Chase said. "Surely you know that."

"I was fifteen when I got pregnant, sixteen when I had her," Sara said. "They made me part of their family. I loved them. I loved my baby. And then they disappeared."

Lorna sighed again. "I'm very sorry, Sara. If I had a forwarding address, I'd give it to you. Or I'd contact them myself."

Sara hung up the phone and went to Abby's computer, switching it on. She wouldn't give up, she just wouldn't. She hadn't tried to find George or

Eva in years, hadn't thought she had a right to. Now there were a million new ways to find people, and now, she had money, too.

She found two different sites that looked promising, but both wanted fifty-dollar fees. *"We find anyone,"* the sites said. Sara typed in her credit card. She'd be here for a few more days. That evening, and the next day, she was back and forth to the computer so many times, Jack teased her about which sites she was going onto, but the day after that, she logged on, and there it was: George and Eva Rivers, Boca Raton, Florida. And there below it was an office phone number. And a home phone. There were two addresses.

She glanced at the phone. One in the afternoon. George would be at work. Anne at school. She'd call the office. The phone rang twice and a woman said, "Doctor's office," and Sara chewed at a thumbnail.

"Is George there?" Sara said, and then Sara heard George in the background, a voice so familiar it sent a pulse of longing through her body.

"Who's calling, please?" the woman said, and then Sara hung up.

Suddenly, she had things to do. She called work and told them there was an emergency, that she'd be gone a few more days. "Sara," said Hal. "We need you here." *Hope,* she thought. It didn't die the way people thought. It just went underground and then reemerged.

She knew, but she couldn't worry about that now. She felt fueled, so energetic, she couldn't sit still. Everything had a new meaning. She booked a cheap flight so she could be there in the morning, she started to pack and then the phone rang, jolting her, and she picked it up and there was Scott's voice. "I finally got you!" he said, and she slunk down on the bed again.

"I found us a place!" he exulted. "It just fell into my lap. A client of mine told me he's giving up his place and did I know anyone who might want it? Sara, it's a two-bedroom, right in the West Village, and it's got a sunroom and a little deck and a kitchen as big as Jupiter. I know the building, Sara, and it's perfect—so I told him yes, sight unseen."

"Scott." Her throat was so parched she could barely speak without it hurting. If he'd been there, she would have gone over to him and rested her head along his shoulder, she'd have placed his arm about her, making him hold her tight.

"What, are you mad that I made the decision without you? Don't be, Sara. I had to say yes, but nothing's been signed. And I know you're going to love it. And Sara, I was a fool before. I just want to be with you. I—I want to marry you, Sara. I know I shouldn't spring this on the phone—"

"Scott!" She rested her head against the receiver. "I have to go somewhere first."

"First? What are you talking about? What's more important than this? Go where?"

He was silent the whole time she was telling him, things so stunning even she couldn't believe them. Even when she started to cry, when she was telling him about what Danny had said to her, he didn't speak. And when she was finished, she grew afraid.

"You went to find this old boyfriend?" he said, stung. "Is this something I'm going to go through again?"

"It's nothing like that. I told you I was just riding around." She heard him breathing. "Scott? What are you thinking?"

"I don't know. I—Sara, I thought you were over this. What does it mean?"

"It means I have a daughter. It means I have the right to see her."

"You're going to just spring yourself on her? After all these years? Surely, you must know that would be disaster. Sara, you studied psychology—"

"And I gave it up!" Sara said. "Because it doesn't always help. It doesn't always make things better."

"Sara—"

"I know, I know everything you're going to say. But I'm not a psychologist now. I'm a mother. And she's my daughter."

"I don't understand." She heard his breath through the wires. "Why do you even have to go down there? Why can't you take it slow? Write her first. Or call."

"I can't risk taking it slow. I don't know if her parents want me knowing her—if they'd disappear again—"

"Well, there you have it," Scott said, "you shouldn't do this, then, it'll be a mess." And he suddenly sounded so relieved that she felt something tighten inside of her.

"I have to see her." Sara hesitated. "Come with me, Scott."

"Sara, I don't know this girl and neither do you! She has parents, Sara, she has her own life and you're going to disrupt it. What do you think is going to happen?"

"I can have a relationship. Maybe I can move down there and be nearer to her."

Scott was quiet for a moment. "I don't want to move there. My work is here."

"Well, maybe she can come here—who knows what can be arranged? I just want her to be a part of my life. I just want to see her."

"What about my life?" he said. "What about our life together?"

"This is our life together—"

"No, it's your life. Your decision." His voice was so far away, floating from her. "If you have a relationship with this girl, then don't I have to have a relationship with her, too? What if I'm not ready for that? What if I just want it to be me and you?"

"She's my daughter!" Sara stared at the phone. She thought of the place they were planning to get together, big and sunny, filled with light, and then she thought of her daughter, a girl who had been frozen in time for years and years.

"We're either a couple or we're not," he said.

"What does that mean?"

"It means don't go," he said.

"I have to."

"Sara," Scott said, and his voice was suddenly so sad that it worried her. "This is too much for me. You call me, Sara, when you've figured out what you need to do."

She put both hands around the receiver. Was this a mistake? Was this just dreaming, Sean Young aching over her worn photographs of a mother who never existed? "Scott," she said, and then the silence grew and they both hung up the phone.

The house ticked and settled, and then she got up, and her whole body felt so heavy, as if she had thickened in the space of the conversation. She would finish packing, and by the time her parents came home, she would be gone. No one could tell her she wasn't doing the right thing. She would miss Scott, but by the next morning, she would be in Florida and she would see her daughter.

chapter

twelve

Anne stood outside the high school, waiting anxiously for Flor and June, clutching her journal to her chest. They used to all walk home together, the three of them giggling and carrying on, gossiping about school and clothes and the boys they secretly yearned over. The Triple Threat, they called themselves. Lately, though, they were more like the Double Trouble, and she was the odd girl out. Though she had casual friends at school, Jasmine in her algebra class whom she sometimes ate lunch with, Ryan in history who regaled her with tales of the computer game he was developing that he hoped would make him rich, when she walked home most days, she walked alone.

She rubbed at her bare arms, wishing she had worn more than a T-shirt, that her legs were in jeans rather than bared under a short plaid skirt, but changing this morning would have involved going back into the house, having Eva trail after her and ask her questions.

She spotted Flor, languidly climbing down the stairs, walking as if she were Miss America, nodding her head at the other kids who were staring yearningly up at her. What would it be like, Anne wondered, to feel that way about yourself? To be that lucky? Flor's eyes roamed the crowd and then met Anne's, and instantly Anne perked up. "Flor!" she called, waving, and Flor hesitated, looked around some more, and then ambled over.

"Want to go to the park?" Anne asked. "Or want to come to my house? Hang out?"

Flor considered. "What's June doing?"

"She went home during history. Period cramps."

"That rat! She doesn't have her period! We're on the same schedule. She should have told me! I would have skipped out, too."

"She skipped?" Anne said. June had been doubled over at her desk, had winced when anyone even looked at her. And more importantly, June hadn't let Anne in on the ploy.

"That June is really something," Flor said admiringly.

"So, do you want to hang out?"

Flor studied Anne, considering. She tapped one finger on Anne's journal. "You are so queer," she said. "It's bad enough we have to write for school. I can't believe you actually like to do this and you bring it to school, yet. Me, the only stories I need to make up are the ones for my parents."

"I didn't say we had to write together," Anne said.

"Maybe I'll go home and clean my room," Flor said.

They started to walk home, and even though Anne was matching her strides to Flor, she couldn't help feeling that she was tagging along, that somehow they weren't walking together. She looked at Flor who was slightly smiling, and then she cleared her throat. "What're you thinking about?" Anne asked, and Flor started. "Oh, nothing," she said.

Despair washed over Anne. She tried to think of something interesting to say, something that might draw Flor into a conversation or at least an animated response. "I heard they might have a dance at school—" she said.

"I know. I've already been invited. Bob Ross. I rate a cuter boy than he is, though."

Anne glanced down at her feet. Red cowboy boots. She had bought them with Flor and June last year, but now they were scuffed and a little uncomfortable. "We should go shoe-shopping one day," she said as they rounded the corner toward Flor's block.

"Sure," Flor said, waving her hand. She pointed to Anne's shoes. "You still have those boots we all bought?"

"Don't you?"

"God no." Flor shook her head. "But they're okay for you," she said magnanimously.

They turned down another street, Flor's block. "See you," Flor said.

Stung, Anne slowly walked home. She took the long way, circling past the town, along the stretches of beach and boardwalk. Her pace lengthened and she began to relax. Road rapture. She felt like she could walk for years without stopping.

She cut down Forest Street and then headed toward Bank Avenue.

She missed Flor. She missed June. It was like that movie about the pod people. Something had taken her friends over, changed them without her even noticing it, and worse, it hadn't changed her. Flor and June were going out with senior boys, who trailed after them in school, confused and bothered, and if those boys happened to see Anne, their eyes skimmed right over her like she was the fat on top of some soup. The only time the other girls called Anne was to brag about this boy liking them or that one asking them out, or when they needed an alibi to cover their tracks. They had a new patina about them, a shimmer like a force field. Anne couldn't get close. June kept love notes in her bra to take out and swoon over. *"You are so beautiful you make my eyes hurt,"* one note said. Flor had a whole brown paper bag of fortunes from this boy Richard who sat behind her in math class and was in love with her. *"You will fall in love forever with a boy named Richard." "You will ask Richard out for a date on Saturday." "You will wear Richard's ring."* And she had seen one note nudged to the bottom of the bag: *"You will kiss Richard's balls."*

The only notes Anne had were notes her mother left her. *"I'm happy you're my daughter. I'm so proud of you."* She found them tucked in her junk drawer under her bangle bracelets, sometimes at the bottom of a shoe, and once in a bag lunch she had made for herself. She loved the notes, but she never mentioned them to her mother, because the one time she had, her mother got this bright, expectant look on her face and said, "And?" as if Anne were supposed to respond in a certain way. So rather than risk getting it wrong and disappointing her, Anne had just shrugged, which had ended up hurting her mother anyway.

Anne rounded the corner to her block. Here, nothing ever seemed to change. She could count on Mrs. Morton hanging up her wash on the clothesline even though everyone in their right mind had a dryer. She could count on Mr. Thrommer sitting on the front porch reading the newspaper. Anne knew she herself didn't change either and everything she did to rectify that mistake backfired.

Because she looked tragically young, she spent mornings in the girls' room vying for a position at the mirror, carefully applying mascara and blush and lip gloss, the same way everyone else did, but on her, the mascara freckled under her eyes. Her lipstick faded back into her skin. Sixteen and she looked twelve. A junior and she could pass for eighth grade. June, watching, had laughed. "You look like a kid wearing her mother's makeup," she said, and put the blush on Anne herself. "That's better," June said. But later, in history class, Mr. Reynolds had asked Anne with great concern if she needed to go home. "Your cheeks are so flushed," he said. "do you have a fever?"

"Fever! She's on fire!" said Sal Nelson, who sat behind her. He tugged Anne's short carroty ringlets and then made a sizzling sound. The other kids cracked up, and while Anne slunk lower in her seat, Sal was spurred on. "What did you do, put your hand in an electric socket and it went right to your head?" he said, laughing.

Anne concentrated, willing herself to be invisible, gripping one hand in the other so she wouldn't reach up and try to smooth her hair down flat, which would only call more attention to it. Her hair! God, her hair! She had always hated her hair. She had ironed it, and straightened it, had once poured a solution of Jell-O and water through it and worn a nylon stocking on her head, but her hair always sprang back curlier than ever. "There must be a way to tame it," her mother kept saying, showing Anne photos in magazines, buying her clips, but Eva always threw her hands up when the clips sprang free, when the curls that had been jelled down grew rampant again, as though Anne's hair and Anne had both disappointed her. Anne kept her hair just to her chin, and every time she went to have it cut, she was in misery because she saw the perplexed look on the faces of the cutters, the way they didn't know what to do with such a wild mop, either. "Short. Very short," they suggested, and the one time she had agreed, she had ended up looking like a pinhead.

Anne tugged at a curl, trying to will it to straighten. Eva was blessed with a sheet of shiny blond. Complete strangers were always stopping to compliment it, like it was the eighth wonder of the world. The pictures she had seen of her father when he was young showed he had glossy black waves. She cursed her genes, cursed whatever ancestor's recessive code had given her her pale skin that wouldn't turn gold in the sun the way her friends' skin did. Cursed the way any attempt she made to look older—makeup, clothing, even the way she walked—ended up making her look younger instead.

"Who do I look like?" she had asked her mother.

"You look like me. I've told you that. You look like Dad."

Anne had studied Eva. "You always say that, but how is that true? I don't have your coloring or Dad's. I don't have your eyes. I don't think I'm anything like you."

"Your great-aunt Ada had red hair," Eva had told her.

"She did? Do you have a picture?"

"Not in color. And listen, I don't look anything like my parents, either."

She looked up, shoulders hunched, in time to see Eva, blond hair flashing, getting ready to go someplace in the car, and Eva looked at Anne, delighted. "I was just saying to myself, who's that pretty girl coming toward me?"

"Mom." No one ever called Anne pretty and a mother saying it didn't count. The boys at school ignored her, the other girls never thought to consider her competition. "You have no style," June had told her critically. "You so don't know how to dress that even my help wouldn't help you." Even Eva fussed with Anne about combing her hair or putting on a nicer shirt. But right now, her mother was so happy to see her that Anne couldn't help but feel cheered.

"Are your friends coming over today?" Eva said. "I miss those girls."

"Not today." Anne wished her mother would stop asking. What was she supposed to tell her? My friends don't like me anymore? My friends outgrew me? The only friends I have are the casual ones at school?

"I was just going shopping. Going to treat myself to something. Come with me."

Anne hesitated.

"Come on," Eva urged. "We'll go to Saks and spend some money."

Saks was cool and quiet. Eva couldn't stop talking about her class today, how she had had the children draw portraits of themselves as if they were animals. "You'd be surprised how many kids were dinosaurs!" Eva said. "One girl was this tiny little insect—a cockroach of all things!—and I felt so bad until she explained to me that she was more powerful than anyone because everyone knew cockroaches could survive a nuclear blast!

Anne picked up a soft blue suede glove and held it against her cheek.

"Let's go upstairs and look at the dresses," Eva said.

They took their time going to the elevator, stopping at every counter. Eva plucked up glittering earrings and held them against her lobes. Anne tried on a few felt fedoras that sat on top of her curls rather than on her head and she finally gave up. They were passing the maze of makeup counters, the perfume sprayers, when a saleswoman in a burgundy lab coat beckoned them over. She was tall and angular and as pale as a sheet of paper. "I have just the thing for you," she said in a bright voice to Eva. "Be the first to try our brand-new line and get some wonderful free samples."

"Free samples!" Eva winked at Anne. Anne used to love when Eva brought home tiny pots of sample face cream, the golden tubes of lip gloss. "Doll makeup," they used to call it, and when Anne had put it on, George had called her Dollface.

They both approached the counter. Eva plucked up some moisturizer and then the saleswoman peered at her. "It's past time for you to start using our latest line," she said.

"What line?" Eva tapped some sample moisturizer on her wrist and sniffed at it. "Mmm, smell this," she said to Anne.

The woman pointed to a display case of bottles, all the same burgundy as her lab coat. Matura, they all said, in tiny gold script. The woman held up a small tube. "You won't believe the difference one little tube can make. I swear by this cream. This is true anti-aging technology for the menopausal woman." She leaned forward so Eva could see her perfect skin, and then, with great sympathy, she held up a mirror, positioning it so

Eva could see herself. "See those lines by your eyes? Those crinkles on your neck won't go away by themselves." She took the moisturizer from Eva's hand. "This is for younger skin."

Anne saw her mother visibly flinch. She looked up at Eva as if she were noticing her for the first time. Her mother's hair was beautiful, long and silky and buttery yellow, but in this odd, bluish light, her mother's skin looked like crepe paper. The lines around her mouth and eyes suddenly seemed dug deeply in. Startled, Anne drew back. Mom's in her fifties, she thought. By the time I graduate college she'll be sixty. Sixty! How could her mother be sixty so soon? It struck her like a slap.

"Anne! Hi!"

Anne turned. Doreen, the girl who Anne sometimes had lunch with, smiled at Anne and started walking toward her. Anne smiled back. It felt funny to see Doreen outside of school, here in Saks. "Who's that?" Eva asked with interest.

"Doreen," Anne said shyly. "My friend from school."

"Your friend!" Eva said approvingly, and her approval made Anne brighten, too.

"My good friend," Anne lied.

Beside Doreen was a slender woman with shining blond hair cropped at an angle, the same heart-shaped face as Doreen. "My mom," Doreen said. Peering at the cosmetics, she snickered. "Matura!" she said, delighted.

"You must be Anne's grandmother," said Doreen's mother, turning to Eva.

"Actually, I'm her mother," Eva said quickly, and Doreen's mother looked appalled. Doreen squinted at Anne as if there were now something wrong with her.

"Oh, of course," Doreen's mother said quickly, but Anne could see how flustered she looked. "We're just shopping for things for our vacation," she said. "We're going to the Rockies. Do you hike?"

"Oh God, no," Eva said. "It's all I can do to get up in the morning!" She laughed and Anne felt her stomach plummet. Couldn't her mother see no one else was laughing?

Doreen's mother politely smiled. "Well, we had better get going," she said.

"I'll see you at school tomorrow," Anne said.

Eva grew more animated. "Oh, are you leaving now? We were just about to leave, too. Would you like to come back to the house with Anne?"

"Mom!" Anne said.

"My house is always open to Anne's good friends," Eva said, and Anne could have sunk through the pale rose carpeting.

Anne saw the way Doreen gently tugged at her mother's sleeve, drawing her away. "Another time," said Doreen's mother awkwardly. "We have errands."

"Well," Eva said. "It was so nice to meet you, Doreen." She took both of Doreen's hands in hers, impulsively squeezing them. Doreen quickly removed her hands. "I've heard so many, many wonderful things about you from Anne."

"You have?" Doreen said.

"Mom——" said Anne.

"I'm sure we'll see you again," Eva said, "I look forward to it." Doreen's mouth fell open a bit. She gave Anne a quick, sidelong glance, as if she were taking her measure, as if she didn't know her anymore, and then she followed her mother out of the store.

"Why did you do that?" Anne asked. "Say all those things? You don't know her!"

Eva looked perplexed. "But you do. You told me she was your friend!"

"Not really. Not yet—we're just in-school friends. We have lunch once in a while. How could you invite her to the house like that?"

"Well, sometimes you have to push these things. Make an in-school friend an out-of-school one. Don't look at me like that—I just wanted to make her feel welcome. And I was just trying to help you." The saleswoman scooted back, smiling expectantly, and Eva leaned across the counter. "I'll take the face cream," she said.

Eva charged the cream and took the burgundy bag. "You'll come back a changed woman wanting more," the saleswoman said, smiling. "I guarantee it."

Anne didn't feel like shopping anymore. "Why don't we hike in the mountains?" Anne blurted.

"Hike? And break my legs?" Eva said.

Anne picked a skirt from the rack, plucking at the ruffled hem.

"She must have had her daughter when she was fourteen," Eva said abruptly.

"Why'd you wait so long to have me?" Anne asked.

"It's just the way things happened."

Eva took the skirt from Anne and put it back on the rack. "It's not really me," she said.

They only shopped for a little while longer.

"I'm tired," Eva admitted. "Let's get home to your dad," she said, and then Anne thought of her father, the way he came home and was tired, the way he fell asleep in the chair after dinner, the way his glasses got thicker and heavier on his nose. She hated the way he referred to himself as "your old man," almost as if he were proud of his age. It seemed stunningly unfair and terrifying that she had such old parents. We choose our fates, Flor had told her. We create our own reality. Flor believed in reincarnation now, and all that New Age stuff. She was sure you chose your own parents before you were even born, that you did it to give yourself a life lesson. But why would Anne have chosen such old parents? What possible lesson was there to be learned in that? Eva coughed and thunked her chest. "I can't get rid of this pesky cough," she said.

"Maybe you should call the doctor," Anne said, and Eva laughed. "You don't have to call the doctor over every little thing. You talk like I'm dying."

Anne gave her mother a sharp look. Dying! She hadn't thought about that! What would happen to her if her mother did die? she worried. What if her father died? What would she do? She felt a sharp pull of tears and blinked hard, stricken.

"Allergies, honey?" Eva asked, but Anne shook her head. There was a girl in her math class whose father had dropped dead of a heart attack in the backyard while he was barbecuing hot dogs. A year later, her mother had died of cancer, and now she lived with her aunt and didn't crack jokes the way she used to. Where would Anne go if something happened? She had a grandfather on her father's side who was ancient, whom she saw once a year, for barely a week at a time. He didn't really know her and she didn't really know him. Would she end up in a group home sharing a room with a girl so tough she'd take to carrying a nail file for protection? Would she end up in foster care with some awful family who would treat her more like a slave than a daughter? Surely, no one would adopt someone her age, someone right on the cusp of independence. Someone who looked the way she did. She scratched at her arm, uneasy.

As soon as they got home, Anne headed for her room. "Is everything all right with you?" Eva studied Anne. "Would you like to talk about it, honey?" Her mother's voice scratched against her like kitten claws.

"I'm going to go in my room and write," Anne said.

"You're always writing, can't you talk to me for a minute?" her mother asked.

Anne hesitated, filled with grief. She started to open her mouth but the words were jammed in her lungs and only a sound came out. "Mom—" she started to say, but her mother had already turned away.

"All right, all right," Eva said affectionately, "I can take a hint," and she left the room. Anne saw her mother in the hallway, taking out the tube of anti-aging cream from the bag, squinting at it, then digging her glasses out of her purse to read the fine print. Anne turned away. She could see both their reflections in the mirror, her wild mop of hair and ragged features and her mother's aging beauty, and both images made her want to crumple up and die. She bent, plucked up her sweater from the floor, and draped it over the mirror so that when she passed by it, all she would see was soft green wool.

She was starving. She glanced at the clock. Nearly six now. She had been writing so furiously, she had lost track. She put the notebook carefully under her mattress and then came out into the living room. Eva was huddled around George, talking quietly, the two of them conferring like a matched set of worry dolls. She knew what they were discussing. His practice wasn't doing so great, hadn't been for a while, and now that a cut-rate dental clinic had opened right near him, she heard him telling her mother that it was doing even worse. He came home later and later, past dinner, taking every emergency case that came his way because if he didn't, the clinic would. Most nights, he fell asleep in his chair watching TV, like he was a cliché instead of her father. When her parents were together like that, instead of making her feel relieved to be let alone, it made her feel as if they were purposely ignoring her, blaming her for the lines on their foreheads, for her mother's white hairs threaded among the yellow. And the thing of it was she didn't have a clue what she had done to get blamed.

"Hi, Daddy."

He looked up, startled. "Hi, sweetheart," he said.

"This Friday, for our day, can we go to Spitfire's for dinner?"

He blinked at her. "Sure," he said. "Sure we can." And then he and Eva were silent, waiting for her to leave, and so she wandered into the kitchen. Something was boiling on the stove and she lifted the lid. Beef stew. Bubbling with carrots, a scrim of fat along the top. Disgusting. She grabbed a handful of potato chips and sat at the kitchen table.

She and her father had their day together once a month. Or whenever she wanted. "Just give me a few days' notice," George told her. "You're my number one priority." They went to a fancy place for dinner, just the two of them, or out bowling, or to a movie, loading up on Twizzlers and popcorn.

Anne ate another chip. When she was little, they didn't have to plan a day. He was always taking her places on the spur of the moment, jangling the car keys and saying, "Come on, princess, let's go." Museums, zoos, the botanical gardens. He didn't care if she talked. He never said, "A penny for your thoughts." And oh, the way he looked at her! As if she were the most special person on earth! Anyone could see how much he loved her. And how much she loved him. Well, she could wait until Friday. Maybe she didn't go skiing, but her mother took her shopping, and her father took her to dine.

By Wednesday, Anne was feeling so out of sorts, she wasn't sure what to do with herself. She spotted Doreen going toward class, walking with another girl, and for a moment she felt the same flicker of embarrassment she had had in Saks when Eva had tried pushing them together. "Hi, Doreen," she said. Starting, Doreen pointed at Anne and then whispered something to the other girl, and they both burst out laughing.

Anne veered the other way, her head down.

Room 242. Writing and composition. Anne grabbed a seat in the first row, which wasn't difficult since just about no one wanted to sit that close to Mr. Moto. Instead, the class congregated to the back, keeping heads lowered, voices mute.

Often, Mr. Moto was late. He'd rush in, with no excuse or apology, and instantly start the class. A few times, he had ended the class halfway through, his long, bony fingers stroking his brow, and then he had dismissed everyone, saying curtly, "I have nothing more to give today." Mr. Moto was famous at the high school. Everyone had names made up for him. The more stupid boys called him Ichobod Crane because he was so tall and lanky, with a shock of yellow hair and tiny blue beads of eyes, and an Adam's apple that moved and shivered up and down his throat like a blob of mercury. He had lived for ten years in Prague, and he had actually published a novel called *The Long Rust of Winter,* a book he never failed to talk about in his lectures, though it had been published over fifteen years ago, and he hadn't published anything since, and when Anne had tried to order it on-line, she was dismayed to find it wasn't even listed.

When Anne had found out she was in his class, she was both terrified and exhilarated. She began to work harder than before, studying her stories, rewriting them until her fingers cramped. She read biography after biography of the writers she loved: Fitzgerald, Carson McCullers. A lot of them were loners like she was. A lot of them suffered self-doubt, too. When she read how Fitzgerald drew picture after picture of Gatsby until he felt he knew his character, she tried to draw her latest character, a waitress named Carolyn, over and over. When she read that Richard Price (oh, how she had loved *The Wanderers*) regularly gave his characters Rorschach tests, she did the same for Carolyn.

Carolyn, she decided, had amnesia. Carolyn woke up on the side of the road and made up a new name and re-created herself. Walking into a diner, she got a new job, a new name, while she struggled to figure out who she was, and when people asked her about her life, rather than reveal her confusion, she made up stories about her life. She even started to believe them. *"You can be anything you want,"* Anne wrote. *"Clouds don't part, bells don't ring to announce it. The future is more subtle than that."*

She had it planned. No one in the class ever turned in more than two pages at a time, and even then, they bitterly complained about it. But when she had fifty pages, she was going to give them to Mr. Moto. She was going to tell him it was part of a novel. God, she couldn't wait.

Mr. Moto strode in five minutes late, his hair raked back and damp. He frowned at the class as if his lateness were their fault. "This week I want an original essay on a theme I choose," he said. Anne took out her notebook and the boy next to her groaned. "Temperance," he said. "Something all of you could surely use an education in." He tightened his tie and frowned again. "Five hundred words," he ordered. "Typed."

"Moto taught at a boys' school before this one." Ron Cotter, who sat beside Anne, snickered. "Bet he wasn't too temperate then, if you catch my drift."

"Ron, would you care to stand in front of the class and enlighten us with your wit?" Mr. Moto asked. "All of you, read until the bell," he ordered.

Anne stared at the page, the words swimming in front of her, and then the bell rang and everyone sprang to their feet.

"Ah, the Exodus," Mr. Moto said dryly, parting his clasped hands like the Red Sea.

Anne sat at her desk that evening, trying to write. Temperance. She couldn't write about that. She didn't drink. The one time she had tried, standing behind the school with June and Flor, sipping beers from cans Flor had stolen from her dad's stash, Anne had thrown up in the bushes. "Oh God," she had said, standing, and then she had seen how sly and soft June's face looked, how Flor was listing, and the two of them were giggling as if they had a great secret Anne couldn't understand even if she tried. But still, Anne didn't begrudge anyone else wanting to drink. She could understand wanting escape, wanting to get out of your own life, but that was something she could do with writing.

She tapped her pen. She wanted him to see how good a writer she was. "I'm showing this to my publisher," he might tell her. She imagined herself giving readings, her parents in the first row, her mother making friends with everyone, telling the woman next to her, "I used to nag her when she shut herself up in her room, but not anymore!"

Why did she have to do a dull, boring essay? Why couldn't she write a short story instead? She looked through her Carolyn story. She thought about what might make Carolyn want to drink and then she thought about Eva. Maybe Carolyn had been a kindergarten teacher in her other life, and something reminded her of it. Maybe she had a memory of how she had been fired for drinking in class at the end.

She wrote in a fever. Four pages, and then six, and then she pushed back the pages and sat back, amazed and finished. She touched the words with her fingertips as if they were living, breathing things.

Friday was sunny and clear, the sky hard and blue, and George had come to work early. His last patient had asked him what he thought about the new dental clinic. " 'Course I'd still come here for the important work," she said, touching George's arm.

Well, the last patient had come and gone, a woman who had casually admitted that she didn't like to brush her teeth. "You don't like to?" George asked, amazed. Now, the office was hushed. George wanted nothing more than to go home and soak in a hot bath and go to sleep, but tonight was his dinner with Anne and nothing was going to make him miss that, not lack of sleep, not nerves, not the dull ache in his lower back. No, he'd go and be charming and order dessert, and if his daughter wanted to go to a movie afterward, well, he'd do that, too, if he had to pinch his thigh to keep himself awake.

George had a jacket in the closet. He had the tie Anne had given him for his birthday, bright red and printed with dancing Elvises, tucked in the pocket, and he had arranged his schedule so he could get out early. He missed his daughter. He found everything about her interesting, even the sullen teenage stuff. He could wait for it to pass.

He hated it whenever people talked about how parents only have their children for a little while and then they're gone. How every step a child took was one step away from you, every milestone another stone on your grave. "God gave us teenagers so we can break away and lose interest in them, the same way they do in us," one of his patients had said dryly. Well, George wasn't like that. His wonderful surprise had been falling in love with his daughter as a baby, and he hadn't stopped falling. He couldn't imagine not being crazy about her, not being interested in everything she said and did when she was in her twenties and thirties and forties, too, for that matter. Growing up didn't mean banishment. He had patients who had terrific family relationships their whole lives. Daughters who married and lived half an hour away from their parents. Daughters who brought their kids over every Sunday, and sometimes even more. There was such a thing as lifelong respect in a family. Relationships could be honored. It was all in the way you played it, wasn't it?

Dinner was at eight, and it was just seven. George was getting ready to change when the doorbell rang. Maybe it was Anne. He had told her to meet him at the restaurant, but she had been so excited that morning, that he supposed she couldn't wait. He opened the door and there was a woman he didn't know. "I called," she said defensively and winced, one hand flying to her cheek. "I kept getting the machine." She looked around at the dark rooms in the back. "You can take me, can't you?" she said miserably, and she looked so sad and defeated that George ushered her in.

He glanced at his watch. "I was just on my way out—" he said. "My daughter—"

"Oh, ow, ow, ow," said the woman, "I can go back to the clinic, I suppose—" And then George took his jacket off. He had some time to take a look, to do what he could, and still be able to make it to dinner. "Just let me make a call."

He called home, but no one picked up. Eva said she was taking herself to a movie, and Anne had probably left for the restaurant. But just in case, he left a message. "I'll be a little late, honey, can't wait for our dinner," he said. He called Spitfire's, and asked a waitress if she'd look out for Anne, if she'd tell her what happened. "Yah. Sure," the woman said and hung up.

George walked the woman to an examining room. He snapped on latex gloves when the woman held out one hand and grabbed his wrist. "I'm allergic to latex," she said.

He peeled off the gloves. "Good you told me," he said, thinking, oh God, why hadn't he asked that? What was the matter with him?

The woman's name was Meg Emberlon, and when she opened her mouth, George flinched. There was a definite swelling by her molars, a raw tenderness, and he touched it, and she jerked away from him. "Oh, don't!" she cried.

"Let's take some film," George said.

He took the film, but before it even developed, he knew what he'd find. Abscess. He cleaned it out as best he could, he gave her a prescription for an antibiotic and set her up with an appointment for tomorrow.

He didn't notice the time until after Meg left, thanking him so profusely he was almost embarrassed. "That's what I'm here for," he told her.

He rubbed his wrist thoughtfully, and then he glanced at his watch.

Fuck. Oh fuck. He was an hour late and Anne was waiting for him.

He called Spitfire's again. "The reservation for Rivers?" he said.

"Your party's here," the waitress said and hung up on him. He dialed again, and this time the line was busy. Well, he'd drive there. He'd explain in person.

By the time George walked into Spitfire's, Anne was finishing a burger. She had gotten dressed up, had clipped back her hair with a golden barrette. She looked small and beautiful and his heart broke to see her, but she didn't even look up at him when he sat.

"I'm sorry," he said quietly. "I am so sorry. There was an emergency."

He tried to reach for her hands, but she pulled them away. "A burger at Spitfire's!" He tried to joke. "You could have ordered lobster."

"I don't like lobster."

"Want to order dessert?" he said.

She pushed her plate away, and when she looked at him, she looked so unhappy, he couldn't bear it. "I'm not hungry anymore," she said. "I want to get out of here."

She was silent the whole way home, looking out the window the entire time. George kept offering alternatives. A mall. Miniature golf. "What do you say we go to a movie?" George said, and Anne looked at him as if he had three heads.

"I want to go home," she said, biting down on her lower lip.

"Radio?" he asked, and she ignored him, and as soon as they got home, she walked inside, past Eva, and slammed the door of her room. "What happened?" Eva asked.

"No dinner," he said sorrowfully, and then he told her.

In the morning, Anne was up and out of the door before her parents woke. George had tried to talk with her last night, knocking on her door, but she shut her eyes, pretending to be asleep. She waited until she heard her parents go to bed, before she got up again, and wrote at her desk, the one thing that was making her happy, that saved her.

Monday, in class, Mr. Moto was already there. He smiled thinly at Anne which she took to be a great sign, and she took her seat. He said nothing about the papers, but Anne could see them in a pile on the corner of his desk and her heart skipped. She tried to concentrate on what he was talking about today—"Huck Finn is a parable," he intoned—and Anne rested her chin on her hands. It wasn't until the bell rang that he started handing out the essays. "Just trying to avoid a mutiny," he said dryly. She heard the hisses, the moans, the audible sighs as kids took their papers. She knew he could be ferocious in his comments. "Anne," he said and put a paper on her desk.

There wasn't a mark on it. Amazed, she looked at the page. Was it perfect? She glanced at the boy next to her who was scowling at his first page, which was covered in red, slashed and arrowed and mangled. "Fuck-ing shit," he muttered. She looked back at her paper. Nothing. She glanced at the sentences and felt a rush. There was that phrase she had labored over, how Carolyn had found the coffee "warming her like yesterday's sun." How deliciously happy the words were making her. In wonder she turned the page, and it was clean, too. She couldn't help laughing out loud, and then she turned the next page, and the next until she got to the very last page and saw the huge, humbling red F.

"Despite clear instructions, only you among everyone in the class did not follow the assignment but went off on your own merry tangent. I asked for an essay, not a story. Your puerile prose makes me cringe and there's little grasp of proper style. The characters are so flat they can't possibly draw breath. If I could have marked this lower, I would have. As it is, I did you a favor by giving you an F."

Her legs were buckling and she blinked back the tears. Kids were shuffling out, complaining to each other. One girl was waving her paper like a flag. "B!" she called out.

Surely this was a mistake. She stared up at Mr. Moto, but he was sifting papers into a pile on his desk, humming to himself.

She waited. Every sound seemed amplified. Her breath. The scrape of her shoes on the floor as she shifted weight. "Mr. Moto." Her voice sounded foreign to her.

He kept shifting papers. "Yes?" he said.

"There must be some mistake—" she said, fumbling. "I worked so hard on this story. I wrote and rewrote—" She paused, catching her breath. "I want to be a writer." Her words speeded up, like a car out of control. "Maybe I could show you other things I've written, maybe it's just this one story—" And then he looked up at her, and she saw how eerily blue his eyes were, like beach glass worn smooth from the salt water.

He sniffed at her with disdain. "There's a very famous story I'd like to share with you," he said dryly. "You're familiar with I. B. Singer, of course?"

Anne had no idea who he was talking about, but she nodded.

"I. B. Singer said he wasn't scared of a burglar breaking into his house and taking something. What he was scared of was a writer breaking in and leaving him a manuscript to read."

Anne stared at him and blinked. What did that even mean? She couldn't read any meaning in his face. He walked to the door, opened it and stood there, waiting for her to leave. "Your grade was exactly right.

You didn't follow the assignment. I did you a courtesy even reading it."
Haughtily, he raised one brow at her.

"I want to be a writer," she repeated, her voice a whisper.

"Pardon me," he said coldly, "but you don't write that well."

Dazed, Anne retreated. She walked out of his classroom, down the
crowded hall, her books clutched to her chest, and when she got to the
front door of the school, there seemed nothing more to do but walk out
of it and keep walking.

The whole way home, she wept. A few cars beeped, a voice called out,
"You okay? Hey, girlie, you okay?" But she ignored it and kept walking.

She assured herself that he was wrong, that he didn't know good writing if it turned around and bit him in the butt. She thought of Carolyn, living on the page, how she had labored and labored to get the words right so
she would feel them deep inside of herself. How much pleasure she had
taken in the writing, as if she were in this whole other magic world.
Really, if he was such a hot writer himself, what was he doing teaching
here in some crummy little high school instead of a college, at least? Why
wasn't he home writing? She tried not to let her mind go anywhere near
the thought that he might be right, that maybe she didn't have talent after
all. It was too terrible to contemplate. Because if she couldn't write, if she
wasn't talented, then what was left her? Where was her comfort?

Inside the house moved and settled. She went to her room. She took the
story out of her backpack, ready to rip it to pieces. And then she glanced
down, she saw her words again, Carolyn the waitress pouring coffee, and
for a moment, the pages breathed. Wrong. Wrong. Surely he was wrong.
She folded the story in half. She bent and tucked it in between her mattress
and box spring, on top of her journal. Then she went to the bathroom to
splash water on her face. She'd take a walk, all the way to the Rite-Aid and
back, and by then, the dangerous shaking feeling inside of her would be
gone.

* * *

Eva scooped up her daughter's laundry. She had come home to an empty house, but had spotted Anne's things. Anne must be out walking. How that girl could cover ground! She'd get upset and just storm out and walk and walk for miles and then come back, the anger or sadness or whatever terrible emotion she had been feeling walked right out of her. And if Eva felt shut out, at least she was relieved that Anne felt better.

Puddles of clothes were kicked in the corner of Anne's room, dresses were slung on chairs and doorknobs. *Seventeen* magazines spilled over the bed with an ad for a hair straightener circled, and there was a half-eaten jelly sandwich on the desk. George had already called her twice today, once to tell her his office manager had come in two hours late, and the second time to tell her they were so backed up he wasn't sure he would make it home for dinner and not to hold it for him, that he'd grab something later. In the background, Eva could hear his phones ringing, she could hear the buzz of talk, like bees swarming around him, and worst of all, she could hear the exhaustion in his voice.

"I'm worried about you," Eva said. "And I miss you."

"Doctor—" Eva heard.

"I've got to go," George said, and then the line went dead.

A vague irritation prickled along Eva's spine. Here she was, brushed off by her busy, worried husband, as if she weren't involved in the worry, too. Here she was, picking up after her daughter yet again. She felt a pulse of heat. Hot flashes. Menopause. "Getting old, old girl," she tried to joke to herself.

The only thing making Eva happy now was her job. She couldn't wait to get to school tomorrow, for all those clamoring children, all so in love with her, it made her giddy. Fifteen friendly faces instead of the sullen one of her daughter. Just thinking about school made her excited. At the beginning of every month, she surprised the kids by changing the room around as dramatically as possible. She knew just how she wanted to do her room this month. She'd paint each wall a different color, and one wall would be that new blackboard paint so the kids could scribble all over it if they wanted. Any kid who walked in would just about go crazy with excitement. The other teachers thought she was a bit eccentric, that she went overboard. She didn't speak in that "teacherly" voice the others sometimes affected, a tone they told her commanded children's attention. Like little soldiers, Eva thought dryly. She didn't walk into her class on the first day with the fierce look in her eye all the other teachers said was mandatory for keeping control. "Don't smile until mid-year," they advised, but Eva just laughed. It didn't matter what the other teachers said to her because she had seen how they copied some of the things she did, how one of the other teachers had come in dressed in costume one day the way Eva sometimes did when she wanted to read a particular story, how another even wore roller skates to teach the kids about wheels and what they did. Eva wanted to make a time machine this year; she'd paint a box silver; she'd attach knobs. She'd have the kids go in and she'd have artifacts from different years. Wooden teeth that she'd swear were George Washington's. A Pilgrim costume. A space suit she'd sprinkle with gold dust. Letters she'd age by crumbling them up and smearing on a little dirt. She'd swear they were from Paul Revere. The kids would die from happiness.

The weather was too hot and sticky for all this cleaning, but if Eva stopped moving, she'd think about what was going on with Anne.

The other mothers she knew told her that this was all perfectly normal, par for the course for a teenage girl. All kids yanked away the umbilical cord. Her friend Jennifer's daughter crossed the street and walked the other way when she saw her mother coming. Her friend Adelle had overheard her son call her "the dried-up old bitch" on the telephone, and when she had confronted him, he had said mildly, "Well, I guess the truth hurts." "Not more than this does," Adelle had said, smacking him across the face, instantly horrifying them both. Eva would never hit Anne, would never even raise her hand, but God forgive her, that sure as hell didn't mean that sometimes she didn't feel like it.

The other mothers she knew, though, were undeniably different from Eva. They were in their thirties, while she was approaching the end of her fifties faster than she would like. Once she stopped talking about Anne, she didn't have much else to say to these other mothers, and the sad fact was she probably had more in common with these women's mothers than with them.

She and George didn't know what to do about their daughter. Anne, her sweet, dreamy little Anne, used to listen to them, used to obey. She used to have friends, two girls they liked, who were always hanging about the house, or tying up the phone, but then these girls had disappeared, and if they had replacements, Eva didn't know them.

She swept up notebooks, and pens, and then tore off a piece of paper and wrote on it: *"I love you!"* She tucked it into the edge of Anne's mirror.

She was stripping Anne's bed when she noticed how lumpily the mattress was settling. She straightened it and saw a book poking out under the mattress. *Don't,* she told herself. She pulled off the sheet, the pillowcases, and then resettled the mattress and the book fell out. *Put it back,* she told herself, and then she saw the typed pages poking out, and she couldn't help herself. She sat back on the bare mattress and began to read.

A waitress was pouring coffee, making friends with a housewife, but the waitress wasn't telling the truth. It just sounded like truth. Eva couldn't stop reading. The housewife had been a kindergarten teacher and she was talking about a short skirt, finally saying, "It's not me," and Eva started. My God, that was something she had said to Anne the week before. She blushed, as if she had been complimented, because really, wasn't it a compliment to find yourself in your own daughter's story?

Eva turned a page. Why had Anne hidden this? It was pretty good, wasn't it? And how could she get her to tell them about it? She kept reading. The housewife was drinking, pouring booze into the coffee, and Carolyn, the waitress, kept serving, and the dilemma was, if the waitress turned a blind eye, she'd have a friend, but if she didn't, the woman would leave and God knows what. The story ended with Carolyn outside, spiking her own coffee with booze, and then not taking a sip, so you didn't know what was going to happen. Eva turned the page, and then saw a scribbling of red, a huge red F.

Shocked, Eva blinked. F? How could this be an F? Was she going crazy? Or was the teacher nuts instead? She read the note and then sat back. Wait, wait, here it was. Anne hadn't followed directions. She hadn't done the assignment. It didn't matter how good it was if she didn't fulfill the assignment. She leafed back through the pages and suddenly words jumped out at her. Weak adjectives. Funny constructions. Why hadn't Anne taken more care? Poor character development. Well, yes, she could see that. Carolyn's motives weren't quite clear. Eva let the papers settle on her lap. She was about to put them back in place, under the mattress, when she heard the front door open, heard the clack of Anne's shoes and suddenly there didn't seem to be any real reason to do anything but wait.

Anne strode in, her hair damp from the outside, and as soon as she saw the story on Eva's lap, her face changed. Eva waited to be accused of snooping, but Anne simply stood there. "What's wrong?" Anne said.

"You got an F," Eva said quietly.

Anne's mouth snapped shut and then opened again.

"Why didn't you follow directions?" Eva asked.

"What?" said Anne, astonished.

"You didn't do what your teacher asked. There were sloppy mistakes—"

"I did more than what he asked for—"

"And it got you an F!"

"It's a good story! I know it is! I worked so hard—I wrote ten times more than anyone. He's wrong! He just didn't see it!"

Eva looked at the paper again. "Maybe if you redid it. Showed initiative—"

"I did show initiative! I wrote a story!" Anne grabbed the paper out of Eva's hands so hard it ripped. "Did you even read it?" she asked Eva. "Did you like it—even a little?"

"Well, yes, but that's not the point. Honey, you can do better," she said, and then she saw Anne's face folding like a flower. "I know from my own class, I'd rather see a child trying and trying until he gets something right than just giving up on it after the first try." She tried to think of an example. "Bill Broomer," she said. "Couldn't tie his shoes and instead of running around with them hanging out and tripping over himself, he missed a playtime activity so he could sit in the corner and just practice and practice and get it right, and when he did, I swear I couldn't tell who was happier or more proud, me or him!"

"I'm not one of the kids in your class," Anne whispered. "This isn't tying shoes."

The door opened again, and George called out, "Anyone home?" his voice tense and weary. "Cancellations so I'm home early," he said, his voice growing louder as he came toward them, and then he stopped at the door of Anne's room, looking from Anne to Eva. "What's wrong?"

"Daddy," she cried. "I wrote this great story—"

Eva handed the paper to George. "An F?" George said.

"Read it!" Anne cried. "Just read it!"

"I told her to rewrite it as an essay, to give the teacher what he asked for—"

George glanced at the paper and then rubbed at his temples. In the hall, the phone rang, and George stepped out to pick it up. "Yes," he said shortly. "You're sure? Yes. You'd better come in then." He hung up and sighed. "I can't believe this but I've got to go back to the office. Another emergency. Does it ever end?" He looked at Anne.

"You're not going to read it?" she asked.

"Honey, I can't read anything right now. I think your mother's right on this one."

"Daddy—"

"Just redo it."

As soon as Eva was out of the room, Anne shut the door. For a moment, Eva stood there with George, wondering what Anne was up to. And then they could hear the whir of the computer going on, the soft tap of Anne's hands on the keyboard.

Relieved, Eva rested her head against George's shoulder. "She'll be *fine*," she said.

For two days straight, Anne worked on her essay. She sighed heavily, she kept glancing at the clock, but she did it. And when she came home with an A on her temperance essay, Eva and George made a huge deal out of it, reading it, exclaiming over how well it was organized, how intelligent it sounded, how even Mr. Moto's comments ("Clearly stated. Good segue.") were something exceptional, especially since Anne had told them how he never liked anything, much less gave praise. "You should be so proud of yourself," Eva said, giving her a hug.

"I thought it was so dull," Anne said quietly. "I wrote it in my sleep."

"Keep up the great work," George said and rushed off to work.

*   *   *

Anne's grades improved. If she didn't come home with friends (and Eva kept encouraging her to join clubs), well, she now came home with fresh surprises. College catalogs tucked under her arm, but always to schools as far away as she could find them, New York City, Maine. Books about different professions, ambitions Eva never knew anything about. *So You Want to Be a Veterinarian* lay by the tub, with a bookmark in the chapter about exotic reptiles. *Today's Advertising* was shoved under Anne's bed, with passages underlined in yellow. *Get the Big Picture. Make It Pop.*

"At least she's thinking about her future," Eva said to George, but a day later, she found books kicked under Anne's bed. Books left in the backyard.

In bed, at night, holding hands, they talked quietly about Anne, how she was doing in school, what she might become in her future. They had long since stopped talking about telling Anne she was adopted. *What did it matter?* Eva thought. The fact was that the people who raised and loved a child were the parents. The rest was just biology. People formed bonds in all sorts of ways. Husbands and wives. Friends. If you wanted to get scientific, well, couldn't you say that everyone shared the same basic matter, the same cell matter and memory—wasn't everyone family in one way or another?

"She'll be going to college before we know it," Eva said. She knew what that meant. The thrill of being on your own. Boyfriends that turned serious, and then jobs in cities that might be clear across the country. Phone calls and visits rather than the day-to-day presence. Eva gripped the blanket. "I'm not ready to let her go," she said.

chapter

thirteen

S ara stood on the sidewalk, unable to move, the shiny heat blanketed
around her. She couldn't think anymore if this was the right thing to
do, only that here she was and it was finally happening, and terrified
or not, she would see it through. Eva and George's house was big and
white with a shady porch and a fancy oak door, a walkway made out of
intricate mosaics, and everywhere she looked was something special.
Exotic plants and a well-tended lawn, a small brass angel on the knocker
and a rubber welcome mat cut to look like wrought iron. She licked her
lips and tasted sugar from the tea she had had that morning. Everything
seemed a rebuke to her, reminding her of what George and Eva could give
her daughter, and what she couldn't.

Struggling to compose herself, Sara rang the bell. She heard footsteps
and her bones turned to water. "Coming—" she heard and she knew that
voice, she remembered how some days she'd call just to hear the loving
way Eva would say "Sara," as if her name were a kind of prayer, or a blessing.

The door swung open and there Eva was, the gold hair still long, but
now faded, the milky skin weathered from the sun, and Sara's anger
flared, making her glad Eva was on the other side of the door.

"Yes?" Eva said quizzically. She smiled pleasantly, the way she would to a stranger, and then her gaze sharpened, she looked at Sara as if she were waking from a dream.

"It's Sara," she said tightly, and then Eva started. Her hand rushed to her mouth.

Sara heard George's voice from the other room, his footsteps, and then there was George, and as soon as he saw Sara, he stepped back. "Sara?" He shook his head as if he couldn't believe what he was seeing.

"Can I come in?" Sara asked coldly, and Eva opened the door.

As soon as she was inside the house, Sara anxiously looked for signs of her daughter. A Mother's Day card on the mantel, schoolbooks on a table. George and Eva used to almost paper their walls with photographs back when Sara was a part of the family, but now the walls were clean. She braced one hand on the wall. "Let's all sit," George said.

He led her into a spacious white living room, filled with green plants. Eva quickly sat on a floral couch, and then George sat beside her, taking her hand. Sara's knees felt like jelly but she wanted to stand tall, she wanted to show them how much older she was now, stronger, that they couldn't push her around anymore.

"What are you doing here?" George blurted.

"I could ask you the same thing."

George looked down at his hand that was holding Eva's. "We live here now."

"You could have told me." Sara fought to keep her voice even. "I went to your house and no one was there. No one even knew where you were. How could you do that to me? Just disappear like that?"

Eva leaned forward. "We thought it would be better."

"Better? Better for whom?" Sara asked. "You stole my daughter."

Eva drew herself up. "You endangered her when you took her from us."

"Anne was mine to take! Maybe I didn't go about it the right way but it wasn't my fault. I was a kid, I didn't know there was a right way. But I do now."

"Sara, you gave her up! You signed away your rights! You knew that!"

Sara lifted her chin. "But Danny didn't," she said.

"What? What are you talking about?" Eva said. "Those papers were signed." Her eyes were wide, innocent, but Sara could see Eva's hand gripping her leg.

"I saw Danny," Sara said. "And I found out that he didn't even know there was a baby, that he didn't sign any papers. That his name was forged. He would never have given up Anne! He would have fought to keep her—fought you! And without both our signatures, you'd never have gotten Anne, you'd never have been able to disappear."

"How does he know now what he would have done at sixteen?" Eva cried.

"He knows. And so do you."

Eva looked as if she were having trouble breathing. She met Sara's eyes. "What does Danny want now?"

Sara was quiet. She didn't want to lie, but she couldn't tell the truth, couldn't risk giving them a reason not to let her see her daughter. "I'm the one who's here now and what I want is to see Anne."

"And then what?" Eva leaned back into the couch as if she could no longer keep upright on her own.

"Maybe that's for Anne and me to figure out."

"Anne doesn't know about you," George said.

"You never told her?"

Eva jumped to her feet. "Anne'll be home any second. Instead of springing this on her, can't George and I discuss the best way to break this to her?"

"Please," George said, standing now, too. "Whatever mistakes we made in the past, think of Anne. Let's work this out. Eva and I can arrange something."

"I used to be willing to do anything for you," Sara said, voice cracking. "I used to imagine finding you and Eva again, convincing you to make things go back to the way they were, when we were all so happy. What did I know? I was a kid. But I'm not a kid anymore. And now the only one I care about is Anne."

"Then let us prepare her—" Eva said. "There's no need to tell her every detail—"

There was the sound of a key in the lock. Eva jumped up and grabbed Sara's arm, the first time she had touched her, and Sara shook it loose. "Please," Eva said. "Don't say anything. I'm begging you."

Sara hesitated. If she didn't tell Anne right away would they disappear again? If she didn't tell her daughter would she ever have another chance? She looked at Eva's beseeching face and something soft and small formed in the pit of her stomach. "You tell her this week or I will," Sara said, and then the door opened, and there was Anne.

Her daughter was nothing like how she had imagined her, but how could she be, when all these years the Anne Sara had clung to was as small as a minute, a pearly baby in her arms, smelling of powder and milk. This girl was grown and Sara thought she was beautiful, small-boned and thin, with a riot of short russet hair, dressed in baggy, drab clothes, and for a moment, Sara felt as if time had gone all out of whack, free-floating her someplace she might not belong. She looked at Anne again, at that delicate, lovely face, and then she started. Anne had been born with slate-colored eyes, and all this time, whenever she had been drawn to a girl, whenever she had wondered about her, she had been drawn to grey eyes. Fool that she was, she hadn't thought about eyes changing color, because her daughter's eyes were now the same startling green as Danny's.

"Is something wrong?" Anne asked. Her eyes flew to her own shirt, to her loose cotton pants.

"You're Anne," Sara said. She held on to the edge of the end table so she wouldn't spring across the room and embrace her daughter. Anne looked at her curiously, and then she looked from one parent to another before she glanced at Sara again.

"Last time I looked," Anne said. She walked over and stuck out her hand for Sara to shake. "How do you do?" she said politely, and Sara glanced down and saw the raw, bitten nails. Sara took Anne's hand and held it, and as soon as she did, she wanted to wrap her arms about her daughter and never let go.

"Why is everyone looking at me like that?" Anne said.

"This is an old friend of ours," Eva blurted. "Sara Rothman."

Interest faded in Anne's eyes, and it was more than Sara could bear.

"More than a friend," Sara said, and Anne's glance darted her way again. Sara ached to move closer, to touch her daughter's skin, to smell her hair. She had to force herself to look away. She dug in her purse and found a receipt for aspirin and started scribbling her hotel address on the back, her hand shaking so badly she could barely form the letters. Then she thrust the paper out to Anne. "This is where I'm staying." Anne started to hand the paper to Eva, but Sara reached over and folded Anne's hands over it. "You keep it," she said.

As soon as Sara stood outside, she wanted to rush back inside. She wanted to grab Anne and tell her who she was, what she had been through. Instead, she couldn't move. Mosquitoes whined past her ears. The cab was gone. She didn't have a cell phone to call another. There was nothing to do but start to walk and hope that it was toward something.

"Why'd she give me this?" Anne said, slouching on the couch. She put the paper on the table next to her. "Aren't we going out to eat?" She glanced up. "Why are you both looking like someone died?"

"Anne," Eva said, pacing. "Honey. This is very hard."

"What is?" Anne grabbed for a peanut from the bowl on the table.

"Remember how you always asked where you got your hair?"

"My great-aunt Ada's to blame."

"No, honey. That's not who you got it from."

Anne took another nut, a fat salted Brazil, and bit into it. She waited for her parents to argue with her that she was spoiling her appetite, but they were staring at her so hard, it suddenly made her anxious. The nut, sweet and salty both, split in her mouth. And then George leaned toward her and began to talk, and as soon as he did, Anne couldn't move. He must have been speaking in a foreign language because none of the words made sense. *Adopted. Birth mother. Losing touch.* The nut felt lodged in her throat.

"We should have told you years ago," George said finally.

"We love you," Eva said. "We thought it wouldn't make a difference."

Anne bolted to her feet. "Of course it makes a difference!" Anne cried.

"No, no, honey——" Eva said.

"Shut up, shut up, I don't believe you!" She grabbed for a napkin and spit the nut out into it. "Why didn't Sara keep me?"

"Sara was a baby, herself. How could she have kept you?"

"What about my real father?" She glared at George, who stepped closer to Eva.

"He wasn't around——" Eva said. "And even if he was, he was sixteen. What kind of life would you have had?"

"I don't know! My life?" Anne cried, mouth trembling. "Why is she here now, after all this time? Am I supposed to be grateful?"

"She just wants to know you——"

"I don't want to know her! I don't want anything to do with any of you!" Anne reached for the front door and Eva grabbed to close it, and then the glass shattered into thousands of little mirrors sparkling on the floor, and Anne leaped over them out onto the walk.

Anne ran along the streets, panting. The wind was sharp, a razor skimming her skin. Her sneakers slapped on the pavement. *Liars,* she thought. *Liars.* She was furious. All those stupid made-for-TV movies about kids finding their birth mothers, about birth mothers finding them, everyone dissolving into tears of happiness as if they had finally been completed. *"I didn't grow under your heart, I grew in it."* What a bunch of treacly shit. All she knew was that she didn't want her life with her parents, and she didn't want a life with this woman, either. And she certainly didn't want to meet some guy who said he was her father and expected her to love him.

She ran harder and then she was crying, folding down onto her knees. Sara was her real mother and she didn't know anything about her, whether to hate or love her or feel anything at all.

Anne felt like one of those orphans in the stories she used to write, one of those lost girls, and the only difference was that the girls she wrote about had money to travel, had freedom to do what they wanted, and here she was stuck in Florida.

She got up, not bothering to brush her knees, and walked slowly back to the house. George and Eva were standing by the door, the glass still sprinkled around them, and as soon as her parents saw her, they straightened. "Don't say anything to me," Anne warned and George closed his lips. Anne averted her face so she wouldn't have to see either one of them. Still, she felt them watching her, even after she entered the house.

She went into her room and shut the door, and when she heard her parents talking, she clapped her hands over her ears. She grabbed up her journal and a pen and then dashed *liar* onto the page, flinging her pen and then her notebook to the floor.

She stayed in her room, coming out only to use the bathroom. She heard a truck outside, trying to park. The voice of a workman putting in new glass. The TV turning on. She wouldn't open the door when her parents knocked, wanting to tell her dinner was ready, that they were going to bed, and please would she come out and talk? "Honey?" George's voice was smooth and slow as syrup.

"Anne, please," Eva said. "Honey, we need to talk about this."

She stayed silent. The knocking went away.

She didn't sleep. At three in the morning, she crept to the living room, but the piece of paper that had Sara's address and number on it was gone. There was sparkling new glass in the front door. She went to the kitchen and took a chunk of cheddar cheese from the refrigerator and broke off some Italian bread and ate standing up by the door, the blue light spread over her like a blanket. She went back to her room and sat up, thinking. Her parents were two strangers and everything she had thought she knew about them was wrong. Who were they, then? And more importantly, if she didn't know who they were anymore, then who was she?

At five, she dressed in the quiet house and made her own lunch, and even though school wouldn't start for another three hours, she went out the door. Let them wonder where she was. Let them wonder what she was going to do.

At school, she moved in a daze. She couldn't dare open her mouth to speak for fear of what might fly out. She was stumbling down the hall to her third-period math class when hands grabbed at the back of her shirt, making her jump.

"Hey, hey, it's me! What's gotten into you?" Flor stood in front of her, frowning. "I was just trying to help. I mean, did you want your buttons all open like that?" Flor asked. "Let me fix you up before you give everyone a free show." In gym class, she stood in the outfield while everyone around her played softball. She didn't hear people shouting her name, until the ball flew out from center field and struck her in the face. "Are you all right?" A few girls crowded around her, but Anne brushed them away.

And though she meant to go to her last-period history class, she found herself standing outside the front of the school, a strange new roaring in her ears, and then she started walking along the road.

She had another mother. There was a whole other side to her she knew nothing about. The thought bounced around in her head. Another person who was somehow like her, who might instinctively understand.

She came home, and as soon as she saw her mother, Anne walked toward her. Eva smiled hesitantly, acting as if nothing had happened, as if this were the most normal day in the world. "What a day today," Eva said. "Three different kids threw up."

"I want Sara's number. I want to go see her."

Eva's smile faded. "Are you sure?"

"I can't find the paper she gave me." Anne's mouth tightened. "Did you throw it out?"

She saw her mother swallow hard, and then Eva went to the other room and came back with a piece of paper and slowly handed it to Anne. "You know," she said slowly, "everyone has different versions of the past, of why they needed to do what they did—"

Anne slipped the paper into her jeans. Abruptly, Eva stopped talking.

"Do you want me to drive you?" Eva said finally. "I could go with you, if you want."

Anne shook her head. She didn't want her parents having any part of this. She'd go see her mother and find out what she felt for herself.

"You know how much we love you," Eva said, but Anne was gone.

Anne had to change buses twice to get to Sara's hotel, a Howard Johnson's, which was not in the greatest part of town. VACANCY, the red neon sign flashed. The desk clerk, a young, bored-looking guy with bad skin, was reading a racing form when Anne walked in. He didn't look up, didn't even blink when she went right to the elevator. *I could be anyone,* Anne thought, amazed.

Sara's room was on the second floor, down the hall to her right. Anne put her hand up to the door. She could still turn around, go back into the heat of the day. She could go home and walk in the house and have her mother's eyes boring into her wondering what had happened and the only person who would know would be Anne.

She raised her hand to knock on the door. She had an ink scribble on one hand and she quickly spit on one finger and rubbed at it until it was gone. She sucked in a breath and knocked and the door opened and there was Sara and this time Anne looked at her as if she were trying to find out something. There was Anne's same red hair, but while Anne had clipped her hair short to control the curl, Sara's length flaunted it. While Anne tried to tan, Sara's pale skin was so striking Anne couldn't stop looking at it. And then Sara smiled, the first time Anne had seen it, and the right corner of Sara's mouth tilted up higher than the left, the same way Anne's had ever since she was little. "Like a broken parentheses," Flor used to tease her. Anne's hand flew to her own mouth and she took a step back.

"Anne," Sara said. "I've been waiting for you."

There was no place to sit except the bed, which seemed far too intimate. There was an old wooden chair orphaned in the corner that looked as if it would crash to the floor if you dared to sit on it. "This is strange, isn't it?" Sara said quietly. "But I'm glad you came."

Anne's tongue lay thick and heavy in her mouth. Her breath came in pinches. Outside, a car spit gravel in the parking lot. "Get some ice," she heard a guy shout.

"I don't know what to say," Anne said. She kept standing, folding her arms about her chest, holding on to herself, as if any moment she might fly away in all directions.

"You don't have to say anything yet if you don't want to," Sara said.

Anne shook her head. "Want to sit?" Sara motioned to the bed, but Anne backed away, leaning against the far wall. She felt as if she were under a hot light. The way Sara was looking at her made Anne feel as if everything about her was wrong: her hair, her clothes, her face. "You're staring at me," Anne finally said.

"I can't help it."

Anne tried to smooth her shirt, pasted along her back.

"Did your parents tell you anything more about me?" Sara asked.

"No." Anne couldn't bring herself to look back at Sara, to meet that gaze, as intense and pointed as a laser beam. Instead she shifted her weight, staring at the far wall, at a pastel picture of mallard ducks, all in flight, and for a moment, she wished she could join them. "You can ask me anything," Sara offered.

"How old are you?" Anne blurted.

"Thirty-two."

Thirty-two! Younger than anybody else's mother. Anne did a quick subtraction in her head. Thirty-two meant that Sara had gotten pregnant when she was fifteen, only a little younger than Anne was now. Anne couldn't imagine herself pregnant, couldn't begin to think what she'd do if the same thing happened to her, though it wasn't likely since she had never even really kissed a boy, let alone slept with one. She didn't know any girls her age who had gotten pregnant, though she had heard vague rumors, followed by even vaguer rumors of abortions. Everyone had to take sex education class, everyone knew about condoms and pills. "There's no excuse for an unwanted pregnancy," the sex ed teacher had told them, and now, thinking about it, Anne reflected: *There's no excuse for me.* Her hand rested on her belly, and abruptly she took it off.

"You don't know how long I've imagined this," Sara said.

"Why? You gave me up."

"Don't say that," said Sara, "I didn't give you up, not the way you think. I loved you. I loved your house. I even loved your parents."

"You loved my parents?" Anne said, astonished.

"I was family." Sara leaned forward, as if she were going to tell Anne a great secret. She started to tell Sara how she and George and Eva had done all these things together, how they had gone miniature-golfing and to plays, how Eva had taught her how to make crème brûlée, how George had taught her to drive, and Anne flinched, because all she could remember was how Eva had whisked her out of the kitchen when Anne asked if she could cook something, how George had given her one lesson and then, when she had banged up the car, wouldn't teach her again. "You came back to see them," she said.

"I came to see you."

Anne was quiet for a moment. "Who's my father? Does he know about me?"

"It's complicated. He's married. He has a whole other life. But you have me."

Anne stared down at the floor and then back at Sara. "Do I have grandparents?"

Sara nodded and looked weary. "What?" said Anne. "Why do you look that way?"

"Because it's hard. It's always been hard for everyone. I was only fifteen when I got pregnant, sixteen when I had you, and my parents wanted none of it to have happened."

"They don't want to know me?"

Sara didn't say anything and Anne felt something chipping deep inside of her.

"I have to go," Anne said, and Sara moved toward her, upset. "Oh no. Please."

Anne looked toward the door. "Why did you come here? What do you really want?"

"I want to see you. I wanted to know you."

Anne yanked at the door, and suddenly she felt Sara's hand on hers. She tried to jerk her hand free, but Sara's grip tightened, holding her in place. "Will you come back?"

"I don't know—" Anne said.

"We don't have to meet here if you don't want. We can meet at a diner, go to the movies, or for a walk. Whatever you'd like, whatever would make you feel comfortable."

"I said I don't know."

"I'll be here," Sara said. "You can call me anytime."

And then Anne was off, out the door and down the hall, and the one time she dared to look back, there was Sara, standing in her doorway, lifting her hand up in a wave, but when Anne tried to move her own arm, it stayed stuck at her side.

Outside the hotel, everything looked different. The sidewalk had a huge jagged crack she didn't remember from before. The sky was a weird metallic-orange color and none of the clouds looked real, but like Styrofoam. Everything familiar now seemed strange and new and terrible, as if her old life had been ripped apart. Her parents weren't her parents. Her father was missing in action. Her mother was a stranger. And now she felt like a stranger, too.

Anne had hoped for an empty house, but as soon as she got home, she could hear Eva talking on the phone, bright patter like pennies spilled in a jar. "Oh, she's here, I'll call you back—" Eva said, the shine suddenly gone from her voice, and then, before Anne could even settle herself, Eva was in the room with her, her face a map of concern. "How did it go with Sara?" Eva asked. Anne just shook her head. "I don't want to talk about it." She went right to the bathroom and locked the door, rushing the water in the shower, while she sat on the toilet and tried to think.

"Anne?" Eva knocked on the door a few times and Anne put her head in her hands, shutting her eyes, and then she heard George coming home, and he came and knocked on the door, too. "Come out now," he said, and she slowly got up and opened the door. George and Eva were standing there. "Come talk with us in the kitchen," George ordered, and she followed them, reluctantly, sitting down at the table. Her parents scraped their chairs closer to her. "What happened with Sara to get you so upset?" he said.

"I don't know."

Eva and George exchanged glances. "What did she tell you?" George said.

"She said she loved you." Anne felt tense and miserable. "That she lived with you."

"She didn't live with us," Eva said. "It was an open adoption. She was over a lot."

"But why did that all stop?"

"Well, because—because it had to. Because Sara did something really terrible."

"What did she do?" said Anne.

There was that funny look again between her parents. "Tell me," Anne said. "I have a right to know, don't I?"

Eva exhaled. "Fine. What does it matter? If I don't tell you, she will." Eva rubbed her forehead. "She tried to kidnap you."

Anne sat up straighter. "She did what?"

"She took you on a Greyhound with her. With no money and no food," Eva said.

"She took you across state lines," George said. "You could have died!"

"I might have ended up with her—" Anne said in wonder.

"It was a crime!" Eva said. "If we were anybody else, we could have put her in jail, we could have ruined her life if we wanted. But we didn't. We let her off the hook, even though all our friends said we were crazy. We did what was hardest for us, leaving the practice, moving down here, and maybe it was difficult, but at least everyone got a new start."

Anne leaned against the wall. What must it have felt like to be on that bus, young and terrified and on the run, a baby jostling on your lap? It was better than any story she herself could have come up with. And it was a story about her.

"Anne? Honey? We know it's terrible, what she did," George said. "You don't have to see her again. You're not obligated."

"I *want* to see her," Anne said, and then before she could see her parents' expressions, she left the room.

The next day, right after school, instead of going home, Anne showed up at Sara's. Her parents would probably give her grief about it, they'd put her on the hot seat wanting to know every detail, but she knew they wouldn't stop her. Not that they could, anyway.

Sara didn't seem surprised to see her. Her hair was held back by a red bandana headband and Anne couldn't take her eyes off how cool it looked.

"Oh great, you're here!" Sara said, as if they had actually made plans. "Want to see a movie?"

"In the middle of the day?"

"Sure. Why not?"

They walked a few blocks to the triplex and bought tickets for a movie called *Good Gone*. They looped their feet over the back of the chairs and shared popcorn and Raisinets. Through the whole movie, a thriller about a man trying to convince himself his wife isn't a secret agent, Anne couldn't concentrate. She was too aware of Sara beside her. Instead of watching the film, Anne watched the hole in the knee of Sara's jeans, she watched the way Sara's feet tapped on the floor. Every time Sara laughed, her hair bounced, but Sara didn't bother to try to hold it back the way Anne would have.

Afterward, they walked on the sidewalk, stopping to look in windows, and when they passed an ice-cream place, Sara stopped. "Hungry?" she said, and they went inside. The parlor was gleaming black and silver chrome with plush black booths with minijukes in the center. The waitresses were all in snappy checked uniforms. "Let's grab a booth," Sara said. As soon as they sat down, Sara began talking. The only time she stopped was to order, but when Anne's sundae came, she couldn't touch it. Anne sat there, clumsy, eyes glued to Sara, listening to stories about Danny, about George and Eva, and the whole time Sara was talking about her parents, Anne felt as if Sara were talking about people Anne had never met before. She couldn't imagine Eva anxious and unsure of her mothering skills the way Sara was telling it.

"Oh, she was," Sara said. "She barely put water in the tub because she said you could drown in three inches. I filled the tub and got in there with you, bubbles up to our chins. We could lie beside each other on the daybed for hours, not saying a word. She worried because you were so quiet but I knew you were saying volumes."

"It still bothers her that I'm quiet."

"I'm quiet, too. There's nothing wrong with that."

Anne shifted in her chair. "Did you love my father? My real father?"

Sara looked down at her hands and then back at Anne. "More than anything."

Anne shredded a piece of her napkin, studying it carefully. "What was he like?"

Sara was still for so long, Anne was sure she wasn't going to get an answer, and then Sara glanced at her hands and then back at Anne. "He was smart, but not book smart. Funny. He'd stand outside my window nights and I'd just know he was there. I'd feel a change in the air. Do you understand?"

Anne nodded.

"When you were a baby, I'd lay you down on the bed and study you," Sara said. "I just wanted to find something of his in you—his eyes, an expression, something, anything, but I never could. And then I just fell in love with you for yourself."

"I don't look like him at all?"

"You have his eyes. Exactly his eyes. And you have beautiful features all your own."

"Are you married?" Anne blurted. "Do you have other kids?"

"No, not married. And no other kids. You're my only one," Sara said quietly.

"Do you have a boyfriend?"

"Well, I thought I did. I thought I was in love, that I might even get married, but now I don't know what's going to happen."

"Why? How come?" Anne asked, and then Sara grew quiet. "I think my coming here—" She stopped talking. "Maybe it's over now," she said. "I don't know."

"Is it because of me? Are you sorry you came?" Anne said, alarmed.

"Never," Sara insisted. "I'm not going to lose you for anything or anyone. Not ever again." She glanced down at the napkin in her hand and crumpled it into a fist, tossing it into the ashtray. "Come on," she said. "Let's get out of here."

Anne began seeing Sara as much as she could, and when Anne couldn't see her, she called. She couldn't believe her good fortune! Sara was so young and hip. Everything about herself she had always hated was transformed in Sara into something special, as if Sara were a fun-house mirror, and every time Anne looked at her, all she saw reflecting back was her own best self revealed like magic. The hair Anne despaired over became something unbelievably cool. The pale skin that made her friends badger her about hiding it under fake tans became strikingly exotic, something to show off rather than to hide.

She felt her parents watching her, but they never said one thing when she got on the phone, when she grabbed her jacket and went out the door, not coming back until hours later, her cheeks flushed. Still, she heard them talking at night. "What does she want?" she heard her father say, and Anne wondered, did they mean her or Sara?

Anne never asked Sara what her plans were, but she didn't have to. She saw Sara looking through the want ads, and every Sunday, Anne looked through them herself, wanting to help, and when George nodded at her and said he was proud she was looking for a summer job, Anne sighed, and thought how little he knew about her. Or Sara.

One day, Anne and Sara were shopping, trying on clothes in a huge dressing room, and Anne pulled her jeans back on, and Sara said, "Whoops, those are mine."

Anne looked down at the jeans. "We wear the same size."

"Keep those jeans, if you like them better."

Anne ran her hands down the denim, soft and faded. "I like them better," she decided. Anne wore Sara's jeans every day. She stopped drying her hair with a dryer and let it dry naturally, scrunching it to make it as curly as Sara's, and when she came home from school one day, she stopped at Kmart and impulsively bought herself the same kind of red bandana Sara wore. She spent half an hour in the bathroom at home, trying to tie it around her hair just the right way. She studied herself. She was starting to like her coloring, starting to want to grow her hair, too. *Presto chango,* she thought. Transformed.

When she came out of the bathroom, Eva blinked at her. "You like your hair like that?" Eva asked, reaching up to smooth Anne's hair down. "I love it this way," Anne said, moving out from under Eva's fingers, and quickly fluffing her hair out.

"Where did those old jeans come from?"

"From Sara," she said. "Aren't they fabulous?" And Eva flinched.

That night, Anne couldn't sleep. Stories kept traveling through her mind, waking her: A baby fussed on a bus. Two people became so close they were communicating telepathically, and then they began to morph into each other. *Same hair,* she thought. *Same eyes. Same person.* Finally, Anne got up, turning on her light, and went to her desk, and it seemed as natural as breathing to pick up her journal and start to write again. Never mind that that stupid Mr. Moto had told her about her lack of talent, never mind the way he had sized her up brutally and dismissed her as if she were no more important than a dust mite floating by him. She could no more stop writing now than she could stop breathing. But her writing felt different. Now her heroines weren't orphans. Now they had another person along with them. A confidante.

A best friend.

She had written six pages when she heard a noise. Talking. An undercurrent she couldn't quite make out. She tucked her notebook under her mattress and padded into the hall and saw her parents' door was open, but the front door was open, too, and for a moment she was afraid. Then she saw them, sitting on the front porch, sipping tall drinks, and looking so old and frail that she suddenly felt terrible.

"Mom? Dad?" she said. "What are you doing up so late? Couldn't you sleep, either?" She wanted to sit out on the porch with them, but Eva brusquely stood up. "It's late, honey, go back to bed."

"I don't need much sleep anymore."

"We all need sleep," George said. "Come on. We're coming in soon, too."

And then her mother bent and kissed her. Her father stroked her hair back, and rippling through her was a strange, awful feeling, as if she were being pulled in two different directions and there was only enough of her to be in one. "Good night then," Anne said and then she went into the other room and quietly dialed Sara's hotel. *Call me anytime,* Sara had told her.

The next day, in first-period math class, Bob Shoulton, who had once asked Anne, with great concern, if she had overdosed on her ugly pills that day, complimented the dress she had on, a short black mini she had bor-rowed from Sara. "Socko dress," he decided. Startled, she looked closer at him, to see if he was making fun of her, but he was smiling, his face relaxed. Later that day, she was in the girls' room, washing her hands, when Crystal Lafarge, the head cheerleader, came in and Anne felt Crys-tal's gaze sliding up and down her, centering on the bandana in her hair, but all Anne had to do was think about Sara, and the look slid off her as if she were made of Teflon. Two days later, to Anne's surprise, Crystal came to school with a bandana headband, and a day after that, another girl did, too, and then another.

After school, Flor caught up with her. "Are you doing someone?" Flor asked. "Because you have that look."

"You're crazy," Anne said, but she flushed, pleased that Flor would think she might actually have a boy interested in her.

"Like that dress," Flor said, "it's different than what you usually wear. It's you." Flor walked with her, idly talking. "There's a group of us going to hang out at Bobby's this afternoon," she said casually. "Maybe you could go."

Anne glanced at Flor to see if she had heard her right. Flor never invited Anne anywhere, never even thought to. "Can't make it," Anne said cheerfully. "I'm meeting a friend."

"Oh?" Flor said, and then they were walking past Burger Heaven and there in the window, at a corner table, in a short paisley dress and high boots, her long hair wild about her, was Sara. "Wow, look at that babe," Flor said. Flor's eyes were glued to Sara, right up until Sara spotted Anne and waved happily, and then Flor turned her stare to Anne. "See you," Anne said, and she pulled open the door and walked inside.

Anne slid into the booth just as Sara got up. "Be right back," Sara said. "Just going to the ladies' room."

Sara was gone so long, Anne took out her notebook and started to write. Carolyn, the waitress, the one Mr. Moto loathed, was out on the town with the housewife she had met, and the two of them were spilling their hearts out, bonding, telling each other everything.

"What are you writing?" Sara asked, and Anne jumped. She looked around dazed. She had been so deep into her writing, she hadn't heard Sara's footsteps. Anne quickly closed the notebook.

"I just like to fool around," Anne said.

"It didn't look like fooling around to me." Sara sat down. "Could I see?"

Anne pushed the notebook aside. "No, no, forget it. It's horrible."

Sara shrugged. "Okay," she said, and reached for a menu, and suddenly, the fact that she didn't press made Anne want to show her. She nudged her notebook forward.

"Just read a little," Anne said. "No more than a page."

The whole time Sara was reading, Anne was so nervous, she could hardly sit still. Sara finished a page and turned another, but Anne didn't tell her to stop. She anxiously watched Sara's face for reaction. Sara slowly shut the notebook and studied Anne. "You hated it?" Anne asked.

"I loved it," Sara said.

"You did? You're not kidding? Really?"

"Really. You have talent."

"My English teacher, Mr. Moto, said I couldn't write at all. He gave me an F."

"He's completely insane. Look at this line," Sara said. " 'The spoon made whirlpools of cream in the coffee.' " I like that." She shrugged. "Your teacher doesn't know what he's talking about."

"Do you write?" Anne hesitated. "Is that where I get it from?"

Sara laughed. "Some people think I write. I wouldn't know what I'd call it."

"Can I see?"

Sara laughed even louder. "The right whites," she said. "Blanc de blancs."

Anne looked confused. "I don't get it—" she said doubtfully, and Sara laughed again.

"Catalog copy," Sara said. "I'm a hack." She grinned, cheerful. "Turn on red. The skirt flirts with possibilities in deepest crimson."

"That's what you do?" Anne laughed. "That's your job?"

"You're the real writer. I don't have that gift. But you—" Sara shook her head in admiration. "You're the real thing."

*   *   *

Anne got home by ten. "Where were you?" Eva said, but Anne was too fired up to say anything more than, "Library." She couldn't wait to get to her room, to write. "*You have talent,*" Sara had told her. "*You're the real thing.*" All those days and days of yearning to be something else, someone else, and here was Sara telling her she was real. What did it matter what Mr. Moto thought? What did it matter that her parents didn't see it?

Sara did.

Anne lay on her bed, her mind zooming. She started thinking about another Carolyn story, about the waitress discovering she had a long-lost daughter. "*By five, she found her.*" That was the first line.

She suddenly bolted up. Oh shit, shit, shit. Oh holy fuck. She forgot she had a book report due for Mr. Moto, and she hadn't written one, she hadn't even chosen a book for it. Shit. She couldn't get another failing grade, not from him, not from any class. She got up and flicked on the light by her desk. Shit, shit, what was she going to do? Drumming fingers on the desk, she tried to dredge up a book she had recently read, something she might write about. She thought about Sara, on the Greyhound, with her as a baby clutched in Sara's arms, and then suddenly, she clicked on her computer.

She made up a book, *Forget Me Not,* and an author, H. R. Fleebling, a novel about a woman who kidnapped her daughter and brought her on a Greyhound bus and got away with it. Then, fueled, she started to write her book report. "*Forget Me Not* is lyrically written, beautifully told," Anne wrote, "this book makes you believe that happiness is possible." She wrote for twenty minutes, printed it out, and then went to bed.

When she handed it in the next day, Mr. Moto looked at her with hooded, lizard eyes. She was too keyed up with everything that was going on to worry about it, not that day, or even the next, when she was in his class again, and he approached her desk, looming over her, so she lowered her eyes. *Here it comes,* she thought. *Another F.*

"Well, this is a surprise. Another deviation from your usual poor performance," he said, and she glanced up at him. He was still holding the paper, one hand over the grade. Around her, the other kids slumped in their seats, trying to be inconspicuous.

"Probably the book you chose made the difference," said Mr. Moto, fluttering the paper in his hand. "And your sticking to the facts, fiction certainly not being your forte. I'll have to check that novel out myself," he said and put the paper down on her desk. "Now, as for your work, Mr. Laprodose," Mr. Moto said to the boy who sat behind Anne, "shall we discuss your little adjective problem?" And then Anne dared to look at her grade, and every other voice in the classroom disappeared.

Anne stared, astonished. She had only thought she'd pass, but her nerve had made her pull off something even greater. A. It was an A. The first he had ever given her. "Good job," he had written. She touched the paper and laughed so loudly, the girl in front of her turned around. "What's so frigging funny?" she asked Anne, who laughed even louder.

George could barely get to work anymore. He hated to go to work, but he hated to come home, too, because as soon as he did, he felt the tension in the air. He didn't know what was happening, only that things were snowballing. He couldn't concentrate at work. Patients were noticing, canceling. He was losing some of his practice. But worse than that, far worse, he was losing Anne. He used to come home and find her everywhere. Now he was hyperaware of every change in her. He noticed a new tone in her voice that he couldn't pin down. He noticed she was wilder-looking somehow. Her hair was longer, curlier, and he hated it. What he hated more, though, was the way she ran to Sara, the way her whole body changed when she got on the phone, how he didn't even have to hear her say "Sara" to know that it was her on the line, and then the two of them talked for hours.

He knew it was natural for Anne to want to know her birth mother. He knew every book, every statistic, said it was important for adopted kids to trace their roots, to know where they came from, but the one thing those books and statistics didn't take into account was a birth mother who had tried to take the baby, who was trying to take her now, at least in spirit, and Anne, sixteen and impressionable, the age when most kids wished they didn't have parents at all, seemed more than willing to go. His heart tumbled inside of him. *Come back, come back,* he wanted to shout to Anne. *Don't go.*

He used to think he could reclaim her. As soon as his work problems were settled, he could devote himself to her again, he could take her places, the way he used to. All he needed was time. Anne went to movies and out to dinner with Sara—he and Eva would take her there, too, if she'd let them.

It was a beautiful night. "Let's all go take in a movie," he offered, but Anne was flying out the door. "Gotta go," she said.

"Go?" George said, baffled. "Go where?"

"You know where she's going," Eva said quietly. "Where she always goes."

"What's wrong with scheduled visits? With limited time? With visiting her when she's right here in this house with us?" George asked.

Eva stared at him. "You sound the way Sara's parents used to when we proposed open adoption." She sighed. "I deal with this all day. She's never home, but neither are you these days, and you expect it to work out all right."

"Eva!" he said, but she turned away from him, and he suddenly felt pained with loneliness, and he reached for her. *Come back,* he wanted to say to her, too. "Come sit outside with me," he said, but Eva was halfway to the kitchen. "I'll be outside," he called to her, and he sat out, waiting for her to come out, too, sitting until it got cool and dark, until the neighborhood emptied out, until it seemed like there was no one else in the world but him.

chapter

fourteen

It was three in the morning in her hotel room and Sara was awake, sitting cross-legged on her bed, ticking off all the amazing things she knew about her daughter. Anne's favorite color was blue. Anne's favorite writing pen was a black fineline Pilot. She doused her popcorn with grated cheese and peppered her fries. Every little detail was a revelation, and the more she knew about Anne, the more she wanted to know.

She couldn't imagine leaving her; she had to find a way to stay. "I think my parents are pissed at you," Anne told her, and Sara didn't tell Anne how Eva had called the other night to ask Sara when she was planning to leave.

Sara thought of being back in New York and she felt undone. That whole life paled before this one. The only thing that mattered to her in New York was Scott.

Scott. She thumped fingers on the bedspread. When she was at her parents', she had missed him so much it made her a little crazy; he had been like a glass of water on a table too far away from her, and there she was dying of thirst. This was the first time he had been in her thoughts since she got to Florida.

She reached over for the phone and dialed Scott's number. It rang a few times and then, abruptly, she hung up the phone, sitting back on the bed. What would she say if he answered, that she missed him, that she wanted him to come here? And what if he said no?

She had been here a month already and her money was dwindling at an alarming rate. She made her lunches from the vending machines, she went to the diner for dinner and filled up on grilled cheese, the cheapest thing on the menu. She would find a way to stay here. She could get a job, an apartment. She was determined to save enough money to hire a lawyer and see just what her rights concerning Anne were. Her rights. What a thrilling phrase!

She slid down into the bed. *Sleep,* she told herself. She'd find a job if it killed her.

At first, she felt ridiculously hopeful. She had found Anne, surely she could find a great job, too, but as she scanned the listings, her hope grew as small and skimpy as the listings. There was an advertisement for a copywriter for an automotive firm, an editor for a supermarket flyer, nothing terribly exciting, but still, they were jobs with steady pay, with benefits, work that might anchor her here with Anne. She'd call them all.

"Just hired someone," a voice told her when she called about the editorial slot. "Sure, come by," said a woman at the automotive firm, "but I should tell you that the pay is only a bit above minimum wage." Sara hung up. With pay that low, she'd have to take on two other jobs just to barely scrape by, and then she'd have no time to see Anne at all.

Sara spent two weeks calling places. She and Anne never really talked about her staying, but she couldn't help seeding her conversation with things like "don't worry," and every time she did, Anne's face was so bright, it made Sara even more determined.

By the next week, Sara began to panic. Her money was almost gone. She could probably let her New York City rent slide for a month, but her landlord gave people problems if they wanted to sublet, and in the time Sara had been there, he had even evicted two people on the first floor, and although it had taken months and months, it hadn't been pleasant. No, she couldn't risk that. And the hotel would want more money soon, too. She bought the paper every day, she made blind calls, she tried other employment agencies, but still she had no job. She could cash in her plane ticket, which would tide her over for a while, but then what if she didn't find a job after that?

She sat with her head in her hands, trying to figure out what to do. *Madame,* she thought. If she still had her job, she could go back to New York. Just for a while. She could ask for a raise, she could save more money and take her time looking for work down here. She could have more time to talk to Scott, to try to work things out. Maybe he'd come here with her. The thought of leaving Anne made her crazy, but it was the only way.

She picked up the phone and dialed. Hal probably had fired her already. He probably would make his secretary talk to her. To her surprise, though, he answered.

"Sara?" Hal's voice was rushed. "When are you coming back?" he said.

That evening, Anne bounced happily into the room, a red Gap backpack like the one Sara carried slung casually on her shoulder. "You're not ready?" she asked.

Oh God. The movies—Sara had been so preoccupied she had completely forgotten.

"I've got a stash," Anne said, tapping the backpack. "Mars bars, chips. Soda. Maybe we can make it a double feature, sneak into another one, like last time."

Sara smiled weakly. How could she do this? How could she convince Anne it was the best thing to do? "Anne—" she said, and as she looked at her daughter's bright happy face, her mouth went dry. "Sit," Sara begged.

Anne glanced at her watch. "Okay, but we'll miss the previews," Anne said. She plunked down on the bed, bouncing on the springs, making them squeak. "Looks like someone let the air out of you," Anne said. "Hope it wasn't my parents. What a fight I had with them this morning over coming here!"

She wanted to say it right, to take her time and sound calm. "I have to go back to New York," Sara said. "Just until I can save money, and until I can get some work here." Anne grew still. "It's just temporary," Sara insisted.

"We're leaving here?" Anne asked uncertainly.

"No, no, of course not!"

Anne's backpack slid off her shoulder, thunking to the floor, but she didn't bother to pick it up. "I don't know what my parents would do if I left—I know they'd try to stop me, they'd make it so rough—" She rubbed one thumb along her fingers, deep in thought.

"Anne—"

"But I don't know what I'd do if you left me here." Her voice speeded up. Her shoulders rose with her breathing. "I can always go to school in New York, right? Or maybe I can get a job."

Sara threw up her hands. "Anne, you can't quit school! And you're not listening to me. Even if I thought it was a good idea, which I don't, I can't take you. You're a minor. It'd be kidnapping! And this time, the charges would stick. I have to do everything right!"

"Is leaving me right? I thought we were best friends!"

"Anne! I'm not your best friend!"

Anne's neck snapped back, as if Sara had slapped her. Her mouth crumpled. "You *are* my best friend! We think alike, we dress the same— we are the same—"

"Anne, I *can't* be your best friend! I'm your *mother*—I have to be responsible!" Sara reached to touch Anne, but Anne jerked away from her so hard, she knocked Sara's brush off the dresser, and then Anne knocked everything else from the dresser, too, keys and loose change and Sara's Gap knapsack, the same as Anne's, and then Anne whipped around to face Sara. "My *mother?*" Anne said, incredulous. "I don't need a mother! I *have* a mother, thank you very much. I need a friend—something I thought you were!"

"Look, I made a lot of mistakes when I was a kid—I'm trying to do things right—"

"Now I'm a mistake?" Anne cried. "I hate you! I wish I never heard of you at all!" Anne sprang up from the bed. She strode to the door and yanked it open.

"Anne! Oh God, I didn't mean—" Sara cried, but Anne was gone.

* * *

Anne didn't know where she was going. Her heart was a hard little marble inside of her, rolling crazily around in her chest. She couldn't go with Sara, couldn't stay here without her, either. Couldn't go home and face her parents' relief when they discovered Sara had left her. She dug in her jeans. Ten bucks. Her just-in-case money Eva always made her carry, because you never knew what could happen. *You never do know,* Anne thought, helplessly. Ten dollars wouldn't get her very far but at least it was something. She walked along the road, sluicing her tears with her fingers.

She didn't believe for one moment that Sara would come back. People could say things all they wanted, but it didn't make them true. She felt so alone. Where was there a place for her? She used to have friends. She used to feel like she had parents. She used to have Sara. She looked out across the highway, at the cars zooming past her.

But she still had a father.

He floated up in her mind, a tracking blip on a radar screen, growing louder, more insistent. She could go find him, show up at his doorstep and present herself and he'd have to take her in because she had nowhere else to go. He had loved Sara, maybe he'd love her, too. Sara had said he lived in Pittsburgh. He shouldn't be so hard to locate, and she had all the right in the world to find him. And he had no right to turn her away.

She stood out on the road and jabbed out her thumb. Who cared about dangers? What more could happen to her that hadn't happened already?

Eva was at home waiting for George, waiting for Anne, who was late, and Eva didn't have to wonder where she was. She knew, all right. And she knew with whom.

Eva had lost her daughter. All this time, all this distance, trying to make sure that that would never happen, and here it was. She had tried so hard not to feel that she and George were just borrowing Anne. Eva was the only mother who didn't let her child run far on the playground, but who traipsed after her for fear her daughter would be stolen from her. She always tried to know where Anne was. To keep tabs.

Eva remembered once, when Anne was only three, she had taken her to a department store to shop. Anne had been sitting quietly at her feet while Eva looked at dresses, and then, Eva had reached up to get another size, turning her back on Anne for just a second, and when she turned around, Anne was gone.

Never had she been more terrified. She stared across the sea of racks, the milling crowds of people. The air tightened around her. "Lost child!" she shouted, because that was what the magazines all told you to do, but the only thing that happened was that other mothers clutched their children closer to them, averting their faces from her as if what had happened might be catching. The people without kids looked at her as if it were her fault, as if she must be a bad mother not to keep better track of her own child. She finally grabbed a saleswoman, who made an announcement over the PA and sent salespeople out to comb the store, and all Eva could think of was that she had read how people could take children into the washroom and cut their hair in the stall, how they could fit wigs on small heads and inject drugs and the child you had known could walk right past you and you might not even know it. All those thoughts flooded through her, cold as a stream. She sat in the back room, numb with fear, and then after an hour, a saleswoman had led Anne to her by the hand. Anne blinked up at her and Eva leaped up and then crouched down by her daughter so she was at eye level. She cupped Anne's face, stroking back her hair, staring into her eyes. "Where were you? Oh honey, I was so worried! Were you scared?" Anne gazed impassively at her and Eva turned to the salesgirl. "Was she crying?"

The salesgirl patted Anne's head. "She was sitting under a row of evening dresses playing with a beaded hem."

Eva started. "She was?"

"She said she was there the whole time."

"I don't understand. If she was there the whole time, then why did it take you so long to find her? Why didn't you have me paged sooner?"

The salesgirl gave Eva an impassive stare. "No one in the dress department thought she was missing. She was just sitting happily playing, so they thought her mother must be nearby." The salesgirl shrugged. "Usually, missing kids cry for their mothers."

Eva felt as if she had been slapped. As if there must be something terribly deficient in her that her own little girl didn't know enough to cry like other little girls when her mother wasn't in sight. She left the store holding Anne's hand so tightly, Anne began to whimper and complain. "You're hurting me, Mommy." A woman walking past gave Eva a funny look, but Eva didn't care. She kept her hand clamped around Anne's, and the whole way home, she kept watching Anne in her car seat from the rearview mirror.

By eleven, George was home, but Anne still wasn't, and Eva's worry turned to anger, and in a way, she was glad because at least she didn't feel so helpless. Instead, she felt fueled. Determined, she called Sara, punching down the digits, but no one answered. She leafed through the phone book, calling the friends of Anne's she could remember—Flor, June—but Flor was out on a date, and when she called June, June's mother answered and said, "Oh, Anne! We haven't seen her around here for such a long time!" And then June's mother told Eva that June had the flu and was fast asleep.

"I'm calling Sara again," George said, "she's as bad as Anne in all this," and just as he reached the phone, it rang.

"George?" Sara said, her voice tight with worry. "Is Anne there?"

They all met at the police station. It was the second time in her life Sara had been in such a place with George and Eva, but this time, she wasn't the one in trouble. This time, the cops were polite and concerned. "This way, ma'am," a cop said. He was young, chewing gum, making it snap and pop. The air about him smelled like Juicy Fruit. Eva and George were already sitting around a desk, talking to a cop who was typing something into a report, and when Sara came in, they didn't look at her.

Sara sat beside George and Eva. "Maybe we should call people she knows—" Sara faltered and Eva shot her a look.

"Don't you think we've done that already?" Eva said, her voice sharp. "Of course we've called. All her friends."

"Who did you call?" asked the cop, and Eva rattled off names and Sara sat there feeling lost because she couldn't remember Anne ever mentioning these people.

"Any other names?" the cop asked Sara and she shook her head, shamed that she couldn't come up with any.

"What places did she like to go?" the cop asked.

"Bowling," said Sara. "The movies."

"What bowling alley?"

Sara blinked. "I don't know—"

"The Wal-Ex," George said. "We used to go to the Wal-Ex all the time."

The cop tapped his pencil. "Any allergies or anything we should know about?"

Something pulsed in Sara's stomach. She remembered newspaper stories about kids who were lost who needed medication, who could go into shock if they were so much as stung by a bee. Helplessly, she looked over at George and Eva.

"No, none," said George.

"Scars? Birthmarks? Tattoos?"

Again, Sara felt that same swimmy helplessness. *I know her,* she told herself. *I do.*

"A tiny scar, by her right thigh," said Eva. "She fell from a bike."

"Was she upset about anything?" the cop said, and Eva looked down at her hands and then at George. "We have some family issues—" she said.

"She was upset that I was leaving," Sara blurted.

Eva stared at Sara. "You're leaving? When were you going to tell us this?"

"She wanted to go with me," Sara said, but to the cop, not to George and Eva because she couldn't bear the way they were both looking at her.

"You come here, disrupt our lives, get Anne all agitated and confused, and then you just leave and we're here to pick up your pieces? Is that it?" George said.

"I was coming back! I was going to do the right thing!"

"Is this why she took off?" the cop said. "To go after you?"

Sara turned to the cop. "She doesn't know my address in New York City. She wouldn't go there without me. She was just upset."

"I see." The cop looked at Sara.

"When will we know something? What will you do?" Eva said.

"Well, with kids, we don't usually do anything. Not for forty-eight hours. They usually come back." He stood up and nodded at them. "But we have the report. Look, I'm sure she's just upset, that she'll come home, her tail between her legs. I wouldn't worry. Call us if you hear anything more. And we'll be in touch."

"We'll go every place she's ever been," George said to Eva. "I swear we'll find her."

They all walked out together, Sara trailing behind Eva and George. No one talked, but then Sara saw George reach out and grab Eva's hand, pull her close, and then he put his arm about her, and she put hers about him. They pressed together like a seam. When they got to the front door, Eva pulled the door open and then stopped and suddenly began to weep. Her hands flew up to her eyes. "Eva," George said, and held her, stroking her back, so tenderly that Sara felt like a voyeur, and then Sara saw that George's eyes were damp, too. "My baby," Eva said quietly. *My baby,* Sara thought, but she kept silent. She wavered, unsure what to do, and then Eva snuffled, digging into her pocket for a handkerchief, and when she looked at Sara, Eva looked tamped down.

"I'll help you find her," Sara said, and Eva held up her hand.

"No, you've done enough," Eva said wearily. "Just go. Go home to New York City the way you planned. Just go and leave us alone."

"No," George said. "You stay. Please. Stay and help."

Eva looked at him, startled. "George!" she said.

"We need all the help we can get, Eva," he said. "Even if it's Sara's."

They drove around the town, Sara in the backseat. George drove to the bowling alley and went inside, and when he came out his face was so drawn that he didn't have to say one word, both Sara and Eva knew Anne wasn't there. They drove to the school, to a mall, to a dozen places Sara didn't know about, and at each one, she felt more despairing.

Finally, George and Eva drove Sara back to her hotel.

"There's nothing more you can do," Eva said. "Just go. We'll call you."

"I'm staying," Sara said.

By Friday morning, Anne was in Pittsburgh. It had taken her two days to get there. The first ride, a woman who barreled down the road in her little white car, took her across two states. At the side of the road, Anne gulped the soda she had packed, which was now warm, the fizz gone. She ate the candy and chips until she began to feel ill from the rush of sugar, the tang of salt, and then she threw them away. Her next ride was with a middle-aged woman who lectured her about hitching until she dropped Anne off at a diner in Virginia, and by then Anne was starving. She sat at the counter and scanned the menu for whatever would be the cheapest and the most filling. "Corn chowder," she said, which turned out to be watery broth with a scrim of oil across it and not a kernel of corn in sight.

"Could you please pass the salt?" she asked the person next to her, a burly man in a Yankees baseball cap. They started talking, and he told her his name was Charlie, and that he was a trucker.

"Are you crazy traveling alone?" he said. "I have two girls about your age and I don't even let them out of the house after seven, let alone hitch by themselves."

"You sound like my parents."

"Well, good. I would hope so. They must be fine people, then." He studied her and bit into his burger, chewing thoughtfully. "Why Pittsburgh?"

"My father is there."

Grabbing his napkin, he swiped it across his mouth. "Your father," he said. His brow furrowed. "How come your father didn't send you money to take a bus?"

"I want to surprise him. I can't do that if I ask him to pay."

"What about your mother? She in on this surprise?"

Anne played with the salt shaker. "She doesn't want me seeing him. They're not together anymore."

"Ah—I see. That's the way it is, then." The trucker took another bite of his burger, considering her. "I'm going to Pittsburgh," he said finally. "I'll take you."

"Really? You will?" Anne brightened.

His truck was shiny and red, with "Orson's Sausages, The Links You Love!" scribbled on the side in bright yellow letters. "Up you go," he said, taking her hand, helping her step up into the truck. There was a compartment in the back, with a pillow and a soft red blanket. She intended to stay awake, to talk to him, to tell him stories she'd make up so he'd be glad of the company, but as soon as she sat on the seat, her head lolled, and the next thing she knew he was gently shaking her. "We're here, sleepyhead," he said.

And then she was there. Dropped off in the center of town, by the university, in the middle of a bright day, students spilling all around her. Pittsburgh wasn't anything like she expected, not grey and unfriendly looking, not with a cloud cover of smoke. No, the city was green and leafy and sparkling, and there was a crunchy apple smell to the air. Anne strode down the street and two people passed her and gave her smiles so friendly, she had to turn around to make sure those smiles were really directed at her. Amazing, she thought. A good omen if her father lived in such a nice place.

She stopped at a phone booth and called information for Danny's address. "It's 5525 Howe Street," said a voice. She could find it.

She started walking, stopping a woman to ask for directions. She reached in her pocket to check how much money she had left. Five. No six dollars. But there was something else. Three twenties and a scrap of paper. A phone number scribbled down. "You call if you need to," it said. "Charlie."

Anne carefully tucked the bills and the number back in her pocket. He was a nice man. She bet his daughters didn't realize how lucky they were to have a father like that.

She turned down Negley and walked a few blocks. Howe. The street was lined with trees. There were a few people milling around, talking, walking dogs, riding bikes. A jump rope lay curled on the lawn of one house, a red tricycle was parked on a front stoop. She shivered. She hadn't dressed warmly enough. And she was starving again.

Anne's father's house was brick with a sort of ramshackle garden in the front, and a gold door knocker in the shape of a lion. Anne stopped in front, heart hammering. She wasn't going to throw herself on these people the way Sara had with her parents. *We're not alike,* she thought. *I was wrong.* She was going to scope these people out, figure what to do. She stood in front of his house and then the door opened and a woman with cropped yellow hair came out, a tiny baby, bottom heavy with diapers, held against her chest in a Snugli, and she opened the mailbox by the door, riffling for the mail. The woman hummed.

Anne froze. A baby. She didn't know there was a baby. She stared in wonder. She couldn't tell if it was her half brother or her half sister, but it didn't matter. It was incredible that such a person existed. And then, she stared at the woman. Her father's wife. The woman he preferred to Sara, and that seemed impossible to her, too, because this woman wasn't as pretty or cool as Sara. This woman was wearing a frumpy floral dress and had a faceful of freckles. And then suddenly, this woman was looking at Anne.

"Are you lost?" the woman said. "Can I help you?"

This was it. All Anne had to do was say who she was. All she had to do was ask to see her father, but she couldn't do it. She lost her nerve. "Looking for Rushmore Street," she blurted, feeling suddenly ridiculous.

"Rushmore? Can't say that I know that street," the woman said. "But if you go up there, that's the main drag. I'm sure someone could help you there."

Anne nodded. She walked to the end of the street and then turned around. The woman was gone. Anne circled back around, standing in front of the house again. All she had to do was walk up four stairs and press her finger to the bell. All she had to do was open her mouth and say her name. What was the matter with her that she couldn't?

She walked to the side of the house and sat down, circling her knees with her arms, resting her head. The grass was cool and green. There was shade from a maple. Inside the house, she could hear music, a swell of piano notes that made her shut her eyes for a moment. Drifting, she was half-asleep, the occasional insect a kind of lullaby.

Someone shook her. Anne's lids fluttered and she looked up and there was the blond woman, the baby in the crook of her arm. The woman stooped down, and as she did, the baby laughed and cooed. "You don't live around here, do you?"

Anne started to lie, but the woman's gaze was so clear and steady that she thought better of it. "And there's no Rushmore Street, now is there?" the woman asked, and Anne dug her hands in her pockets.

"Well, you look harmless enough. I'm Charlotte. This little one's name is Joseph. Why don't you come inside and we'll figure out what to do with you."

Charlotte's kitchen was bright and cheerful with a big green clock in the shape of a dinner plate, the numbers different foods, and the hands a fork, spoon, and knife. "Isn't that clock fun?" Charlotte said, following Anne's gaze. "My husband's surprise."

My husband, Anne thought. She tried to imagine her father buying something for his wife, thinking: oh, she'll love this. Meaning, oh, she'll love me.

Clumsily, she sat at the Formica table. There was a big old-fashioned baby carriage in the corner and Charlotte gently lowered Joseph into it, and then wheeled it closer to Anne. "He likes to be part of things," she said. She bustled around, opening cabinets, finally pulling out a can of Campbell's soup. "Beef okay?" she said. Anne, whose mother never fixed soup that wasn't made from scratch, nodded. She was so hungry she could have eaten the can.

The baby cooed, a peal of sound, and Charlotte turned to him and smiled. "You peach," she said.

"Is that your baby?" Anne said carefully, and Charlotte burst into laughter.

"Now who else's baby would it be?" Charlotte asked. She reached into the cupboard again. "And these," she said, taking out oyster crackers.

The soup was hot and sugary tasting, the oyster crackers were too salty, but Anne ate every bit, scraping the bowl, not protesting when Charlotte filled up her bowl again.

"There's thirds if you're still hungry after this," Charlotte said. And then she studied Anne. "What's your name?" Charlotte asked.

* * *

Danny was in a meeting about ways to make the bank staff more efficient when someone came in and told him he had an urgent call. He didn't like that word, *urgent*. It made his heart jump, his thoughts race. *Charlotte,* he thought. *Joseph.* If something happened to either one of them, he didn't know what he'd do. He walked out of the meeting and strode into his office, picking up the phone. "Hello?" he said quickly, and then he heard his name, he knew the voice, and he had to sit down to hear it again.

"Sara," he said, resting his forehead against the receiver. He sat down, trying to think what to do. "Sara," he said again, trying to compose himself.

"I'm sorry to call you at work. I'm sorry to call you. Did Anne come there?" Her voice rushed over him like a tide.

"Anne? Who's Anne?"

"Our daughter Anne."

His mouth went dry. Anne. He thought of that day at his house when Sara had come by on her bike, a shock because he had never thought he'd see her again, he had never imagined she might want to see him, and for a moment, he had been so ridiculously happy. Sara! Sara was here! And then she had told him about Anne and then everything that he had struggled so hard to build up, to make right in his life, seemed to falter.

"Why would she come here?" he finally said.

"I found her, Danny. I went to Florida to find her. She knows about you. She ran away and we all think she might have come to your house."

His house. Charlotte opened the door to everyone. She said even salespeople deserved common courtesy. How many times had he come home to find her with one of the runaways she helped at the church center? How many times would an extra place be set for dinner? Danny rubbed at his forehead. "I'm going home now to see," he told her.

"Wait, wait, here's a cell phone number. You'll call, if she is?" she begged. Her voice cracked and he felt pulled toward it. "We can fly up if she's there," Sara said.

She waited. He knew she was expecting him to tell her to come to the house, to stay if she needed, but how could he do that? The last time he had seen Sara he had told Charlotte they were friends from school and that was that, and Charlotte had believed him. They had gone out to dinner that evening, and when he hadn't been able to eat a thing, Charlotte had asked him, her voice rich with concern, if he was coming down with the flu because he was acting so strange.

"I'll call you," he said.

He hung up the phone, trying to think what to say to Charlotte. Maybe the girl wouldn't show up at his house at all and to warn Charlotte would just needlessly upset her. Why would Anne show up, anyway? He hadn't ever tried to contact her. She hadn't tried to contact him. And he had told Sara he couldn't consider bringing Anne into his life; surely Sara must have explained that to Anne.

But if he didn't tell her, and Anne arrived, Charlotte might never trust him again.

He phoned her, and as soon as he heard Charlotte's voice, warm and welcoming, he relaxed. "We have some company," she told him, and he shut his eyes.

"Who?" he said.

"Another runaway, it looks like. A little skittish, but she told me her name—Anne—and she ate three bowls of soup and then fell asleep in the den." Her voice was sure and calm.

"I'll be right home," he said.

"Honey, you're working! You don't have to come home!" Charlotte said, surprised. "Anyway, I already called the church and as soon as she wakes up I'll take her over there and we'll figure out the best thing to do for her."

"I'm coming home," he repeated.

The whole way driving home, Danny felt panicked. Charlotte didn't see anything out of the ordinary about any of this. Charlotte was so big-hearted, she was just the kind to take Anne in, the same way she would any lost soul. The same way she had taken him when he was floundering around, tense and miserable, his life feeling as if it were about to break into a thousand pieces. What would he say? What would he do? Danny swerved, beeping the horn at another driver. How could he ever explain it to Charlotte?

He parked the car. He used to hate dusk, used to think it was the loneliest time of the day and he'd do anything to avoid it. Go to the movies. Go take himself out to eat. Go pick up a woman and spend the night with her. Anything so he didn't have to be by himself. So he didn't have to think about the mess of his life. But then he had met Charlotte, he had married her, and the dusk had been his favorite time, because it was when he'd come home to his own family, when he'd see his house—his house!—the wooden plaque with "The Slades" hand-painted across it in his own careful script, the flowers Charlotte had planted so there'd be a blaze of color about the house. And then he'd see Charlotte, beautiful and smiling, he'd smell the delicious dinner she had cooked, and there was never a moment when she wasn't delighted to see him, when she didn't make him feel that she was the lucky one to have him, instead of the other way around. He felt as if he had spent his whole life yearning for this and he hadn't even known it, not until it was here, love and family and home, and maybe it was because it was such an unexpected gift to him that he couldn't help worrying that any minute, like everything else in his life, it might be wrested away from him.

He walked inside, and there was light and warmth in the house, music playing from the radio, and now, the icing, he heard the baby. He looked at his boy and sometimes all he wanted to do in this life was make sure Joseph knew how much he was loved. His little boy. His baby.

Anne was his baby, too.

"I'm home—" he said tensely, but only Charlotte tiptoed out.

"The girl's still sleeping," she said in a low voice. "I already called the church and they said they can talk to her, get her to consider going back home with her family."

She rested her head against his shoulder. "Know how I can tell we belong together?" she teased. "My head fits perfectly right here."

He stroked her hair. "I just want to wash my hands," he said.

He didn't go into the bathroom. Instead, he walked to the den. His blood felt as if it were thrumming inside of him. *Please,* he thought. *Please let it not be her,* and as soon as he opened the door and saw the spill of red hair on the pillow, the lopsided mouth, he braced one hand against the doorjamb. He was looking at Sara.

Slowly, he closed the door. He felt like crying. He walked heavily to the kitchen and there was Charlotte behind him, and she looked up at him. "What? What's wrong?" she said. "Oh, honey, did you have a bad day at work?" And she placed one hand, warm, against his cheek, and then, because there was no longer any reason not to, he started talking, telling her, and she took her hand slowly from his face. She kept her eyes on him.

She was so still, he began to worry. He had seen her this upset only once before, the first time she had gotten pregnant, when she had been so happy that the obstetrician used to joke with her that she was the only one he knew who even liked morning sickness. And then one day, during a routine visit, when she was three and a half months along, they hadn't found a heartbeat. The baby had quietly died inside of her. "It's a blessing," the doctor had told her. "Usually that happens when there's something very wrong with the baby." But it was the first and only time Danny had seen Charlotte doubt God, something he himself doubted from the time he was twelve, the one and only prickly difference between them. She believed and he did not, could not. She had taken to her bed, not being able to get up until, desperate, Danny had called the priest and begged him to come over and talk to Charlotte. He had stood in the doorway listening to the priest tell Charlotte this baloney, that it was God's will, that no one could understand God but God himself, and it was prideful to even try, and then Charlotte had gotten up, and after that Danny never said one bad word about religion again to Charlotte. He never stopped her from going to church Sundays, never stopped her from trying to tease him into coming, too, and sometimes he did go, just so he could sit beside her and think how lucky he was, how his blessing was not from God, but from her.

"There's a child?" Charlotte said quietly. "A child born out of wedlock?" And Danny wished he could disappear. "You think that Anne is your Anne?"

"I thought Sara had an abortion," he said, and Charlotte drew in her breath. She stepped back from him.

"An abortion? You would have let her get one?" Charlotte said.

"I didn't know that was what she was planning. All I knew was she didn't want to see me. Didn't want anything to do with me."

"Well, thank God she didn't have one," Charlotte said. "Thank God."

Danny was silent. "I never wanted to hurt you. I wanted to keep this from you, Charlotte, to protect you. I swear I tried. I don't know what to do now." He looked toward the doorway. "You don't have to do anything about this. I'll take care of it. Sara and the girls' parents said they'd fly in and get her. Things will go back to normal."

Charlotte looked at him. "Nothing's normal anymore."

"No, no, don't say that—" He didn't know what to say to her, how to make it right. He was ruining everything again. "You can't touch a thing without making it die," his brother used to taunt him. The broken-winged birds he'd find in the backyard would die before he even made up a box for them. A bike he had spent two whole Saturdays trying to fix had burst a tire the first time he took it out for a spin. He had been sent by his mother to buy a few things for the house once—butter, bread—and by the time he got to the store, he had lost the money. He hadn't known what to do, so he simply slipped the items under his jacket and hoped for the best. Of course he was caught. Of course his mother was called and charges were threatened, and in the end, Danny and his mother were asked not to come to the store anymore. And when Danny and his mother got home, his brother had come after him, furious, shaking his finger. "You'd better stop screwing up!" he had shouted. "You'd better stop thinking of yourself! You're killing her! Everything you do kills her a little bit more!"

Danny had told his mother about Sara being pregnant only because he was beside himself, because he didn't know what else to do, because he thought maybe she could help. He was nearly weeping. "Please—" he begged, and she had gotten up without speaking to him and gone into the other room and sat there in cold, rigid silence, as if it were all happening to her, and not to him, and in that moment, Danny had known he was lost.

Charlotte shook her head, and when she looked at the door, he couldn't help it, he grabbed Charlotte's arm. "Don't go," he pleaded, and she looked at him, astonished.

"Go? Go where? What are you talking about?"

"I know I lied to you. You have a right not to trust me. A right to be angry, but please, we can work this out. We can get things back to the way they were."

She stepped back from him. "Sometimes I think I don't know you," she said.

"I'm sorry—"

"And sometimes I think you don't know me, either."

"Charlotte—"

"Your daughter is sleeping in this house and you're here in this kitchen. Don't you want to go in and talk to her?"

"I'm going to talk to her—"

"That time Sara came to your mother's house, you didn't tell me the truth about her, did you? You didn't tell me she was your old girlfriend. You didn't tell me how serious things had been with you. What did you think I would do if I knew?"

"I'm sorry. I'm so sorry."

"Did you still love her? Is that some of it? Did you want to leave me for her? Is that why you couldn't tell me anything about her?"

"Don't talk like that."

"She was beautiful. And very smart, you told me. And she was your first love. I know what that means."

"Charlotte. It was sixteen years ago."

"And all I have to do is look at your face and see it's upsetting you like it was yesterday. You think time matters? You think love goes away?" Charlotte brushed a hand through her hair. She smoothed her blouse. "I've gotten a little plump. I'm a housewife with a baby and I wear what's practical rather than in fashion. I don't have the time I'd like to have to read."

"Charlotte, who cares about that?" he said, but she lifted up her hand.

"Your daughter is sleeping in our den, and your first love is about to come to town to get her. You tell me the truth, now. Should I be worried?"

"Charlotte, of course not." He touched her arm. "I love you."

She considered him. "You have a number to reach these people?"

Danny nodded.

"I want you to call them. They have to come here. All of them. As soon as possible."

He stared at her. "You want them to come here?" he asked, astonished.

"No," she admitted. "I don't. I feel like screaming. I feel like asking God to help me not throw away everything good because right now I just want to walk right out of this house with Joseph and not come back."

He stroked her face. "Charlotte," he said, and she drew herself up.

"I'll make a meal. When they get here, we'll sit and eat and talk this all out. It's the only way." She started moving about the kitchen, looking in cabinets, in the freezer. "I was saving these chicken fryers for Sunday dinner." She looked at him. "You invite them," she repeated. "All of them." She reached for a glass and it shattered on the floor, a million shiny shards. "Oh!" she said, as if she had been cut. He crouched down by her and helped her pick it up, but she wouldn't meet his eyes.

He cupped his hands about her face and kissed her but her lips were cool, her kiss distant. She pushed him from her. "It doesn't mean I'm happy about this," she said. "It doesn't mean I understand or I'm not angry with you, because I am. It just means they're coming here." She stepped back from him. "You call them, first. Then, you better go talk to that poor little girl in there," she said.

He spoke briefly to Sara, was put on hold while she checked and made reservations. "Best we can do is tomorrow late afternoon," she said, "Please. Don't tell her we're coming. I'm afraid she'll take off again."

He nodded because he couldn't speak. Sara, here in his house. Sara.

He put the phone down. He could hear Charlotte in the kitchen and all he wanted to do was go to her, wrap his arms about her and sway her to him. All he wanted was to feel her hands on his face, to feel there was no one in his life but his wife, even as he felt Sara, like an undercurrent, rising to the surface. *No*, he thought. He knew if he walked in there, she'd just point him back out again.

Danny walked to the room where his daughter was. He stood in front of the closed door for a long time. What was he going to say to her? How could he possibly explain? How could he even know what he wanted to do? He knocked and a voice full of sleep said, "Come in."

She was sitting up, her red hair—Sara's hair—rumpled, her clothes in disarray, and as soon as she saw him, her eyes grew huge. He couldn't believe it. This girl in his house.

"Are you my father?" she asked.

"I'm Danny." He thought suddenly of his own father, a man who left his family without a second thought, who drove off toward a new life and ended up dead. God, how he had hated him. How he had wanted him back, too. "I'm your father."

Her eyes narrowed, as if she were measuring him up.

"You look just like your mother," he said.

"Ha. Some mother," Anne said. "Abandoned me twice." She studied him. "And you abandoned her."

He shook his head. "No, she didn't. And neither did I."

"Uh-huh. Do you still love her?"

Danny started. It was the second time that day someone had asked him that.

"I love my wife," Danny said. "I love my son."

Anne picked at the tufts in the spread. "What about me?" she said. "Did you love me?"

"I didn't even know Sara had had you."

She stared at him, making him feel uncomfortable, as if he should know the right thing to say or do.

"You want to forget about me now?" Anne said. "Just like you forgot about Sara."

"You think that?" He looked at her. "I never forgot her. And I won't forget you."

"You don't even know me. You said that yourself."

He swallowed. "Tell me everything about yourself," he said. "And then I will."

He tried to concentrate on what she was saying, but the whole time he felt as if he were watching a movie of his life, the way it might have been, as if he had gotten up and left the theater to get something, and when he had come back, he had missed so much of the story, it wasn't quite making sense to him, and his mind was trying to patch in what was lost.

"You would have raised me," Anne said, shaking her head. "It would have been such a different life having you and Sara as my parents."

"It would have been a harder one," he said. "Two young kids, no money, struggling. We wouldn't have been able to give you half of what your parents did."

She blinked at him. "How do you know?" she said quietly. "How do you know how it would have turned out?" Helpless, he shrugged.

"Can I stay here for a while?" she asked. "Just until I figure out what to do?"

"I don't know if that's going to be possible," Danny said quietly.

"Why not?"

"Because legally you can't. Because I have a family. And so do you."

"Family! I don't even know what that means anymore!" Anne jumped up, digging in her pockets.

"What are you doing?" he asked, and she turned from him, her face pinched.

"I'm checking how much money I have." He saw the crumpled bills, and then he saw the panic in her face. "Don't look at me like that," Anne said. "You don't have to worry. I'll be out of your hair in ten minutes. I'll find someplace to go." She crouched down and searched out her sneakers under the couch, tugging them on, tying the knots so fiercely one snapped in two.

He touched her shoulder for the first time, this slight young girl. "You can stay here tonight," he told her and her whole body relaxed again.

"I could get to like this den," she said hopefully.

Charlotte made a simple dinner. Hot dogs. French fries. Grape juice. "Comfort food," she said cheerfully, and all Danny could think was, well, who was getting comforted? Certainly not Charlotte, who averted her eyes every time Danny tried to meet them. And it sure as hell wasn't Anne, who picked at her hot dog and maneuvered her fries about the rim of her plate. No one talked about Danny being Anne's father, or Anne running away. Instead, Charlotte kept up a patter about the weather (God, the weather!), about how it was supposed to rain again. "I won't have to water the lawn, then," Danny said, and instantly felt ridiculous. Only the baby remained sunny, settled next to Charlotte in the carriage, babbling his own secret conversation.

When they were all as finished as they were going to be, Charlotte started clearing away the plates, and when Anne jumped up to help, Charlotte lifted her hand. "No, no, you're a guest——" she said.

"I'm family."

For a second Charlotte's mouth wobbled, the way it always did when she was struggling with something, like the words she wanted to say wouldn't come yet, and were crowding behind her lips. Anne stood there, glancing so anxiously from Charlotte to Danny that he suddenly didn't know who he felt worse for, his wife or this young girl. "Hey, the more hands the better," Danny said, and grabbed some plates to clear himself, and when he glanced over at his wife, he saw her mouth had gone soft again.

There wasn't much to do. Dishes piled in the dishwasher, pots soaking in the sink, and then Anne began yawning, her hands cupped over her mouth. "Looks like it's time for you to hit the hay," Danny said. "Come on, I'll set you up in the den."

He brought her some clean linens, a blanket, a pillow. Then Charlotte appeared, holding up a green nightgown. "Nothing's more uncomfortable than sleeping in your clothes," she said.

They didn't stay up much later than Anne. Only long enough to bathe Joseph and put him in his crib, to watch a bad movie on TV about a young couple who find a million dollars, and though they sat close together on the sofa, neither one of them said very much. "Let's go to bed," Danny said.

They usually slept spooned together, one of his arms flung about her, keeping her close as his heartbeat, but tonight, they both lay on their backs, blinking at the ceiling. He couldn't sleep. God. He just couldn't sleep. And then he heard noises. Anne moving about the house. The pad of her feet. As exhausted as his daughter was, she couldn't sleep either. *His daughter,* he repeated to himself, suddenly as startled as when he first found out she was in his home. When Joseph was born, he was there in the delivery room, holding Charlotte's hand, as terrified as she was, and as soon as Joseph had come out, dotted with vernix, eyes wide open, Danny had burst into tears. *No one tells you what it's like,* he thought, *how mixed up in the fierceness of your love is sadness because you know from the moment they're born, they're moving steadily away from you.* Right now, he knew everything there was to know about Joseph, that he laughed if you tickled his feet, that he loved it if you blew raspberries on his sweet little belly, that his cry when he was hungry sounded different—longer, more plaintive—than his cry when he wanted to be held. Oh, yes, Danny knew everything about his boy, but he was smart enough to know that soon, he wouldn't. And right now, he didn't know much of anything about his daughter. And soon, she'd be leaving. And how was he to know it wouldn't be for good, that all he might have is this one small slice of her time? He slid down against the pillow. Then there was a loud thunk, and then he turned to Charlotte.

Charlotte's eyes were open. "Guess we're all up now," he said quietly and she nodded.

They heard a door whine open and then shut, and then the house was quiet again, and *how funny,* he thought because as soon as it was, he missed the noise of Anne. And he wondered how much more he'd miss when she was gone and what that would mean for him.

He called in sick the next day. He had been so conscientious, had barely missed an afternoon of work for a doctor's appointment, let alone a whole day, but to hell with the office. His only thoughts were of Anne.

Charlotte had gone out before he was even up, coming home with enough groceries for months. Almost instantly she started in the kitchen, and he could still hear her, the clang and rattle of pots. The lilting babble of Joseph. And then, suddenly, she started to sing, some top-forty song that had a lot of "Jimmy, Jimmy, Jimmy" in it, her off-key voice winding around him, moving him closer to her.

He puttered around the house, waiting for Anne to wake. He did chores, fixing the garbage disposal, rewiring a lamp, watching the time. One hour passed, and then another. Soon, Sara and Eva and George would be here, coming for Anne, and every single feeling he had about that was as tangled as the wire on this lamp.

"Hey."

He knew it was Anne standing there, leaning against the wall, in the same clothes she had worn yesterday, her hair wild about her face. But for a moment, in this raw morning light, the way she was standing, he swore he was seeing Sara again, when she was sixteen, and it confused him so much he stepped back, banging his leg against the table. He shook his head as if to clear it. There she was, his daughter, a thing as strange and astonishing as thinking he had seen Sara herself.

"What?" Anne asked. She watched him as if she expected him to say something—which he gladly would have if he could've figured out what in hell would be the right thing to say. "I keep thinking," she said. "Maybe we could do some things together while I'm here. Get to know each other. Go to a movie. Or go bowling." Her face brightened. She looked brand-new, full of hope.

"I'd like that," Danny said, though he knew there was no time.

"Do you bowl?" she asked.

"Terribly."

She laughed. "See? We have something in common," she said, and then the doorbell rang, and Anne froze. Suddenly, she didn't look so brave anymore, suddenly she looked ten years old. "Did you call the police?" she whispered. "Are you turning me in?"

"No, no—" he said, but she cocked her head, and then they both heard Charlotte.

"Come in, you must be tired from your trip," Charlotte said, and her voice was so warm and friendly Danny could have cried. And then he heard Sara's voice, and then two more voices, and Anne touched his arm, like a small shock. "We got an earlier flight," Eva said. Anne's eyes grew large. "They all came here together?" she whispered, incredulous. "They don't even talk." Her gaze darted around. "What do I do?" she said. "What do I do now?"

"We'll go in together," he said, and to his surprise, Anne reached for his hand and clasped it, linking her fingers with his so tightly that later he'd find faint marks.

They walked into the room and two older people were there, older than he expected for Anne's parents, and behind them was Sara, and as soon as he saw her, he felt even more confused. Time peeled back. Beautiful. She was still beautiful.

"Dan," Charlotte said, and he looked at her, dazed. She had Joseph in her arms and she handed the baby to him.

The older couple looked over at Danny, and for a moment, he was a kid, when all he had to do was stand in front of anyone's parents and feel their disapproval. The man thrust out a hand. "George," he said. "My wife, Eva. I think we owe you thanks."

Eva turned to Anne. "Thank God, you're all right," Eva breathed.

Anne dropped Danny's hand and stared at the floor. Nobody else moved.

"We came all this way," Eva said. "Won't you at least talk to us?"

"Why? What good will it do?" Anne said.

Charlotte cleared her throat. "I have to go to the store and pick up a few things I forget, and Joseph could use the air. Why don't you all go out in the backyard and talk?"

She took the baby from Danny's arms, making him feel suddenly weightless.

"I'll be back," she said. Charlotte grabbed her purse and then, as she passed, Anne reached out one hand and very lightly touched the baby's head, and the baby looked at her, eyes bright with surprise.

chapter

fifteen

⁓

They were all in the backyard except for Sara and Danny. There was
a foot or so of living room between them, and suddenly Sara wished
for an ocean. This was the first time she had been alone with him
since that day she had biked to his old house, and she didn't trust herself to
look into his face. If she saw his mouth, she was afraid she'd want to touch
it. If she glanced at his eyes, she was afraid of what she might read in
them.

"Sara," Danny said, and she finally looked his way, and there, just for a
moment, was the same heady pull in her stomach she used to get when she
was fifteen. But she wasn't fifteen anymore. And neither was he.

"Please," Danny said. He shifted his weight, avoiding her eyes. "Can
we sit down?"

She sat on the couch next to him, the nubby fabric scratching her bare
legs. "Charlotte's very nice. Is she okay about all of this?" Sara asked.

"She gives everyone the benefit of the doubt. Especially me." He tilted
his head, studying Sara. "Anne looks like you," he decided.

"That's funny. I see you in her. She has your eyes."

"Are you taking her back to New York?"

"She's not mine to take," Sara said, and as soon as she said it, she felt a
curl of pain. She took a deep breath. *Look at all the ways you can lose,* she

thought. She couldn't go on talking about this, didn't want to upset herself or anybody. She tried to think of something to say.

"It looks like you have a terrific little boy," she said.

Danny brightened. "Isn't he fantastic? We're so nuts about him. And my mother just dotes on him."

"She could have doted on her granddaughter," Sara said quickly, and then Danny flinched and she realized how sharply the words had flown out of her mouth. *Frances,* Sara thought. A lean, tired woman standing outside one chill day lying to a sixteen-year-old girl, lying to Danny, doing everything to keep them apart. *It's just what love does to you,* she had said. *Sometimes you do things you might never imagine yourself doing.*

Danny picked up a glass candy dish from the coffee table and turned it around in his hand. "I was angry, too, Sara," he said. "After I saw you, I hated her. But how could I accuse her with Charlotte there? I just went back home with it all bottled up inside of me, but the further away we got, the bigger it grew. By the time we got home, I was half crazy. I dropped Charlotte off at the house, then told her I just had to swing by the office, and then as soon as I got there, I called my mother and had it out with her. I got so angry, I punched a hole in the wall."

"Danny—" Sara stared at his arm.

"She didn't apologize, didn't think she had done anything wrong. I told myself that was it. That I couldn't forgive her. That this was too big. I didn't want her having anything to do with me or my family for fear she'd spoil that, too, and I told her if she told Charlotte, I'd call her a liar. I thought I'd feel better, but Jesus, I couldn't sleep. I had this burning in my gut, and Charlotte kept asking what was going on, why my mother had been so short with her when she had called that morning. Then, I blew up at Charlotte because I couldn't find the baby's bottle. Joseph started wailing, and Charlotte gave me this cool look that was worse than if she had stabbed me.

"I made a decision. I knew I had to let the anger go if I wanted to be happy. It doesn't mean I forgive it. And I'll never forget. But the next day, I called my mother and talked to her like nothing had happened. And we haven't talked about it since."

"Are you happy, Danny?"

"What a funny question," he said, putting the candy dish down. "When we were kids, when I thought you didn't want to see me anymore, I sure wasn't. I was a mess. I left high school, left Boston, and roamed around, trying to figure out how to feel better. I drank a lot, did some drugs, I went through girls like Kleenex, and the only thing they all had in common was they looked like you. I was just trying to rewrite the script, but it always had the same finish. None of those girls was you and we always broke up. Then my brother died, and I had to come home, be the man of the family, and I still wasn't over you." He leaned forward. "My mother was so grief-stricken, she couldn't go anywhere by herself. I had to take her, like her chauffeur. I didn't mind. I'd drive and it was so good not to feel anything, not to have to make any decision except which route to take."

Danny started telling Sara about all the places he didn't mind taking his mother to. The cut-rate shops she liked to browse through. The supermarkets. And he told Sara how he hadn't even minded running his mother over to church on Sundays, because otherwise he'd be sitting stunned, in front of the TV with a beer in his hand, trying to concentrate on whatever was on, trying to wonder how his life had gone so wrong. "That's where I met Charlotte," he told her. "At church. My mother always wanted to stay for the meet-and-greets they had afterward. Watery red punch. Store-bought powdered donuts. Everyone all decked out in hats and ties, the whole nine yards. I never wanted to go, and I certainly didn't have anything to say to anybody, a heathen like me, but I sat on one of the chairs, waiting for my mother, killing time, and every time, Charlotte would come over and strike up a conversation. She'd talk about a movie she had seen. A book she had read. Sometimes she talked about something going on in the community—a chocolate festival she was helping to organize, a new pet store that was opening that specialized in exotics. She made me talk, and even though I barely said two words, she treated me like I was the most interesting person on the planet, and she kept inviting me places I didn't want to go. Picnics. Potlock suppers. Square dances."

"Square dances! You used to walk out of any place that even thought of playing country music," Sara said. She tried to imagine him, moving with that easy grace of his.

"Sometimes things change, and you don't even see it coming." Danny half-smiled. "I kept turning her down, but it never stopped her from asking me again the next Sunday. Finally, I went because it filled up the time. Because it was something to think about other than you. And then after a while, I went because I wanted to. I wanted to be with her. She could find fun in the simplest things. Even going to the Thrift-T-Mart to look for toasters. She's the happiest person. She's got faith and hope about life, and it's catching. She makes you feel good just to be around her." He leaned back on the sofa. "She's good for me, Sara. She saved my life."

"Then you are happy."

Danny looked away from her. "I have a wife who loves me more than I deserve to be loved. I have a house and a good job and a beautiful little boy."

"You love her?"

"Yes," Danny said. "I do."

She was surprised at the hurt, and then there was a sound from the back of the house. A door slapping open and then shut again. "That doesn't sound good," Sara said.

"I think Anne thinks we should have been her parents," Danny said.

"That would have been something, wouldn't it?" Sara said, struggling to keep her tone light. They were both quiet. Outside, in front of the house, someone laughed loudly. Danny touched her face, and then she reached up her hand and covered his with it.

She expected him to move away, but instead, Danny leaned toward her so their foreheads were touching, so she felt his breath against her face, coffee and cigarettes, and then Sara kissed his nose, the way she used to when she was just fifteen, so shy and scared, she didn't know what else to kiss, and then he closed his eyes, distressed, and she kissed his mouth, and he moved closer to her, holding the kiss, cupping her face in his hands.

A car beeped outside and Danny slowly pulled away from Sara. He stood up, dazed, and walked to the window and waved, and when he turned back to Sara, he looked like a different person to her. The yearning in his face was gone. All his features seemed put back into place. She felt as if she had been shaken roughly awake from a dream she had wanted to keep dreaming.

Charlotte came bustling through the door, holding up a bottle of wine. Her gaze skittered from Danny to Sara, and she frowned. "Well," she said shortly. "Shall we see if things look better on a full stomach?"

Candles flickered on the table. A gleaming silver platter of chicken sat between long plates of green beans and sweet white corn. The chairs were all pushed so closely together that you couldn't help but touch whoever you sat next to. Anne kept her arms stiffly folded across her chest, her gaze down. What had happened outside? Sara wondered.

When everyone was seated, and when Joseph was wheeled in in the big carriage, placed by Anne, Charlotte held out her hands. "We usually say grace, all right?" she asked. Eva reached for Anne's hand, and Anne tucked it into her lap, but Sara reached across the table and took Danny's hand, warm and smooth, cool only where his wedding band was. "Bless this gathering," Charlotte said. "Amen." Hands released, but for an extra second, Sara held on to Danny's and when she let go she still felt his warmth.

Sara's stomach was in knots and she couldn't eat, but she picked at the food, wanting to be polite, swallowing half a forkful of yams, a sliver of chicken. Charlotte got up, her chair scraping. "I'll just get more butter for the bread," she said. As Charlotte headed into the kitchen, she touched Danny's cheek, the top of his head, and when she came back, she trailed her hand along his back as if each touch were a marker.

Joseph squealed. "What's my little guy up to?" Danny said. His voice lifted, he looked at his son with such pure, open delight, that Sara couldn't help but smile.

Anne leaned over the carriage and held out her finger and Joseph grabbed on to it, squealing louder. "Hey, you," she said, and she laughed, the first time since she had arrived at the house.

"Will you look at that!" Charlotte said. "I do believe he's in love."

Joseph made a buzzing sound and Anne looked up, delighted. "Doesn't it sound like he's saying my name?" She laughed again, and tickled the baby. "I'm your half sister," she told him.

327

No one spoke at first. "Of course you are," Charlotte said quickly. Anne's face lit up and then Joseph reached out for Charlotte so eagerly that he bounced in the carriage.

Eva took the napkin from her lap and threw it down on the table. "I'm sorry. I don't mean to spoil this lovely dinner, but I just can't keep pretending that everything's fine." She turned to Anne. "Why did you come here, Anne? To a stranger's?"

"Maybe you two are the strangers," Anne said. "This is my real father."

Danny looked pained. "Anne, you can't stay here."

Sara tried to speak. "You have to go home with Eva and George."

Anne snapped around toward Sara, eyes flashing. "Why did you come here?"

"I wanted to make sure you were all right—"

"You don't care about me! You blew me off in Florida! You got all chummy again with *them*—" Anne said, nodding at her parents. "Did you come here for Danny?" She wheeled on Danny. "Is that why you were even nice to me? To get to *her*—your true love?"

"That's ridiculous!" Sara said, but she suddenly felt Charlotte's stare.

Danny started to rise and Anne grabbed his arm, holding him in place. "No, don't go," she said, then she turned to her parents. "Everyone is always leaving me," she cried.

"No one is leaving you," Sara said.

"You did! And you are now! You came here to give me back to my parents! You're my mother! Why aren't you fighting for me?"

"I did fight for you!" Sara shouted. "You don't know what you're saying!"

"I know exactly what I'm saying!"

"She did fight for you, Anne," Eva interrupted. "So hard we had to leave."

"Right. You left to keep me safe—"

Eva shook her head. "No. We left to keep *us* safe. We weren't afraid she'd harm you—not as much as we were afraid she'd win you from us! That she might have the right."

"Eva—" George said, but Eva waved her hand at him.

"Oh, my God. You did know," Sara said, astonished.

"Know what?" Anne said.

"Not for sure," George said. "Never for sure."

"Never for sure what?" Anne cried.

"The adoption papers," Eva said. "Danny needed to sign them and he didn't. We were almost sure his name was forged by his brother." Sara sank down in her chair.

"What?" Anne's voice thinned. "Are you all crazy? How can I believe anything any of you say? You've all lied to me and to each other."

"You were this little baby. We loved you so much, Anne—so much—we would have done anything to keep you, even something wrong," Eva said.

"You all got to choose for me! When do I get to decide who I want to be with?" Anne glared at Sara. "I don't care what's right or legal! I'd never go with you now—never!"

"I'd never make you, now," Sara said quietly.

"Why are you even here?"

"She has a right to be here," Eva said slowly. "If it weren't for her, we might not have gotten you in the first place. And if it weren't for her, we wouldn't have found you now."

"You have to come home with us," George said. "Where else can you go?"

Anne threw her napkin to the floor. "Nowhere," she said, defeated, and then she got up and slowly left the room.

Charlotte, head down, began gathering the dishes. "Charlotte—" Danny said, and began to help her. They could all hear Anne banging around in the other room, moving chairs, pacing, and then George got up, slowly. "It'll be all right," he said, but his voice sounded pounded down. "It's by default. She doesn't have anyplace else to go."

"Default or not," Eva said. "We're taking her right home. I'll go make reservations."

Charlotte started doing the dishes. Sara gathered her purse, her sweater. She couldn't stop trembling, and when she came back through the dining room, she saw Anne, sitting by Joseph's carriage, her finger caught in his grasp.

"Time to go," Eva said, coming into the room, and Anne gently pulled her finger free. Joseph whimpered.

"Looks like he's going to miss you," Charlotte said, and Anne shot her a look, as if Charlotte didn't understand anything.

"I prefer to say my goodbyes here," Charlotte said. She handed Sara a square of tinfoil. "Peach pie," she said. "It'll kill the taste of the airline food."

"Thank you," Sara said, but she meant thank you for having me in your house. Thank you for being so good to Danny and Anne.

Charlotte walked them to the front door. She didn't try to hug Anne or shake anyone's hand. "Safe trip," Charlotte said, and then she met Danny's eyes, holding his gaze. Sara saw how Danny cupped his wife's face in his hands, lingering, just for a moment, before he slowly stepped outside. And then, when they all were outside, Charlotte quietly closed the door, head lowered. Danny walked them to the car, stopping at the lip of the lawn, watching all of them, except for Sara, get in. "Anne—" he said, but Anne averted her face, and Danny sighed, helpless.

"This didn't turn out the way I thought it would," Sara said.

"I don't care. I'm just glad I got a chance to know her. Even for this little while."

"I didn't mean just with Anne," Sara said. She felt the words ball up inside her stomach. "I think—seeing you and her together was harder than I thought it would be."

She looked into his eyes. "I'm sorry. I should just shut up."

"No, no. I'm glad we're talking. We could always talk."

She studied his face, hesitating. Really, what difference did it make what she said now? "It could have been a whole different life for everyone," she said.

"Sara," he said, and as soon as she heard the tone in his voice, she knew she had made a mistake.

"You don't have to say anything," she said. There it was. The flip side of love, of happiness, was knowing that it was going to end, no matter what you did, and you were powerless to stop it. "I'm glad you have Charlotte. Glad you got to meet Anne. And I'm glad we saw each other."

He put his hands deep in his pockets, planting his feet in the grassy lawn, and for a moment, she wondered if he seeded and sprayed it, if he tended his lawn as carefully as he did his family. She bet he did. *Look at him,* she thought. Good and decent. Responsible and loving. The kind of man she would have grown old with. Everyone had thought she was crazy to love him, that he was wild, that he had left her in the lurch, that at fifteen she could no more recognize real love than she could the elements on the moon. But she knew now that she had been right to love him because look how he had turned out.

One car drove by, and then another, the tires squealing on the pavement, and Sara heaved a breath. "I have to go," she said. "They're waiting for me."

"If I could move, I'd go back inside so I wouldn't have to watch you leave."

"Danny?"

"That fifteen-year-old guy who was in love with you is still inside me," Danny said quietly. "I can feel him when I look at you, Sara. If I'd known the truth back then, I swear I would never have left you and Anne. Ever." Danny stood there on the grass, not moving, looking at her so hard, he was trembling.

"Danny—"

"I love Charlotte," he said. "I'm thirty-two now and she's my whole life."

Sara tried to swallow. "Then I'm glad you're happy," she said.

"You'd better go," he said. "They're all waiting on you."

Sara walked back to the car, got in, and shut the door. Outside the window, she saw that Danny was still there, only now he was in the middle of the road, and she could see he was crying, his cheeks damp, his beautiful face crumpled. She cried, too. She didn't care what anybody thought. She didn't mind that George and Eva were sitting in the front seat, that Anne was right beside her. Helpless, she grabbed for her tissue. Anne was right here in this car, but Anne was gone to Sara, and now, Danny was really gone, too, growing smaller and smaller. She put one hand on the window and he raised his up, but there was all that distance between them, all that time, and their hands didn't meet and touch. And then the car turned the corner, and he was farther away, and then he disappeared.

At the airport, they had to separate, going to different terminals. Eva awkwardly hugged Sara. "Thank you," George said, but Anne refused to look at her.

"Anne," Sara said, "please let me just talk to you." And Anne turned forcefully away, walking toward the check-in. Never had Sara felt so helpless.

"She's not happy with us, either," George said to Sara.

"Will you let me know how things go?" Sara pleaded.

Eva took Sara's hands in hers. "I'm so sorry—"

"Me, too." Sara looked down at her shoes and then back up at Eva. "Thank you for telling me about the papers. For telling Anne. I needed to know."

"I think I needed to tell."

Sara let go of Eva's hands. "I can't say goodbyes anymore," she blurted. "I'm afraid now they're too final."

"Then we won't," Eva said. Sara didn't walk them to the gate. Her flight wasn't for another hour, so she sat in the waiting area. She had forgotten to give them their share of Charlotte's pie. She opened the foil but the pie was pretty squashed. Picking at it, she took a few bites, sparkling sweet, and then she covered it back up.

She'd be coming back to New York in the middle of the night, a time when the city felt most lonely to her. If she called Scott, he'd come and get her. She hadn't called Scott in weeks now. Hadn't even thought about it. She got up and found a phone. She dialed and Scott answered on the second ring, his voice sleepy, and for a moment, all she wanted to do was tell him, *come and get me.*

"Scott," she said.

"Sara!" he said. "Wait. Let me just turn the computer off so I can give you my full attention." She heard something rattling. "I missed you," he said. "Ah, here we go, done. I'm all yours, now." She still heard the tap of his keys.

"Are you coming home?" he said.

She rubbed her fingers against her temples. "Yes."

"Are you coming home alone?"

A man stood behind Sara, rummaging in his coat for his cell phone and then dialing.

"Yes," she said. She thought of the clamor in Charlotte's house, the cozy warmth. Then she thought of her apartment, how no matter where she turned she could see every corner of it, even the bathroom. She thought of all the apartments she and Scott had seen and he had rejected, how he had chosen one for the two of them and she hadn't even seen it.

"Oh thank God, thank God," Scott said.

Sara drew in and let out a long breath and told him what had happened.

"Are you upset about this? Don't be," he soothed. "This is a good thing."

"A good thing? Anne won't even talk to me, now—"

"Look, you did what you could. You made the effort. That's the important thing."

"Sara? You there?" Scott said.

Sara shut her eyes and then opened them. A woman glided past, her coat brushing against Sara.

"I can't just let this go, Scott."

"Come on, what else can you do?"

"I feel like I gave her up for adoption all over again."

"But now it's an adult choice. It's the right choice."

"Yes, it is," she said. "But do you think that makes it easier?" She heard Scott's sigh, heard the fast tap and patter of his computer keys. Why couldn't he stop work to talk to her now? Why couldn't he just focus on her? "Honey, you went down there, you saw the girl, you made the connection. It didn't work out, what are you going to do, keep making yourself unhappy for years? I think it's for the best. Now we can get on with our lives."

"This is my life."

"I meant our life together."

The man on the cell phone hung up, laughing heartily to himself, patting the pocket where he put his phone. Sara felt a headache forming, small as a dime, spinning on its axis, not sure where it would fall and settle, and suddenly, all she wanted to do was go home to her apartment alone, to make herself some peppermint tea and relax herself enough to sleep. She couldn't think beyond that.

"I want to go home alone," she said.

"Oh, of course. You're emotionally exhausted from seeing that girl."

Sara's throat tightened. "That girl is my daughter." She leaned against the phone. "Scott," she said. "Do you ever want kids?"

"You think we should be talking about this now?"

"I just want to know. Is there ever a chance you'd want them in the future?"

"Come on, this is nuts, talking about this now. You're upset. We're not face to face."

"You don't, do you?" she said. "Not Anne. And not one of our own, either."

"Sara—"

"No. Tell me the truth. Please, Scott. Just tell me."

He sighed, deep and heavy. "Okay," he said. "I don't want a teenage girl in my life."

"What about a baby? Our baby?"

He was quiet again and this time she didn't hear his typing. "Scott?" she said.

"I don't want babies," he said finally. "I can't imagine I ever will. Some people don't, Sara, and they're still good people. Does that make me a criminal?"

"No," she said slowly. "But it doesn't make me a criminal for wanting those things, either. For needing them. And maybe it makes you wrong for me."

"Are you breaking up with me?" Scott said, stunned.

She hadn't realized she was until he said it. She tried to swallow, tried to take in enough air to talk. She had to speak fast before all the good things about Scott welled back up to the surface, before she remembered how nice it was to wake up next to him, how kind he could be, how funny. She'd have a good life with him, but would it be a great one? She thought of Danny, how she had felt just standing out on his front lawn with him today, every cell switched on, and she wanted to feel that way again with someone. She wanted to believe it was possible. "Yes," she said, and as soon as she said it, she felt her life stretching out in front of her. She felt how alone she might be now.

"I wish you had never found that girl," Scott said bitterly.

"I wish I had found her years earlier."

"I don't understand it. Or you, Sara. I don't understand you."

"I know," she said.

"I guess there's nothing else to talk about, then," Scott said, his voice miserable.

"I guess not," she said.

"Goodbye then, Sara," he said, and gently hung up.

Sara kept the receiver to her ear. Around her, people swirled. She'd go home now. Maybe she'd call a friend when she got in. Or maybe she'd just be with herself tonight. See what it felt like to her, see how she might be able to get used to it.

She called her parents the next week. "Please, can both of you get on the line?" she asked. She told them about Anne and the whole time she was talking both her parents were so silent she wasn't sure they hadn't hung up. "Mom? Dad?" she said, and then she heard Abby sigh.

"Sara—" Jack said and then stopped.

"You don't need to fix this," Sara told him.

"I don't even know what to say about this," Abby said.

"Neither do I," Sara said. "But I just wanted you to know. I wanted to tell you."

When she hung up, she got juice from the fridge and drank as if she were parched. She sat on her couch and put her feet up, thinking about the conversation. It was the first time one or both of her parents hadn't told her that things would work out for the best, that she should focus on her future. She stretched out and shut her eyes. All she wanted to do now was sleep.

* * *

At home, Anne stayed in her room. The whole plane ride, she hadn't said two words to either Eva or George, keeping the headphones clamped on, going to and from the bathroom, and each time she reseated her eyes were red. "Give her time," George said. George came home from work an hour early, just to be with Anne, even though she clearly wasn't interested in either one of them. "I'll be in the kitchen," he'd call to her. Or he'd knock on her door and say, "Who wants to go to the beach?" but Anne never did. She always had some excuse.

Sara began calling, but Anne refused to speak to her. As soon as she heard Sara's name, she shook her head. "I have nothing to say to her," Anne said, and went to her room and closed the door tight.

"I'm sorry," Eva said to Sara.

"Is she okay?" Sara asked.

"Are you?" Eva asked. She couldn't get the image out of her mind, of Sara crying in the backseat of their car. *What have we done?* Eva had thought.

"Sure. I'm just fine." Sara's voice sounded shaky.

"Anne will be, too," Eva said, and tried to believe it for all of them.

Sara called every few days, and although Anne would never get on the phone with her, Eva and Sara always talked. Sara stopped asking if she could speak to Anne, and at first Eva thought it was in deference to her, and then Eva realized it was in deference to Anne, and somehow that touched Eva more. Instead, Sara directed all her questions to Eva. "Is she eating?" Sara asked. "Is she going to school? Does she sleep okay?"

Eva gave a small laugh.

"Is something funny?" Sara said.

"You never asked questions like that when you were sixteen," Eva said. "You wanted to know if she had been waiting for you. If she had said your name yet."

"I want to make sure Anne's okay."

"I know. And you're asking just the kinds of questions any mother would ask."

"Thank you for saying that," Sara said. "Thank you."

There was silence on the wires again. "Well, I won't keep you—" Sara said, and her voice was so soft that Eva felt a pang. She felt the way she used to when she had first met Sara and all she wanted to do was take care of her.

"Tell me how you're managing," Eva said. "Talk to me a little about yourself now."

"Really? You want to talk about me?"

"Tell me about your job. About New York."

Sara told her about Madame, she told her she had broken up with Scott. "Oh, I'm sorry," Eva said, but Sara interrupted.

"No, don't be," Sara said. "Maybe I could have been happy with him, but never happy enough. Does that make sense?"

"Yes," Eva said. "It does."

They talked for only a little longer. Their voices wound down, and then finally Sara said she had to go. "Can I call again?" she asked.

"I'd like that," Eva said, and she meant it. Even after Eva hung up, she sat by the phone, and then she got up and went to Anne's room, and knocked on the closed door.

"Honey? Do you want to talk?" she asked. "Can I come in?" She opened the door. Anne was on her bed, writing, papers around her. "Do you want to talk?" she repeated, and Anne shook her head.

"You lied to me," Anne said. "How can I believe anything you say to me now?"

Eva felt her life was out of balance. Sara wouldn't see a lawyer now, but things still hadn't turned out right, because now neither one of them really had Anne. Eva didn't try to push Anne into talking to her; instead she began to leave her little notes, the way she used to, tucked in her lunch bag, on the refrigerator, simple things. *"Hope your day is great!" "Made your favorite lunch." "I love you."* She glanced into the wastebaskets, but the notes were never there, and fool that she was, she told herself Anne had read them, that maybe Anne had even saved them. *Like I would,* Eva thought.

One day at school, the parent of a little boy had come to the school furious and, instead of talking to Eva first, had gone right to the principal to complain that Eva hadn't let his son do his special job of door holder that day. "Because he kicked another boy," Eva explained, "he has to learn there are consequences." But even though the principal had mollified the parent, she lectured Eva about being more on top of things.

"He kicked a boy!" Eva repeated.

"Perhaps you should have called his parents and told them of the incident, rather than letting them be surprised," the principal said. "Perhaps you should have been prepared."

Perhaps you should ride to town on a broomstick, Eva thought, but she stayed pleasant. "Oh absolutely," Eva agreed.

She drove home, irritated, upset that she had lied to the principal, that she had pretended to go along with her. She stopped at the bank to get money. *"You lied to me,"* Anne had told her. Oh yes, another thing she hadn't been prepared for.

Eva made a decision. She went to the safe-deposit box and got out all the letters and photographs she had saved when she and George had first contacted Sara. She hadn't looked at them since the day she brought them here, not knowing what else to do with them, and she couldn't look at them now. She stuffed them into her school book bag, wedged between her lesson plans and her appointment book. She didn't know what had possessed her to save all of them, and a few times she had even considered throwing them out, but she had never been able to. They didn't feel like hers anymore, and they didn't need to be under lock and key anymore, either. What did she have left to hide?

As soon as she was home, she went to Anne.

"Anne," Eva said, knocking on her daughter's door. She could hear music. "Anne!" she called louder. *"This is my house."* The thought flew in her mind. It was a thing her mother used to say to her when Eva was an adolescent acting up, disturbing the equilibrium. *"This is my house and as long as you live in it, you live by my rules." Well,* she thought, *who said rules were right?*

Eva, book bag in hand, opened Anne's door. Anne was on her bed, headphones on, books around her. A storm of paper was on the floor. She sat up and blinked at Eva.

Eva began taking the letters and photographs out of her bag and placing them on Anne's bed. "These are for you. I should have given them to you years ago."

Anne looked at her quizzically. "What's all this?"

"Go look," Eva said.

There were the first letters from Sara, written to George and Eva. There were copies of all the letters George and Eva had written to Sara. "Dear birth mother," it said, and Anne stared at Eva. Eva rubbed her arms as if they were cold. "What can I say, I'm a pack rat. I never could throw anything out," Eva said.

Anne lifted up a photo. Eva and George, when they were young, standing next to Sara who was round and as big as a beach ball. She picked up another photo, a faded one. Danny, swaggering in blue jeans, his thumbs hooked into his belt loops. And then there was a photo of Sara holding Anne up, the two of them staring at each other. "Oh my God," Anne said, and then Eva sat on the edge of Anne's bed.

"We were our own odd little family," Eva said. "We did everything together at first. Went to the doctors, went to dinner, sat around sipping lemonade in the backyard." Eva fingered one of the photos. Sara, young and startled looking, Eva with one arm around her, the baby on a picnic blanket, twisting her head, looking toward Sara. "I loved her," Eva said simply. "And not just because of the baby. I really did love her and want her in our lives." Eva traced a finger over the photo. "But not as much as you did. Whenever you saw her, you just about went crazy. You cried when she left the room, lit up when she reentered. She used to make up these little songs for you and all she had to do was hum a few notes when you were cranky and you would calm. I'd try and you'd get restless. It made me jealous sometimes."

"It did? You got jealous?"

"Of course I did." Eva nodded. "Sometimes I picked you up and you would scream and I'd take it personally." Eva put the photo down and studied Anne. "I spent so much time reading child care books, talking to other mothers, trying to figure out what I was doing wrong. I always thought maybe because I was an older mother, my instincts were rustier. Or sometimes I thought it was because I didn't give birth to you, maybe I had to study harder at raising you. It's taken me all this time to realize maybe I was so busy trying to force connections between us that I just didn't let you be yourself. That just because we were so different didn't mean we couldn't have a bond. I just felt I never had you, so how could I let myself risk losing you to Sara, or to anyone? How could I let you go?"

Anne looked at her so hard, Eva faltered. "What do you tell her about me?" Anne finally said. "When she calls?"

Eva shrugged. "I tell her that you're here, or you're at school."

Anne fiddled with a photo. "And what does she say?"

"She says she wants to talk with you," Eva said.

"You're friendly again all of a sudden?"

"We have a common bond," Eva said quietly. "You."

"She's not really interested in me. She wouldn't take me with her," Anne said.

"I wouldn't have let her," Eva said. "It wasn't her choice to make."

Anne pushed the photographs away from her. "It wasn't my choice to make, either."

"You can throw them away if you want to," Eva said, going to the door to leave. "They're yours now. And anything you want to ask me, anything you want to know, you can ask me that now, too. No one's going to lie to you now about anything." Then she stepped out into the hall, closing Anne's door, leaving her alone with the letters, which Anne promptly kicked to the floor.

At four in the morning Anne bolted awake. She had fallen asleep in her clothes, waking and drifting again, and now she was really up. She leaned over the bed and clicked on her table lamp, surveying the mess of papers.

She had been so furious since she had come home. She had waited for Danny to call her, to check and see if she had gotten home all right, the way any father would, the way George certainly did. When she was half an hour late, George was on the front porch, his car keys in his hands. "I was ready to call out the search party," he said, and he was only half joking. But Danny hadn't called. The phone had stayed silent. She had waited for Sara to show up, in a car, the motor running, bags packed, ready to take her, just the two of them, off someplace, but the only cars that came up her street were the neighbors' cars, old and familiar and going nowhere more exciting than to work or the supermarket. The phone rang and rang, but it was never for her, it was always for her mother. Mail came, bills and advertisements and magazines. Everyone was living another life.

She swung her legs over the bed, the floor cool against the soles of her feet, making her toes flex. The house was so hushed, it was a little spooky. She switched on another light and her gaze darted around the corners of her room, the way it had when she was a little girl and so scared of ghosts she couldn't speak. There were the letters, still scattered on the floor where she had left them. She'd throw them out. She'd burn them. She'd rip them into confetti. Lies. All of it lies. She crouched, gathering the letters up, and then she saw a small red heart drawn in the corner of a page. She saw Sara's name, surrounded by exclamation points. Her legs wobbled and she hinged down onto the floor. She glanced at the paper. *It's the middle of the night,* it said, *and I don't know what to do.* Well, it was the middle of the night here, too, and suddenly, she didn't know what to do, either. She didn't feel angry anymore, but confused and sad, and so lonely she couldn't bear it. Maybe she could read a few letters before she decided what to do with them. She picked up one of the sheets, pale blue parchment, and slowly unfolded it.

"Dear birth mother," it began. Anne couldn't stop reading. She settled back against the bed, and picked up another letter. It was like reading a novel about herself in letters. Real and immediate, a whole other missing life unfolding before her, a drama centering around her that she couldn't even remember. Sara's letters were so desperate it made Anne feel scared to read them. Eva's letters were so effusive, so full of longing and need that for a moment, Anne didn't recognize the letters as her mother's. There was her father's scribble, and a little drawing he made of the house so Sara would know what it looked like. Anne traced a finger over the drawing. It was as if everyone suddenly had identities she knew nothing about. She sifted through the photos and then her hand stopped. It was just a snapshot of her and Sara lying together on a blanket in the grass, facing each other. She must have been nearly newborn in this photo because she was so impossibly small, curled in a tiny blue dress, a pacifier taking up most of her lower face. But the thing that struck her was the way she was looking at Sara, eyes locked onto Sara's eyes, her face alert, full of wonder, and Sara—Sara was radiant. *We look like we're in love,* Anne thought. She stood up, studying the picture.

Anne found her wallet, and slid the photo into a pocket. She put her wallet back in her purse and returned to bed, and shutting her eyes, tried to sleep.

At school, everyone just thought she had been out sick. "Feel better?" one teacher asked, and Anne shrugged, because the truth was, she wasn't sure. She didn't wear the red bandana in her curls anymore, the way Sara did. She didn't dress the way Sara had, but she didn't dress the way she used to, either. Her clothes felt wrong. She felt wrong, so she ended up belting an old dress of hers with the red bandana. She clipped back one side of her hair and let the other be wild, and then staring into the mirror, she felt as if she were transformed again, only she wasn't sure into what. In the cafeteria, Flor flopped down beside her, picking at the hot dog school lunch.

"No food for you?" Flor said. "Are you on a diet?"

Anne shook her head.

"Did you have the flu that's going around?" Flor asked her. Anne shrugged, because how could she explain anything to Flor that Flor'd understand?

Flor waved her fork thoughtfully at Anne. "Girl, snap out of it," she advised.

Anne couldn't snap out of anything. She dreamed through her classes, sneaking peaks at the photo in history class, and then again during math, and every time she looked, instead of feeling comforted, she felt more and more confused. She couldn't concentrate, not in English, not in gym, not even when she was called to the guidance counselor's office to talk about college. The counselor pushed brochures of colleges at her. "Is going away to college something you're interested in?" the guidance counselor probed. It was the second time someone had mentioned that to Anne. Anne studied the first brochure, a brick building covered with ivy, a bunch of kids with their heads thrown back, teeth as even and boxy as niblet corn, laughing as if they had heard the funniest joke in the world. "Writers don't have to go to college," Anne said. "They just have to live."

The guidance counselor blinked at Anne. "You don't think going to college is living?" she said. "Believe me, some people go just for the experience rather than the education." She pushed the brochures toward Anne.

"How do you think you'll write if you're waitressing all day long? It sounds romantic, but believe me, it's not." Anne thought of going away, of being so far away she'd never have to come home, and then to her amazement, she felt a sudden clip of fear, as if there were nowhere now where she might feel at home, no people whom she might really belong to. "Take the pamphlets," the guidance counselor said. "You never know how you'll feel about this later."

That night, Anne couldn't sleep again. The college pamphlets were in her purse. She hadn't even been able to take them out and put them on her desk. The letters and photos were still on the floor. She sat at her desk and tried to write but couldn't. Everything coming out of her pen sounded fake. *"Write about what you know,"* her teachers told her, *"that will make it real."* But she suddenly felt as if everything she had ever known had been wrong, that she didn't really know what was true anymore, and maybe no one else really did, either. She crouched down and dug out all the letters Eva had given her and sifted through them. There, at the bottom, she pulled out a notebook. A journal. "I felt her kick today. I am in love." Sara's writing. Anne put the pen down and padded into the kitchen, glancing at the clock. Two. She picked up the phone and dialed.

"Hello?" Sara's voice was groggy with sleep, and as soon as Anne heard it, she gripped the phone tighter.

"It's me. It's Anne."

She couldn't believe she was doing this. She didn't even know what she wanted to say.

"Anne! Are you okay?" Sara said. "Is everything all right?"

"You want me to call another time—"

"No, no—don't hang up. Please don't hang up!" Sara interrupted.

No one spoke for a moment. The wires hummed.

"I read your letters," Anne said. "The ones you wrote to Eva when you were pregnant with me. I read the ones she wrote you, too."

"The letters—" Sara said, her voice full of wonder. "She kept the letters—"

"She gave them to me." Anne's lips were dry and she licked at them. "Why did you lie to me?" Anne finally said. "Why did you act like you were going to be a part of my life?"

343

"I didn't lie. I'm still a part of your life!"

"How? How are you a part of it? You don't live near me. I thought you came down here for me!" Anne felt a fresh flare of anger. She breathed hard. "You didn't have the right to just show up! To say things you didn't mean, to screw everyone up!"

"I never meant to hurt you," Sara said. "I needed to find you. I couldn't think about anything else."

"You found me. Then you left me!" Anne cried.

"I didn't leave you! I just had to leave Florida. That's different."

Anne sat down on a chair by the phone, resting her head against the counter.

"What does that even mean?" Anne said. "Are you coming back here to visit? Are you inviting me to come there?"

"Would you want that? I'd be there now if I had the money to get there," Sara said slowly. "And I'd invite you in a flash if your parents would allow it."

"Why is it up to them?"

"Because they're the ones who got to raise you. They get to make the decisions."

Anne shut her eyes.

"Would you let me call you?" Sara asked. "Could I write you? Or you write me?"

"I don't know," Anne said. "Maybe. Maybe I will."

"Anne?" said Sara. Her voice was like the skip in one of her father's old records. "We all always loved you."

Anne quietly hung up. Never had she felt so far away from everyone. From Sara. From her parents who were sleeping in the bedroom.

The kitchen felt so empty that when she turned around, she was startled to see Eva, in robe and bare feet, a sheet of paper in her hand, and then Anne couldn't move. "Have you been here the whole time?" Anne asked, and Eva nodded. "You heard what I said?" Anne asked, steeling herself. Eva nodded again, but she didn't look angry. Instead she just stood there. "I read the letters," Anne said. "Why did you save them?"

"I saved everything."

"Did you reread them?"

Eva shook her head. "No, I don't think I can."

"Then what's that?" Anne asked and Eva lifted up the paper. "I did my own rereading," Eva said, and then Anne saw Mr. Moto's scrawl on the page.

"That's my story," Anne said. "The one you both hated. But I threw it out."

Eva shook her head. "I took it out of the trash. I thought maybe you could read it later, compare it to what you were writing now and see how you've improved—an old teacher's trick." She folded the page carefully, as if it were something to be treasured. "It's wonderful, Anne. I should have seen how wonderful it was. I was so wrong—"

Anne started to cry. Eva slowly walked over to Anne and put her arms about her, but she didn't say anything. She didn't even move except to keep her arms about Anne, so warm and steady, Anne felt herself softening, and she finally rested her head against her mother's shoulders. Eva held Anne for as long as Anne needed to be held and for the first time, too, Eva let go of Anne first.

George left work after half a day. One of his patients, who arrived two hours late, complained that she had to reschedule. "Maybe I should find another dentist," she said.

Ordinarily, he'd have put his smock back on. He'd have his hands back in her mouth, examining her jaw, taking film. He'd care about his practice more.

"I can recommend one, if you need," George said, and left his dental smock hanging on the door, and the woman's mouth slowly closed.

He drove home to his daughter. Let his patient reschedule. Let it all go to hell. He wanted to see Anne.

He was always surprised to find her there. He didn't know what he expected anymore. That the house might explode. That Sara would come back. He pulled into the drive. There was Anne reading on the porch. "Anne!" he called and she looked up at him, wary.

"Come drive," he told her. And then Anne put the book down and shyly got into the car. "Drive and you can go anywhere," he said, the same words he had said to Sara when she was this age, too, and he was hoping Sara would learn to drive away from them, that she'd have so much fun, the thought of coming to their house would seem an imposition on her. Anne lifted her chin, her eyes shining. She took a right turn. "Like a pro!" George told her. "Keep going! Keep going! Soon you can take the car on your own."

"Really? You'd let me do that? You'd trust me?"

He stroked her hair, amazed that she let him. He loved her, God how he loved her, and now, he was giving her permission to leave him, and hoping, with all his heart, that she'd find her way back.

Anne woke up, shivering from a dream, not sure where she was. The room came back into focus. This is my house. My parents are here. *My mother saved my writing.*

She could hear a lawn mower roaring outside. Swinging her legs over the bed, she went to her bureau, pulling open her sock drawer, digging for two pairs that matched. Her fingers touched paper and she pulled something out, a folded slip of blue. She opened it, and there in Eva's handwriting was a fortune. *"Lucky are the parents who have a one-of-a-kind daughter."* She laughed out loud. She folded the fortune over, and held it in her hand.

Sara sat in her apartment staring at the phone. She picked it up and started to dial Anne and then slammed the phone down again. This was ridiculous. She had done this so many times since Anne's last call that her wrist ached. "Control yourself," she said out loud. She knew if she made Anne feel cornered, she'd lose her forever, and if she pressured Eva and George, they would turn away from her, too. Her hand hovered over the phone as if she could make it ring by sheer willpower.

She didn't feel like sticking around the apartment.

* * *

Betty's Books wasn't very crowded for a Friday night. She wandered over to the magazine section, then when she'd had her fill, she went over to the fiction section, pulled out a book that looked interesting. As she passed the nonfiction section she pulled down a few books from there, too. A biography of the scientist George Fenyman, and a book on the psychology of desire. She sat down on one of the plush chairs to read for a while.

She was planning to read the fiction book first, but she started leafing through the psychology one instead, and was soon lost in a chapter called "Everyday Eros."

"Excuse me, is that your newspaper?" someone said, and Sara looked up. A woman was standing, pointing to the paper on the floor by Sara. "Not mine," Sara said, and then she looked past the woman, and there, staring at her, was Scott.

Flustered, Sara got up, and as soon as she did, she lost her place in her book. It tumbled from her lap onto the floor. "Scott," she said, and he gave her a tight smile, as if he were biting down on something hard. "How are you?" she said.

"I'm good," he said, and then another voice interrupted.

"Scott?" And a woman, tall and exotic looking, appeared, grabbing for Scott's hand. "Honey, I want to show you this book," she said, and Sara's smile tightened, but the woman didn't seem to even register Sara. She tugged at Scott, who lifted his brows at Sara and then let himself be pulled away.

It stung. She was surprised how much. Her heart drummed, sounding in her ears. She didn't want to stay here anymore. Even though she couldn't afford it, even though she'd be short of money all next week, she went to the checkout counter and bought both books. She walked home, twenty blocks, beginning to pant. If the books weren't so heavy, she would have run. Before she even got the key in the lock, she heard the phone ringing. The key stuck, and then she was inside, grabbing for the phone.

"Hi, darling," Abby said, and Sara sat down and told her about Scott. She knew Abby'd berate her for letting Scott go, but she knew she had done the right thing, and she knew that all the disapproval, all the promises to take away the pain, wouldn't change her mind about it. Abby didn't say much the whole time Sara was talking, though Sara heard these odd clicks and catches in her mother's throat, as though she were choking back-words.

"Well," Abby said slowly. "Staying with Scott is something I would have done. But you're braver than that."

"You think I'm brave?"

"You went out there and found your daughter even though your father and I told you not to. You went even though it cost you Scott. I'm glad you didn't listen to my stupid advice. I look at you and I'm amazed."

"Mom?"

"I wish I had had it in me to be like you. But some people can't. You've always risked everything, Sara."

"And lost," she said bitterly.

"No, you didn't lose," Abby said. "You found your daughter. You found you didn't want to be with Scott." Abby drew in a breath. "Tell me more about her."

"You really want to know? After all this time?"

"I'm asking, aren't I?" Abby said.

"I know, but why? Why now?"

"I don't know. All these weeks you've been in Florida, I've thought of nothing but what a mess you were making. Then, when we didn't hear from you, I started wondering what was going on, why you were there so long, what was happening. And then after you called us and told us, I couldn't stop thinking about it all. Your father and I talked about it, and then I imagined all these scenarios, and then, as soon as I did that—" Abby paused.

"She became a person to me."

"She is a person, Mom. An amazing person."

Abby cleared her throat. "Did you know I held her? When she was newborn."

"I knew."

"You did?"

"I pretended to be sleeping. I heard you and Daddy talking."

They both laughed. "Well, then," Abby said, and then Sara heard another voice, her father's. "Your father's waving at me. He has something he wants to tell you."

"How's my baby?" Jack asked.

"Your grown daughter's fine," she said, then she noticed something oblong and brown by the refrigerator. A waterbug, the size of her big toe. Recoiling, she lifted her feet up.

Jack cleared his throat. "Sara, you know I didn't think much of what I saw of your little job—"

"Daddy—" Sara said. "It's not a little job." The bug skittered under the baseboards and disappeared.

"No, no, let me finish. But what I saw was you did it on your own and I'm really proud of you. You know how to stand on your own feet."

My own feet, Sara thought. She remembered how when she was little, she'd stand on his feet and he'd waltz her around, making sure her feet never touched ground. Flying, she had been flying, a lovely illusion. *"You can stand on your feet,"* he had said. If Sara could have wished for her father to ever have said anything to her before, this would have been it.

"I want to give you a loan. Just a loan. For a better apartment," Jack said.

"I can't take a loan—"

"Sure you can. And you'll pay it back. I'm an accountant, remember? I know about money. Maybe you could even get a two-bedroom."

Sara looked down at the baseboards. If you had one roach, you had thousands. "What am I going to do with two bedrooms? Are you planning to stay with me?" she asked.

"No," Jack said. "But Anne might."

It startled Sara, hearing her father say Anne's name. "Mom?" she said. "Daddy?"

"Oh honey, don't sound so astonished. Don't you think we've been talking about this? Can't parents make mistakes?" Abby said.

Sara rubbed at her arms. She had seen graffiti in the bathroom at the bookstore; *"Mistakes are God's way of calling you to attention,"* it had said. Well, maybe that was true.

Sara smiled. She picked up the psychology book she had bought and ran her hand over the smooth cover. "I think I want to go back to school," she said.

It was winter again, and Sara was walking home, a knapsack loaded with books slung over one aching shoulder. Back in grad school full time at City College, and it felt great. Paying for it herself, too, with a little help from a loan and a terrific financial package. Paying back her father, too, a little at a time. Never had she felt so excited. She couldn't wait to get up in the morning, to get to class. Even studying was, well, exhilarating. In a few more years, she'd be a psychologist. Already, she knew she wanted to work with teenage girls. "I know how you feel," she'd tell them, and she'd mean it.

She sidestepped a snowdrift, manuevering the frosty streets. Fifteen minutes and ten blocks and she'd be at her apartment, a small one-bedroom with an alcove just big enough for a single bed with a soft peach comforter her parents had sent. "You said Anne liked this color," Abby said. After two months, Abby even called Anne, phoning Sara immediately afterward to tell her. "I told her she doesn't have to call me grandmother," Abby said.

"Did Daddy talk to her?" Sara asked, and Abby grew quiet.

"Not yet," she said. "It's harder for your father. But he made me repeat everything we said to each other."

Anne had never had a chance to see the peach comforter, let alone sleep under it. Every time an opportunity came up for a visit, something happened. Sara had invited Anne to New York for Halloween, thinking she'd love the big raucous parade in the Village, but then Anne came down with the flu. Thanksgiving time, Sara was planning to go there, but then she was the one who got sick, and by the time she was well, Anne was back in school. "Oh, Anne, I'm so disappointed," Sara told her.

"We'll figure something out," Anne said, and it sounded so casual that Sara felt a pang of insecurity. Bundling deeper into her coat, Sara crossed the street to her block. Next year, Anne would be in college. If she was anything like Sara had been, she wouldn't be coming home so often, she'd want to use her breaks to be with her friends. Or with a boyfriend. Anne's life would be knit together so tightly that all the lost time Sara had hoped to make up for wouldn't be much more than a loop if she were lucky. Pained, she pulled her coat tighter.

There Sara was. 409. A small brick building with a rusting gate. Scott would have hated it, she thought wryly, he would have found fifty things wrong before he even stepped inside, including this sticking door, but Sara pushed the door expertly open with the toe of her boot, and happily entered.

The night stretched out in front of her. Maybe tonight she'd call a friend, go out and have dinner. That new Thai place. Or the Mexican. Maybe see a movie. Grabbing her mail, she headed upstairs.

Inside her apartment, she dumped her books on the table. Then she slid onto the couch, curling her legs under her, riffling through the mail. *Damn.* Bills. More bills. A letter from her mother. A newsletter from the National Cheese Society.

And then an envelope, pale blue with a flower in the corner, fell out. She opened it up. "Dear friends," it said, and Sara thought, *good God,* one of those corny holiday form letters she always made fun of, and she cringed, about to throw it out, when Danny's name jumped out at her. Sara propped herself up in the bed and read:

> *What a busy time it's been! Danny was promoted (just call him Mr. Regional Manager!) at the bank and we celebrated by taking the whole family to the Poconos for a week of hiking, camping, and just plain old relaxing. And Charlotte got her own promotion, too, to something even more exciting than Danny's—to new mother-to-be! Our little Gift from God will be arriving in June, and we're hoping it's a little sister to join her handsome brother Joseph and her beautiful half sister Anne!*

She turned the envelope over, but it was typed and she couldn't tell who had sent it to her, and really, what did it matter. They had thought of her. And then, another envelope fell out from her pile of mail, a small grey square, and she opened that one up.

PLEASE JOIN US FOR
ANNE RIVERS'S GRADUATION FROM HIGH SCHOOL.
DINNER FOLLOWING AT ARNOLDOS.
RSVP.

Sara had just been on the phone with Anne a few days ago, but why hadn't Anne told her about the party? Or the invitation? She turned the card over. *Please join us,* it said, and all she had to do was look at the signature, as familiar to her as her own palm print. Eva's delicate scrawl. *I know this is early but I just want to make sure you aren't signing up for a trip around the world!* Eva had invited her, and maybe Anne didn't even know that yet. Sara got up and wrote the date on her calendar, almost like a promise she was making to herself.

It was hot again. Ninety-five degrees in June, twenty degrees hotter than it was in New York, and when it started to rain, a light sun shower, Sara hurried into the restaurant, two gaily wrapped presents tucked under her arm. All the preparation and planning she had done to get here, and her plane had been delayed for an hour, and then there was a stopover and another delay in Ohio, and she couldn't believe it, she had missed the ceremony, the one thing she had been imagining for weeks and weeks. And worse, she couldn't shake the vision of Anne looking around and not seeing her there. What could Anne possibly think except she had been slammed again? Flustered, she glanced at her watch again. Dinner. She was still in time for the dinner.

Sara squinted across the room. Four in the afternoon and the restaurant was dimly lit, all potted ferns and barnwood walls, a floor so black it looked like midnight. She could barely see in front of her, let alone find someone she knew. Eva told her they had rented a private room, but Sara wasn't sure where the room was, and she didn't see a hostess. Abby and Jack had even been invited, but Sara wasn't surprised when they didn't plan to go, when they hedged with excuses. "Why should our first meeting be in a crowd?" Abby said on the phone one night. "That's not right." Her voice stopped and stuck, then Sara heard Jack draw in a long breath. "What are you going to do," Abby said quietly, and it was then that Sara heard the pain in her mother's voice, the regret. "But we bought her a gift. An antique pen and pencil set. Perfect for a writer. Perfect for writing to her grandparents. And we sent her a nice check."

"She'll know we're thinking about her," Jack said.

"I'll know that, too," Sara told him.

Now a man in a sparkling white tuxedo jacket suddenly appeared, raising one brow at Sara. "Rivers party?" she said, and he nodded, bored, and led her to a door, pushing it open, making her blink at the sudden light, the flurry of noise.

Sara stood on the sidelines, looking for a familiar face among all these people. She felt suddenly nervous, as if she were on a first date. A woman walked by Sara, beaming. A man in the back threw back his head and laughed out loud. Her own graduation hadn't been so happy, she remembered. Eva and George had already vanished with Anne. Her parents took her out to dinner, Abby smiling too hard, Jack overly boisterous, and Sara pretending that she really did have something to look forward to, that her dreams weren't like hard roots now, frozen under winter ground.

A waitress whisked a tray full of champagne past her and Sara grabbed one. "Everyone is sitting down for dinner," she murmured to Sara, as if she were sharing a great secret.

"Where do I sit?" Sara asked, but the waitress was gone, winding through the crowd, and Sara suddenly felt as if she were in one of those dreams where she was out in public, stark naked, but only she knew it. Everyone else just passed her as if she were a ghost.

She tried to get some bearings. She hadn't seen any placards telling where her table was, so she looked around for an interesting-looking one. There by the corner was a smallish one, with a man with ginger-colored hair and a deep tan, a few women in bare summery dresses. The singles table, Sara thought, the one for people without babies, people without great loves. For a moment, she felt sorry for herself, and then she straightened. She had had both. She walked over. "Hi, I'm Sara," she said, and the man brightened and the women nodded.

"Bill, Anne's neighbor," he said.

"Monique," said one of the women. "I work with Eva at the school. What's your connection?"

Sara smiled. This was too complicated for a party. "Friend," she said simply.

The woman clinked glasses with Sara. "Ah, here's to friends, then," she said, and then she looked over Sara's head. "The happy mother!" she said, and Sara turned around, and there was Eva in a pale blue sheath, her long blond hair held back with a glittering rhinestone clip. Jumping up, Sara hugged Eva.

"You're not sitting here, are you?" Eva asked, puzzled. "You sit at the table with us."

Monique gave Sara a curious look. "Hey, how's she rate preferred seating?"

"Anne's birth mother," Eva said simply, making Sara start.

"Now *this* is interesting," Monique said, looking from Sara to Eva, but Eva was guiding Sara through the crowd.

"Thank you," Sara said. "For saying that. For inviting me."

Eva waved a hand. "I'm happy you're here," Eva said, scanning the crowd. "Where's George? I know he wants to see you," she said, and then she turned back to Sara. "Did she tell you? University of Michigan. Just found out."

Michigan, Sara thought. She didn't know whether to feel relieved that the college wasn't all the way across the country or disheartened that it was still far.

They moved to the long table at the back of the room, and Eva said, "There she is—" Sara looked over, and for a minute, she didn't recognize her. Anne's hair was almost as long and curly as Sara's now, her lips were shined, and she was wearing a simple green dress that brought out her eyes, green like Danny's. "She grew up, didn't she," Eva said wistfully to Sara, and then, as if Anne had known they were talking about her, Anne turned, and shrieked, "Sara!"

"Maybe not so grown-up, after all." Eva laughed.

Anne threw her arms about Sara and then stepped back. "You came!"

Sara handed Anne the gifts. "One's from my parents. One's from me."

"You didn't have to—" Anne said, but anyone could see the delight on her face. She held Sara's package up to the light, as if she could see through it, then she gave it a gentle shake. "I can't wait to see what it is!"

In all the years Sara had bought Anne presents for her birthday, gifts tucked in the back of her closet, like homing devices, she had always bought quickly, impulsively, because it felt so painful. This time, though, she had spent weeks trying to figure out what to get Anne. She had prowled store after store in the city, and in the end she had bought Anne a perfect creamy pearl on a silver chain. She had loved imagining Anne opening it up, Sara carefully taking out the delicate chain and fastening it about her daughter's neck. A necklace as small and slight as a whisper that could even tuck under a T-shirt so Anne might wear it everywhere, so she'd feel it brushing against her skin and always be reminded of Sara.

"You're coming to the house after dinner, aren't you?" Anne said to Sara. "I'll open it there."

"Of course I am."

And then Anne was looking beyond Sara, over her head, and Sara turned to look, too, and there was Danny, coming toward them, lean and handsome in a dark suit, and beside him was Charlotte with a baby in her arms, her hair longer, a halo of curls. Joseph, in a little suit and red bow tie, toddling alongside.

"We'll always be connected," Danny had said to her when they were kids. *"We'll always know where the other is."* And in a way, he had been right. They would be connected, they would see each other, but now it wouldn't be because of the two of them. It would be because of Anne. At Anne's college graduation. At her wedding. Maybe, someday, at the birth of Anne's own child.

A knot rose in her throat so quickly Sara swallowed hard to stop it. Dipping her head, she pretended she had to find something in her purse. She blinked hard, hopeful she wouldn't cry, and riffled through her tiny purse, waiting until she could lift her head again.

Danny hugged Anne first, and then Anne flung one arm about Sara, too, and for a moment, Sara's hand grazed Danny's and their eyes met. "It's good to see you, Sara," he said. Neither one of them moved away. Not yet. Not until George walked over, beaming and proud, motioning every-one.

"Come on, everyone, sit! Sit!" he ordered. He pointed to places. There and there and there. "Sara, right over there!" he said, pulling out a chair for her and then Sara sat, and for another moment again, all of them were here, together.